More praise for
Murder in Hell's Kitchen

"Harris knows a lot about cops and a lot about women and she knows how to plot a good mystery. *Murder in Hell's Kitchen* is so believable I keep expecting to read more about the case in the morning papers."
— STEPHEN GREENLEAF

"If you enjoy police procedurals, look no further than *Murder in Hell's Kitchen*. Lee Harris has captured perfectly that fine line between devoted and jaded that detectives involved with the species' 'ultimate crime' tread every day. An absolute knockout of a novel about law enforcement officers as human beings."
— JEREMIAH HEALY

"With *Murder in Hell's Kitchen*, Lee Harris delivers an engrossing procedural that offers a vivid and richly detailed perspective on New York City and its detectives. Series heroine Detective Jane Bauer is a fresh and appealing protagonist—smart, sensible, and believably complex. A winner of a book that rings with authenticity."
— JONNIE JACOBS

By Lee Harris
Published by Fawcett Books:

MURDER IN HELL'S KITCHEN

Lee Harris

FAWCETT BOOKS • NEW YORK

A Fawcett Book
Published by The Ballantine Publishing Group
Copyright © 2003 by Lee Harris

www.ballantinebooks.com

ISBN 0-449-00734-0

Manufactured in the United States of America

First Edition: April 2003

OPM   10   9   8   7   6   5   4   3   2   1

To Phyllis Westberg
with sincere thanks

As cold as any stone.

—*King Henry V*, Act II, Scene 3, Line 26
WILLIAM SHAKESPEARE

Hot as hell.

—From *Recipe for Coffee*
CHARLES MAURICE DE TALLEYRAND-PÉRIGORD
1754–1838

ACKNOWLEDGMENT

With more thanks than I can express to
James L. V. Wegman

MURDER IN
HELL'S
KITCHEN

1

FOR SEVEN DAYS the picture had haunted front pages and small screens. In the overcast haze of a fall afternoon in downtown New York was the eerie image of the wheelchair with its small, lifeless occupant alone on the grass. The photograph had become the symbol of the dangers of a city so preoccupied with its own needs and wants that it ignored or overlooked a killing in its midst, that it passed alongside death and never stopped to look even once.

The City Hall Park Murder, as it came to be called, had promised to be the case of a lifetime, the capping of a career, the most fitting of departures. But that was a week ago. Today Jane Bauer's life was upside down and she hadn't thought of the little figure in the wheelchair for at least eight hours. She looked at her watch once again.

"We'll get there," Det. Martin Hoagland said.

"I know. I just can't help looking."

He was traveling north on Riverside Drive to avoid the problems on the Henry Hudson Parkway, which ran just west of the drive along the river of the same name. At red lights, he edged forward, then shot across. They drove along the western end of the Twenty-sixth Precinct, the Two-Six, her first assignment out of the Academy. Almost twenty years had passed since she had put on her blues, "the bag" as most cops called it, for the first time and reported there in the center of Harlem. Before graduation, still wearing her cadet grays, she rode for a week as the third person in a radio motor patrol car in the Two-Six so that the sergeant in the car could assess her ability to handle "jobs." He had been impressed and she had gotten the assignment at the Two-Six on graduation. Her father had beamed with pride; her mother had barely accepted it with tight-lipped apprehension.

They passed the street where she had seen her first dead body in a fifth-floor walk-up during a twelve-by-eight, a midnight-to-eight A.M. shift, early in her career when she was given the crap details. Just stay with it, kid, the veteran cop on the scene had said as she tried to control her trembling and her queasy stomach. Don't leave till the body's picked up, the area secured, and all the paperwork's done. If the smell gets too bad in here, just light a cigar. Then he laughed and wished her a nice tour.

Looking out the window Jane thought that she could relive her entire career by driving the streets of Manhattan. Who would have thought nostalgia was so easy to come by?

"I'll pull into Emergency and wait for you there," Marty's voice said, piercing her recollections. They were long past the Two-Six now.

"You don't have to wait, Marty. I can take the subway back."

"I'll wait for you."

It was the kind of firm reassurance that tended to settle stomachs in times of less distress. Not much would work this afternoon.

She thanked him in her head, her apprehension growing as they approached Columbia Presbyterian, the huge hospital complex just south of the George Washington Bridge overlooking the Hudson River and, on the other side, New Jersey. Marty turned and turned again, pulling in close to the Emergency entrance.

"Go," he said as the car came to a jerky stop in front of the door at the covered dock, now almost empty of ambulances.

She went.

Her heart was pounding as she made her way through the sick and the bored to the woman with the records. "John Bauer. I'm his daughter."

"Yes, Ms. Bauer. Your dad's been admitted. You can go up to see him." She wrote the room number and floor for her on a slip of paper and gave brief but good directions.

Jane ran. Arrows on floors and walls directed her around corners and down halls to the elevators and past frequently visited units. A rainbow of color coding indicated one specialty after another. The elevator took forever to arrive. Then it stopped on every floor. Then she ran again.

Her gun was in her large shoulder bag, which she held tightly to her side as she looked at room numbers. Two more. She slowed, trying to calm herself, not wanting her anxiety to become his.

The door was open and she walked in. A curtained bed stood near the window, and her father, a little pale, rested in the nearer bed.

"Janey," he said, seeing her, his face lighting up. "You didn't have to come, honey. I'm just fine."

"You look pretty good," she said grudgingly, edging up to the bed.

"I'm just fine. I'll be outta here tomorrow."

"What happened? You forget to take your medicine?"

"Nah. I took it just like you set it up for me, one of these, one of those, one of the other."

"Then what happened?"

"They gave me too much is what happened. They overmedicated me," he said, articulating the word carefully. "Doc'll come by; you'll talk to him."

She sat down hesitantly. "You were taking too much?"

"That's what he said. Gave me palpitations. Made me dizzy. Got my stomach all upset. I thought I ought to come in and they decided to keep me overnight. It's nothing, Janey. Believe me."

She started breathing again. "You look pretty good."

"Better'n you look." He laughed. "Like you've seen a ghost. You shouldn'ta come all this way. I'm fine. Really."

"Who's your doctor?"

"Swinson, Swenson, something like that."

"Mind if I go find him?"

"Be my guest. Look at you. You look like you're the one needs a night in the hospital."

She felt like it. She went down to the nurses' station and asked for the doctor. He was there, writing on a clipboard.

"I'm John Bauer's daughter."

"Glad to meet you. Dr. Swenson." He offered a slim, pale hand. "Good thing he came in when he did. We're cutting down his medication. That should do the trick. You're the police officer?"

"I guess he talked about me."

"Didn't talk about anything else. He's fine, Miss Bauer. Officer. Once we get the medication straight, he'll be fine."

"He said he was taking just what he was told to take." She wanted to hear him say it, that they had made a mistake, that it wasn't her father's fault, that they had put her father's life in jeopardy by prescribing the wrong amount of drugs.

"He probably was." The doctor looked at her directly. He was a thin, bony man with pale gray eyes behind large thick glasses. "Sometimes the medication needs a little fine-tuning. This should do the trick."

"Thank you." She went back down the hall to her father's room.

"You get the whole story?" he said. He seemed in a good mood, just missing his usual robust color.

"Confirmed every word you told me. I'll come by in the morning and pick you up."

"Don't bother, Janey. Madeleine'll come for me. She's got nothin' better to do. You go to work. You got a big case to work on."

She considered letting it go by. He had been so excited when she was picked for the City Hall Park Murder team. She could tell him another time but he was sharp; he would pick up on the delay and be hurt that she hadn't taken him into her confidence. "I'm off the case, Dad."

He stared at her, shaking his head as if to push away spiderwebs that had clouded the transmission. "What's that you said?"

"They took me off the case. I just got the word yesterday. A telephone call and I'm on a thirty-day assignment as of this morning. I'm on a steal with a new task force."

The phrase captured his attention, his eyes widening. "What kinda task force?"

"The mayor wants to clean up old unsolved homicides. We got a lot of briefings today. Tomorrow I'll get to look at a file."

"That's terrible, Janey. It's a waste. They need you on that City Hall case. Who cares about an old murder that happened in the Dark Ages? Some cases are so old they got whiskers, for cryin' out loud."

"Too many unsolved homicides, Dad. Someone's got to give them another look. Get the averages up."

"They know you're pullin' the pin?" He loved cop lingo.

"Probably."

"You shouldn'ta said anything. You should've kept it to yourself. You'd still be on the case."

He was probably right. "Don't worry about it. Just rest; get a good night's sleep. Marty's downstairs waiting to drive me home."

"Thanks for comin', honey."

She smiled, then bent and kissed his stubbled cheek. He hadn't felt well enough to shave this morning. "I'll call you tomorrow. Take care of yourself."

"You too, darlin'."

She had Marty drop her off at the new apartment. It was closer to where he was going anyway, and she felt like seeing it again. She had taken possession only two days ago and had the key with her. It was down in the

West Village, south of Fourteenth Street, not far from Abingdon Square. The building was old, what was still called "prewar" more than half a century after that war had ended, with beautiful floors that would be scraped and refinished before she moved in at the end of the month, thick walls that kept sounds within them, fine details in the moldings, and, her greatest joy, a working wood-burning fireplace.

As she got out of his car, she thanked Marty again. It wasn't so much that she entrusted her life to him; it was a long time since either of them had drawn a weapon. It was that when the ordinary miseries of life exploded, he was there. That was what partners were all about.

She turned the key, pushed open the heavy door, and went inside. There was an echo of emptiness as she walked, the smell of fresh paint. It was clean, had just needed the paint and the work on the floor. The kitchen had been updated recently and the appliances were nearly new and actually filled the space as though designed for it. All four burners of the gas stove worked. That would give her a third more firepower than she had in the old place. When she got some money together, she would change the floor, maybe put in some fancy tiles with a little color. She was almost forty-one. It was time to live like a grown-up.

There were two bedrooms, the smaller one perfect for an office or a den or a guest room. Dad would enjoy staying over, helping her hang curtains and pictures. She walked over to the windows, moved them up and down, then locked them.

The master bedroom was exceptionally large, with a closet she would have trouble filling. The apartment was expensive but worth it. The new job would pay just enough more than this one paid to cover what it would cost. It was the kind of job she had occasionally dreamed about, an office of her own with a door that closed, a full-time assistant, an hour every day for lunch, not when you found a minute to stuff a sandwich or a piece of cold pizza in your mouth. That elusive quality called dignity.

She stepped into the bathroom. This was where you sensed the age of the apartment. The floor was a mass of white hexagonal tiles, the door on the medicine chest painted over so many times that it no longer closed. She wrote notes on a pad to leave for the workmen. The mirror was slightly wavy, making her look as though she had just stepped through the glass and hadn't completely re-formed on the other side. She smiled and her mouth smiled back in two sections. Time to go home.

The old apartment was little more than comfortable. In a big old building on Broadway in the West Eighties, it was of a comparable vintage to the "new" one but without its charm. It was simply old, with dripping faucets that were beyond repair, a four-burner stove with only three working burners, a floor that creaked, a stain along one bedroom wall that worsened occasionally. And then there was the elevator. She was glad when it worked.

Jane had continued to live with her parents in the Bronx while she worked at the Two-Six and put away her money. The apartment was a gift to herself when she moved on. Like other new officers, she had been reviewed monthly by her regularly assigned sergeant. She made good progress and a few good arrests, but nothing outstanding—drugs, purse snatches, stolen cars. She wrote tickets for parked cars and moving violations. The Two-Six was an "A" house, a high-crime area. As she became more familiar with the territory, she found it easy to determine where to make quality arrests, the kind that looked good on your personnel record. She began thinking about a career path. Did she want to be a boss or did she want to be a detective? It didn't take her long to realize that it was the gold shield she wanted. The street didn't scare her, and she focused on drug arrests in areas where they affected the lives of the working people. She came to be known as a heads-up cop, respected and liked by most of the people in the precinct. Two and a half years into her career, she applied for a change of assignment.

About six months later, when she was twenty-four, she was transferred to Chinatown, the Fighting Fifth. The station house was a hundred years old and crime was rising in the precinct. There were drugs on the streets, and the Chinese gangs were out of control. In their level of violence, the Chinese gangs made the old Mafia types look like amateurs.

That was when she moved out of her parents' apartment and into this one in Manhattan.

In the living room two cartons were already packed and pushed against the wall, more of a symbolic gesture than a real beginning of the packing job. That would get done, as most of the things in her life got done, in a flurry of work, a twenty-hour day with no time off for anything but coffee and a couple of snacks.

There was only one message on the machine, telling her about Dad. The hospital had been thorough, for which she was grateful, calling and leaving messages at both numbers. She dropped into a chair with her mail and closed her eyes for a minute before starting through the envelopes. There was nothing of importance, and she closed her eyes again.

She had been angrier than she would ever have admitted to her father when her boss took her off the City Hall Park case and dumped her into a group of losers to satisfy the mayor's latest whim: raise the percent of cleared cases. Make the commissioner look good. Make the mayor look better, raise the status of the department, but keep the overtime down. Right.

It wasn't entirely a hopeless pursuit, but nearly so. The cases were cold. Besides the routine annual check—the Detective Division 5 reports, always called DD5s—to update the file and keep the squad commander happy, many of the cases had lain dormant for many years. A few of them were famous, and the best detectives on the job hadn't cleared them when they were fresh. Most of the cases never had a chance. The victims were old men and women who lived alone, whose bodies were found when the smell of decomposition awoke their neighbors. They were people whose histories were permanently buried in the past, people too poor to have heirs waiting to benefit from their deaths. They had long since ceased to be thought of as human beings and were now a collection of various colored forms, facts, and reports, or at best a memory in the mind of some retired detective. Science could learn a lot from dead bodies but it couldn't tell you what language was first on the tongue, whether it had been married, if it had living children, if it had a smile for everyone it met or found fault even with people who tried to help. Science couldn't tell you whether the body had nearly starved itself to death out of penury or hopelessness or just plain laziness. And the chances of finding answers five or ten years after death were slim.

The park murder had been, in its morbid way, a thing of beauty. The photograph alone was hypnotic. The eye traced the beams of sunlight, the shadows threatened, the metal side of the wheelchair flashed light. The little woman, almost invisible in the photo, had died of a stab wound, a knife in the stomach, inserted under the blanket that covered the lower half of her body. The killer must have stood in front of her, leaned over her, stuck the knife into her gut, forced it up toward the heart, and left. She must have seen him. Had she known him? Had she spoken to him? Joe, what are you doing here? Nice day for a concert in the park, don't you think? And then sudden death.

Or had it been random? Had some crazy acted on impulse or challenge, proving to himself or his gang that he could kill someone and get away with it?

No purse had been found at or near the crime scene. Either the killer took it with him or she left it home. But what home? She was without identification, but she had a few dollars in bills and coins in her jacket pocket. The team was unable to determine her identity. Her prints were not on file. No one fitting her description had been reported missing since the homicide. The wheelchair, they learned, had been stolen from a hospital. Someone's hard work failed to obliterate the number etched into one of the vertical steel supports, and it was traced. The hospital's property-marking system yielded one small bit of information: it had been missing from Bellevue for almost five years, not the only one, the clerk admitted. They were pretty pricey, and chances were it wasn't stolen by a person who needed it but by someone who could turn it into cash. The victim might have been the one who bought it from the thief, might even have commissioned him to steal it for her, meaning that the Bellevue connection was a dead end.

Jane started to get up from the chair, annoyed that she had let herself become involved in the case that was no longer hers. Forgetting that today's mail lay in her lap, she saw it spill to the floor as she rose. She gathered it up swiftly, noticing that a small envelope had freed itself from behind another.

It was handwritten on thin, crinkly pale blue paper in blue ink. The sealed flap provided an address halfway across the country, but no name. Something made her shiver, the flicker of a remote possibility. The address meant nothing to her, but that didn't calm her. What was remote was not always impossible. This was the wrong moment for the long arm of the past to reach into the present. I can't deal with this, she thought, at least, not now. Too much was happening, too much going on. There was Dad and the move and the new assignment. She knew those were just excuses, but she needed something to allay the panic. She carried the mail to the kitchen and put the small letter at the bottom of the pile on the counter. Along with the City Hall Park Murder, it could wait.

2

THE NEW SQUAD was meeting at nine o'clock Tuesday in lower Manhattan, where the island tapers off and the East River and the Hudson River merge as they empty into the ocean. It is the home of courts, federal, state, and local, a short walk from Chinatown and Little Italy, a stone's throw from the Brooklyn Bridge.

A large area on the third floor of 137 Centre Street had been set up for them. The building was diagonally across the street from 100 Centre Street, the home of criminal courts and Central Booking. There wasn't a cop in Manhattan who hadn't spent far too many hours of his life there, mostly waiting and drinking bad coffee.

A few detectives were already milling around when Jane arrived at a quarter to nine. She had seen them all yesterday at the all-day briefing, but she recognized one from her tour in Manhattan South Burglary back in the eighties. Approaching him to say hello, she wondered what indiscretion had landed him here among the misfits on the job. He likely didn't know himself, and had been stewing over it ever since he got the word.

They walked over to the coffee machine together and then he excused himself and left the area. Sipping her coffee, Jane glanced at her new temporary home. Along one long outer wall were the team offices, each with a window. Two large offices obviously intended for the brass formed one of the short back walls. The second long side of the room had doors that opened out to the hallway, where the elevator and stairs were, and a good-sized kitchen complete with stove, refrigerator, and a couple of tables, one already stained with fresh coffee.

The center of the large suite functioned as a briefing area, with about twenty chairs facing the two large offices, in front of which a lectern stood. When Jane finished her coffee, she took an end seat in the second row.

A small, diverse group had assembled, men and women, black and white, old and less old. The only other person in the group, a trim black woman wearing a skirt suit and high-heeled shoes—a desk job for her, out of the bag and the weather—took a seat at the other end of the third row. There wasn't much chance they would serve on the same team; the overriding goal of diversity would distribute them in separate groups.

Someone cleared his throat into a microphone, and Jane looked up to see a man in plainclothes and shaped like a block of ice at the lectern. What appeared to be a lieutenant's shield was pinned to his jacket. "You wanna find seats, detectives? It's nine o'clock and we wanna get the show on the road."

There was some last-minute scurrying at the coffee machine and then silence.

"I want to welcome you to the task force. I'm Lt. Ellis McElroy, and I'll be your second-in-command. That's my office"—he pointed behind him to the office on the right— "and I'm always available. I want you to know I'm happy to be here, we're here for a good reason, we're a great group of detectives, and I look forward to meeting and working with every one of you. Now it's my pleasure to introduce Capt. Frank Graves, who will tell us all what's going on."

There was a smattering of applause as Francis X. Graves rose from the chair he had been sitting in, mostly hidden behind the huge McElroy. Graves, who was known to most detectives on the job, was also a familiar face on the evening news. He had been blessed with the kind of looks Hollywood admired, a muscular body and a head of perfect silver hair that saw the stylist's brush and scissors more frequently than most women's. He was in uniform today, probably for the last time, and when he smiled, his teeth were enviably even and unstained.

Frank Graves, with his long and upwardly mobile career with the NYPD, was maneuvering toward his ultimate goal, chief of detectives. Having worked in and directed a number of special units, he had gotten his ticket punched in all the right boroughs. From here on up it was all about exposure and politics. Raise the rate of cases cleared—with results—publicize a couple of dead cases brought to life and followed with successful prosecutions, and the prize might be his.

He spoke for about ten minutes, amazingly an engaging speaker. Although Jane anticipated everything he would cover, she found herself listening, a tingle of excitement arising at the prospect of success. His voice was cultured, his words motivating, his phrases well-turned. He understood politics as well as a senator, seduction as well as a suitor. When he finished, he removed his glasses and turned the floor back to the second whip, who held a printout in front of his face.

"OK, we are twelve detectives, and I will read the names of each team and the office you will occupy. You can go back there and get your file from Annie. Annie, you want to give us a wave?"

A thirtyish woman smiled and waved her right hand.

"Team one, Salazar, Jones, MacDougal. That's your room down there." He pointed to the most distant office on the long wall. The black woman rose and joined two men, and all of them ambled down to the appointed office. "Team two, Bauer, Defino, MacHovec. Room two."

Jane got up and joined her new partners as McElroy called out the names of the third team. When she got to the door of the second office, the police administrative aide, known universally as the PAA, was just arriving with a thick file.

"There you go," Annie said. "That's your baby," and

she dropped the file in Jane's hands and walked toward the next door.

Jane put the file on one of the three desks in the office. "I'm Jane Bauer," she said to the thin, dark-haired man already in the room.

"Gordon Defino," he said, grasping her extended hand.

"And Sean MacHovec makes three."

At the door was the last third of the team, a man of medium height, fading sandy-colored hair, and a blond brush mustache. He looked a mess, mismatched clothes, worn cuffs, tie loosened. "What'd you guys do to end up on the fuckup team?"

Defino shook his head. "Take a desk. We can talk about fuckups later."

It seemed good advice. Jane sat at the desk she had put the file on. She opened the top drawer and took out the key, then opened the large file drawer on the bottom right and put her bag in it. The bag was lighter today than usual. Instead of the heavy Glock that she normally carried, she had substituted her off-duty five-shot .38-caliber Smith & Wesson Chief. Then she took off her raincoat and hung it behind the door on the coat tree, noting that it looked like an antique.

"I'll take this one," MacHovec said, leaving Defino with the desk near the window.

"Fine with me."

She could feel the tension between the two men. Defino was a sharp-looking detective, MacHovec a slob with a polyester shirt pulling out of polyester pants, a tie that had seen too many dinners with splashy food, a jacket from the Dark Ages.

"How do you want to begin?" Defino said.

"With coffee." MacHovec grinned. "I'll get it. Regular?"

"Black," Jane said.

MacHovec left the room and Jane looked at Defino and smiled. "He'll be OK. First thing, let's go through the file from the bottom. I can read the beginning aloud so we all get the picture. Then we can take pieces and rotate."

"Suits me."

"And then we'll divide up the work. Maybe start by finding the detective who originally caught the case."

"We'll have to recanvass."

"No problem."

MacHovec came back with three Styrofoam cups of coffee and set them down on Jane's desk. "First thing, we oughta get supplies," he said. "There's a cabinet over near the coffee machine."

"Yeah, why don't we do it before the rest of them make a dash for it," Defino said with irritation.

Jane knew what was coming next. MacHovec was a recognizable type. He would stock up on pads and pencils beyond anything he could reasonably use, and when he left this evening, half of it would accompany him home.

It was a bad start. Jane capped her coffee cup and they walked across the briefing area to the tall green cabinet. She stood back and let MacHovec go first. If there were some prized goodies he was after, let him have them and maybe he'd settle down.

Sure enough, he grabbed enough pads for a year's notes, and a handful of pens and pencils, and started back to the office.

"Where'd they dig this guy up from?" Defino said, standing aside to let Jane in first.

"One of the rag shops in the outer boroughs," she said, taking a pad, a box of paper clips, a couple of pencils, a couple of pens, and the Detective Division forms they would need to file their reports. She would have to remember to lock her desk every night and take the key or MacHovec would go searching to see if she had something he needed.

By the time she and Defino had collected their supplies, the other teams began to descend on the cabinet. MacHovec was in his shirtsleeves when they got back, sitting on his desk and drinking his coffee.

"The phone works," he said. "Looks like they got this set up pretty good."

Each desk had a multiline phone set. Jane wrote her number down. Dad would be home around noon and he needed to know how to reach her. The in baskets on all three desks were half-full, and they all started reading and tossing while they finished their coffee. There was a sheet on fire safety, on parking (practically none), on how to use the voice-mail system. There was a list of every detective in the squad, useful phone and fax numbers, and several pages that explained the squad's mission. It sounded familiar, as though it might be a copy of Graves's speech.

There was one electric typewriter in the room and one computer terminal. That was pretty good. And the desks looked remarkably new. Aside from a couple of loose paper clips and an eraser, Jane's desk was empty and un-marred. No old coffee stains, no carved initials, no decades of history in its drawers.

The men were on the phone giving their new numbers to their wives. Defino spoke in a low voice, MacHovec in a louder one. Jane dropped the cup in her wastebasket and hoped she could avoid partnering with MacHovec when they went out in the field.

They hung up at almost the same moment.

"Want to start?" Defino said. "Looks like a four-pounder."

Jane pulled the fat file over. "Suppose I read as a start," she said. "I'll pass the exhibits around when I get to them."

Defino walked over and closed the door, then returned to his desk. He had a notebook open to the first page and a ballpoint next to it. "Let's get started. This'll take all day."

It was a reasonable time estimate. The folder, like most homicide files at the end of an investigation, was fat and heavy, laden with interviews, sketches, crime scene pictures, autopsy reports, and forensic reports. What was different here was that this file was fat at the beginning. Usually a homicide investigation began with an empty jacket with only an assigned case number. Little by little, interview by interview, piece by piece of information it would grow. This time it was almost complete, lacking only a viable suspect and the crucial piece of evidence for conviction. All the rocks had been turned. The witnesses had given their opinions, asserted what they knew to be true.

They would work from the bottom up. Each new addition to a file was placed on top. The topmost sheet in this case was a DD5 from the detective who had last checked on the case, some seven months ago, the routine annual check of open cases. Jane turned the file over and opened it as though it were a Chinese or Arabic book, from left to right. Then she flipped over to the first sheet, the report of a body found in the hallway of an old law tenement on West Fifty-sixth Street, and started to read.

The call had come in on a spring morning four and a half years ago from the first person in the building to leave for work that day, Henry Soderberg, who lived on the second floor. The body of Arlen Quill lay sprawled inside the front door of the building, making it impossible for Mr. Soderberg to pass. Rather than go back upstairs, he knocked on the door of Mrs. Elaine Best, whose threshold was inches from Quill's shoes. She had screamed at the sight, let Mr. Soderberg in, and allowed him to use her telephone as she whimpered in her nightdress. The call was logged by 911 operator 173 at 7:27 A.M.

The sector car from the Midtown North Precinct arrived four minutes later. Officer Ned Carr was first on the scene, ascertained that Quill was dead—of a knife wound, it was later determined—and notified the dispatcher at Central that he needed an ambulance, a supervisor, and other assorted units. He also called the station house desk officer and requested a response by the squad detectives.

Because of the position of the body in front of the door to the street, the people living in the building had to be detoured around the crime scene to a back door and a roundabout route back to the street. Mr. Soderberg was the first to leave, followed by Margaret Rawls from apartment 3A. Officer Carr tried to keep her in the building until the detectives came, as the deceased had lived on her floor, but she was adamant that she must not be late for work and she left.

The detectives arrived less than a minute later. The catching detective was Charles Bracken, and his partner was Otis Wright.

"I know Otie," MacHovec said at that point. "He retired last year."

"Is he in the area?" Jane asked.

"I don't know. He could've moved south. He's got family in North Carolina. Maybe South Carolina. I can never tell the difference."

"What about Bracken?"

"Never heard of him."

Jane returned to the file. "Looks like it took the crime scene unit a long time to get there."

"It was rush hour," Defino said. "They were coming down from Fordham Place in the Bronx. Lots of traffic."

That was true. The crime scene unit was housed in the Forty-ninth Precinct in the Bronx. By the time they arrived, everyone in the building was up and knew what had happened. While the crime scene people did their work, Bracken and Wright began canvassing the people in the building, starting with Mrs. Best.

The bottom line on Elaine Best was that they got nothing out of her. Noted in the DD5 was the fact that she remained in her nightclothes the entire time the detectives were in the building. She whimpered more than spoke. She was retired from a secretarial job and lived on Social Security and a small income, and this, she assured them, was the end. She would start packing today and get out of this building and this city as soon as she could arrange for movers. She had seen Mr. Quill from time to time but did not know him except to say hello. She knew nothing about him, couldn't remember when he had moved in, and wasn't sure what floor he lived on. Aside from those few grudging statements, she whimpered almost constantly like an ailing animal and repeated over and over that she hadn't killed him. The detectives reassured her that she was not a suspect, but it made no difference in her demeanor. They gave up and went upstairs, presumably to search for a good lead.

The interviews with the tenants about the victim revealed a nondescript man who had lived in apartment 3B for more than a year and less than two years. In the words of his nearest neighbor, Miss Rawls, who was interviewed that evening, he was "a sad man." He looked sad, he acted sad, he said little to his neighbors. On weekdays he left for work about eight o'clock, dressed in a suit "like a banker or an accountant," Miss Rawls volunteered. His shoes were always shined. "I notice people's shoes," she said in her gentle southern speech.

It was Henry Soderberg, interviewed when he came home from work the day of the homicide, who seemed to make the most observant remarks of all the tenants. Quill looked to be in his early thirties (this confirmed by documents on his person). He was about five-ten, dressed for business, wasn't talkative but wasn't hostile either. He went to work regularly, didn't bother anyone, and didn't make any noise. Mr. Soderberg was in a position to know this last personally; he occupied the apartment under Arlen Quill's. "Hardly hear him come home," Soderberg said. But when he did hear, it was generally between six and eight in the evening. If Quill listened to music or television, if he sang in the shower or talked on the telephone, he did it at low volume. "He was a great neighbor," Soderberg was quoted as saying. "I didn't know he existed."

The place where he worked, the Golden City Hotel on Sixth Avenue, hardly knew he existed either. He had a job behind the scenes in the banquet department as an event planner, where he attended to the details of weddings and conferences. He was good at his job, never missed a day in the four years he had worked there, never elicited a negative comment from the people he dealt with, mostly on the telephone. "He had a nice telephone voice," the detective had dutifully written in the interview with a coworker. But Quill had never been known to have lunch with anyone or socialize after work. He usually ate at his desk, cleaning up carefully after himself. In answer to the question of who might have wanted him dead, there were only shrugs. He got along, apparently, with everybody. On one of the last days of his life, he voiced an uncharacteristic complaint: he thought he heard the scurrying of rodents in the empty apartment upstairs.

"The whole thing sounds like a push-in," MacHovec said. "Quill comes home late from work, he's at the door, goes for his key, a guy comes up behind him, follows him inside, kills him, and goes."

"His wallet was in his pocket," Jane said. "What was the point?"

"The perp heard a sound from the whimpering lady's apartment and got cold feet. He killed him for nothing. Not the first time that's happened."

"It's possible," Defino said.

"Which means we gotta look into push-ins in the area, see if we can pin this on a known perp. They get any latents off the door, the door handles, glass? Anything?"

"The prints of the cop that answered the call," Jane said.

"They never learn," MacHovec said.

It was true. Cops destroyed more crime scenes than onlookers did, certainly more than the perps themselves.

"So we got anything that points to someone besides a random push-in?" Defino asked.

Jane turned the pages. "He had an ex-wife."

"That sounds promising." Defino started to look interested. "Kamikaze divorce?"

"Let's see."

The separation and divorce decrees were among the papers in Quill's apartment, along with several snapshots of his former wife. For a plain, quiet, apparently uninteresting man, he had had a beautiful wife who obviously enjoyed posing for the camera. There were pictures of her in bathing suits, in street clothes, in elegant dinner dresses, and a small white wedding album, now in the property clerk's warehouse, whose contents were in an envelope in the file.

The men agreed she was a knockout. Laura Quill had been twenty-nine at the time of her ex-husband's death and appeared to have an airtight alibi. She and her new husband, Terry Thorne, were on a cruise at the time of the homicide and didn't return until several days later.

"So she hired a killer," Defino said.

"Why?" Jane asked. "Quill didn't leave much. She didn't ask for alimony. It looks like she got divorced and remarried in the same week. He's the one who should've killed her, except it looks like he still loved her. Look at this. Here's a napkin from their wedding, 'Laura and Arlen' in silver on pink. He saved all this stuff. She broke his heart when she left him."

"Good morning!"

The greeting took all of them by surprise. In the doorway was the whip himself, his gorgeous face smiling.

"I'm Frank Graves. Glad to meet you."

They went through the introductions, but it was clear that Graves knew every name before he popped in. "We're having lunch together today, courtesy of the task force special petty-cash fund. We want to get to know you, have you get to know the other teams. Anything you need?"

"A hot lead," MacHovec said, and Graves laughed.

"You'll find it. I've got all kinds of faith in you guys. See you at noon. They're setting up tables in the briefing area."

"Free lunch," MacHovec said. "Could be worse."

Defino got off his desk and moved around a little, working his hands in and out of fists to get the circulation going. "There's no such thing as a free lunch. Remember where you heard it first."

3

JANE'S FATHER WAS home and in good spirits when she called just before noon. Madeleine, his longtime friend and neighbor, had picked him up at eleven as promised, and he had already been home for fifteen minutes when the phone rang. Madeleine was making lunch for him, and he was feeling really good.

She hung up in better spirits herself. The catered lunch was being set up buffet style on a long table, and the briefing area was filled with small tables and chairs. The whip was already seated at one table and the second whip at the table that MacHovec and Defino had taken. She didn't want to eat with either MacHovec or McElroy, and as she looked around, holding her tray, she accepted an invitation from another table.

They introduced themselves, and the one who had invited her, Jim McCaffrey, said, "Welcome to the OSS."

"I'm missing something."

"Old Stiffs Squad."

"Got it." She smiled and looked down at her plate, a nice assortment of hot foods, salads, and a warm biscuit. Dessert and coffee would come later. "What's your case?" she asked them.

"Coupla girls got whacked alongside the Bruckner Expressway."

"I remember that one. We've got the guy in the West Fifties, looks like a push-in."

"I wonder how many of these'll get cleared with results," the man called Rob said.

"None of them today, that's for sure," McCaffrey said.

They talked through lunch, Jane feeling that these three men were all preferable to MacHovec, but that was the luck of the draw. They all cared about the victims. There had been a lot of news when those bodies were found about a year ago. Boyfriends had been questioned, girlfriends, families, teachers, employers. It looked as though someone had picked them up to give them a ride and decided to rape and murder them.

She began to wonder how the cases had been distributed, whether this team had rated a better case than her own. She wasn't even sure, in her own mind, what a better case was. Did it mean the case was more likely to be cleared or that the victims were more sympathetic?

Both Graves and McElroy approached Jane's table, although there was no empty fourth seat. Graves pulled up an extra chair and left it there for McElroy. It was all hype and cheerleading. We're counting on you, anything you need is at your disposal, you've been carefully selected, fresh start, new angles. "The PC is very interested and backing us all the way." It had the hidden suggestion of promotion to first-grade detective for results. They had heard it all before.

Back in the office, MacHovec had a foil box full of food to take home. Jane turned her face so he wouldn't see her breaking into a laugh. Cheapskate of the month.

"Look," she said, "let's divide this file up and each read a third and pass it along. We've got the basics now. It's more efficient that way and we can stop and talk about anything at any point."

"Sounds good," Defino said.

Jane divvied it up, keeping the bottom or earliest third for herself, handing the middle third to Defino, and the most recently collected material to MacHovec. For the next couple of hours it was pretty quiet except for pages turning and MacHovec yawning.

Around three-thirty Defino got restless. "We better

start planning our strategy," he said. "Who goes where, you know?"

"One of us should hang out here," MacHovec said, and Jane sighed with relief.

"We should see Bracken and Wright first," she said. "Then the ex-wife and the people in the building."

"I'll call and see if Bracken is still on the job. He'll probably know where Wright is." Defino picked up the phone and started making calls.

Jane found the phone number for Quill's ex-wife and dialed. After several rings an answering machine picked up. At least Mrs. Thorne was still available. She hung up and waited for Defino to get off his phone.

"He's on the job and he'll see us at ten tomorrow. We can check in here first and then go uptown."

"Suits me." Good, she thought. Things are starting to move.

When they broke up at five, she took the rest of her portion of the file with her, something to read tonight. Outside everyone and his brother was going home. She walked over to the City Hall subway station and got on the Lexington Avenue uptown. At Grand Central she shuttled over to the West Side and caught the number one train on the Broadway line going north. When it reached Fifty-ninth Street, she heard a barely intelligible announcement that the train would go no farther. Half the crowd grumbled while the other half, numbed by the daily misery of trying to get to and from work in a hostile subterranean world, moved silently out of the train.

Jane went up to the next level. The crowds were stifling. From this point she could walk home in less than half an hour and leave the underground menace behind. It seemed better than waiting for another train. She climbed the stairs to the street and got her bearings. A stroll up Broadway would do it. As she waited for the light, it occurred to her that she was only a few blocks away from the building where Arlen Quill had been murdered. She was in no hurry to get home, and she had eaten enough for lunch that she could get through the evening on leftovers. Why not take a look?

She turned abruptly and walked west. At Ninth Avenue she turned south and walked to Fifty-sixth, then turned west again toward Tenth. The block was a row of colorless old buildings with a shared lack of individuality, probably looking shabbier inside than outside.

Fifty-sixth Street was near the northern end of the section of the west side of Manhattan now called Clinton, named after the park of the same name a little farther south. The park was home to a statue of DeWitt Clinton, a long ago mayor of the city and governor of the state. The name of the area, which covered most of the west Forties and Fifties over to the Hudson River, was relatively new, having for nearly a century sported the more picturesque name of Hell's Kitchen, an area so full of murderous gangs around the turn of the last century that police officers were sent on patrol only in groups of three.

Several fables explaining the origin of the old name existed. The one that appealed most to Jane claimed that during a blistering heat wave one summer in the late nineteenth century, one cop allegedly said to another that this place was as hot as hell. It was hotter than that, his partner asserted. It was as hot as hell's kitchen. The name stuck until late twentieth-century gentrification brought upscale residents into the west Forties and Fifties. These people, with more money and finer sensitivities than their predecessors, preferred to live with a more gentrified name and Clinton was officially adopted.

When she got to Quill's house she stopped. One of the tenants interviewed had referred to it as the haunted house. Fire escapes lined the front of the building. The windows were large and for the most part uncurtained. The only signs of life were the plastic bags of garbage on the curb.

Three steps led up to the front door. She mounted them and opened the door. On the right were mailboxes and doorbells. She had been in a thousand entries just

like this in the last twenty years. The stairs were straight
ahead and there, on the left, the door to Mrs. Elaine Best's
apartment. She pressed the buzzer next to the door.

An elderly man opened it, a cat at his heel.

"I'm Det. Jane Bauer." She pulled out her shield and
photo ID case. "I'm looking for Mrs. Best."

"Don't know any Mrs. Best."

"How long have you lived here?"

"Almost four years."

"I guess she moved."

"If you're looking for the woman who used to live
here, I heard she died."

"Sorry to have bothered you."

"No bother." He gave a little smile as though her brief
visit had been a welcome interruption from the television
set that sounded from another room. He closed the door
and she retreated to the mailbox area. She had a list of
the tenants at the time Quill was murdered. There were
seven apartments on the four floors of the building, but
only six of them had been occupied at the time: Mrs. Best
on one, Mr. Soderberg and a middle-aged man, Hollis
Worthman, on two, Quill and Margaret Rawls on three,
and a younger man, Jerry Hutchins, in 4A. Four B, the
apartment directly over Quill, had been empty.

When she took out the list and compared it to the
names on the mailboxes, she realized that all the names
were different. She walked out to the street and checked
the number above the door. This was the number of the
building where Arlen Quill had been murdered four
and a half years ago, yet not one person who had been
there at the time of the homicide still lived there. This
was certainly a rent-controlled building. Rent-controlled
tenants in New York had been known to tolerate condi-
tions almost as bad as Third World prisons or battlefield
accommodations—no heat, no electricity, no water, ver-
min and filth, attacks by the landlord's goons—all to
hang on to a cheap apartment. What had made these five
leave?

She went back in. There was no Hutchins, no Soderberg, no Worthman, no Rawls, no Best. No law of averages could account for a clean sweep of this building in less than five years. Twenty percent of the general population of the United States might move every year, but rent-controlled tenants in Manhattan did not.

Jane left the building and turned north on Tenth Avenue. Something was wrong or crazy, and whichever it was, it had to be investigated. She walked briskly, feeling very good after a merely routine day. There was something here, something the detective working the case had not noticed. In his annual review, he had not called back any of the tenants, not that he was required to, and he would be totally unaware that they were all gone from the building.

Throughout the mile-and-a-quarter walk home, her mind buzzed with possibilities. In her apartment she changed into pants and a sweatshirt and started packing, as though the walk had provided the momentum to keep moving. The new apartment was hers. As soon as she was packed and had a mover, she could get out of this place and start making fires every night. Sooner was better than later.

She didn't stop until all but a handful of dishes were packed, till the few pictures on the wall were in cartons, till the pots and pans were taken care of. It hadn't been all that difficult, and she had been free to think, free to direct the rush of energy generated by her discovery to meaningful physical work.

Where had they all gone? And more to the point, why had they left?

At nine o'clock she called it quits, put some ice in a glass, and poured Stoli over it. She was hungry but not in the mood to cook. She boiled some water, measured out spaghetti, and reheated the meat sauce that was left in the fridge from the weekend.

The colander had disappeared. It was not on its shelf or in the sink. She searched fruitlessly before realizing it was packed. She started to laugh. Some days it was hard to win. Luckily it was near the top of a carton, and she pulled it out in time to catch the spaghetti. She was starving. The catered lunch on Centre Street seemed like yesterday. She poured the sauce over the spaghetti, which was on the one dinner plate she hadn't packed, and carried it to the table that had been old when she moved in to this place. But she would move it anyway, scratched and burned as it was. There were too many expenses involved in getting settled; a new kitchen table could wait, as dinner could not. She inhaled the mass of food in front of her and dug in.

The phone rang just as she was finishing. She grabbed it, still sitting at the table.

"Jane? It's Flora."

"Flora. How are you? I haven't heard from you in ages."

Flora Hamburg had made it on the job when women didn't. If ever someone marched to her own drummer, it was Flora. About sixty now, she had become a cop when pretty women on the job were snapped up to assist men moving to higher places, and plain women went almost nowhere. *Plain* would have been a compliment to Flora. Matronly, tough, rarely without a cigarette dangling from her lips, she had succeeded because she was smart and for no other reason. Her clothes looked like leftovers from the Salvation Army, and if she owned a handbag, no one ever saw it. An unfashionable shopping bag held whatever she chose to carry to work. Her weapon, which she was rumored to have drawn to good effect on several occasions, flapped on her hip. Jane had met her at the Policewoman's Endowment Association when Flora was still a lieutenant and Jane was still in blues. For over fifteen years, Flora had kept an eye on Jane.

"More to the point, how're you? I've been hearing things. Is it true you're retiring?"

"It's true. I've got a few months left."

"Where're you going?" the gravelly voice asked, blowing smoke.

"I've got a job with an insurance company."

"Yeah, yeah. Lots of money and an office with a window."

Jane smiled. "Right."

"Your initiative or theirs?"

"They came to the union looking for a few good men. I accepted the invitation."

"Why didn't you come and talk to me?"

"It seemed the right time. I didn't think you'd approve."

"Well, you're right about that. You should think about this, Jane. You're only forty. The hard work is all behind you. How's your dad?"

"He's OK. Got some heart problems, but he's pretty good."

"You're giving me heart problems. I hate to see you go. If you wanna talk, you know where to find me. Not next week. I'm going to Atlantic City to make some money."

"Thanks, Flora." She hung up feeling the old conflict. But although Flora knew a lot, she didn't know everything. The decision to leave had not been all about pensions and more money.

"Run that by me again." Defino's thin face was one big frown.

"The five tenants living in Quill's house at the time of the homicide are all gone. I walked by the building yesterday when my subway train stopped for good at Fifty-ninth. The woman on the first floor, Mrs. Elaine Best, she's been gone or dead for almost four years. I didn't talk to anyone else. We have to talk to the super or the owner before we do anything else."

"We've gotta be at Midtown North at ten." He glanced at his watch. There was plenty of time. "MacHovec, how 'bout you dig up a super or landlord while we're gone?"

"Sure thing."

"And maybe start looking for the other tenants," Jane said. "If they're not in the building, we'll have to find them to reinterview them."

MacHovec started writing down names. "As good as done," he said airily.

Jane wasn't so sure.

* * *

"So you've got the Quill case." Charlie Bracken was a big man with dark, graying hair, a gut, and sharp eyes. He was wearing a worn sports jacket, the pockets stretched out of shape, and dark gray pants. He pulled another chair over to the desk. "Sit down. Can I get you some coffee?"

They said yes, and Bracken brought three Styrofoam cups back and a handful of sugars and whiteners. Defino put everything in his and stuck a wooden stirrer in it and kept it moving.

"Broke my ass on that case. Looked like a push-in but it didn't feel right. Nothing was taken. Wallet, keys, watch, money. Everything was still there." He shrugged. "Guy had an uncontested divorce, ex-wife was out of the country when he was killed, coworkers said he was a nice guy, did his job, never said much. Most of 'em didn't care much whether he was dead or alive, but no one *wanted* him dead. Other people in the building didn't know he existed."

"Pay his rent on time?" Defino asked.

"No complaints. His apartment . . . what can I tell you? Not scrubbed clean but everything in place, checkbook up-to-date, food in the fridge, stuff in the freezer, extra rolls of toilet paper in the closet, clean sheets on the bed. Looked like he was planning to stay awhile."

"Any girlfriends?" Defino asked, and after a moment, "Boyfriends?"

"Nah. I got the feeling he hadn't gotten over his wife yet. She's a looker. Met her second husband at work. He also got divorced to marry her."

"The other woman remarry?" Jane asked.

"Not at the time of the homicide."

"The other tenants," she said. "They all clean?"

"As clean as anyone in New York. There was one guy. . . ." He opened a drawer and took out a dog-eared file folder and opened it. "On the top floor . . . there was only one tenant on four; the other apartment was empty—there was a guy named Hutchins. Something about him. He didn't fit. Came from out west some-where. Talk to him, he never laid eyes on Arlen Quill."

Defino said to Jane, "Tell him."

Jane watched Bracken's face warm with expectation. A detective never lost interest in his old cases. "I went by the house yesterday," she said. "The names on the mailboxes were all different. None of the tenants from the time of the homicide are living there."

Bracken's eyes narrowed. "Crazy."

"Yeah."

"The woman on the first floor, Best is her name, she died maybe six months after Quill. Stroke, I think. She was a funny old gal, wore a black wig with bangs, looked like Mamie Eisenhower. But the others, last time I checked they were all there."

"When was that?"

"Six, eight months after the homicide. I never called any of them again after that."

"We've got someone on our team checking them out," Defino said. "We need to reinterview them if we can find them."

"Four people moved out in four years," Bracken said. "Rent-controlled building. Doesn't make sense."

"That's what we thought."

"Makes you wonder. I didn't hear anything bad about the landlord. He owns a bunch of buildings on the West Side. No complaints about heat, no fights that I heard about. He sure as hell didn't move his family into Quill's apartment. I even went up to a couple of his other build-ings and asked around. Nothing."

"Sounds like you did a thorough job," Jane said.

"So why did they move? Don't tell me coincidence. I don't buy coincidence. I know people get shook up when they trip over a body, but what red-blooded New Yorker gives up a rent-controlled apartment because a guy got stabbed downstairs?"

"We'll be lookin' into it." Defino tapped his pen on the desk. "Anything you want to tell us? Anything make you feel antsy, besides the guy on the top floor that came from the west?"

"Everything made me feel antsy. If it wasn't the ex-wife and it wasn't the landlord, and it wasn't another tenant, and it wasn't someone at work, then who? And why didn't the perp rob him?"

"Maybe Mrs. Best heard the scuffle and called out. Maybe her cat started making noise and the perp thought it would wake up the tenants." Jane threw out the most obvious reasons.

"She swore she didn't hear anything. OK, maybe she heard and said something through the door and didn't want to get involved any more than that. So she can't admit she heard something and didn't make a call."

"You got names and addresses pulled together or do we go through the file?"

"Do I have names and addresses." Bracken leafed through his papers. "I'll get them copied. Sit back and enjoy your coffee."

"Doesn't take much to grab a wallet," Jane said when he was gone.

"Who knows? Could've been a first-timer, got cold feet."

"A perp in training. That was good that Bracken talked to tenants in other buildings. Sounds like he did a first-rate investigation."

Bracken was coming back, carrying more papers. "There you go. All the names and addresses in one place, landlord, super, tenants—but like you said, they're not there anymore—people at work, ex-wife. You don't for any reason want to interview her yourselves, give me a call. Sexy perfume that woman wears." He looked down at the sheets in his hand. "And some others. It's all here. Save you some time."

Jane took it and ran her eyes over the names on the list. Nothing stood out. "Thanks. This'll help a lot."

"Think Otis Wright could add anything?" Defino asked.

"Ah shit, poor Otis. He didn't retire. He's on medical

extend leave. I can tell you he's not coming back. Emphysema. Just a matter of time. I'll give you his number but I wouldn't bother him at this point." He took back the top sheet and scribbled something. Then he gave each of them his card. "Call me anytime. If you turn anything up, I'd like to know. Any reason they picked this case?"

"Not a clue," Defino said. He stood and offered his hand to Bracken, who shook it, then shook Jane's.

"You got your work cut out."

That was no exaggeration, Jane thought as they walked down the stairs to the main floor.

4

THEY WERE BACK at Centre Street before noon. "We could have lunch," Defino said, "or we could go upstairs and ask MacHovec if he wants to have lunch with us."

Defino wasn't a very subtle man. "Let's have lunch."

There were plenty of places in the area where you could eat quickly and comparatively cheaply. All the courts were on or near Centre Street, and jurors never went very far to eat. For what they were paid, they could hardly afford a sandwich. Lawyers and cops were also regulars, everyone in a hurry, everyone trying to beat the clock.

They grabbed a table for two before the crowd got there. Defino ordered a hamburger and fries and started drinking coffee right away. Jane ordered a salad and a diet Coke.

"That fill you up?"

"Almost."

"I guess that's the point."

"Right."

"Always looks like more work than it's worth."

"That's the point, too."

Defino smiled. "If my wife ever divorces me, it'll be because I can eat anything and she can't. Without gaining weight. It's a struggle for her every day. I don't even think about it." He took the ketchup and poured it generously over the fries and burger. "That guy over there? Sitting alone near the wall? Defense lawyer. Tried every trick in the book to get me to back down on my story about a year ago. I didn't give him an inch. Jury came back in twenty minutes with a conviction. Makes you wonder. Guy must have no self-respect."

"It's a job. I do things all the time I don't want to do."

"We all do."

"What got you on the team?"

"You mean how did I fuck up?"

"Whatever."

"The truth is, I heard about it and I volunteered. I wanted to get away from my old squad for a while. You?"

"I got pulled off the City Hall Park homicide. I'll hit twenty years soon."

"You pulling the pin?"

"It's still a few months away. I got the feeling this was my punishment."

"So what do you think?"

"Always like a good homicide," she said.

"So where do we go from here?"

"Depends on whether MacHovec got anywhere while we were gone. I think we have to talk to those tenants."

"I agree. So if he didn't get anywhere, that's what we do this afternoon. What did you think of Bracken?"

"I liked him. He looks like a good man. Still . . ."

"Yeah?"

"I'd give Otis Wright a call. You never know."

MacHovec was out to lunch when they returned but, surprisingly, he had had not just a busy morning but a productive one. A sheet of paper left on Jane's desk contained an annotated list of names, addresses, and phone numbers, starting with the landlord and super, which they had just picked up from Bracken. There was a date of death for Elaine Best, approximately six months after the Quill homicide, the cause listed as a stroke. Her age had been seventy-nine.

The space next to Hollis Worthman's name was blank. Worthman had lived above Mrs. Best. Across the hall from him, Henry Soderberg, who discovered Quill's body, had, with quotes around the words, "met with an unfortunate accident," probably the words of the landlord or super. Soderberg had died a couple of months after Mrs. Best. The other tenants, Miss Rawls on three and Hutchins on four, apparently moved but left addresses for their security checks to be sent to.

Jane handed the sheet to Defino. "I think I can tell you why the tenants are all gone. After Best died of a stroke, Soderberg died of some kind of accident. That would make three deaths in the building in less than a year. The others probably got scared. Anyway, it looks like MacHovec is good for something."

"A telephone detective. Good at making phone calls."

"That's OK with me."

"So we have Hutchins on four, Rawls on three, and Worthman on two who are presumably alive and living somewhere else. We'll have to track them down."

"I think we should talk to the landlord in person, find out what this unfortunate accident was, and see if he knows where the other three went."

"I got the time."

Jane called the landlord. A secretary answered and said Mr. Stabile would be back from lunch by one-thirty, which was a few minutes away, and he was free and was always happy to work with the police. This last she said as though reading from a script. Jane said they would be there in half an hour.

MacHovec returned before they left and filled them in on a few details. He had informed the landlord that some detectives would be interviewing him, which most likely accounted for the secretary's agreeable disposition. A landlord who cooperated with the police generally felt somewhat secure in the event that tenants banded together to protest the kinds of things that tenants were forever protesting.

MacHovec said he was trying to find someone at the post office who would look up Worthman's forwarding address, and he would keep at it. If he had no luck, he would call in a favor from a postal inspector he knew. He also said the super got cold feet after Soderberg died and quit his job but returned, humbled, about six weeks later, having used up his savings. He was still on the job.

The landlord's office was on the ground floor of a large, prewar apartment house on West Eighty-sixth Street, half a block from Riverside Drive. Jane and Defino tinned their way onto the subway—showed their shields—getting there about two-fifteen. The building was a couple of blocks from Jane's apartment and of the same vintage. The West Side was increasingly divided between sixty- and seventy-year-old buildings and brand-new ones, but this block of Eighty-sixth was solidly old, tough as a fortress.

"I guess I expected Detective Bracken," Stabile said after they had introduced themselves. "I thought he was working on this case."

"He was," Jane said, "and he's still the detective in charge, but we're reinvestigating the case."

"Really. I see." His welcoming smile faded to nervousness. "Why this case? Aren't they satisfied that it was some mugger off the street?"

"We're just trying to put a name to him, Mr. Stabile. And we have a few questions."

"Anything at all." He opened his hands in a gesture of complicity. "Can I give you some coffee?"

Jane turned it down as Defino accepted. The secretary brought a cup for him.

"We understand that Mr. Soderberg had a fatal accident. Can you tell us about that?"

"Mr. Soderberg," Stabile said, looking confused. "I thought you were here on the Quill case."

"We are. But we're interested in the death of Mr. Soderberg as well."

"I see." He looked very unhappy. "It was horrible," Stabile said, his forehead forming furrows. "He fell down the stairs."

"Where?"

"In my building." His eyes darted from one detective to the other.

"Where was he found?" Jane asked.

"On the second floor at the bottom of the stairs."

"And who found him?"

"I believe Miss Rawls did, when she came home. It was a terrible shock."

Defino was shaking his head. "Soderberg lived on two, isn't that right?"

"That's correct, apartment two B."

"Then what was he doing falling down the stairs from the third floor?"

"I couldn't tell you, Detective. He must have gone upstairs for something."

Defino's skepticism was all over his face. "Did you tell Detective Bracken about this?"

"No."

"Why not?"

"I didn't think it was necessary. It had nothing to do with . . . anything."

"Wasn't Mr. Soderberg the one who found Arlen Quill's body?"

"I believe so, yes. I think that's what I heard."

"And it didn't strike you as strange that the person who found the body had this kind of accident?"

"I never connected the two." Stabile looked very troubled. "It happened almost a year later, and I had a building full of frightened people. The others moved out, you know. They're gone. It took me a while to rent out those apartments. Miss Rawls moved out before the end of that month. She'd been there for years. Years," he said again. "There was a lot of income involved in that building."

"Was there a police investigation of that accident?" Jane asked.

"I don't know. I couldn't tell you. Miss Rawls called for an ambulance. They came and took him away."

"Was he still alive then?"

"I don't know. She must have thought so, if she called an ambulance."

"Any other accidents after that one?"

"None, none at all." The phone on his desk rang and he looked at it with distaste till it was answered elsewhere. "That's a safe building, everything up to code."

"Was there a lawsuit over the Soderberg incident?"

"No, there wasn't. It was simply an accident."

"I see," Jane said. She flipped a page in her notebook. "Was Mr. Quill's apartment occupied at the time Mr. Soderberg had his accident?"

"It wasn't. His estate held on to it for a while."

"His estate?"

"I think there's a mother somewhere. It took her some time to clean it out. She kept it for several months."

"Was anybody home when the accident happened?"

"I don't know. Mrs. Best had died. She was the very lovely lady who lived on the first floor. Mr. Worthman lived on two, across from Mr. Soderberg, but he went to work every day. He may not have come home yet. Miss Rawls was living on three when she found him. Mr. Hutchins was on four. I think he had irregular hours, but I couldn't tell you any more than that. I wasn't in the building very often."

"Where can we find the super?" Defino asked.

Stabile wrote something on a piece of notepaper and

pushed it across the desk. "Derek lives down the block from that building in another one that I own. You can find him there."

Jane closed her notebook and Defino picked up on it. "Thanks for your time, Mr. Stabile. We may be contacting you again."

"Anytime," the landlord said, smiling again. "Always at your service."

They walked back across Eighty-sixth Street to Broadway. The subway stop was at the corner, the number one Broadway line that ran in a straight line all the way from South Ferry at the foot of Manhattan to Two Hundred Forty-second Street near Van Cortlandt Park at the lower end of the Bronx. Jane had lived and occasionally nearly died on that line for more years than she could count.

"You live up here, don't you?"

"Two blocks from here. I'll have to get used to a whole new bunch of takeouts when I move."

"Where're you going?"

"The Village."

"That'll be a change."

"I'm looking forward to it."

"How'd he strike you?"

"Nervous."

"Holding back?"

"Maybe."

Defino looked at his watch. "Want to talk to the super?"

"Absolutely."

They took the train to Fifty-ninth and walked the same route Jane had walked last evening.

"Still Hell's Kitchen up here," Defino said.

"Just what I was thinking."

The building the super lived in was closer to Ninth than Quill's building and looked identical to it. They found Derek, a pudgy black man with a scraggly beard and work clothes, in his ground-floor apartment.

"You the cops?" he said when he saw them.

"Mr. Stabile call you?" Defino asked.

"Yeah. Said you might come by. This about that murder a coupla years ago?"

"Mr. Quill. You remember that?"

"Man, I can't never forget it."

"I can believe it," Jane said. "Must have been awful."

"Yeah, it was. You wanna come in?"

"Sure."

The inside was a mess, a big room that had never seen a vacuum cleaner, never had anything thrown away or replaced.

"You can sit here, miss," Derek said, removing a pile of nondescript items from a wooden chair and putting them on the floor. He offered Defino a chair from the kitchen and then he sat on a sofa with just enough uncluttered space for one man's bottom.

Jane introduced herself and started the questioning. "We heard there was a tragic accident in that building a few months after Mr. Quill was murdered."

"That other man, Mr. Soderberg, yeah. He fell down the stairs. That poor lady on three, she found him when she came home from work."

"Did the police talk to you after that?"

Derek looked scared. "The police? What they want to talk to me for?"

"Just to find out what happened."

"What happened? That was a accident. He fell down the stairs."

"Seems a little funny to me," Defino said, screwing his face into a look of skepticism or even disbelief. "He lived on two, didn't he?"

"Yeah."

"So how come he fell down the stairs and landed on two? What would he have been doing one flight up from where he lived?"

"He was changin' a lightbulb is what he was doin'."

"Changing a lightbulb?"

"Yeah. He was always complainin' 'bout those missin' lightbulbs. Someone was comin' in offa the street and stealin' them. He kep' sayin' it was dangerous, you didn't have enough light."

"How'd he reach the ceiling?"

"He had a little chair or somethin'. I don't remember exactly what."

"Isn't that your job, Derek? Changing lightbulbs?"

"It's my job, sure, but I gotta see that lightbulb's missin'. I can't be everyplace at once." He sounded very imposed upon, as though he were being asked to do more than his contract required.

"Where were you when it happened, Derek?" Jane asked.

"Me? I was here. I was watchin' TV."

"Who was the lady who found him?"

"That Miss Rawls. Nice lady. She about as scared as anyone I ever see. She called a ambulance. I heard it come and I went down to see what happened. They took him away."

"What happened to Miss Rawls?"

"She picked up and moved out. Left the same night."

"You know where she went?" Defino asked.

"Yeah, she went to live with a friend. She give me the address."

"Do you still have it?"

"Nah. I threw it away. She come back a coupla days later, moved her stuff out. I never saw her again."

"I heard you moved out, too," Defino said.

"I was scared. Too many people die in that house. I went to stay with a friend but he threw me out after a few weeks. Mr. Stabile, he took me back. I been here ever since."

"Did you know Mr. Soderberg?" Jane asked.

"I knew 'em all. They all nice people. They nice to me at Christmas."

"How did Mr. Soderberg get along with the other people in the house?"

Derek shrugged. "I couldn't tell you that. I never heard no shoutin' or nothin'."

"Do you remember Mrs. Best?"

"The lady on one? I remember her."

"Did she die in the house?"

"Yeah."

"Who found her body?"

Derek took a deep breath. "Somebody called. They didn't see her for a while so Mr. Stabile asked me to open the door."

"That must have been pretty awful," Jane said.

"I never wanna do that again, I can tell you."

"It's been rough on you, Derek."

"It sure has."

"How are the people who live in that building now? You get along with them?"

He smiled, showing a couple of missing teeth. "I get along with everybody. Just ask Mr. Stabile."

$$5$$

THEY WENT DOWN the block to the building where Quill had lived and died. All seven apartments were occupied now, and they turned down Derek's offer to go inside the apartments of their choice. They had no warrants, and there wasn't much they could learn almost five years after the victim's death. The file contained sketches of Quill's apartment, but it was clear he had not been attacked there, nor had he died there.

As they walked up to the fourth floor, Derek prattled

away about who had lived where, what a nice person he was, who lived there now.

"How do you get to the roof?" Defino asked.

"Up there." Derek pointed. The stairway became little more than a ladder from the top floor to the roof.

"You keep that door locked or open?"

"Locked most of the time."

"Was it locked or open when Mr. Quill died?"

"Prob'ly locked, but I don't remember no more. You can ask that policeman was here after the murder. He tell you."

"What about when Mr. Soderberg died? Was it locked or open that day?"

Derek raised his shoulders. "I couldn't tell you. Prob'ly locked."

"Who else has the key to the roof?"

"Mr. Stabile."

"Any chance Mr. Soderberg was out on the roof the day he had the accident?"

"I don't guess so. Nobody goes out there 'cept me."

The interior of the building had a new coat of paint, and the stair treads looked as though they had been repaired or replaced recently. Maybe Stabile had put some money into the building in order to attract renters.

They went downstairs, stopping on two, where Soderberg's body had been found.

"Is that where Mr. Worthman lived?" Jane asked.

"Yeah, that was his place."

"You have any idea where he went when he moved out?"

"I think maybe back to his family in Harlem."

"Is Mr. Worthman black?"

Derek nodded his head.

"How long did he live here?"

"Long time. Maybe twenty years. More'n I been here."

They went downstairs and out to the street. Derek left them, walking slowly back to his building.

"I wonder if Bracken ran a check on Derek to see if he

has a record," Jane said. "Let's check the case file and, if not, call down to NCIC."

"Sounds good. Want me to sign you out?" Defino asked. "Seems like a shame for you to go all the way downtown just to turn around and go back up."

"Thanks. I don't mind. Give me a chance to think."

MacHovec had spent a busy afternoon. The medical examiner would send over a copy of the report on Soderberg's autopsy tomorrow. "Lotta broken bones," MacHovec said, looking at his notes. "Head injury probably did him in."

"Any chance he was pushed?"

"There's always a chance. Also a chance it was a suicide. But the ME's office labeled it accidental. Looked like he was up on a stool to reach a lightbulb."

"You get anything on Worthman?" Jane asked.

"Not yet. You?"

"He's black. The super thinks he went back to his family in Harlem. Maybe we should try the phone book."

MacHovec grinned. "I'm good at that."

They sat down and began comparing notes. MacHovec had the name of the friend Miss Rawls had moved in with, but he hadn't been able to reach her by phone. He also had a forwarding address for the man from the West, Jerry Hutchins, and had come up with a local phone number from Cole's Directory, but again, there was no answer.

"I'll try them from home tonight," Jane said, taking the slips of paper and copying the information. "They'll be home from work."

MacHovec had also checked up on the landlord's record. It was amazingly clean. He had been cited for a minor violation in another of his buildings two years ago, but aside from that, he seemed to manage well-run buildings. Either he had a cozy relationship with inspectors or his buildings were up to building code. There were no records of anyone who lived in Quill's building at the time of his death ever taking a complaint downtown.

Defino was just starting to type up his DD14s, the forms for recording additional information, when the second whip knocked on the doorjamb and came inside.

"Just touching base," he said. "Anything I can do for you?"

"We're doing OK," Defino said.

"You're on the Quill case, right? I looked that one over. Everything's a dead end there. They questioned every mugger in Manhattan about that homicide. Got nowhere."

"We turned something up," MacHovec said.

"Oh, yeah?"

"Another suspicious death in that building."

"OK!" McElroy said with feeling. He sat on the nearest desk. "Let me in on the secret."

MacHovec gave it to him, and McElroy almost beamed. He had something to take back to his boss.

"Hey, it sounds like you're really onto something. Any chance this was a homicide?"

"A chance," MacHovec said. "The ME came down on accidental death."

They talked about it for a couple of minutes and then McElroy left.

"Just enough to let the whip know we're on the job," MacHovec said. "I'm on my way. See you guys tomorrow."

"Were you holding your breath?" Defino asked when he was gone.

Jane laughed. "I was. I was afraid he'd give McElroy everything and then we'd find out tomorrow it was all worthless. But what he said was OK. He was right. It was just enough."

"Go home," Defino said. "I'll be using the typewriter for the next half hour."

Before she left she called the mover. They had a cancellation for Saturday morning. Could she be ready by then? She said yes and took a deep breath. It was really going to happen.

The steam was puffing up in little spurts as she entered the apartment. The sight of the packed cartons startled her; they seemed so out of place. She wondered if leaving this apartment for the last time would affect her. This was only the second real home in her life, and after she left her first home, she watched her mother get sick and die there. She had pleaded with her father to leave then, to find a small, clean new apartment in a safe neighborhood, but he would have none of it.

She had never felt that kind of fierce affection for a place, but she knew he felt it, and as long as he was able, he would stay there, and she would see to it that he could.

The answering machine was blinking and beeping, and she pressed the play button as she took her coat off. It was a man's voice: "Jane." A brief silence. "I've been missing you. I just wanted to hear your voice." That was it. The mechanical voice told her the call had come in less than five minutes ago. She dropped her coat on a chair and pressed the replay button.

"Jane . . . I've been missing you. I just wanted to hear your voice."

So I heard your voice and you heard mine on the recording. There was never anything simple about the man. Had he called early so as to miss her or had he called as late as he could, just as he was leaving for home, hoping to catch her as she walked in the door? How many hours or days had he thought about calling before picking up the phone?

She hung up her coat and listened to the message a third time. "Jane . . . I've been missing you. I just wanted to hear your voice."

"Miss you too, Hack," she said to the machine. The voice still did it to her, hit her where it hurt most. She had done the right thing, breaking it off, but righteousness was a cold bedfellow. She let thoughts of him enter her mind as she changed her clothes and went to the kitchen to scrape up some dinner. The relationship had been long and warm and rewarding. Even the end was not bitter. Maybe the breakup was the greater reason for her deciding to take the new job. In a high-rise office building there was no chance of crossing paths. The insurance business was another world, one he would not enter.

And soon there would be another apartment. Would he call this number in a few weeks or months and hear a robotic voice telling him the number had been changed? Would he think she had married or moved in with a new boyfriend? Would he dial the new number to find out?

Nothing was simple. If this apartment—the wood and plaster and thick coats of paint—had not left a permanent mark on her, maybe his presence in it had. Maybe that was what she would miss in the end, knowing that Hack had walked these floors, lain in her bed, cooked for her in the kitchen, that they had been here together, that he would never set foot in the new place.

It took her long enough to decide to make it end. Several months ago his daughter began to ask pointed questions about where he spent his evenings. Discretion went only so far; she had suspicions, which meant his wife did. Something had to change, and Jane made the decision. They would stop seeing each other, and he would stay with his family. Afterward she had to keep herself from calling, as he had only minutes ago, just to hear his voice, to hear him say something comforting, something to carry her through a tough time. His number was still number two on her speed dial. No one had come along to fill the slot, not that she was looking. She was forty when men her age were looking for girls half of hers.

Enough, she thought, taking out the one dish, the one knife, the one fork. It was good that she would be moving in a few days. Maybe in a couple of weeks she would call and leave her new number, just so that he could have it.

Come on, Jane, she instructed herself. It's dinnertime. Get on with it.

* * *

It was while she was in Chinatown that she had decided to go to college. *Decided* wasn't exactly a fair way to put it; Flora Hamburg ordered her to get a degree.

"Go to school, girl," she said. "There's no future for you if you don't."

Jane didn't want to. It would be years of hard work, and she wasn't convinced that it would pay off, although she knew now that it was the way to go. She registered at John Jay College of Criminal Justice, a division of CUNY that catered to cops and firemen by offering the same courses twice a day, morning or afternoon, and then again in the evening to fit in with changing tours of duty. One week she sat in on the morning class; the next week, when she was working days, she attended the evening class. Luckily the college wasn't far from the apartment, which made it easy.

About halfway through college, when she had left Chinatown for OCCB, the Organized Crime Control Bureau/Narcotics Unit down on Ericsson Place, she sat down next to an older student in one of her forensics classes. She hadn't seen him before—maybe he came days when she came nights—and they talked during a break and after class for a few minutes. He seemed interested in her career but said nothing about his own, just told her his name was Hack. She figured him for an executive in the security business.

It was more than a year before she ran into him again. It happened on St. Patrick's Day, when an Irish cop she had dated a couple of times invited her to the annual Emerald Society bash for a traditional green beer after the parade. The place was wall-to-wall cops, most of them, like her date, smashed. She looked up and saw the man from last year's class standing in front of her, wearing the uniform of a lieutenant with a couple of medals on his chest.

"Jane Bauer," he said.

"Lieutenant." She was nearly speechless.

"Nice to see you again. How's the degree coming?"

"Very well, sir."

"No 'sir,' OK? I told you the name was Hack. You were in Manhattan South last year, OCCB. I always liked that place. I used to take my daughter to see the horses in the stable downstairs."

She was amazed at his memory. "They're still there."

"Where are you?"

"Still in Manhattan South. I'm on the burglary squad now."

"Behind the Academy. Maybe we'll run into each other. I spend a lot of time down there. Enjoy the party. It was good seeing you again."

She felt dazzled. She watched him walk away, grasp someone's hand, pat someone else on the back. She felt a sexual draw that had happened only once or twice before. But he had said "daughter," and that meant wife, and she didn't want to get into that kind of situation. Flora would kill her, and Flora was right.

That was more than ten years ago, and Flora hadn't killed her because Flora didn't know.

Looking through her few pieces of mail reminded Jane that she would have to let the post office know of her change of address. And the credit-card people and the stores where she had charge accounts. The details of moving went far beyond hiring a van with a few strong men.

At the bottom of the pile of mail was the little letter on crinkly paper. Once again she left it unopened. This was not the time. She had dinner to eat and calls to make to try to locate the missing tenants in Quill's building.

"This is Catherine Phelps. Who is this, please?" The voice was not that of a native New Yorker. It had probably started life in the South, although Jane guessed its owner had lived here for some time.

"This is Det. Jane Bauer of the New York Police Department."

"My goodness! That is a surprise. Has something happened?"

"No, ma'am. We're just trying to locate someone you know, Miss Margaret Rawls."

"Margaret. Well. It's a long time since I've heard from Margaret."

"Do you have an address for her?"

"May I ask why you want to find her?"

"It concerns a homicide that took place in a building she lived in a few years ago."

"Yes, I remember that very well. Her neighbor was murdered in the downstairs area."

"That's right. We'd like to talk to her about it."

A "hmm" came across the line. "Well, I tell you what. I don't like doing business over the phone. I'm sure you can understand that. If you want to come and show me some identification, I'll tell you what I know."

"How about first thing tomorrow morning, Miss Phelps?"

"That will be just fine. I usually leave for work about eight-fifteen. If you can be here before eight, we can talk."

The address wasn't far. Catherine Phelps lived on West End Avenue in the Seventies, and Jane could walk it in fifteen minutes or less. Getting up early was preferable to knocking herself out tonight and not getting any packing done. There were linens and clothes still to be taken care of, a couple of small rugs to be rolled and tied. In fact, everywhere she looked there seemed to be something else that needed to be packed.

That left the number for Jerry Hutchins. She dialed it and waited while it rang several times, finally answered by a youngish-sounding man.

"I'd like to speak to Jerry Hutchins."

"Who?"

"Mr. Hutchins, Jerry Hutchins."

"No one here by that name right now."

"Maybe someone by that name stayed at your address a while back. I really need to talk to him."

"Hey, babe, anyone in New York could've lived here a while back. Hold on."

There were voices in the background. It almost sounded like a bar on Saturday night. Then another man said, "This is Al."

"I'm trying to find Jerry Hutchins."

"Jerry Hutchins."

"Yes."

"It kind of rings a bell."

"Does he live there?"

"If he does, it's news to me. But it wouldn't be the first time someone's lived here without my knowing it."

"Do you know where I can find him?"

"When do you think he was here?"

"About three or four years ago."

"Four years! Lady, in this place that's a lifetime."

"Al," she said plaintively, "I really need to find him."

"OK, hang on and I'll ask around."

Maybe it was a dormitory, not a bar. The voices sounded male, and there was a lot of laughing. She waited over a minute before he came back.

"You're right, he did live here for a while. But he's been gone for a long time."

"Tell me, Al, is this a hotel? All Jerry gave me was a phone number."

"Nah, we're a loft downtown. People stay awhile, then move on. Jerry was one of them."

"You have any idea where he went?"

"He left the city. Went back to where he came from. One of the guys thinks maybe Omaha."

"OK, thanks, Al."

"Hey, a pleasure. Call anytime."

Not likely.

She worked for the next hour. Going rapidly through a box of more or less important papers, she was happy she and Hack had never written each other letters. He gave her gifts that she treasured, things that she used or wore and would continue to do so, but there was almost a sense of relief that their relationship was not documented on paper, little notes or long letters folded into envelopes, precious missives that would demand rereading, that would evoke all the wrong emotions.

The floors, bare of the rugs, looked odd. She saw for the first time how the sun had bleached the uncovered areas in the living room, how the shape of the rug remained like a memory.

Every step along the path to moving out made her more eager to leave. She was tired of this place; weary was a better word. She found that she hated the glossy paint on the trim around the doors, hated the fact that not one door closed. How had she put up with it for so long? The apartment seemed like a gift when she moved in, and, happy at her newfound independence, like a woman newly in love she had ignored or been blind to all its faults. Now it seemed shabby and worn, a place she could hardly remember liking.

She picked up the Manhattan phone book to put it in a carton and remembered Hollis Worthman, the black tenant on the second floor. She went through the Worthmans, but found no Hollis and no *H*. Looking at the addresses, she picked one in the Thirty-second Precinct in Harlem and dialed it.

"Hello?" It was the voice of an old woman.

"Is this Mrs. Worthman?"

"Yes, it is."

"I'm trying to reach Hollis Worthman."

"Hollis? My son Hollis?"

"I believe so."

"Hollis died, dear."

"Oh, I'm sorry to hear it. My information must be wrong. Can you tell me when it happened?"

"It's more than four years ago now. Hard to believe it's that long."

"Was it illness?" Jane asked, as long as the woman seemed content to keep talking.

"You mean was he sick? No. My boy was a healthy person. He wasn't sick a day in his life. It happened in the street. It was a mugging. I don't know why they had to kill him. He gave them his wallet and his watch. They were just mean. All the young people nowadays, they're mean."

Jane felt a quickening of her heart. Another death from unnatural causes. "I see. Where did this happen?"

"Just on the way to the little grocery store. It's around the corner from us. He often took a walk there at night. He liked the exercise." Her voice trembled.

"I'm very sorry, Mrs. Worthman. I apologize for the intrusion."

"You're quite welcome. I wasn't doing much anyway."

Things were in good shape by the time she was ready for bed. The medicine chest was empty, and all the old leftovers in the refrigerator were in the garbage. The few canned goods and cooking necessities were packed as well.

In her slippers and robe she made a circuit of the apartment, looking for things she had missed. There were two more evenings before moving day. As she passed the answering machine, she stopped. There were no old love letters, no tapes, and no videos. She pressed the play button and listened to his voice one last time. Then she erased the tape.

6

JANE RANG THE bell to Catherine Phelps's apartment on West End Avenue at a quarter to eight. She identified herself through the intercom and made her way in a shaky elevator to the ninth floor. When she walked down the hall, she held her ID in front of her. The door opened and a woman, perhaps in her fifties, scrutinized the ID before smiling and inviting her in.

"I've got coffee for you, Detective Bauer. Just drop your coat on a chair and come sit at the kitchen table. Can I give you an English muffin?"

"No, thanks." Jane did as she was told and took a seat in front of a tall mug of coffee. She had had breakfast at home but this was a nice way to hold an interview. "You said you knew Miss Margaret Rawls."

"I did. Knew her for years. Tried to get her to leave that place she was living in and move up here, but she wouldn't have it. Said the rent was just right and it left her enough money to take a nice trip every summer."

"When was the last time you saw her?"

"You want a date?"

"As close as you can get."

"Well, I'm not too good on dates, but it was a few years ago. She called me one evening in a panic. She sounded over the edge, I can tell you that. There'd been a murder in her building some months before and it had left her looking over her shoulder everywhere she went.

Then someone else in the building died, but I can't remember the circumstances."

"Do you remember if it was a man or a woman?"

Miss Phelps closed her eyes and tilted her head downward. She could have been praying. "A woman, I think. Died of old age. But you know, it was very unsettling, the way they found her there."

"I understand. Then what happened?"

"Margaret said she'd stick it out. Then one day something else happened, a mysterious death, and she found the body, poor thing. That was when she called me and asked if she could move in, just until she found something permanent."

"Did she tell you anything about the mysterious death?"

"I guess he tumbled down the stairs is what she said. Don't ask me for any names. I've got a head like a sieve. But coming home and finding that poor soul . . . it was the last straw."

"Did she move in with you?"

"She did. She grabbed a suitcase and took a cab up here."

"How long did she stay?"

"A couple of weeks. I don't think it was as long as a month."

"The coffee is very good, Miss Phelps. I really appreciate it."

She smiled. She was a well-proportioned woman wearing a gray wool suit with an antique pin on the lapel. Her fingernails were manicured and polished with a shade of pale pink. Antique gold rings decorated many of her fingers, and several gold bracelets were visible at the cuff. A light scent perfumed the air. "I enjoy a good cup of coffee," she said.

"Where did Miss Rawls go when she left you?"

"She sublet an apartment, as I remember, somewhere around here. I never got to see it because she didn't stay very long. She said her sister called her one night and said there were several openings in the company she worked for, and why didn't Margaret come back to Tulsa."

"That's Tulsa, Oklahoma?"

"That's right. The sublet was only for a couple of months, so she could find a place without feeling rushed. When it was over, she picked up and moved back home."

"Do you know where she went?"

"I've got the address right here for you." Miss Phelps pushed a piece of paper across the table. "She went to live with that widowed sister who called her. They'd always been close, and it seemed like the right thing to do."

Jane looked at the address and phone number. "Then I should be able to find her here?"

"I should think so. But I have to tell you, we're no longer on the best of terms. After she moved back, we just lost touch. I didn't expect regular letters or phone calls, but I certainly thought she'd send Christmas cards. When she didn't, I crossed her off my list."

"Well, I thank you for your help."

"Anytime. Always happy to do my part."

Jane took her coat and went down the hall to the elevator.

Downstairs she made a brief detour and went to the post office to change her address. Then she called in and said she'd be late. It was after nine when she got to the Centre Street office. Defino was just as she had left him yesterday, sitting at the typewriter as though he had been there all night.

"Got something?" he said, turning around to say hello.

"Got an address and phone number for Margaret Rawls, and I'm starting to get a lot of bad feelings." She told them about her call to find Jerry Hutchins and the conversation with Hollis Worthman's mother.

"So of the three you've got one a homicide and two left the city," Defino said.

"That's the way it looks. What's the time difference between here and Oklahoma?"

MacHovec checked a card. "One hour and thirteen hundred seventy road miles."

"Better wait an hour then for Miss Rawls. Nebraska's at least an hour, too, but you can call Information and see if Hutchins is listed. If he's not, we'd better see if we can find out anything from the place where he was working. It should be in the file or on that list Bracken gave us."

MacHovec was already on the phone asking for Hutchins, J., Jerry, Jerome, or Jerold. There was a lot of silence, and his pen didn't move. He got off the phone and said, "*Nada*. I guess maybe he could live in a suburb. Why don't I call the Omaha police first and see if they have anything on him?"

"And maybe they'll look in some suburban phone books."

"Omaha's across the river from Iowa," Defino said. "He might commute from out of state."

MacHovec wrote it all down and got on the phone. Jane walked over to where Defino was sitting at the typewriter. "This case is giving me the chills," she said.

"Too many deaths?"

"And too many disappearances."

"You think Bracken should've been onto it?"

"That's not it. He had no reason to go back and reinterview the tenants. He talked to them early on. There're plenty of DD Fives on them. He knew Mrs. Best had died. She was the first. So he was still back at the building six months after the Quill homicide. But I'm starting to feel . . ." She didn't like what she was feeling.

"I'm listening."

"I'm not sure what homicide we should be investigating."

"Soderberg was a possible; Worthman sounds like a homicide."

"Sean can dig up the Sixty-ones and Fives on Worthman." Sixty-ones were original complaint reports, formally called Uniformed Force or UF61s. That would be the first report on the homicide.

In twenty-four hours they had fallen into roles as surely as if they had been assigned. MacHovec would handle the phone and do the research. Jane and Defino would do the legwork.

"Maybe you should call the woman in Tulsa. She might respond better to you."

"Sure." She got her notebook and opened it. "I'll call Quill's wife too. Maybe I can set up an interview for today. And then there's Bracken's partner, Otis Wright. Sean can get that started."

"I'll tag along if you set something up with the wife," Defino said before turning back to his typewriter.

Before calling the wife, Jane took a sheet of unlined paper and sketched the house on Fifty-sixth Street, putting in the names of the tenants. It was a lopsided picture, with four occupied apartments on the left side and only two on the right. There was no apartment on the right side of the ground floor, and only Soderberg and Quill had lived on that side. The sketch didn't provide any insights, so she pushed it aside, leaving it where she could look at it, and called Laura Thorne, Arlen Quill's ex-wife.

"This is Laura Thorne," a pleasant voice answered.

"Mrs. Thorne, this is Det. Jane Bauer. I have some questions to ask you about Arlen Quill. We're reinvestigating his murder."

"I told the police everything I knew when it happened. That was a long time ago." The voice turned less pleasant.

"I'm sure you did, but I'd like to talk to you myself. Can I stop over this morning?"

"I'm very busy this morning. Perhaps we could look at a day next week."

"Next week is pretty far away. Suppose we try for lunch hour today?"

Laura Thorne exhaled in resignation. "Twelve-fifteen," she said. "I'll wait for you in the lobby of my office building. I assume you know where that is."

Jane read off the address. It was a large building on the west side of Sixth Avenue.

"Fine. I'm wearing a black coat with a red silk scarf."

"I'll see you at twelve-fifteen."

Defino relinquished the typewriter, and Jane typed up a Five on Catherine Phelps. When she was finished, she called the Tulsa number Miss Phelps had given her. The woman who answered had a sweet southern voice.

"I'd like to speak to Margaret Rawls," Jane said.

"Who is this, please?"

"This is Det. Jane Bauer of the New York City Police Department. It's not an emergency. There's nothing to be concerned about. I need some information from Miss Rawls."

"I'm Miss Rawls's sister. I'm afraid my sister passed away, Detective."

And stopped sending Christmas cards to Catherine Phelps. "I'm sorry to hear that. Can you tell me the circumstances of her death?"

"May I inquire why you are asking these questions?"

"We're reinvestigating the murder in the building your sister lived in. It seems a strange coincidence that she died, as well as the man whose body she found."

"Well, then. Margaret died in a traffic accident. She was hit by a car. It was a hit-and-run. She never had a chance." The voice choked up slightly.

"I see. And when did this happen?"

"About . . . it must be nearly three years now."

Jane was aware that Defino had stopped what he was doing and was watching her, listening to her responses. So was MacHovec.

"Ma'am, did your sister ever talk to you about the murder in the building she lived in in New York?"

"She talked about it a lot. It was the reason she left New York and came home. She'd lived there for a long time but that murder unnerved her. And then what happened afterward."

"What are you referring to?"

"She came home one day and found the body of a neighbor lying on the floor in the hallway. She moved out that night."

"I spoke to Miss Catherine Phelps this morning," Jane said.

"Yes, she's the one Margaret moved in with for a while. She's a good woman and a good friend. I'm afraid I never really informed her of Margaret's death."

"Ma'am, could you tell me your name, please?"

"Yes, of course. I'm Nancy Hopkins."

"Mrs. Hopkins, did your sister tell you anything about the third death in the building she lived in?"

"That would be Henry. She said he fell down some stairs. That's all I can remember about the accident, but what was so terrible for her was that she knew him."

"She knew him?" Jane said.

"Yes. She told me all this when she came back. She'd been on her way to have some dinner one night when she ran into him doing the same and he suggested they have dinner together."

"I see. Did they do that on other occasions?"

"I think they did. I don't want to make too much of it, but Margaret was a lovely-looking woman with great charm. I think they found each other interesting, although I wouldn't say they had a serious relationship."

"But they knew each other," Jane said.

"Yes, they knew each other."

"Did she say his death was an accident?"

"That's what she was told. But she didn't stay around very long to find out how it happened."

"Did she ever go back to the building again?"

"You mean to visit? I don't think so. I don't think she had any real friends left in the building, just neighbors. She must have gone back once to get her things. When she came home, there was a truck with her furniture."

"Can you tell me anything about the accident that killed your sister?"

"I wasn't with her when it happened. I only know

what they told me. She had left work and was getting her car from the parking lot. That's where the car hit her."

"In the parking lot?"

"That's right."

"I thought you said it was a traffic accident," Jane said, looking down at her notes.

"What I meant to say was that she was hit by a car. I must have picked the wrong word. Margaret was walking toward her car when she was hit. The police said there were no witnesses. By the time people got there, the car that hit her was gone."

"Can you give me the name of the detective who investigated the accident?" Jane asked.

"Yes, I remember his name very well. It was Johnnie Roy Anderson."

"Thank you, Mrs. Hopkins. I assume they've never found the driver of the car."

"Not that they've told me. It was probably some young fella who ran away when he saw what he'd done. I don't expect they'll ever get him. Maybe when he's old and gray he'll come forward because of his conscience. I've heard of that happening."

"It does happen sometimes. I'm sorry for your loss, Mrs. Hopkins. Thank you for your help."

Jane put the phone down and looked around the small office. MacHovec had just put his phone down and both men were looking at her.

"Dead?" MacHovec said.

She nodded.

"Suspicious circumstances?" from Defino.

"Hit in a parking lot as she was walking toward her car. No witnesses, no suspects."

"Wow," MacHovec said. "Maybe we better take out more life insurance working on this case."

"But there's a connection between the Rawls woman and Soderberg. They went to dinner sometimes."

"Interesting," Defino said. "I wonder how Hutchins died."

"Hutchins is dead too?" Jane swiveled to look at him.

"No, just a bad joke. Sorry. If we find him alive, at least we've got a suspect."

"A busy one," MacHovec said. "That makes five suspicious deaths, right?"

"If you include Mrs. Best. Four if she died of natural causes." Jane looked at her sketch of the building. "I've never had a case like this before."

"Got you goin', huh?" MacHovec said with a wicked grin.

She felt a flicker of irritation, but he was right. "All I can think of is questions."

"And the big question is why," Defino said. "You got anything, Sean?"

"Omaha police'll look into it and get back to me. And the autopsy on Soderberg should be here before noon."

"We'll be gone before noon," Jane said. "We're meeting Quill's ex-wife at twelve-fifteen on Sixth Avenue in the Fifties. Doesn't matter. She's not going to give us much time. She sounded very defensive."

"Hey, if she paid to have Quill killed, she could've paid to have them all killed."

"But why?" Defino said.

Why, indeed, Jane thought. She pushed the notebook away and called her dad.

7

THEY ALLOWED PLENTY of time so they wouldn't be late, taking the D train up to Fiftieth Street, then walking north past Radio City to the office building Laura Thorne worked in. It was a section of Sixth Avenue with one glass-and-steel building after another, buildings that held thousands of people each on weekdays, people who clogged the streets and subways and buses in the morning and early evening.

They crossed to the west side of the street and found the door to the massive lobby behind which were banks of elevators.

"We're early," Defino said. "Black coat, red scarf?"

"That's what she said."

"That her over there?"

The woman standing to the side of the information desk was blond and very pretty, wearing what she had promised and black high heels. They walked toward her and she saw them and watched them approach without a hint of recognition.

"Mrs. Thorne?" Jane said, showing her shield and photo ID.

"Yes."

"I'm Det. Jane Bauer and this is Det. Gordon Defino. Where would you like to go to talk?"

"Not here. Come with me. They're holding a table at a little place around the corner."

They headed toward Seventh Avenue, Laura Thorne leading the way so that she scarcely looked as though she was walking with them. The coffee shop was almost full, but there was a table in the back that was empty, and she walked directly to it and sat so that her back was to the door. Jane and Defino sat opposite.

After sitting, Laura Thorne stood and took off her coat and silk scarf, folding them carefully on the chair next to hers. She was wearing a good-looking suit of black wool with a white silk blouse showing at the neck and an interesting handmade silver pin on one lapel. Her nails and lips were an exact match. Her wedding ring was a row of diamonds of a good size, and on her other hand was a silver ring in a fluid free-form. Her face was made up with care, the eyes very prominent, only a hint of color in the cheeks. Her scent crossed the table like an invitation, and Jane remembered Bracken's comment.

"Mrs. Thorne," Jane began, "we're reinvestigating the murder of your former husband. Can you tell me exactly when you married him and the date of your divorce?"

Laura Thorne looked stunned. If she had prepared herself for this meeting, it was not to answer this question. She looked at Jane for a long moment with a wide-eyed stare, and then she smiled. It was a beautiful, practiced smile, but she said nothing.

"Could you answer the question?" Jane asked.

"You're joking."

"I'm quite serious. When did you marry Mr. Quill and when were you divorced?"

"I can't really remember. Uh, we were married in June 1993, I think. The divorce was . . . I don't know the date."

"Can you tell us a year?"

"It was about a year before he was murdered. We were separated for some time before that. I stayed in the old apartment and Arlen moved out. He moved into the place where . . . where he died."

"When did you meet your present husband?"

"While I was still married to Arlen. It's why we broke

up. I fell in love with Terry and that was it. My marriage was over."

"When did you marry Mr. Thorne?"

"May seventeenth, 1996." She smiled nervously. At last she had remembered one date.

"Where were you when Mr. Quill was murdered?"

"I've given all this information to the police. Terry and I were on a cruise in the Caribbean. I didn't know Arlen was dead until we got back." She motioned a waitress to come to the table, and she ordered a salad and tea. Jane and Defino declined. "I hope you'll excuse me but I must have lunch before I get back to work."

"What was your relationship with your former husband after you married Mr. Thorne?" Jane asked.

"We were never on bad terms. I didn't ask for alimony, so we had no quarrels over money. I kept a small bank account in my name, and we agreed that it was mine. Arlen kept everything else."

"Did he enjoy his job?"

"That's a hard question to answer. Arlen wasn't a person who came home and said how much he enjoyed things. I don't think he really liked his job, but I don't think it ever occurred to him to look for something he might like better."

"Was that a source of trouble between you?"

"I wouldn't put it quite that way. Arlen was a man who plodded along. He did his job well. No one ever complained about him or the way he worked. He put in his hours, picked up his paycheck, and came home at night. Sometimes we went out to a movie, sometimes we had dinner out, sometimes we watched television. A few times a week we made love. I don't think Arlen ever thought about where he was going. He cared for me a great deal. Unfortunately, I was bored."

"Did you think about where you were going?"

"All the time." She said it as though it were her defining statement. Her salad arrived and she began to eat it in small, careful mouthfuls, patting her mouth from time to time with the napkin. The tea steeped in a small metal pot. After a minute or two, she poured it and sipped it without adding sugar or lemon.

"You were saying that you thought about where you were going," Jane said.

"I did. It was very important to me. If you had seen me when I married Arlen, you wouldn't recognize me. I didn't know anything, and that's how I looked. I learned a lot during my marriage to him. One of those things was that I had to change my appearance. I worked at it. I started doing exercises, I changed the kind of clothes I wore, I had my hair cut a different way." She stretched out her hands as though to appreciate her manicure. Every nail was perfect.

"Arlen loved me very much. It was a terrible blow to him when I said I was leaving. But he was a dead-end man with a dead-end job. He would have stayed in that job forever. Terry has an important position, and he keeps moving up. I've taken a few giant steps myself."

It didn't surprise Jane. Everything about this woman was careful and studied.

"The only pictures of you in Mr. Quill's apartment look the way you look now," Defino said. "Didn't he keep any of the old ones for sentimental reasons?"

She allowed her lips to smile very slightly. "I burned them. I wouldn't have them around. Arlen was very angry when he found out."

"Can you think of anyone who might have wanted to kill Mr. Quill?" Jane asked.

"Not at all." She pressed the napkin against her mouth again. "I thought this was supposed to be a mugging or a push-in or whatever they call it."

"We don't know," Defino said. "Nothing was taken from Mr. Quill. He had his wallet when he was found, and there was money in it. We were hoping you might have thought of someone who had a grudge, a reason, an argument with him."

Laura Thorne shook her head. "Who would have cared? I don't think Arlen made enough of a difference in anyone's life that they would want him dead."

* * *

They left her to finish her salad and tea, to pat her mouth dry and pay her bill. They walked west until they found a small restaurant with lasagna on the menu in the window. Defino wanted pasta and Jane didn't care. A very harried waitress pointed them toward a tiny table that was being cleared and they sat.

"What a climber," Defino said. "Talk about moving up the social ladder. That woman used Quill as a stepping-stone."

"The coat was cashmere. I touched it as we were walking. I feel sorry for Quill. But there's no motive. If there was money hidden somewhere, she would have killed him before the divorce."

"She'd have no claim after she remarried."

"Funny that she didn't remember when she married him. I thought women remembered things like that." There were dates in Jane's life that she would never forget, none of them a wedding.

"My wife gets mad at me when I forget the year. And it was a lot longer ago than this broad was married."

"She has no reason to remember," Jane said. "She'd rather forget. She was an ugly duckling, and she doesn't want to be reminded of those times."

"You think she's a dead end."

"Too soon to say. I hope to God they find Hutchins alive."

"They won't," Defino said. "It's that kind of a case."

It was two-thirty when they got back to Centre Street. MacHovec was on the phone, and Defino had a message to call his wife. Jane took the opportunity to call her dad. He was feeling fine, had gone out for a walk, and was having dinner with Madeleine tonight. His voice was strong and he sounded good.

"I hear there's no progress on the City Hall Park Murder," he said when he'd answered all her questions.

"I haven't even had time to think about that," Jane

said. "It's a week and a half. If they haven't cracked it by now, it may be a long time."

"You could have done it, Janey."

"Let's see if I can crack the one I'm working on now. It's a case that really grabs you, Dad. I think it's got more to it than the other one."

"The other one had visibility." He was always sure that if she did something that was noticed, she'd end up running the detective division. It was hard to disabuse him of his fantasies, and Captain Graves had a leg up on the job.

"At least here the press isn't looking over our shoulders all the time."

"You tell me about it when I see you."

She promised she would. MacHovec was off the phone, and Defino was arguing with his wife about something. When he saw Jane hang up, he wound up his call.

"Got the autopsy on Soderberg," MacHovec said. "No surprises. His injuries were consistent with falling down the stairs. Could he have been pushed? Yeah. Could he have fallen off the stool? Yeah. The ME flipped a coin on it and made it an accident."

"Don't they usually steal lightbulbs from the downstairs socket?" Jane said. "Seems like a long walk up just for a bulb."

"Maybe Hutchins snatched it," Defino said.

"And take away light he needed to get upstairs?"

"He needed a lightbulb," Defino said. "He took one."

"Anything on Hutchins?" she asked MacHovec.

"He doesn't have a Nebraska driver's license, but they'll check Iowa. No rap sheet. This guy's gonna call around the high schools, see if Hutchins went to any of them. It'll take some time, but he offered to do it. You ever notice how polite these guys are in the Midwest? They seem to get a kick out of helping the big-city detectives."

They started to talk about it when a cheer went up in one of the nearby offices. It sounded as if someone had hit the lottery. They went out to the briefing area just about the same time everyone else in the squad did. A couple of doors down, three detectives were going crazy, shouting and yodeling their excitement. Lots of high-fives and handshakes.

The black woman walked over to Jane and said, "They cracked their case."

"How . . . ?" She couldn't believe it. "How'd they do it?"

"Two of them walked in to question a friend of the victims and he got scared and confessed."

"What case was it?"

"The girls dumped at the side of the Bruckner Expressway."

It was the group Jane had had lunch with yesterday. She started toward the gathering crowd, but Captain Graves, smiling like a proud poppa, was on his way.

"Guess we won't get the gold medal," MacHovec said behind her.

"We should have such luck."

But she knew it wouldn't happen to them. The murder of Arlen Quill was not a pickup and rape. There was more to it than that. Much more.

Not a hell of a lot of work was done for the rest of the afternoon. Before the day was over, every TV station had set up cameras and lights in the briefing area, and Graves, every silver hair in place, had given a statement, smoothly worded and delivered, and then introduced the three detectives who were the new stars of the task force.

MacHovec suggested with disgust that the whole thing had been a setup to promote the squad and help Graves on the road to the chief of D's office. In spite of his undis-guised hostility, Jane couldn't entirely discount what he said. As the man in charge, Graves looked damn good.

The new heroes of the squad were gracious in victory. Jane got a hug from one of them and an offer of cham-pagne from another. At this rate, the celebration might last through the weekend. And then what? MacHovec said irritably that all three would be promoted and out of

Centre Street in a week, maybe even get a chance to pick
their new commands. Jane wasn't sure what he was so
upset about. He had the job of his dreams right now. He
never had to leave the chair behind his desk except to go
for coffee and the men's room, which appeared to be the
life he had always wanted.

"You think MacHovec's right?" Defino said next to her.

"That it's a setup? Graves would be out on his ear if it
ever came to light."

"Yeah, I guess so." He sounded defeated, and she
wondered whether she was the only one who hadn't se-
cretly dreamed of being the first to solve their case.

Omaha called back later in the afternoon. They had
found the high school Hutchins had graduated from,
but he had dropped from sight after that. A call to the
home he had lived in during high school found someone
else using the number for the past seven years. The detective was checking other Hutchinses in the phone book
and would get back to MacHovec tomorrow.

The noise in the briefing area was so loud they could
hardly talk, and Defino, who had been in a foul mood
since his phone call home, wanted to leave, but there
wasn't a chance of that. He'd have to walk right by
Graves to get to the stairs or elevator.

"All right," he said, "let's see where we're at. Omaha
is working on Jerry Hutchins."

"Check," MacHovec said.

"We've got the autopsy on Soderberg and it's
inconclusive."

"Right."

"What about this guy Worthman? The one who moved
back to Harlem and got mugged?"

"I'll go over to One PP tomorrow and get the file,"
MacHovec said, referring to police headquarters at One
Police Plaza.

"The woman who was a hit-and-run in Tulsa."

MacHovec yawned. "I talked to the detective, Johnnie
Roy Anderson, while you guys were out. He'll get the file
and call me back. He remembers the case. It's still carried

as a vehicular homicide, officially, but maybe it was just a hit-and-run. He said it almost looked like a homicide except who would want a nice woman like Miss Rawls dead?"

"Or a nice man like Hollis Worthman," Jane said. "Or a nice man like Henry Soderberg. Anything on Bracken's partner?"

"Otis, yeah. I called him. His wife said he'd love to meet with you. She said he's doing fine."

"OK," Defino said, sounding a little more upbeat. "When do we go?"

"I'll get you a time." MacHovec keyed a number and had a brief conversation. "I made it ten o'clock tomorrow," he said. "Give you some time to get out to Queens. Otis is black, by the way."

"If he can talk to us," Jane said, "I don't care if he's purple."

The call from Flora Hamburg the other night had troubled her. Flora wanted to know that Jane's decision to retire had not been made either quickly or lightly. When you've spent half a lifetime on the job, if you haven't grown to hate it, you probably love it. Jane loved it.

Working the streets in Harlem, then Chinatown, and later in Manhattan South Narco, she had built a reputation for herself, made the kinds of arrests that drew notice, received a few commendations, and eventually, on her assignment to the Manhattan South Burglary Squad, was awarded her gold shield. Now Detective Bauer, she put together everything she had learned on the street: the junkies, the fences, the informants, the hows and the whys of how crime worked. She knew which secondhand shops would buy jewelry cheap, no questions asked, which antique dealers would close their eyes and hand over cash, which stamp and coin shops would buy old gold and silver to be made into scrap and resold to jewelers. She used everything she knew for a couple of spectacular arrests that netted her no promotion but got her a mention in the *Daily News*.

And it was close to the Academy, and she did run into Hack, and something got started and neither one of them ever looked back.

When the noise died down on Centre Street, she signed out.

8

SHE WENT TO the new apartment before going home. The floors, now sanded and polished, were so beautiful she didn't want to step on them. The new buildings she had looked at had floors of square parquet. Some people kept them natural; others stained them a darker brown. But these floors had character. They were patterned with a thin, dark border that ran around the whole room a foot or so from the wall, and the sanding and polishing made the design almost a work of art. It would be a shame to cover them with anything larger than a small rug.

She went through the apartment one more time, finding that her small requests had been attended to. The window that stuck now opened and closed effortlessly. The few imperfections in the paint were cleaned up. A note on the mantel assured her that the fireplace was in good working order.

After her checkup, she went down to the super's apartment and told him she would be moving in on Saturday.

That was fine with him. She buttoned up her coat and went out into the cold evening.

She had always loved lower Manhattan. From Fourteenth Street down to the Bowery it was the part of the city that was most appealing. The streets here ran amok; the famous grid of uptown Manhattan didn't exist below the single-digit streets. On the east, the island bulged into Alphabet City; on the west it narrowed, eliminating some streets and squeezing others into strange patterns. Parallel streets inexplicably crossed; others came to an unexpected end. The monotony of numbered streets no longer existed. The havoc that began below Fourteenth Street increased around Washington Square Park. If a map was superfluous uptown, it was a necessity downtown, where nothing was predictable. Jane knew the streets because she had worked them; she even loved them, some of them, anyway. Now she would live there. For as long as the Centre Street job lasted, she would be able to walk to work if the weather allowed. Chinatown was also accessible, as were Washington Square and all of Greenwich Village. She enjoyed walking, especially in that part of New York. When the new job started, she would be back to the subway, this time paying her way, but it didn't matter. She would earn more, and she would allow herself luxuries and pleasures that she denied herself now.

When she went down into the subway for the ride uptown, she pulled out her shield as automatically as she always did and rode for free.

There were no messages waiting tonight, not from Hack and not from anybody else. Not that she expected him to call back. It had been a moment of opportunity, a moment, perhaps, of weakness, being alone in his office, something reminding him of her, and before he knew it he had the phone in his hand and he was keying the number. She knew this about him, that he hadn't forgotten. She knew it because she felt the same. She was glad that she shared an office now, that there would be no momentary lapses, no chance to pick up the phone and have an intimate conversation with anyone. Look at poor Defino, his day ruined after talking to his wife.

After dinner, she began throwing things away: papers, letters, magazines, half-used packages of food she hadn't even known she owned. She felt a little like Old Mother Hubbard when she was finished; the cupboard was bare. She would eat one more dinner here, two more breakfasts. There was enough left to do that. When she was finished with dinner, she wrote checks for the few bills that lay on the kitchen counter, remembering that she would have to find a closer branch of the bank next week, that she would need new checks printed. There was no end to details.

And then there was nothing left in the kitchen except the little envelope of crinkly paper. She thought about whether this was the time to open it, whether she should take care of old business in the old apartment and start everything fresh in the new one. But this was not something she could take care of as easily as she could write a check and get rid of a debt. She put the envelope in her handbag and turned on the TV to catch the news, see the guys in the squad get their minute of fame.

Otis Wright lived in a private house in Richmond Hill, a brisk ten-minute walk from the J train station on Jamaica Avenue and One Hundred Twenty-first Street. Years ago the population had been white, Irish, Jewish, Italian, and German. Today it was mostly black, both American and Caribbean, as well as Indian. It was one of those old neighborhoods of low buildings with storefronts at street level, a nail store, a drugstore, little restaurants, a grocery. She remembered an old partner once calling such buildings "taxpayers." In the old days, the family business was downstairs and the family's life went on upstairs.

She spotted Defino half a block ahead of her as she

walked south on Lefferts Boulevard but wasn't able to catch up to him till he stopped and looked around on the next corner.

"Morning," he said as they met.

"You know where we're going?"

"Yeah. Left at the next corner onto Ninety-fifth Avenue and A Hundred Twenty-first Street. Want to stop for coffee?"

"Not now. They'll probably give us some."

They started walking. "You have kids?"

"No."

"Don't."

Jane laughed. "They giving you trouble?"

"She's giving me trouble," he said, emphasizing the *she*.

"How old is she?"

"Sixteen." He shook his head. "I don't think I was ever sixteen the way she is."

"I was."

"And you turned out OK."

"I gave my folks a hard time. They didn't deserve it."

"Nice of you to own up. I don't think my kid ever will."

"She will, Gordon. She just won't tell you."

He smiled a little at that. They came to the corner and turned left. Here it was completely residential, one small house after another, small, well-cared-for lawns that were autumn drab, here and there a leafless tree in front of a living room window. They walked another block and found the house. They were just on time.

Mrs. Wright was an attractive black woman wearing a black pantsuit with a white blouse. She looked as though she was expecting company. "I have to ask you to be careful where you step," she said after they had introduced themselves and she had taken their coats. "We have tubes all over the place for Otis's oxygen." She led the way into the living room, where a clear plastic line on the floor ended at a chair near the front window. "He has emphysema, you know."

"Charlie Bracken said he wasn't well," Jane said.

"Oh, you've talked to Charlie." She smiled at the name. "Otis, these folks have talked to Charlie Bracken." She made the introductions.

Otis Wright started to get up, but Defino told him to stay where he was. They all shook hands, and Mrs. Wright said she'd bring in the coffee.

"I'm OK," Otis Wright said. "Just need a little oxygen once in a while if I move around too quick."

"We just want to talk," Jane said, sitting on the sofa near his chair.

"This is about the Quill murder, right?"

"That's it. We're on the new squad they've set up to look into open homicides. Gordon and I got Quill."

Wright sat in his chair and looked down for a moment. He was a tall man who had apparently lost a lot of weight. His sweater looked big on him; his face was gaunt. His hair, like his wife's, was beginning to gray. "There wasn't much to grab onto in that case," he said finally, looking up at them. "The body was lying in the front hall of that building over on Fifty-sixth Street. He'd been dead all night when one of the tenants came down and found him. Had a knife in his gut, if I recollect properly."

"He did," Defino said.

"Nothin' was taken, right? Wallet was there, watch was there. If it was one of the tenants did it, we never found a motive and nobody heard anything. I interviewed everyone in the building myself. The two women, they were so scared I thought they'd move out that night. But they didn't." The talk had been too much for him. He reached for the plastic tube and fitted a small breathing piece into his nostrils, sat back for a moment and just breathed. Then he said, "I'm fine. Don't worry about me."

"There were three men in the building, too," Defino said. "You remember them?"

"Yeah."

"Any of them give you a bad feeling? Anything sneaky?"

"Yeah, maybe. But there was nothing there. The guy on the top floor, Hudson or something."

"Hutchins."

"Right. Jerry Hutchins. He didn't fit. Didn't come from New York. Didn't seem right for that place. Doesn't make him a killer."

"What way wasn't he right?"

"He was young," Otis Wright said without hesitation. "The others were . . . well, sad older people."

"Quill wasn't old."

"No, you're right, he wasn't. He was in his early thirties. But he was sad too. Had a gorgeous wife that had left him. You get a look at her? Upscale, wow."

"Yesterday."

Mrs. Wright came in with a tray and set it down on the coffee table in front of the sofa. It was close enough to Otis that he could lean over and reach his cup. The coffee was in a handsome silver-plated thermos to keep it hot. As she poured, Jane could see the steam rise.

"I brought you some nice cakes, too," Mrs. Wright said. "We have a new Caribbean bakery on Liberty Avenue. The old one closed a couple of years ago, but now things are getting better."

"They look great," Jane said.

Mrs. Wright moved away and took a chair apart from them.

Defino got back on track. "From what she told us, she used her husband as a stepping-stone to a better life, hung on to him till she found something better."

"I can believe it."

"But she had no reason to kill him, or have him killed."

"None we could find," Otis said. "She's got a husband who makes more money than Quill, treats her real good, buys her nice things. Why should she get rid of the poor slob she ditched?"

"So what do you think, Otis? You think it was one of the folks in the building, one of those sad people that lived there all those years, or someone at work, or someone who just followed him home, killed him, heard a noise, and ran off scared before he took anything?"

"I gotta tell you, I don't think it was someone in the building. If it was someone where he worked . . . it was a hotel, right?"

"Right."

"We couldn't find anything. He was Mr. Invisible at work. No one knew if he was there or not. They all said he was nice, but they didn't know a damn thing about him. The trouble with someone following him home—" He stopped for a minute and caught his breath.

"They didn't take anything," Jane said.

"Nothing we could find missing."

"Well, Jane and I stumbled onto something," Defino said.

"Yeah?"

"Something crazy. Tell him, Jane."

"I went into the building the other day on my way home. Every name on the mailboxes was different."

"They all moved out? Every one of them?"

"The woman on one? Mrs. Best? She died in her apartment about six months after Quill was murdered. A stroke or something. Then Soderberg, the guy who found Quill's body, he fell down the stairs and broke his neck."

"He's dead too?"

"Right. The southern woman, Miss Rawls?"

"Oh, yeah, nice woman, sweet as sugar."

"She found Soderberg, got so upset she moved out that night to stay with a friend, and went back to Oklahoma a few months later. Got hit by a car in a parking lot, hit-and-run, no ID on the driver."

Wright's alert eyes glistened with interest. He looked at her with disbelief. "Go on."

"Officially, vehicular homicide. The detective said it almost looked like homicide, but who would kill a nice lady like Margaret Rawls?"

"I'm listening."

"Hollis Worthman—"

"The black guy."

"Right. Moved out after Soderberg died and went back to Harlem. I talked to his mother. He was mugged in the street and killed."

"This is crazy," Otis said. "You're gonna tell me they're all dead. That's all of them, isn't it? Except Hutchins."

"It looks like Hutchins went back to Omaha, Nebraska," Defino said, articulating the city and state carefully, as though there were something unusual about it. "But we haven't found him yet. He's not listed in the phone book. We've got a detective calling high schools and checking the DMV."

"This is crazy. I've never heard anything like this. You hear this, Betty?"

"I'm listening to every word and I can't believe it either."

"Damn peculiar. All of this must've happened after Charlie and me stopped working actively on the case, six months after."

"Charlie knew Mrs. Best had died," Jane said.

"Yeah, OK, I remember that too. Skinny old gal wore a black wig to make her look younger. Yeah. It comes back to me now. There was nothing suspicious about her death."

"You take them one at a time," Defino said, "there isn't much suspicious about any of them. Soderberg was changing a lightbulb and fell off a stool and went down a flight of stairs. You get mugged on a city street at night, you don't go looking for any motive besides money."

"But a nice southern lady getting run down in a parking lot," Otis said. "Makes you wonder. And Hutchins disappears. I don't like it one bit."

For a minute they all sipped coffee and ate squares of cake. Jane looked around the room. Half-concealed behind an end table was a small green oxygen tank, probably for taking along when he went outside. It was in a clear carrier case and didn't seem to be connected to

anything. His life and limits were defined by the length
of the plastic hoses. He could no more go down to the
corner for a paper than he could scale a fence or chase
a perp.

"So now that you know everything," Defino said,
"think about it. Think about Hutchins. Either we find
him dead like the others and we got a killer on the loose
or we find him alive and he's our best suspect. What do
you think? Do we find him dead or alive?"

Otis smiled. "This a quiz show or something? I don't
know how the hell you'll find him. Maybe you won't find
him at all. Let me just tell you what I remember. He was
maybe thirty-five, could be a little younger. Not real tall,
kinda thin light straight hair but not blond, and losing it
on the top of his head. Built stocky, not fat, just on the
big side. Nervous is what I remember, but they were all
nervous, every one of them. You don't go downstairs and
see the body of your next-door neighbor and not feel nervous. Plus it took a while before they got the bloodstain
off the floor. But he was nice, polite, knew who Quill
was, hadn't ever been inside his apartment, but that's
New York. Knew him to say hello to, that's about all.
Didn't know he'd been married or anything else about
him. Didn't know where he worked."

"You remember where Hutchins worked? I must have
seen it in the file but I don't recall." Jane had her notebook open.

"He worked . . . lemme think . . . he worked for some
TV company I never heard of, some desk job, didn't have
to dress up to go to work. Dress down, he said. Worked a
computer and the telephone. Seemed like a, you know,
happy kind of guy, except that he was scared"—he
glanced at his wife and changed what he was about to
say—"out of his mind about what happened to Quill. If
he killed Quill, if he killed all those other people, I tell
you, that's news to me."

"Were you on the case the whole way with Bracken?"
she asked.

"Oh, yeah. Charlie and me, we did the whole case together. I only been on sick report a year."

"A year and a half," his wife said from her chair at the other end of the room.

"A year and a half. Yeah. Can't believe it's that long." He adjusted himself in his chair, pulled the oxygen line so it wasn't in front of his feet.

"What did you think about the super?" Jane asked. "Derek."

"Derek. Jeez. A little light on gray matter, I'd say."

"Think he's holding back on something?"

"I don't know if he's smart enough to hold back. I think he's just a guy does what he's capable of, which isn't much." He took a few breaths. "So where do you go from here?"

"I'm asking you," Defino said.

"I wish I was on that case myself." His face had taken on a glow since they had all sat down together. The boredom of sitting in one spot and not overworking himself had melted away. The old tug of the job was still there. Once a cop, always a cop; more so with detectives. Jane wondered fleetingly if she would feel this herself after she started working for the insurance company, after she was earning more and sitting in a plush office without having to run around in cold weather with a gun in her bag.

"I guess you go with Omaha," Otis said. "Guy must drive a car, don't you think? Out there, how else do you get around? If he isn't dead and buried somewhere, you'd think he'd turn up." He looked at Jane. "How'd you trace him to Omaha?"

She explained the conversation with the man at the place where Hutchins had gone after Soderberg died. "If we don't get anything from Omaha, I'll have to go over there and find out which of those guys is the one who knew where Hutchins had gone to."

"That's a possibility," Otis said. "Doesn't seem too much to go on."

"Well." Jane looked at her watch. They had been there

an hour, and it would take about that long to get back to
Centre Street.

"Hey, don't go," Otis said. "Stay awhile. Betty, you
got lunch for these folks? You don't want to go so soon."
He reached for the breathing piece and stuck it in his
nostrils again.

"We can stay a little while, but not for lunch. Thanks
for the invitation."

They made small talk, and Jane caught Mrs. Wright
smiling quietly. It was just job-related gossip, but Otis ate
it up. Tell him about the squad. Who was the whip? No
kidding, I remember Graves. Who's getting promoted?
What other cases? They solved one? How about that.
Nice collar.

Jane had allotted fifteen minutes, but they stayed closer
to half an hour. It was worth it. It was Otis Wright's best
day in weeks, she figured. Finally they got up and went
for their coats.

"Otis get along OK with Charlie?" Jane asked Mrs.
Wright as they stood near the front door.

"Charlie's a good man, the best. They love each other.
He comes out here and visits when he can. There was no
trouble between Otis and Charlie."

"Shit," Defino said when they were out on the street.
"What a way to end up." He reached into a pocket and
pulled out a pack of cigarettes, took one out, and went
searching for matches as they walked.

"You have to end up some way."

"Yeah, but not at that age. He can't be more than in
his fifties."

They got back to Jamaica Avenue and headed for the
stairs to the elevated line. "Want to have lunch here or
wait till we get back?"

"That cake filled me up. Let's get back. Maybe Mac-
Hovec's got something for us."

As they got to the stairs leading to the elevated station,
he looked at the cigarette in his hand as though he didn't
know where it had come from. He said, "Shit," softly
and dropped it, grinding it under his heel.

The train was just coming into the station as they came up the stairs. They were back at Centre Street by twelve-thirty.

9

THEY WERE GREETED—or accosted—by an angry PAA as they walked into the briefing area.

"Where is MacHovec?" she demanded.

"I don't know. It's not my day to baby-sit him," Defino said irritably.

"Well, he's not here, and I'm not his private secretary." She practically flung a pile of message slips at Jane. "He didn't make his rings every two hours; he didn't log in. Who does he think he is, Detective Diva?"

"She's gonna get herself fired," Defino said as they watched Annie stalk away to her office.

"So is MacHovec," Jane said.

"He was going somewhere this morning, wasn't he?"

She tried to remember. "One PP. I forget what for."

"The file on Worthman," Defino said. "That doesn't take four hours."

It was one-thirty. Even if it had taken a long time, MacHovec knew better than to be away from the team or the squad office without making his rings. And if he were home sick, his wife would have made the call.

"What are the messages?" Defino asked.

"Omaha, Omaha, someone named Nuñez at One PP."

"So he got there."

"Let me call back Omaha and see if they've got anything."

Jane sat at MacHovec's desk and found a file folder with a record of his calls. Det. John Grant was the contact in Omaha, and he answered quickly.

"This is Det. Jane Bauer in New York. Sorry Sean MacHovec hasn't gotten back to you. He's doing some digging over at headquarters today."

"No problem. Just wanted to keep you folks up-to-date. Jerry Hutchins has no Iowa license either, and just to cover all bases, I tried Kansas and South Dakota. No luck in either place."

"So either he's not driving or he's not back in Nebraska."

"Looks that way. Now I've been calling all the Hutchinses I can find in the phone book and I haven't run into one yet who admits to knowing our Jerry. You'd think there'd be something after he grew up here."

"So maybe he's back and he's keeping quiet about it and asking all his cousins to do the same."

"Sounds like that could be it. Can I get you or Mac-Hovec over the weekend if something comes in?"

"I'm moving tomorrow, so it's a little complicated. I'll give you my old number, where I'll be in the morning, and I can check the voice mail here every couple of hours; how's that?" She gave him her number, thinking that maybe these complicated new phones had a reason for existing after all.

"Well, that sounds real good, Jane. Maybe we'll talk in the next day or two."

"Anything?" Defino asked as she hung up.

"No license in Iowa, South Dakota, or Kansas. I can't help thinking—"

"So the traveling twosome are back."

It was MacHovec, standing unsteadily in the doorway, a silly smile on his face. Defino opened his mouth to speak, but Jane said quickly, "Get in here, Sean, and close the door."

He teetered a little, then obeyed her, pushing the door so it slammed shut.

"You're drunk, you son of a bitch," Defino said in a low voice. "You've got the whole fucking squad looking for you."

"Had a beer with lunch is all. Looks like I got some messages while I was out solving your crime for you." He looked at the slips on his desk, still smiling.

"The PAA is ticked," Jane said quietly. "You didn't call in or sign in."

"I made all my rings. She just doesn't remember." He dropped a file on Jane's desk. "Worthman. Still open." Then he stuck his hand in his pants pocket and pulled out some scraps of paper, looked through them, and let one flutter onto Jane's desk. "I found Hutchins for you. Stopped at the DMV and ran a search. Here's where his license was mailed."

Jane picked up the crumpled piece of paper. It had Hutchins's name on it, followed by the address of the place she had called Wednesday night. "Nobody there knew him when I called," she said.

"Or admitted to it." Defino had picked up the paper.

"He could be there under another name. I'll go over there tonight and see what I can dig up."

"Let's go now. It's early."

"That's the problem. It's too early. They're probably all away during the day."

"You're moving tomorrow. You can't get over there tonight."

"I'll get there." She turned to MacHovec. "Sean, you have to play by the rules." She was angrier than she let on. If he went off on a bender, he could destroy the case and get all three of them flopped back into uniform. Drunks made very bad partners.

"Always," he said. "I always play by the rules."

She turned to Defino, who was seething. "This stays in this room. That's it. I have to tell you, this was good thinking, checking the DMV in New York. We're gonna find this guy."

"If he's alive."

"He's alive," MacHovec said. "That license was issued this year. June of this year." He looked at his messages. "You call Omaha?"

"Yeah. John Grant said no license was issued to Hutchins in Iowa, Kansas, or South Dakota."

MacHovec grinned. "The Empire State took care of all his troubles."

Defino sat at the typewriter and banged out the interview with Otis Wright. Jane picked up the Worthman file and started through it. Worthman had been stopped on a dark street not far from the apartment he shared with his mother. He had been stabbed and left to bleed to death on the sidewalk. He was barely alive when a passerby found him, and he did not survive the trip to Harlem Hospital. Jane looked at some of the crime scene glossies. He was handsome, slim with graying hair. She looked through the Fives at the bottom of the file. His body had been found about ten o'clock at night. His mother said he had gone out for a walk to pick up a few things at a nearby grocery store. He did that often, she said. He liked walking.

If he did it often, there was a possibility that someone who had watched him was waiting in the street for him to come out and take his walk, then followed him down the block. So it could have been a hit instead of a mugging, but the investigating officers would never connect it to the deaths of former tenants in another precinct at a West Fifty-sixth Street tenement over a period of a year or two.

There were no witnesses to the murder of Hollis Worthman, or at least none that came forward, and no apparent motive. It was just one of those things that happened, and people felt bad about it, both his friends and the people who lived in the area. It was the sort of crime they unfortunately got used to, so if there was no apparent reason for its happening . . . well, that was the way things were, another big-city stranger-to-stranger crime.

MacHovec drank two cups of coffee and took a mint

from the roll he kept on his desk, then went to soften up Annie. He must have been successful because he came back happy. Jane told him about the Omaha detective's wanting a phone number for the weekend, but Mac-Hovec said if Jane checked her voice mail, that would be enough. He had a busy weekend planned. And they weren't going to find anything in Omaha anyway.

Jane tried the number of the apartment where Hutchins had had the license sent. After several rings, a half-asleep man answered, said he was the only one there and he'd never heard of Jerry Hutchins. She would go tonight.

Nothing in the Worthman file indicated anything more or less than a mugging. It was one of those crimes that would remain open forever unless a mugger was picked up with the same MO or some of Worthman's property and a sharp detective made a connection or some friend of the perp ratted him out trying to get a pass on one of his own cases. She was about to ask MacHovec for the autopsy on Soderberg when the second whip came in.

"Well, folks, we're rounding out our first week. Any hot stuff for me before we go home for the weekend?"

"We've got a lead on Jerry Hutchins," Jane said, nodding to MacHovec.

MacHovec told it straight, his professionalism winning out over his ego.

"So maybe he's still here in the city," McElroy said.

"I'll look for him tonight," Jane said. "There's only one guy in the place now, and I woke him up."

"OK. You know how to get hold of me if anything turns up. Don't hesitate. We closed one yesterday. We'd love to close another one on Monday." He held it out like a golden carrot.

"Doin' our best, Lieutenant," MacHovec said.

That must have been good enough for McElroy, because he went on to the next office.

There were no more calls from Omaha, and Jane went back to the Soderberg autopsy. She called Midtown North Precinct and left a message for the officer who had responded to the 911 call. He got back to her a little while later, and she refreshed his memory on the case.

"He was lying there on the landing," Officer Richardson said. "With this little step stool on top of him and pieces of a broken lightbulb around. Looked like what the super told us, that he'd been screwing in a lightbulb one flight up and lost his balance. He shoulda left it for the super."

"Any chance he was pushed?" Jane asked.

"There's a chance, sure. Wasn't anybody else home when we got there except the lady who made the nine-one-one call, and she was a wreck. You want my opinion, I don't think she did it."

Jane didn't either. She thanked Richardson for returning her call and let him go, picking up where she had left off in the autopsy. There were a lot of broken bones, but if Soderberg had been standing high enough up to reach the ceiling fixture, he had gone down a long way. His weight at death was 184 pounds, and the step stool had landed on top of him, possibly breaking a few more bones than the fall itself had.

"See you guys Monday," MacHovec said, and Defino looked up from his work without saying anything.

"Night, Sean," Jane said.

Defino waited till MacHovec was gone. "That son of a bitch is big trouble."

"Let it be, Gordon. He's good at what he does."

"Using the phone?"

"Someone's gotta do it. We'll watch him. If he makes any mistakes in the case, we'll talk about it. What he did today was just to himself. And checking out Hutchins for a license in New York State was good thinking."

Defino didn't say anything, and she was pretty sure he agreed but didn't want to give MacHovec credit.

"Looks like everyone's on their way," he said, looking at his watch. "I'll see you Monday." He pulled the sheet of paper he was working on out of the typewriter. "Hey, if something comes up, give me a call. I don't want McElroy knowing something I don't know." The little smile showed he accepted her truce.

"Don't hold your breath. Hutchins is dead, remember?"

He waved. "How could I forget?"

The phone rang as she was getting back into the Soderberg autopsy. It was so quiet in the other offices, the ring almost echoed. Jane picked it up and said, "Hello?" thinking it must be her father.

"Is this Detective Bauer?" a woman's voice asked sweetly.

"It is, yes. How can I help you?"

"This is Otis Wright's wife, Detective Bauer. He asked me to call you. He doesn't do well on the phone, you know."

"Yes, Mrs. Wright."

"Well, Otis has been stewing about that case since you left this morning. And he has an idea. He said maybe that man Hutchins, the one you're trying to find in Omaha, got his license here in New York State and had someone send it to him."

"Otis hit the nail on the head," Jane said, thinking he was one damn good detective. "A member of our team checked it out this morning, and Hutchins had a license mailed to him at a New York address a few months ago."

"Well, I always said Otis was a good detective."

"He is, and you can tell him I said so. We don't know yet if Hutchins is living here or had the license sent somewhere else. I'm going to try to find that out tonight."

"I hope you'll keep him posted. He's really into this."

"I promise I will."

She smiled as she hung up. Then she went back to the autopsy. She looked for minor details: moles; deformed digits; scars or wounds, new or old, that bodies acquire; tattoos. There was a tattoo mentioned, described as snaky.

She pulled out the photos. One was a full-face picture of Soderberg. She looked at it, holding it away from her at eye level. There was something familiar about the face, although she had never seen it before, never seen a picture of Soderberg till she opened the jacket of this file. It was almost as if she knew him from somewhere, but she couldn't put a name on him.

She moved the glossy around in front of her, as though looking at it from another angle might help. Then something occurred to her. She got out the Quill file and opened it, leafing through it till she found the photos. She took a front-face glossy and laid it on the desk next to the one of Soderberg.

"Holy shit," she whispered. "Sweet little Jesus." They could almost have been brothers. Quill was younger by a good ten years, but they shared the same long, oval face, the high forehead with the hair receding, the prominent nose, the large eyes. On a dark night you could easily mistake one for the other.

She grabbed the autopsy for Quill and looked at his vital statistics. He weighed about ten pounds less than Soderberg, but they were almost the same height. Quill wore glasses and so did Soderberg. She walked out into the briefing area and looked around. No one was there. She walked over to the offices of the whip and second whip. Both were gone. She went back to her own office and cleared her desk.

It was just possible someone had killed Arlen Quill in error. If the real target was Soderberg, the killer had to wait till the active investigation was over and the police presence in the building was gone so that Soderberg's "accident" would go unnoticed. Maybe it was Soderberg he wanted. Maybe they were trying to solve the wrong case.

[10]

IT WAS THE kind of high that only a discovery like this could produce. Jane took a file folder with the phone numbers, the Soderberg autopsy, and some notes. She would be too busy tonight and tomorrow, not to mention unpacking on Sunday, to think about work, although she was sure there was nothing else she would think about all weekend.

At home she ate what was left in the refrigerator before packing the remaining things she saw lying around. Then she took the subway downtown to Lower Manhattan to find the address where Jerry Hutchins had lived.

The trip took her to an old manufacturing building that had been broken up into residential lofts and rented out. The elevator was one of those precarious jobs with a Peele gate, the top half of which rose while the bottom half dropped. It made as much noise as an old truck as it went up to the fourth floor. As she manipulated the gate, someone opened a door to the loft.

"Coming to see us?" He was in his twenties, with a neatly trimmed blond beard complementing blond hair that could have used scissors.

"If this is four, I'm in the right place."

"Come on in." He swung the door wide and Jane went inside. "Anyone special you're looking for, or are you just killing time?"

She took her ID out and showed it to him, watching

the frown form on his smooth forehead. "I'm looking for Jerry Hutchins."

"You called."

"Yes."

"You didn't say you were a cop."

"Are you Al?"

"Al's inside."

About half the loft was what you might call a living room, with a kitchen on the wall that divided the room from what were probably bedrooms in the back. The shaggy blond walked over to a small, dark man, also in his twenties, and whispered to him. The dark man got up from his canvas sling seat and walked over to Jane. He was a head shorter than she and clean shaven. There were men, and a few women, parked on old sofas, pillows, and unmatched chairs all over the room. Some of them began to watch.

"I'm Al. Do I know you?"

He had a strong voice for a little guy. On the phone she had imagined a bigger and older man.

"I'm Det. Jane Bauer, working on a special task force. I'm looking for Jerry Hutchins."

"I told you on the phone I didn't know him. He doesn't live here."

"Where does he live?"

"I don't know. One of the guys said—"

"Which guy?"

Her brusqueness had effect. His self-assurance melted a few degrees. "I think it was Moke." He looked at the shaggy blond for confirmation. The blond shrugged.

"Can you take me to him?"

"I'm not sure."

"This is police business."

"Lemme look in the back."

She waited, wondering if there was a back stairway he might decide to disappear down, but he had to know it was a bad move. Around her, the group was drinking beer, eating out of McDonald's bags, and doing a lot of talking.

"OK if I go?" the blond asked.

"What's your name?"

"Sal. Sal Fortina."

"You live here, Sal?"

"Yes, ma'am."

"You work, Sal?"

"I'm an actor—sort of."

"You know where I can find Jerry Hutchins?"

"No, ma'am."

She wrote his name down. "You can go. Thanks."

When she turned back, Al was leading a sleepy-looking young man with a red beard. "This is Moke. Moke Beardsley. He's the one who said this Hutchins guy was in Omaha."

"I'm Det. Jane Bauer, Mr. Beardsley. Can we talk somewhere?"

"Yeah, sure." He led the way out of the loft, where Sal was still waiting for the elevator, which was ascending noisily. When he had departed, Redbeard yawned.

"I'm looking for Jerry Hutchins."

"Jerry lived here, maybe . . . I don't know how many years ago. A few. That's all I know."

"Where did he go when he left?"

"He told me Omaha."

"He give you an address?"

"What, in Omaha?"

"Yes, in Omaha."

"No." He said it almost angrily. Jane moved a step away from him. His breath stank. "He lived here and he left. That's all there was to it."

"The New York State Division of Motor Vehicles sent Jerry Hutchins a driver's license to this address a few months ago. You have any idea what became of it?"

"Why should I?"

"I think you sent it to him."

"I didn't send it to anybody."

"What did you do with it?"

"I don't know anything about it."

"You want to come downtown and talk about it?" She wasn't sure where she would take him; her office was closed for the weekend. And she was downtown already. She hoped he didn't notice.

"What do you want from me?"

"The truth. I think you sent him that license."

"What if I did?"

"If you did, I think you better tell me about it. Then you're off the hook on this."

He scratched his head, making Jane feel itchy. She had him and they both knew it.

"All I can tell you is, he called up one night and I answered the phone. That's all I did, I answered the fucking phone. This guy says he's Jerry Hutchins, he useta live here, he's coming back soon, and he wants to renew his license. He says the renewal form should be coming here soon, would I put it in another envelope and send it to him?"

"He said he was coming back soon?"

"That's what he said. He gave me an address in Omaha."

Two people walked out of the loft and rang for the elevator. It crept up to the fourth floor, and Jane waited till the couple were on their way down before speaking again.

"Then what happened?"

"He was right. An envelope came from the DMV. I put it in another envelope like he told me and sent it to him."

"How did he get his license?"

"He sent me back an envelope inside an envelope all stamped and everything so I could drop it in a mailbox. I did. A coupla weeks later, his license arrived. I put it in another envelope and sent it to him."

"What did you get for your services?" Jane asked.

He scowled. "He sent ten bucks in the first envelope. OK?"

"It's fine with me. Did he ever show up here?"

"Not that I know of."

"Let's go inside and you find me the address in Omaha."

"Are you kidding?"

"Mr. Beardsley, I'm very serious."

"I don't know what I did with it. It could be anywhere. I could've thrown it out."

"Why don't we go inside and look?"

She followed him back in. He had become docile, and she thought there was a fair chance he still had the address. Maybe Hutchins had promised him another ten if he did another favor.

His room was as disgustingly filthy as she had expected. The smell of unwashed laundry was putrid. He went in while she stood at the door, trying to breathe the air in the hall and keep an eye on him at the same time. He began by moving things, mostly dirty clothes, in a haphazard manner.

"I don't even know where to look."

"Maybe on your desk."

"Yeah." He went over to a table that appeared to have been made of a piece of plywood with a single shallow drawer hammered into the center. He pushed papers and clothes around on the surface, then pulled the drawer open. He rummaged through it as though he expected the sought-for paper to rise out of the debris. He took a handful of stuff and glanced through it without much concern.

"Here it is," he said, pulling a strip of paper that looked like a supermarket bill out of the junk he was holding. "Jerry Hutchins. Take it." He walked to the doorway and handed it to her.

"That's not his name," she said.

"Hey, that's the name he gave me, OK? Maybe it's his girlfriend. That's who he said I should send the license to. That's what I got from him. Now it's yours. That's the last time I do a favor for a guy on the phone."

"Thank you, Mr. Beardsley." She couldn't wait to hit the fresh air.

* * *

"That's fantastic," Gordon Defino's voice said, blowing smoke over the phone. "You got a phone number, too?"

"There's something scribbled here, looks like a phone number. I'll call John Grant tomorrow while the movers are doing their thing and let him know. If he's not there, I'll leave a message."

"What's the girlfriend's name?"

"Looks like Cory Blanding. They'll have to handle this carefully. I don't want Hutchins flying the coop."

"Maybe you should go out there. He's a material witness at least, and he could be our guy. You don't want to stay home and unpack, do you?"

She knew the answer to that one. "You think Omaha's better than unpacking?"

"I figure almost anything is."

"I've got something else, Gordon. This is really something. I was looking at the autopsy report on Soderberg late this afternoon. Something about his picture. I thought I'd seen it before. He's a ringer for Arlen Quill."

"He—" Defino stopped. "Say that again?"

"He's older than Quill, but you put those pictures side by side, Soderberg could be Quill's older brother. I think Quill may have been killed by mistake."

"Jesus."

"Yeah."

"You let anyone know?"

"I was the last one out. If I have a chance tomorrow, I'll call McElroy."

"So you think Otis and Charlie Bracken could have been looking at the wrong homicide."

"Could be."

"Who the hell was Soderberg?"

"There's no file on him because his death was ruled accidental. Give Sean something to do on Monday. But we still need Hutchins. He may have killed Quill, realized his mistake, and knew he couldn't hit Soderberg with all the cops around. So he waited six months or so, pushed Soderberg off his stool, and got the hell out of the building."

"Fits what we know. At least MacHovec won't get any sleep on the job next week."

"Or us."

"Right. Or us. If you hear anything else, you'll give me a buzz?"

"I will."

"Good work, partner," Defino said. He sounded as if he meant it.

The movers missed eight A.M. but not by much. Jane was dressed and ready, and they arrived and wasted no time getting her worldly possessions out the door, into the elevator, and down to the street. She kept her file folder on the telephone table, her eyes occasionally checking to ensure it hadn't been touched. By eleven o'clock, everything was in the truck except the phone, the table it sat on, and the file folder. She pulled the plug on the phone, leaving the table for the movers, took the folder, and went back for a last check of the apartment.

To her surprise, as she stepped into the empty and somewhat dusty bedroom, tears spilled onto her cheeks. She could see herself in her twenties, Chinatown on her mind, moving Salvation Army furniture into this room, in her thirties welcoming Hack into her bed for the first time. She touched the gun on her belt to try to restore some remnant of toughness but failed. This apartment was her youth; it was Chinatown and Narco and Burglary and the Sixth Precinct Detective Unit where they shared the building with the bomb squad. It was getting her gold shield. It was Hack. It was all things gone. She was moving on to middle age, a respectable job, a life without the man she had loved more than anyone else she had known. She could practically smell him in this room, hear him teasing her, loving her, comforting her. She turned and walked into the hall, wiping at her cheeks.

The bathroom was stark, the irritating stain on the sink

just as dark and ugly as the day she first saw it. She opened the medicine chest. The empty shelves were dustier than she had ever noticed. On the second one from the bottom was a bottle of Hack's Motrin. He was plagued with headaches, brought on, Jane was sure, by the guilt of leading a double life. She tucked the small bottle in her jeans pocket and walked out, heading for the kitchen. Maybe the headaches would abate, now that he wasn't seeing her anymore. And maybe not.

"You about ready?" one of the movers called from the door.

"Just checking the kitchen. I'll be right there."

It was empty, as was the living room. She picked up the phone and answering machine from the floor and cradled them in her left arm on top of the file folder like a child going to school with his books. Then she left the apartment, pulling the door closed behind her. Her right hand curled around the Motrin, she went to where the mover was holding open the elevator door, and she rode down with him.

THERE WAS A dial tone when she connected the phone in the new apartment. She kept herself out of the way as the movers reversed their work of the morning, and dialed Omaha.

"Detective Scofield, can I help you?"

"This is Det. Jane Bauer calling from New York." The youngest of the movers turned to look at her. "Is Det. John Grant on today?"

"Sorry, he's off on the weekend."

"Can you get a message to him?"

"I can try."

She dictated it slowly, including her new phone number and the fact that she had a contact for Jerry Hutchins in Omaha. If he wanted more, he could call her. She didn't want anyone else screwing up the works. Grant had done a good job, and whether he moved on this over the weekend or on Monday, she didn't think Moke Beardsley was going to get word to Omaha that Hutchins's cover had been blown. She was confident she had the only copy of the address and phone number.

"I don't know if I can reach him," the Omaha detective said. "But I'll give it a try. You gonna be around this afternoon?"

"Probably for the rest of the day except to pick up something for dinner later on."

"I'll see what I can do."

As the furniture filled the rooms, she liked the apartment even more. The floors were gorgeous. The rugs seemed made for the rooms. When her paychecks started increasing, she would put money into the living room first. By spring it would be on its way.

"Bedroom one or bedroom two?" one of the men asked, holding one end of her desk.

"Two." She followed them into her study and indicated where to put it. Then she went back to the kitchen and called Lieutenant McElroy.

He listened to her long narrative, uttering only grunts and occasional syllables of pleased amazement. "Fantastic," he said at the end. "Have you heard back from Omaha yet?"

"I just called them a little while ago. It's possible he won't get back to me till Monday."

"I think you should plan on going out there," McElroy said. "I'll talk to Captain Graves about it, and we can get the paperwork started. But let's wait till we see if they can confirm Hutchins lives at that address."

"I'll let you know if I hear from him."

"You do that. He could have killed the wrong guy. I like it. You talk to the original detective on the case about that?"

"Not yet. I just saw this at five o'clock yesterday."

"Fantastic," he said again.

"I'll call if I hear anything."

It was three-thirty when she paid the movers. They had all stopped for a bite on the way downtown, so she wasn't hungry, and she wanted to stick around in case John Grant called. There was plenty to do, unpacking clothes and dishes, finding a secure place for her guns, moving furniture to better positions. She was on her hands and knees in the kitchen when the phone rang for the first time.

"Jane? John Grant here in Omaha. Sounds like you've got something."

"A couple of things." She detailed them, grabbing a kitchen chair and sitting on it while she talked, the file folder open in front of her on the table.

"Cory Blanding. Can you hold a minute while I check my phone book?"

"Sure thing."

Pages turned. "There's a Blanding here but it's not a Cory. I'll give them a call and see what I can come up with, but if she's unlisted, she's probably told her family to keep quiet about her whereabouts. I'll try to get into the office for half an hour tomorrow after church, see what I can find. My wife and I are going to a wedding tomorrow afternoon, so I won't have much time, but if I find a number for her I'll give you a ring."

"That's great."

"And maybe I'll take a little ride down to where she

lives and see what we've got. How do you want to handle this?"

"With kid gloves. If she knows we're on to her, we'll lose Hutchins. I want him as soon as possible and alive."

"I hear you. I'll call tomorrow before I tie my bow tie."

She smiled. "Good luck."

She called Defino and McElroy just to let them know they were still making progress, and then she got back to work unpacking. By the time she was ready to find something to eat, the kitchen looked lived-in.

She brushed dust off herself and went into the living room, standing back from the fireplace to appreciate it properly. Somewhere there was a framed picture of her parents that she would put on the mantel. The more immediate problem was firewood. Where in the city of New York did you find it? And shouldn't she have asked that question before she signed the lease?

There would be no fire tonight, not that she had the energy to build one. But now a nice walk through her new neighborhood, a hot meal to bring back and savor in her new surroundings. And then a good night's sleep. She needed it.

John Grant called on Sunday. "Got her phone number and drove down to see where she lives. It's a two- to three-story complex of small apartments, mostly singles, I'd say. I hung around for a while to see if she'd come out, but my wife likes to get places on time, so I didn't see her."

"Any name besides hers on the mailbox?"

"Just hers. How do you want to play this?"

"I may fly out there," Jane said. "My lieutenant suggested it. I can question Hutchins just as easily in Omaha as here, and I'm not sure it pays to bring him to New York."

"Well, I'll be at my desk tomorrow morning. If you need a hotel room, I can get that for you. Meantime,

I'll just pretend we don't know anything about Cory Blanding."

"That's good. We'll be in touch tomorrow."

She knew she wanted to be there when they took Hutchins in. It wasn't that she didn't trust them. They seemed competent as well as polite, but the thought of losing Hutchins at this point sent chills up her back. She'd had plenty of experience getting perpetrators out of hiding, but never one so far from home base.

In the afternoon she read through the Soderberg autopsy report but nothing stood out. There were scratches made by the shards of glass that had been a lightbulb, so whether he had been changing the bulb or the killer had smashed one to use as a prop, the glass was consistent. He had suffered a broken arm many years before his death. Other than that he was in tip-top shape with good muscle tone, weight only slightly over the norm. There was no hint at what he did for a living, no indication why he was home in late afternoon when most men working for a living were still at their jobs.

After reading through the report as carefully as she could, she left the apartment to explore the streets of her new neighborhood. There were plenty of restaurants within a radius of a few blocks, although several of them looked expensive. But there were more reasonably priced places too: bars, coffee shops, ethnic eateries that would give variety, and a certain spice, to her life. Just walking past one of them made her wrinkle her nose with anticipation at the fragrance flowing into the street: cinnamon, nutmeg, maybe a whiff of allspice.

In a supermarket window she spotted packages of firewood. She hadn't expected a forest in the middle of a block, but she would prefer to have a bigger supply than half a dozen pieces of wood.

Sean was on time Monday morning, and both McElroy and Graves wanted the team in Graves's office first thing.

"Sounds like you had a busy weekend," Sean said, opening his coffee. "I thought you were moving."

"I did. And it was busy. When do they want us?"

"ASAP," Defino said. "Got your coffee?"

"I'll get it and meet you there."

Graves's office had no more amenities than the offices of the teams, but it was less crowded. Jane sat in the last empty chair and looked out the window beside Captain Graves. The view was substantially the same as hers. Graves was his usual gorgeous self, well turned out, eyes sparkling. He reached across the desk and shook Jane's hand.

"Sounds like you had a busy weekend," he echoed MacHovec. "You want to bring us up to speed?"

She did it quickly, not making a big deal out of her trip to the loft on Friday night. "Bottom line," she said, finishing, "Det. John Grant has an address for Cory Blanding but hasn't seen either her or Jerry Hutchins."

"But he assumes at least the woman is there?"

"She's got a phone at that address and a mailbox."

"That's a good start."

"Jane," McElroy said, "tell us about Soderberg."

"Right. I noticed a resemblance between his picture and that of Arlen Quill." She took them out of the folders on her lap. "I think there's a good chance the killer of Quill hit the wrong man."

Graves rose to take the pictures. "Amazing," he said. "They could be brothers. I bet you couldn't tell them apart in profile. Especially on a dark night." He passed the pictures to McElroy, who made the appropriate noises. The pictures then went on to Defino and MacHovec. They made MacHovec smile.

"What do we know about Soderberg?" Graves asked.

"Nothing," Jane said. "The ME ruled his death an accident. There was no crime, no file, no investigation."

"But there should be something in the Quill file," Graves said. "He was interviewed after the Quill homicide."

"We'll look at it today."

"And meanwhile we've got a good lead on Hutchins."

"I think someone should go to Omaha," McElroy said. "I'd rather see our people talk to Hutchins than theirs."

"We don't know that Hutchins is there. We think his girlfriend or whatever she is is there." Graves looked at the notes he had made when Jane was briefing him. "He could be in another state for all we know."

"He could be in New York," Defino said. "The guy who sent him the license said Hutchins was coming back. We're assuming he was lying, but maybe he wasn't."

"True." Graves frowned briefly. "But the woman is the key. Unless he's been using credit cards, and he seems to be too smart for that, she's our best bet for finding him. I think Ellis is right. Someone should talk to Cory Blanding. If Hutchins is living with her, that's easy enough to find out. If not, she has to know where he is because she sent him the driver's license. She knows he's got problems and she's careful not to let people know anything about him. But he's gotta have a job, even if he's using another name. And they probably go out together." He looked at Jane. "You want to go to Omaha?"

"Sure," she said.

There was a knock on the door, and Annie stuck her head in. "Detective Bauer, you've got a call from Omaha. Sounds important."

Graves waved her off and she went to her office and picked up. "Bauer."

"Jane, John Grant. I got a look at our friend Cory Blanding. Don't worry; she didn't see me. I watched her door early this morning and saw her come out about eight o'clock our time. That's just a little while ago. I got a snapshot of her but it may not be too good. But I know what she looks like now. Twenties, light straight hair, glasses, nice-looking but no model."

"That's great. What about Hutchins?"

"I stayed a few minutes but he didn't come out. But if she comes out with him at night or something, we'll be able to nab him."

"Good, but don't do it. I'm probably going to fly out."

"Well, that's just fine." He sounded ready to roll out a red carpet.

"I'll let you know as soon as I know."

She returned to Graves's office and gave them the news.

"Get yourself on a plane," he said. "The sooner the better. If we've got cops hanging around where she lives, she's gonna get wind of it sooner or later. Tell Annie to get you a ticket and get the paperwork going. We'll have to expedite it right away."

"I'll do that."

"And you two better come up with something good on this guy Soderberg or we're barking up the wrong tree."

"Right away," MacHovec said. He crushed his Styrofoam cup with a crackling sound.

The meeting was over.

Annie booked her on a late-afternoon flight, and John Grant gave her the name of a hotel halfway between the airport and the city. "About five minutes either way," he said. "We're not New York."

While Annie was getting the paperwork started, Jane sat with Defino and MacHovec as they looked at the Five for Soderberg in the Quill file. Soderberg had discovered Quill's body and left for work before the police could interview him. But Bracken had talked to him that evening, eliciting very little personal information. On the night of the homicide he had been at home from about eight o'clock on and gave the name of the restaurant where he had dinner—alone. It was an inexpensive local place, and Bracken had checked it out. Soderberg ate there frequently and was known there. No one could put a time on when he left, but it seemed to be on the early side.

He was a salesman for an electronics company that checked out, too. He got in to the office early, made calls during the day, and was often, but not always, he was careful to point out, home in late afternoon. That would explain how he came to be changing a lightbulb many months later before the other tenants got home from work. Not that he knew at the time that he was providing this explanation.

Otherwise there was very little in the file on Henry Soderberg. While they were talking, MacHovec picked up the phone and dialed a number from the Five. He listened for a few moments, then hung up.

"Whoever Soderberg worked for, they're not at that number anymore, and there's no forwarding number."

"Terrific," Defino said. "We got nothin' and nobody. This guy must've been involved in something dirty. I hope Hutchins knows something. I hope he did it."

Jane looked at her watch. "I better go now. I've got a lot of paper to process, and I don't own a suitcase, if you can believe that, at least not one I can use. So I have to buy one and get it packed."

"You want me to pick you up and drive you to JFK?" Defino asked.

"That's gotta be out of your way, Gordon."

"Gives me an excuse to leave early. Let me have your address and I'll be downstairs whenever you want."

"Thanks."

She got about two pounds of paper from Annie, some of it with Graves's signature still damp, and started to make her rounds. There were three offices she had to visit, all at One PP. Annie had called ahead that this was top priority, so Jane finished in a couple of hours, probably a record. This kind of procedure usually took forever. Next she took the subway to Bloomingdale's and bought a medium-sized wheelie. She could get enough in there for several days, although she didn't think her trip would last more than two or three. Then she juggled it on the subway back to her apartment, emptied her mailbox, wondering what would happen when the mail piled up, decided not to think about it, and went upstairs to pack. Defino called before she had finished and checked to make sure the time was right. She said it was fine, and when she hung up, she suddenly started to feel very good. She was glad to be getting away from the MacHovec–Defino tension, glad to be going somewhere she'd never been, and glad to be the first to get a crack at Hutchins. If Hutchins was there. If Hutchins was still alive.

[12]

John Grant was at the gate when she walked off the plane, a lean man with pale, thinning hair, a nice smile, and a firm handshake. He led her to the baggage carousel and lifted her new suitcase off the belt as though it were weightless. They walked out into the dark night and into a parking lot.

"It's just up here on the left. How was your flight?"

"I guess it was fine. They fed me something edible and they got me here."

He laughed. "You can't ask for much more, can you? Here we are." He stopped at a maroon van that had enough room for two big families.

"You have a lot of children?" she asked.

"Three and one's off to college. My wife wanted this. Said she couldn't live without it."

She clambered into the front seat and looked down at the world below. "Nice view."

"That's what she likes best. What's the plan for tomorrow? We going to try to take Hutchins first thing in the morning?"

"Are you sure we can see the door to the apartment without Cory Blanding seeing us?"

"Sure as I can be. In fact, she turns the other way to go downstairs, so her back's to me. What are you thinking?" He stopped to pay a laughably small fee for parking, then continued out of the airport.

"Hutchins is a suspect in four homicides, possibly five, but I think the old woman who died first was natural causes. Still, nothing links Hutchins to the murders except the fact that he's still alive."

"And he fled New York, tried to get a New York State driver's license illegally, seems to be hiding out. . . ."

"It's very circumstantial. I don't want to screw this up. Let's stand by and watch the apartment after Cory Blanding leaves tomorrow morning. If he has a job, he's got to come out at some point. Then we can move in on him."

"We can do that. I'll pick you up at the hotel at seven-thirty and we'll drive over."

"Will that give us enough time?"

"Plenty of time." He made a turn, and Jane saw that they were in the parking lot of her hotel.

"That was fast."

"Exactly my point." He hopped down to the pavement and came around to help her but she was already out. He took the suitcase out of the back and pushed the hatch door down. It moved slowly, thumping itself shut.

The hotel had her reservation, and she signed in while John waited nearby. With the key in her hand, she went to get her suitcase.

"How about you take that upstairs and I'll meet you in the bar?"

"That sounds good. I'll be down in five minutes."

"Don't hurry."

She called her dad, who was waiting anxiously for her

call, and told him the little she knew about Omaha and Nebraska. He liked hearing what she said. He hadn't traveled much in his life, and she was his lifeline to the world he would never see.

Downstairs, wearing a different pair of shoes, she found her way to the bar, where John Grant sat at a small round table nibbling at nuts. He rose as she approached, a Midwestern gentleman.

"What's your pleasure?" he asked, signaling to the waitress.

"Scotch on the rocks with a twist, a little water on the side."

"That makes two of us." He gave the order to the waitress, a woman in her fifties with a cheerful demeanor. She walked over to the bar, stopping on the way to say a word to three men at another table.

"Very relaxed," Jane said, taking a handful of nuts from the bowl.

"Who's in a hurry at this hour?" He smothered a yawn. "Just a little tired. It's been a long day. How'd you get involved in a case this old?"

She told him, pausing to toast their hoped-for success when the drinks came.

"Interesting idea, looking into cold cases. We've got a few ourselves, one of them dating back to the Second World War."

"For all I know, we may have some of those, too. But we may be onto something here, now that we have a lead on Hutchins and the possibility that Arlen Quill was killed in error."

"Poor fella. Walks into his house and gets stabbed because he's got the wrong profile. How long've you been with NYPD?"

"Almost twenty years."

"That's the magic number, isn't it?"

"I've got a new job lined up for when I hit twenty. Insurance."

"Well, that should keep you busy in a quieter way."

"I hope so. And it pays more." She told him about the new apartment and the fireplace that actually worked.

"A working fireplace right in your apartment. That must be unusual in the big city."

"It is. I looked for a long time before I found it."

"You chop down your own trees for firewood? In Central Park or wherever?"

"I'm looking for a source."

"Well, we'll send you some of ours. Got lots of trees where we live."

"You look very tired, John. I think you should go home and let me get unpacked and into bed."

"Can't argue with that." He waved to the waitress and settled the bill.

They agreed she would wait outside the hotel for him to drive by in the morning. When she got upstairs, she knew she was even more tired than he had seemed. It had been a twenty-five-hour day.

The waitress poured coffee, shielding the cup from Jane so it wouldn't splatter. There were many acts of simple courtesy that would be rare in a New York coffee shop. She had slept well, the bed comfortable and her fatigue overwhelming her concern that the clock might not wake her at six-thirty.

At twenty-five after seven she stepped out the front door of the hotel into a brisk, sunny morning to see John Grant at the wheel of a black Ford. She was rather glad she would be spared the gymnastics of climbing into the van.

"You're early," he said cheerfully.

"Likewise. Nice hotel. Good breakfast."

"Sleep well?"

"Like a baby."

"We can't be sure when we'll get our next meal, so I have some munchies and soft drinks in the cold pack." He motioned his head to the backseat and Jane saw a Styrofoam picnic container resting there.

"I hope things move fast. I'm better at moving than waiting."

"Least you don't fall asleep."

They drove a short distance and entered the city. John made his way, avoiding the main part of downtown Omaha. At a quarter to eight they were driving slowly down a street with low apartment houses, a few stores, and people already walking purposefully along the street, getting into cars, driving off to work.

"That's her car," John said, pointing to a dusty blue two-door that would never stand out in a crowd.

"Registered in her name?"

"You bet." He pulled into a space across the street and they got out. "Let's stay on this side. The stairs to her apartment are right over there." He nodded toward a break between one building and another. "There are other stairs back the way we came. I think, from where she parked her car, she'll come down these. We can stand under the stairs to the next section and watch for her. Then we'll go on up and start our wait. Unless, of course, he comes out with her."

"That would be nice."

They passed the stairs, crossed over, and walked to the next set nearby. Standing under them, they had a view of Cory Blanding's stairs and, in the other direction, the interior grounds of the buildings, including a swimming pool. The water had been drained but it looked nice, with steps down to the shallow end and a diving board at the deep end. Jane turned around to watch for Cory Blanding. For a minute or two, no one at all came down. Then they heard the click of heels.

"That's her," John said in a low voice. He stepped out from under their hiding place and moved toward her. Then he shook his head. "No luck. She's alone. Come on. Let's go up and keep an eye on the door."

Upstairs, John pointed to Cory's door. He stood next to it and put his ear against it, then walked away. "If he's inside, he's not making any noise. We can park ourselves down at both ends. There are seven doors. Blanding's is third from this end, fifth from the other end. As long as you can count, you're OK." He left and took up a position at the far end of the corridor.

They began a long wait. At nine o'clock, she sat down on the concrete landing at the top of the stairs, her back wedged into the corner the wrought-iron bars made. When a door opened that was not Cory Blanding's apartment, she got up quickly, trotted down the stairs, along the sidewalk to the next set, and then up to where John was waiting.

"There's a gas station about a block back if you need a bathroom," he said.

"I will soon. Want anything from the car?"

"Maybe a bottle of iced tea would be nice." He pulled a ring of two keys out of a pocket and handed them to her. He was driving an unmarked police vehicle.

"You have Cory's phone number?"

He wrote it down.

"I'll try from the gas station."

She enjoyed the walk. It was long enough to stretch her legs and wake herself up. She called her father from a pay phone and he was thrilled.

"A stakeout, huh?"

"A pretty boring one, Dad," she said. "I don't think he's home, and it's going to take us a while to find out for sure."

"Well, you're probably breathing better air out there."

She had to agree. When she got off, she dialed Cory's number. It rang several times before a machine picked it up. "Hi, this is Cory. Leave your name and number and I'll call you back as soon as I can."

Jane hung up. On the way back, she grabbed two iced teas out of the cold pack in the car and gave one to John.

"He answer?"

"Her voice on a machine."

"Either he's out or they're very careful."

"OK. I'll go back to my post."

Around lunchtime John went down to the car and got some sandwiches and a thermos of coffee. While he was gone, a woman left her apartment and walked down the stairs on his side. She was dressed nicely, a pants outfit and low heels, as though she were going to work or to lunch with a friend. Otherwise, there had been no activity for almost an hour.

They ate at opposite ends of the hall. Jane told herself this was not unusual, and it wasn't. Most detectives had spent long periods of time standing in dark hallways, on rooftops, or sitting in smoke-filled cars. One old-timer she knew would entertain himself by melting holes in Styrofoam coffee cups. Another played self-improvement tapes. Everyone had his own technique for waiting out suspects. It was more unusual for the wanted person to step out of his apartment five minutes after surveillance was set up. But she didn't feel good about this one. There was really no reason to believe Hutchins was living in the Blanding apartment. He could be anywhere in Omaha, anywhere in the country. Cory could have mailed the license to him and he could be driving around California or Utah just as easily as sitting inside the third door on the right.

The afternoon passed the way the morning had. They took turns going to the gas station, and finally, around four-thirty, they huddled at John's post.

"I'm going down now and watch for Cory. Let's give it some more time after she comes home. Maybe they'll go out for dinner or some fun."

"Fun," Jane echoed.

"Right. Remember when we had fun?"

"What a day."

He went downstairs and Jane lost sight of him. A little after five he hissed at her from below, "She's on her way."

Jane moved down the corridor to the far staircase and stood where she could see anyone who came toward Cory's apartment. The woman came up to the second floor a minute later, a key in her hand. Cory was about five-four, wearing dark tights and a navy-blue coat over them. Her hair was sandy and straight, her cheeks slightly red from the crisp air. She looked pleasant, ready to smile if you gave her an excuse. A dark shoulder bag hung from her left shoulder, while a bag that might be groceries rested in her left arm. As she turned the key in the door Jane moved silently toward her and was sure she heard Cory say, "Hi," as she stepped inside.

Someone was waiting for her.

13

THAT CHANGED EVERYTHING. If someone was in the apartment, had been there all day, maybe he worked nights. Or maybe he didn't work and Cory supported him, and maybe they would go out in the evening.

Neither Jane nor John had the right to force their way into the apartment. And if they rang the doorbell and asked for him, there was only a slim chance he would show his face.

"I say give it a couple of hours," John said. "This guy's been inside for a long time. If he works nights, he'll come out before midnight. You'd think he'd want to stretch his legs. Lord knows I want to."

They took turns again going to the gas station. Jane called McElroy at home and briefed him. On her way back, she stopped in a little grocery store and picked up two sandwiches in case their stakeout lasted longer than another hour. But she was now wide-awake. The echo of that single syllable, "Hi," had buoyed her.

It grew dark and Jane saw stars above the apartment complex. In New York it was often too hazy to see many stars, but here the air was clear and dry, the distant lights very bright.

About an hour after Cory Blanding came home, the door to her apartment opened and she stepped out into the hallway. "Well, don't forget it," she called back through the open doorway. She shook her keys as she waited for him.

A few seconds later a man emerged, and John started down the corridor toward Jane's end, assuming the couple would move in that direction. The man with Cory was about medium height, with thinning pale straight hair, dressed in jeans and a leather jacket. Cory locked the door and they turned toward the stairs at Jane's post. John moved in quickly from behind and Jane started toward them.

"Jerry Hutchins?" she said as John closed in. "I'm Det. Jane Bauer of NYPD."

The look on his face was more fear than surprise. He turned to bolt in the other direction but John had him, and Jane grabbed his arm. "Let me go," he shouted.

Cory screamed.

"Keep quiet, Cory," Jane said. "We're police officers. No one's going to get hurt. We just want to talk to Jerry."

Cory stopped screaming but her face froze, her mouth open, her eyes wide. John talked quietly to Hutchins, who had given up trying to run.

"We'll just take a quick trip to the station house and ask you a few questions. Is that OK, Jerry?"

"How'd you find me?"

"We'll get into that later."

"Oh, my God," he said, a faint note of hysteria in his voice. "How'd you find me?"

John led Hutchins down the stairs, and Jane and Cory followed. "You can come down and wait for him," Jane said, "but you'll have to drive in your own car. We've only got room for Jerry."

"What're you going to do to him? He's got to get to work."

"We're just going to ask him a few questions."

"Is he under arrest?"

"Not at the moment."

"Oh, God." Her eyes filled. "Should I call someone, Jerry?" she called after him.

"Wait awhile," he said. "I don't know. Jeez, I don't know what to say."

"This is a mistake," Cory said. "Jerry didn't do anything. We were just going out to eat. What are you going to ask him?"

"A few questions."

At the bottom of the stairs they crossed the street to John's unmarked car. Cory stood at the curb watching. Then she started running.

They sent out for pizza for Hutchins, pizza and a Coke. He ate hungrily, finishing a slice and a half before pushing the box away and putting his head in his hands.

"You ready to answer some questions?" John asked.

He nodded but didn't look up.

"You want to tell us your name?"

"Jerry Hutchins." He looked up.

"When did you leave New York, Jerry?"

"About . . . I'm not sure. Maybe three years ago."

"What was your last address in New York?"

He gave the loft address.

"And before that?"

"Fifty-sixth Street, between Ninth and Tenth."

"What made you leave?"

He didn't answer right away. He reached for the unfinished slice of pizza and ate it, crust and all, then drank from the Coke can. "Everyone was dying," he said slowly.

"Jerry," Jane said in a gentle voice, "I want you to tell us about the deaths, starting with the first one."

"Quill?"

"That's the one. Tell me what you remember about Arlen Quill and how he died."

"All I know is I came downstairs that morning because I heard a lot of noise. There were cops there, and that woman who lived on the first floor was crying, more like wailing. She wouldn't shut up. I didn't really see Quill because they had him covered, but the whole scene was really gruesome."

A shudder passed over him and he reached for the Coke again. "I wanted to leave for work but they asked me to stay, so I did, and some detective sat down with me and asked me a lot of questions I couldn't answer."

"Why couldn't you answer them?"

"Because I hardly knew him—Quill, I mean. We talked sometimes, but he really kept to himself, never said much that was personal. I didn't know if he was married or single, where he came from, that kind of stuff. He was a guy, he was quiet, he had a job, and he lived downstairs in the apartment on the other side of the building."

"Where were you the night he was murdered?"

"I was probably home listening to music or watching TV."

"Is that what you told the detective?"

"Sure."

"And you didn't hear anything?"

"I lived on the fourth floor. He was murdered inside the front door."

"Who else in the building did you know?"

"I knew them all," he said. "New Yorkers are funny people. They live somewhere forever and never meet their neighbors. I had come from Omaha and I knew everyone on my street. I didn't know you were supposed to keep to yourself, so I didn't. I said hello to everyone and they said hello back. Even the black guy downstairs. We used to go out for dinner together sometimes. You know what I mean?"

"You were a friendly person." Jane smiled. "That means you can tell us more about the other tenants in that building than anyone else."

"Yeah, sure."

"Let's start with the woman on the first floor."

Jane led him through a series of questions about Mrs. Best, how he occasionally helped her open a jar or change a lightbulb. There was nothing new in his answers.

"What was the next death?" Jane asked.

"Henry Soderberg."

"Did you know him?"

"He was another one that kept to himself but yeah, we talked sometimes."

"Did he ever invite you into his apartment?"

"No."

"You invite him?"

"I did, now that you mention it. He came in for a beer once."

"Did he tell you anything about himself?"

He shook his head. "Not much. He said he'd been married once but it hadn't worked out. Mostly it was like an interview, him asking all the questions."

"You have any idea where he worked? What he did?"

"Electronics sales. Whatever that means."

"Do you know how he died?"

"They said he fell down the stairs."

"Who said?" John Grant asked.

Hutchins said, "It's what people were saying when I got home."

"Did you believe it?" Jane asked.

"Yeah, I did, when it happened. But later . . . I don't know. I don't know what to believe anymore."

"You feel like smoking, Jerry?" John asked. "It's OK to smoke in here."

"Nah. Thanks. I don't smoke." He reached for another slice of pizza and started eating it.

"What happened to make you think Henry Soderberg didn't just fall down the stairs?" Jane asked.

"It's what happened to everyone else."

"Tell me."

He talked about the night Henry died, his conversation with Margaret Rawls, whose name he couldn't recall, who had found him and was hysterical, how she moved out that night.

"She sent me a Christmas card with an address somewhere in Oklahoma, and I sent one to her. Then what happened was, I called her down there to tell her what happened to Hollis Worthman, and her sister said she'd had an accident and got killed. Hey, I was scared shitless."

"Let's back up a minute. How did you find out about Hollis Worthman?"

"I told you, we used to have dinner sometimes. I knew him. He moved out after Henry died and went to live with his mother up in Harlem. But a couple of times we got together—he'd call me or I'd call him. Not too often, just once in a while. And it was, like, my turn to call him to set something up, and his mother said he was dead."

"What did she tell you?" Jane asked.

"He got knifed in the street one night, going to the store. You know what? It happened the night after the last time we had dinner together. It was like a piece of ice went right down my back. I just looked around at the doors in that building, and behind every door there was a dead body."

It was a chilling image. "When did you move out?"

"I started thinking about it when Hollis got killed, or when I heard he'd gotten killed. They were renovating the building by then. For a while I was the only person living there, and it gave me the creeps. You know how it is. You wake up in the middle of the night and you hear noises."

"What kind of noises?"

"Just noises. Creeping around. Rats, mice, who knows? It's just that it's dark and you're in New York and it's not exactly the rich East Side."

She talked to him about the loft, then looked down at her notes. "OK, so you found out Hollis Worthman had been killed. Let's go back to the southern lady, Margaret Rawls."

Hutchins smiled. "Rawls, that was her name. Margaret Rawls. Yeah. Well, I got her phone number down South and I called to tell her. She was friendly with everyone who lived in that building. It was just her nature, I think. And this woman answers and says she's her sister and Margaret was killed in a freak accident." He finished his Coke and scrunched up the can. "And I just saw it. Someone was killing everyone in that building and I was the only one left. Which meant I was next. I moved out."

"I don't blame you," Jane said sympathetically.

John Grant got up and left the room, returning a minute or so later with a fresh Coke. Hutchins had been finishing up the pizza and he was ready for something to drink.

"Anything happen while you lived in the loft?" Jane asked.

"Not much. But I looked behind me a lot. I didn't forward my mail there. I didn't have any credit cards, and I let my mother know where I was so I didn't have to forward anything. I cut off my phone and I didn't have to pay the electric bill anymore. At the loft, we just split the bill that came every month, and one of the guys paid it. I had a driver's license with the Fifty-sixth Street address on it and I changed that. But I was really scared, and after a while I came back here."

He had just wanted to come home, he said. "The thing was, my license expired and I needed a new one, and I didn't want it on record that I lived in Omaha. So I got one from New York." He looked at Jane. "That's how you found me, isn't it?"

"That was it."

"Shit." He put his head in his hands again, and when he sat up he looked as though he had figured out how they'd found him. "You can't keep anything a secret anymore, can you?"

"It gets tougher and tougher," John said.

"So if you could find me, anyone could, right?"

"Not necessarily," Jane said. He seemed genuinely scared. "We can get into files that the public can't."

"But if someone really wanted to find me, they could, right?"

"There's a chance they could."

He shook his head. "I was feeling safe, but now I don't know where to go from here." There was a tremor in his voice.

"Jerry, I don't think anyone's after you, because if they were, they would probably have found you by now. It's over four years since Arlen Quill was killed."

"Even so. They found Margaret, didn't they? And she left New York."

"Why would someone be after you, Jerry? Did you see anything that might put the finger on who killed Arlen Quill or Henry Soderberg?"

"I didn't see anything. I don't know anything. I just lived in my apartment, went to work, that's all."

It was a little too glib. Jane had that itchy feeling she got when someone was holding something back. "Can you describe Arlen Quill for me?" she asked.

He raised his eyebrows as though the question had surprised him. "Maybe five-ten, five-eleven—he was a little taller than me—wore glasses, most of his hair was gone, didn't smile much."

"How old would you say he was?"

"Thirties. Thirty-two, thirty-three."

"What about Henry Soderberg?"

"He was a big guy, six feet probably. Older. Looked like maybe he worked out. He had pretty broad shoulders."

"His face?"

"Big face, big nose, not much hair."

"Did he wear glasses?"

"Yeah, usually. I remember when he came to my place that night he took them off and kind of cleaned them with a napkin."

"Did he ever change lightbulbs in the hall in that building?"

"I don't know. The super did that stuff. Derek was his name."

"You never saw Mr. Soderberg change a lightbulb?"

He thought about it. "I don't think so. Doesn't mean he didn't do it."

"When did Mr. Soderberg come home from work?"

"Different times."

"How do you know? You lived two floors above him."

"I'd come home sometimes and he'd already be there."

"Did you see him?"

"I'd see his mail was gone from his mailbox."

"You checked his mailbox?"

"I just kinda looked to see whose mail was there and whose wasn't. Mrs. Best on the first floor always took her mail in right away after it was delivered."

"I see. You're an observant person, Jerry."

"Just a habit I have."

"You lived on the top floor. Did you ever see the door to the roof open?"

He looked a little uncomfortable. "Maybe sometimes in the summer. You could go up there but it was pretty dirty."

"You ever see anyone up there?"

"No."

"You ever sit on the roof, look at the city?"

"Once or twice. Like I said, it was dirty." He looked at his watch, a black digital on his left wrist. "How long're you gonna keep me here? I have to get to work."

"Where do you work, Jerry?" John asked.

"At a gas station. I'm the night man. I work ten to six."

"There's plenty of time," John said. "Anything else I can get you?"

"I'm fine."

"After Hollis Worthman and Margaret Rawls left," Jane said, "you were in that house all alone."

"Yeah, I was."

"I don't blame you for being scared. It must have been like a haunted house."

"It was."

"I guess Derek was in and out."

"Yeah, he cleaned up, worked around the place."

"What else, Jerry? What else happened in that building that you're not telling us?"

"Nothing. Honest. It was just a big, empty place."

Jane sat and looked at him. He knew who was home from the mailboxes. He had dinner with Hollis Worthman. He sent Christmas cards to Margaret Rawls. He changed lightbulbs for old Mrs. Best. He invited Henry Soderberg in for a beer and got interviewed. He was a regular gadfly, and if anyone in that building knew something funny was going on, this was the guy.

"I don't know anything," he said, uncomfortable that she was looking at him.

"If you saw Arlen Quill walking down the block, would you recognize him?"

"If I saw his face, yeah. If he was walking away from me, I don't know."

"Did he look anything like Henry Soderberg?"

He wrinkled his nose. "Henry's taller, you know? And older."

"But from a distance. Think about it."

"They were . . . You know what? I made that mistake once, now that I think about it."

"What mistake?"

"I was coming down the stairs and I saw—or I thought I saw—Henry Soderberg going down ahead of me, and I said, 'Hey, Henry. How's things?' and he didn't turn around, and when I got to the first floor, I saw it was Arlen Quill."

"So there was something about them. . . ."

"I guess there was. Funny you should mention it. I'd forgotten about that. It happened a long time ago. Is Cory still waiting for me?"

"I'll go out and check," John said. "I think she is."

When the door closed, Hutchins said, "Is that about it? Cory hasn't had dinner yet. It's getting late."

She couldn't hold him; legally he wasn't a suspect. And unless he was very clever, and he might be, he was afraid of being a victim himself. The interview hadn't given Jane anything to link him to the killings. "We may need to ask you more questions," she said.

"Can you tell me what you're after? I don't think I know anything that can help you. I just lived there, that's all."

"Tell me about Derek."

"Derek. He was OK. He kept the place pretty clean."

"Did he ever fight with Arlen Quill? Or Henry Soderberg?"

"Derek didn't fight with anyone. He was this very mild kind of guy."

John came back in. "Cory's still waiting for you," he said. "I got her something to eat from the machine."

"Thanks. I appreciate that."

"Derek," Jane said. "What else can you tell me about Derek? Did he ever go out on the roof that you know about?"

"Sure, he went out on the roof. It was part of his job."

"And sometimes he left the door to the roof unlocked?"

"I couldn't really tell you that. You think someone came in from the roof and killed Arlen Quill and Henry?"

"I don't know, Jerry. It's what I'm trying to find out."

He picked up the empty Coke can and scrunched it a little more. Then he picked up the second one and drained it. He was nervous. "You know, I really want to go. I've answered all your questions. I have to get to work."

Jane looked at her watch. He still had a couple of hours till he had to be at his gas station, wherever that was. She could keep after him and maybe something would come up. He was antsy now. Maybe keeping him here would yield something; maybe it would just get him mad and turn him against her. It was always a gamble, and you never wanted to lose. "I'd like to let you go," she said. "You've been cooperative. I just wonder if there isn't something else you know about Derek."

"I don't know anything about Derek."

"What about Mr. Stabile?"

"The guy who owns the building?" He sounded shocked that anyone would even mention his name. "I almost never saw him."

"Maybe Derek knew more than he let on."

"About what?"

"About the people who lived there, about what they did, who they were, how they felt about each other."

"Derek didn't know anything." He put his head back in his hands. "Well, maybe he did."

Jane held her breath for a second. "What did he know, Jerry?"

"Look, I'll tell you this one thing and then I'm going, OK?"

"I'm listening," she said, without making any promises.

"I told you about the rats."

"Yes."

"Well, I'm not sure it was rats."

"What do you think it was?"

He looked up, his eyes going from John's face to hers. "I think . . . I'm not sure of this, but I think it's possible. You know there was an empty apartment across the hall from mine?"

"I know."

"I think someone may have been living there, or at least staying there sometimes at night."

She felt her heartbeat quicken. "Did you ever see him?"

"No. It's just the noises. And sometimes . . ."

"Sometimes what?"

"Sometimes at night I thought I heard the door close."

[14]

GODDAMN. THAT WAS all she could think of. A hole you could run a tanker through and no one had seen it. Had Charlie Bracken and Otis Wright looked in the apparently empty apartment? And even if they had, if someone was sleeping on the floor, maybe taking his bed with him during the day, it could have looked like an empty, like a place under construction. Maybe it was Derek himself who was sleeping there, mild Derek who seemed to like everyone equally and who had disappeared for a convenient length of time after the death of Soderberg.

After they let Hutchins go, Jane fixed up her notes and faxed them to Centre Street. In the morning Defino and MacHovec would call Bracken and see if he had looked inside the empty apartment, the source of possible evidence that was now gone and irretrievable. Then John drove her to the hotel and they had a bite and a couple of drinks.

"So what's on the schedule for tomorrow?" he asked.

"Just to try to get on a flight home."

"It wasn't a very long visit. We didn't have a chance to show you around."

"But I got what I came for."

"You convinced Hutchins didn't do any of the homicides?"

"I'm not convinced of anything, but he's a lot less of a suspect tonight than he was on Monday. What do you think?"

"I agree. To me, it looks like he's scared. I wouldn't be surprised if he moves."

"I hope we don't lose him. He knew everyone in that building."

"You'll still be able to find Cory. She can't disappear. She has a real job that pays her on the books."

"And we have a killer wandering around, probably still looking for Jerry Hutchins."

"I feel sorry for the poor bastard. I hope they don't find him."

"Me too," she said. Unless, of course, it was all an act and he was the killer. He knew everyone in the building by name. He had eaten with them, had a beer with them, changed their lightbulbs, sent them Christmas cards. He was in a perfect position to know where all of them had gone when they left Fifty-sixth Street. But she could think of no motive. If he had done this, she had to believe he was psychotic, and he seemed pretty normal while they were talking. And how could Cory Blanding live with a psychotic?

"You're having second thoughts about Hutchins."

"You're reading my mind."

"It comes with the job. Leave it awhile, Jane. Relax. It's been a long day, a very long day. Tell me how a good-looking woman like you ended up chasing a guy like Jerry Hutchins out to Omaha."

"I guess I screwed up enough times the right way. I certainly never aimed for Omaha or a cold case."

"I bet you never screwed up in your life."

Strangers were all the same. Keep your face clean and do your job the way you were taught and they draw the usual conclusions. "You ever get involved with anyone on the job?" she said, watching his face for reaction, feeling the need to confide.

The reaction was there, the eyebrows jumping suddenly. "Can't say I have. I'm a pretty dull family man."

"I did. He's a family man, too."

"And he's staying with his family."

"Right." She finished her drink and put the glass down. "I never expected him to leave. I don't know if I could handle a man full-time. The bottom line is, his daughter started asking questions. That meant he had to do one thing or another and I wasn't ready to . . ." She let her breath out.

"Make a commitment?"

"I guess that's it, that and my guilt about his wife. His children. If anyone found out, that would be the end of his career."

"And he's pretty high up in NYPD."

"He is, yes. How did you guess?"

"You don't strike me as the kind of woman who would risk all for a fellow detective."

"I am, actually. Or I was. But I settled down with . . . this man and that was it. It was a wonderful relationship for both of us."

"But it's over."

"It's over, yes." She hated saying it. "He called me the other day just before I got home from work and left a message on my machine. I missed him by a few minutes. I hadn't heard his voice for weeks, and it stirred up a lot of things I thought weren't there anymore."

"What did he say in the message?" John asked.

She smiled. "Just that he wanted to hear my voice."

"That's nice. He must think of you a lot."

She knew that was true, that in those small segments of time, flickers, microseconds, when nothing had a prior claim on his mind, he would think of her as she did of him. She thought of those moments as elevator time, when she stood among people she didn't know, people who wanted nothing from her, and let her mind go where it wanted, to Hack. She could almost feel his presence, his arm against hers, his fingers touching hers, his breath in her hair.

"We were good for each other," she said, not responding to his comment. "A lot of things in my life changed after it was over. I moved to a new apartment."

"A couple of days ago, I think you told me."

"Yes. Over the weekend. And when I leave the job, I'll work somewhere that I'll never run into him."

"Maybe you'll run into someone else."

"Maybe I will."

"Why did you tell me?"

"It's on my mind a lot. Waiting all day for Hutchins, I needed something to think about."

"I spent most of the day trying to figure out how I'll get my kids through college if they pick expensive ones."

"I guess that's on a lot of people's minds these days."

"Not a very sexy topic to spend a day thinking about, but that's the way it is."

She was tired now, the effect of the long day, the long interview, the drinks. She wanted to sleep, then find her way back to New York. "I wonder if Hutchins is at work," she said, "or if he's flown the coop already."

"I'll drive by the gas station on my way home. It's not far out of the way. If he's gone, you'll hear from me."

"There goes my night's sleep," she said with a laugh.

"You think he's gone?"

"I'm too exhausted to think at this point."

"Then it's time to pay up." He looked around for the waitress. "Give me a call when you know what time your flight leaves. I'll come pick you up."

"You're very nice."

"And very tired."

Ten minutes later she was in her room.

It seemed strange to have talked about Hack. Hack was one of the two things in her life she didn't talk about. Her father suspected, she knew, that she had a boyfriend whom she couldn't introduce, but he would never ask, and if he knew, he surely understood why. If it caused him pain, and she felt sure it did, he kept it to himself. On the job, it was a subject she could never even hint at. She had a friend who knew, a girl—a woman— she had gone to school with, but even her friend had never laid eyes on him. Not that she cared. Their being together was theirs; they had never needed anyone outside.

What she hadn't shared with John was the letter on crinkly paper that she had not yet opened. As she turned off the light, she wondered if she ever would.

She thought it was the alarm, far too soon for the deepness of her sleep. But it was the phone and she pulled herself up, fearing the worst about her father.

"Is this Detective Bauer?" a woman's voice asked.

"Yes, it is."

"This is Helen Grant."

A chill went through Jane's body. "John's wife?"

"Yes. Do you know where my husband is?"

Her heart was racing. She pulled the alarm clock toward her and looked at the time. It was two A.M. "Mrs. Grant, John left the hotel between eleven and twelve. He said he was going home."

"He's not here." The voice was just short of shaking.

"He said he would drive by a gas station to look in on someone we interviewed this evening. If you hold on, I'll get the address." She got out of bed and went to her file. She had every piece of paper that John had. She took the address back to the phone and read it off to Helen Grant.

"I know where that is. It wouldn't take more than twenty or thirty minutes for him to get home from there."

"Mrs. Grant, I want you to call your husband's unit and tell them he left here about eleven-thirty, that he was going to stop at that gas station and talk to Jerry Hutchins, the night man. And that he isn't home yet. I'll call the gas station and see if he's there or find out when he left."

There was a short silence. Then the woman said, "Thank you. I'll call the unit."

Jane found the gas station in the hotel phone book. She dialed the number and let it ring. She counted twenty rings, then tried a second time. She was sure Jerry would answer if he was there. It might be Cory, and he wouldn't want to miss her call. She sat on the edge of the bed, feeling fear seep through her veins. Jerry Hutchins wasn't there, and neither was John Grant.

She scrambled into her clothes. Helen Grant would be on the phone for a few minutes. As soon as she got off, a car would be dispatched to the gas station. Jane wanted to be there, too, and she didn't want John's wife going. At best, no one would be there. At worst . . . she didn't want to think about it.

She was throwing pens into her bag when the phone rang.

"Detective Bauer?"

"Yes."

"This is Officer Keller. I'm on my way to your hotel. Thought you'd like to come along to look for John Grant."

"I would, thanks. I'll be downstairs in about three minutes."

"Don't hurry. There's another car on the way to the gas station."

She hung up, dialed Helen Grant's number, and told her quickly what was happening.

"I can drive over there myself," Mrs. Grant said.

"Please stay where you are. We'll call you the minute we know anything."

"Is that a promise, or are you trying to keep me out of your hair?"

She was a cop's wife, all right. "It's a promise. You'll hear from us."

She grabbed the electronic hotel key, stuffed it in her wallet, and ran out to the elevator. There was one sitting on her floor, and she rode it down and went outside to wait. It was cold out but very clear, the kind of sky you rarely saw in New York, where the haze frequently clouded the stars. The air smelled fresh and invigorating. If she had been visiting a friend here or setting off for work, she might have wondered why she had ever wanted to spend her life in New York. Sentences that started with *if*, she thought. There were too many *if*s in her head concerning John Grant and Jerry Hutchins, too many possibilities she didn't want to consider.

A police car pulled into the hotel drive and swung around to stop under the canopy in front of her.

"Detective Bauer?" the young man at the wheel called.

"Yes. Thanks for coming."

He leaned over and opened the door. "Come right in. We'll be there in no time."

[15]

THERE WERE TWO police cars at the scene when they arrived, and a third arrived half a minute later. Men in blue were swarming around the area and in the combination office and snack bar.

"Detective Bauer?"

"Yes. What's happening?"

He was a uniformed sergeant and he offered his hand to shake hers. "Sgt. Mike Fromm. Nice to meet you. Looks like nobody's here. What can you tell me?"

"John Grant left my hotel about eleven-thirty, give or take ten minutes. We'd been interviewing Jerry Hutchins, the night man here, in connection with several homicides in New York. Hutchins left the station house about eight, eight-thirty. We left later. I don't know what else I can tell you."

"Hutchins a suspect in your homicides?"

"He was a possible. After we talked to him, it looked more like he could be the next victim or a material witness."

"Hey, Sarge? I think this could be blood." The man who called was in front of the doors to the workshop.

Jane and the sergeant jogged over. The uniform shone his light on the stain. It looked as much like blood as any Jane had ever seen.

"Move the light," she said, "over that way." She pointed toward the far end of the small building.

"Here's another one." He turned the light toward the scrub brush behind the station.

"John?" Jane called into the blackness. "Jerry? You guys out there?"

"What kind of car was John driving?" the sergeant asked.

"Today it was an unmarked police vehicle." She looked around.

"It's not here. What about Hutchins?"

"We drove him to the station house. His girlfriend has a small blue car, maybe Japanese. She could have dropped him off and gone home."

"Or maybe he never came here tonight."

"Maybe." Her head was buzzing. "And whoever was waiting for him met John Grant." She pulled her coat around her. "Someone with a light come with me?"

The three moved into a standard search pattern, arm's-length distance from each other, the uniforms sweeping their flashlight beams side to side, intersecting in front of Jane. As she walked, she kept calling the men's names, kicking an occasional can and stepping on something she'd rather not know the nature of. Twenty or thirty feet behind the small building was a stand of trees, preventing them from seeing what lay beyond.

When they reached the trees, they stopped. "Let's keep going," she said. "You have any idea how far the trees go?"

Neither of them did.

Walking was harder now, little saplings poking out of the earth, slippery leaves hiding roots and debris that could trip them. She wondered what poison ivy looked like.

"Look at this," the man on her right said. His light pinpointed a stain on some compacted leaves.

Jane knelt and looked at it closely. "I think it's blood." She stood and looked around. "John? It's Jane Bauer here. Jerry? Let us know where you are."

They stayed still for a moment as the two lights swept the woods.

"You hear that?" the man on her left said.

"Yes. Over there."

They walked diagonally left. It had been a moan, or at least a faint sound from a human throat.

"There he is!" The man on her left charged forward, and they followed, dodging branches. "It's Detective Grant," the uniform called.

Thank God. "Get Sergeant Fromm," she told the uniform beside her, "and call for a bus. Ambulance," she amended, not sure what the lingo was in the Midwest. Then she saw John Grant. He lay twisted on leaves and branches, as though his fall had been broken awkwardly and painfully. She got down beside him. "It's OK, John. We're getting you to a hospital." She pulled off her coat and folded it under his head. His hair had twigs and leaves in it, which she brushed away.

"Looks like a bullet in his thigh," the uniform said. "There's a lot of blood."

She took John's hand and squeezed it. He squeezed it back with only a small amount of pressure. "Hang in there," she said softly, her mouth near his ear.

The uniform had taken off his jacket, and they covered John and heard him make a sound. Then they heard a distant siren.

Mrs. Grant met them at the hospital. She was about his age, graying, and very frightened.

"Thank goodness you called me," Jane said.

"He's very good about letting me know where he is and when he's coming home. I woke up and he wasn't there, and I didn't know what to do."

"You did the right thing. He was shot in the leg and there's a possibility there's another wound, but we'll find that out. He's lost some blood, and it was cold out there."

"I can give him blood," his wife said. "We're the same type. I wish they'd let me see him."

"They will. Come and sit down."

"What is all this about? John's never been shot before. I don't think he's ever drawn his gun."

His gun had been missing. "We were interviewing a possible suspect in a New York homicide earlier in the evening."

"Why was John at that gas station?"

"The man we were talking to worked there at night. John wanted to make sure he was at work."

"Where is he now?"

"We don't know." They had combed the woods and not found Jerry Hutchins, dead or alive. Two uniforms had been dispatched to Cory Blanding's apartment, but there was no word yet.

Sgt. Mike Fromm came into the waiting area and went directly to Mrs. Grant. They hugged and he comforted her, telling her John would be fine and they would let her see him very soon.

Then he turned to Jane. "I just got a call from the men who went to the Blanding woman's apartment. Hutchins isn't there."

"Did he go to work tonight?"

"I'm waiting to hear."

"Hutchins may have shot John and taken off in John's car."

"With John's gun."

"Yes." She shook her head. "We were both almost convinced he was a possible victim, not a suspect. Even so, we couldn't hold him."

"We don't know enough yet. They'll be calling me when they've talked to the Blanding woman."

"I'd like to talk to her myself, but I want to see John first."

"It may be a while. He's in surgery. Let me call the men who are talking to her and then let's get over there." He disappeared around a corner.

Mrs. Grant had been watching them. "Did they find the man who did this to John?"

"No." Jane took a seat beside her. "We're going to talk to the girlfriend of the man we questioned this evening. Is there anyone you want me to call for you?"

"I've called my kids. That's enough for right now."

"We'll be back to see John later. He probably won't be in any condition to talk when he comes out of surgery anyway."

Mike Fromm was on his way back. "Let's drive over to the Blanding apartment." He turned to Helen Grant. "Helen, anything I can get you?"

"I'm fine. Just go before it's too late."

Cory Blanding was in her nightgown, a maroon velour robe over it. She sat on a sofa in the small living room, her hair disheveled. She looked pale and scared as Jane and Mike Fromm walked into the apartment. "Can you tell me what happened?" she asked in a quavering voice.

"We're looking for Jerry," Jane said. "He's not at the gas station. Can you tell me where he is?"

She shook her head. "He was there; that's all I know."

"How do you know?"

"Because Jerry went there."

"How sure are you?"

"Where else would he go?"

"How did he get to the station, Cory?"

"In the car."

"How did you get home?"

"He drove me home. Then he went to work."

"In your blue car?"

"Uh-huh."

"Is that how he usually gets to work?"

"Most of the time. He gets home about six-thirty in the morning, and then I take the car to work. Unless he needs it during the day."

"We'll have to put an alarm out for the car," Jane said.

Mike Fromm took the information from Cory. Cory got up to get her bag to find the license plate and VIN numbers. When she sat down, the sergeant went to the phone and called it in.

"What time did Jerry drop you off tonight?" Jane asked.

"I don't know. We had a quick bite when we left the police station. Then we came home. Then he left. Nine-thirty maybe?"

"How do you know he went to the gas station?"

"Where else would he go?" she asked for the second time.

South Dakota, Jane thought. Iowa. California. "Did you talk to him after he went to work?"

Cory thought a minute. "Yeah. He called me."

"You're sure he called you, not the other way around?"

"I'm sure, yes, I'm sure." She seemed overwhelmed. "Why are you asking me these questions? Where's Jerry?"

"We don't know where he is. We want to find him. You're sure you didn't call him, right?"

"He called me. I was getting ready for bed. I remember I turned down the TV when the phone rang."

"How long did you talk?"

"A couple of minutes. He usually calls me about that time."

"What time?"

"Eleven-thirty. Twelve o'clock."

"Are you cold, Cory?" Jane asked. The girl seemed to be shivering.

"I'm freezing. I didn't turn the heat up when I got out of bed."

"You want to turn it up now?"

She got up from the sofa and went to the wall near the front door. She moved something on the thermostat, then came back to the sofa, hugging the robe around her. "It'll take a while," she said.

Jane kept her coat on. It still had debris from the woods clinging to it, but it kept her warm. "What did Jerry tell you about our interview with him?"

"He said he told you everything he knew, how he'd been so scared he'd be the next one killed, how he thought someone was living in that empty apartment in New York, everything."

"Did you know all about it before tonight?"

"Yeah. I knew. He told me a long time ago. And we talked about it sometimes."

"Suppose you tell us everything that Jerry told you about what happened in New York."

She exhaled, looking annoyed, if not angry. Then she set her lips. Then she started her story.

She didn't remember the names of most of the players, but she had the story substantially accurate, starting with the discovery of Arlen Quill's body and finishing with Jerry's return to Omaha. They had known each other before he left, and they had talked about Cory joining him in New York, but it had never happened. About the time she had seriously considered moving east, Henry Soderberg had been found dead, and sometime after that Jerry moved out. There was too much upheaval in his life at that point for him to take on a live-in girlfriend, which meant finding a new apartment that would be suitable. Also, he was scared for a long time, both for himself and for anyone living with him. There had been too many deaths, he told her, too much that was unexplained. And he just didn't understand what was going on.

"What did he do when he came back here?" Jane asked.

"He stayed with his mother for a while. Then he moved in with me."

"Where's his mother now?"

"She died. It was very sudden."

"Is that when he moved in with you?"

"A little while after that, yeah."

"Does he have brothers and sisters?"

"No. There's just Jerry."

"Does he have a good friend that he might go to if he was in trouble?"

"There's a couple, Richie Strohman and Carl Gibbs."

"We'll need their addresses and phone numbers."

She got up and went to the kitchen, returning with a piece of paper she had written on. "He's not with them," she said. "He would know you'd look for him there."

Jane thought she was probably right, but it had to be checked out. "What about old girlfriends?" she asked.

Cory set her lips again. "I don't know anything about them."

"He keep an address book?"

"I don't think so."

"Cory, if you know a name—"

"I don't. I don't." She was almost shouting. "What's happened to Jerry? What have you people done to him? Where's my car? How am I supposed to get to work in the morning?"

"We're looking for your car. As soon as we find it, we'll let you know."

"This is a nightmare," Cory said, her voice breaking. "Yesterday we were just two people living together, and today Jerry is missing and I'm in the middle of a bad dream."

"I know, and we're trying to help, but we have to find out if Jerry took off or if someone took him away."

"Why would anyone do that?" There were tears on her face. "Why would anyone want to hurt Jerry?"

Mike Fromm, who had been standing somewhere behind Jane, came forward and sat in the chair that matched hers. He leaned toward her. "It's possible he just decided to get away," he said in a soothing voice.

"He wouldn't leave me."

"The problem is, we have two cars missing from the gas station, yours and one belonging to Detective Grant, who went to check up on Jerry. It's hard to explain the disappearance of two cars unless there are two drivers. If Jerry drove off, maybe because he was scared after being interviewed at the police station tonight, that would account for one of the cars. Does Jerry own a gun?"

"A gun? No. Why?"

"He might have thought he needed it for protection."

"He never owned a gun. I wouldn't let him own a gun in this apartment."

"Maybe he kept it hidden," Mike Fromm said. "Maybe he came back to the apartment with you after dinner and picked it up."

She shook her head.

"Did he go to a closet while he was here? Did he change his clothes?"

"He didn't change his clothes. We were here for maybe ten or fifteen minutes."

"Would you give us permission to look around the apartment?"

She sat breathing deeply, her mouth moving as though she might burst into tears. "OK," she said.

"Thank you, Cory." He signaled the two uniformed officers and they moved into the bedroom.

"There's no gun," she said in a low voice. "I promise you."

Mike Fromm got up to check the bedroom, leaving Jane alone with Cory. "What kind of work did Jerry do when he was living in New York?"

"He was in sales. He sold advertising for a television company. When he came back here, at first he was afraid to do anything where he had to give his address and Social Security number. He still kind of works off the books at the gas station. And I pay all the bills here so nobody knows he's here."

"Did he ever think he was being watched?"

"He was careful. He always checked. But I don't think so."

Jane took her coat off and laid it on the arm of the sofa. When she sat down again, she made small talk with Cory while the men in the bedroom did their work. When they came out, she could see they had found nothing.

Mike Fromm sat down opposite Cory. "We'd like to set up your phone," he said, "so that if Jerry calls, we know where he's calling from."

"I don't know if I should."

"He may be running from someone who's after him with a gun. We'd like to be able to help him."

"Look at the trouble you got him into already."

"I know, and I'm sorry about that. But if Jerry's in trouble, we'd like to help him."

Her mouth trembled. "I was never supposed to tell anybody anything."

"You did the right thing, Cory. We want Jerry alive as much as you do. If we find him, we'll protect him."

"Go ahead," she said, her voice breaking again. "Do what you have to."

He went to the phone and made the arrangements. Then he and Jane left for the hospital.

[16]

"YOU MUST BE ready to collapse," Mike said as he drove to the hospital.

"I'll catch some sleep later. I won't be flying back today."

"Good idea. I hope John can talk to us. There's a lot we need to know. Two missing cars. And how did the shooter get to the gas station? In a third car?"

"And did he follow John from my hotel, or was he there when John showed up?"

"Which would mean he'd followed Jerry Hutchins."

"I'm probably too tired to think, but I'm trying to figure out who in New York knew I was coming to Omaha, or who knew I was on the case and might have passed along the information."

"You must have interviewed a lot of people."

"Not that many," she said. "The ones we wanted were all dead, except for Jerry Hutchins. There was the owner of the building, the super, the two detectives who worked the case four years ago, some guys at the last place Hutchins lived." She tried to get her brain to function for another few minutes. "Hollis Worthman's mother, Margaret Rawls's friend, and then Margaret's sister. Arlen Quill's wife, but this isn't about Arlen Quill, I don't think." She looked at Mike. "You don't know what I'm babbling about."

He laughed. "No, but it makes sense. Here's the hospital. Let's hope John's doing well."

He was, as it turned out, but he was still asleep. His wife even smiled when she talked to them. She had sat by his bedside ever since he returned from surgery, but it would be a while till he woke up. There had been a second bullet, probably from the same gun, in his back, but it hadn't done much damage. All in all, he was very lucky.

In his room they talked to him, but there was no response. He was hooked up to some IVs, but he was breathing on his own. Jane watched him with feelings of guilt and sorrow. He had been so helpful, so kind to her, and he had ended up like this.

"Go home and sleep, Detective Bauer," Helen Grant said. "John's going to be fine. Come back later and you can talk to him."

It was good advice. They left her sitting in a chair beside the bed, her eyes on her husband.

"I think you should check out of the hotel and go somewhere else."

She knew Mike was right. If Jerry Hutchins had not shot John Grant, whoever had shot him probably knew where she was staying. He might be outside the hotel right now, waiting to see them drive up, waiting to follow her to another hotel or to the airport. She said all this to Mike.

"We can get you out a back way while I sit in the car out front waiting for you."

"Let's do it then."

"I'll go upstairs with you till you're packed and ready. You can use the express checkout, or I'll settle the bill for you. How about bunking in my house till you're ready to go back?"

She smiled, her eyelids closing as fatigue began to take over. "I'm almost too worn out to turn you down, but staying with you would just put your family in jeopardy. Whoever this guy is, he'll find me if I spend any kind of time here."

"My family is my son and me, and he's a cop. He's the guy I'm going to call to get you out the back way."

"OK. Sure. Thanks." She shut her eyes and her mouth for a few seconds. "I haven't had an all-nighter for a long time."

"You can catch up in our guest room. We've—" He stopped as a radio call came in. "This is Sergeant Fromm. Go ahead."

"Sergeant Fromm, we've got a blue Toyota registered to Cory Blanding abandoned about two miles from the gas station where Detective Grant got shot tonight."

"Thanks, Mary. I can't get there for a while, so tell them I said to treat it like the biggest case they've ever handled. Got that?"

"You bet. You just call me when you're ready to go and I'll lead you right to it."

"He's on the run," Jane said.

"Or the shooter got to him. It'll hold till later."

"Suits me just fine."

He came into the room and made some phone calls while she gathered her things together. Having expected to stay only a couple of days at the outside, she didn't have much, and it repacked easily. His son arrived about ten minutes after he was called, a handsome young man named Luke who was tall but didn't look much like his father. It was something she always noticed, who people took after. He had a small overnight-sized bag with him that Mike intended to use as a decoy. Its much-used look resembled her old suitcase at home, just what a New York cop would carry if she hadn't gotten to Bloomingdale's before dashing out to the airport.

When she was packed and Mike had arranged payment for the room, he took the small suitcase downstairs to his car. Then Jane and Luke took the service elevator down and went out the back way. He was driving his own car, and they drove off the hotel grounds using the back exit, the one trucks used when they made deliveries.

Jane didn't look around till they were well away from the hotel. The sun was rising now, light in the eastern sky, cars along the road, most of them heading into Omaha.

"You know what?" she said. "I've got my second wind. Can you take me to where they found Cory Blanding's car? I'd like to see it before I go to sleep."

"You sure?"

"I'm sure. I won't collapse on you."

He smiled and turned at the next intersection. It took about twenty minutes to reach the car, and a crime scene unit was already on the scene, the area taped to keep away the curious. Four floodlights, with black battery packs, provided the detectives with enough light to read by as they examined the car and its contents.

Jane introduced herself to the detectives and asked if they had found anything.

The one named Joe Meyner said, "There's a lot of junk in the backseat, fast-food garbage mostly, but nothing in front. The door to the driver's side was open when we got here, and the motor was off."

"Keys?"

"None."

"Mind if I have a look around?"

"Sure thing. Hope you find something."

So did she. She bent to go under the tape, then walked back and forth, moving farther away from the car with each turn. Luke Fromm joined her.

"What're you looking for?"

"Anything he might have thrown away."

He pulled out his flashlight, although it was fairly light by now, and pointed it toward the ground. The grass was several inches high and weedy and would need to be combed to dislodge its secrets. The area was similar to the brush behind the gas station, where she had searched for John Grant and Jerry Hutchins a couple of hours ago. She didn't think Hutchins was around, but just in case he was hiding from an attacker, she called him a couple of times; there was no response except for the rustling of the wind in the leaves.

"Something over there?" Luke said.

In the beam of the light there was a glitter, glass or metal. They walked over carefully and Jane crouched. "Keys," she said, feeling a rush of excitement.

Luke pulled a plastic sandwich bag out of a pocket and lifted the keys with it. "Looks like he tossed them to keep someone else from driving his car away."

"Could be. Mark the spot where the keys were lying and give them to the crime scene guys, and then maybe I'll be ready to find a place to sleep."

Nothing was new at the car. The trunk was open, revealing more junk but nothing that looked promising as evidence. She gave Meyner the keys and saw his eyes light up. She was sure he would have checked out the grounds himself later, but she was glad to have found them.

"Toyota," Meyner said, looking at them. "Very nice." The smile he gave her was genuine.

"OK," she said to Luke. "Now I think I can sleep."

She didn't, of course, for some time. By the time they got to the Fromms' house, a small house with a beautiful front lawn and a big yard out back, it was after eight, which meant it was nine in New York and time to call in. She reached Defino on the first try and he returned her call, conferencing in McElroy. She detailed the night's events as far as she could remember them. They hadn't read her fax yet, but while they spoke it was delivered to Defino by Annie.

McElroy must have been taking notes, because he asked her to repeat a lot of things. Finally, after almost twenty minutes on the phone, he summarized: "You're telling us that someone knew you went to Omaha, that he followed you when you picked up Hutchins, that he went after Hutchins at the gas station where he worked and managed to shoot a cop and get away with Hutchins?"

"Or Hutchins ran for it. No telling where he is now."

"Jesus."

"Right."

"We got a problem."

"Looks like it. We have to find out who Henry Soderberg was, who he worked for, and whether Derek, the super, knows things he hasn't told us. But you know, I never told Charlie Bracken where I was going, so maybe we can cross him off our list."

"Guess we got our work cut out for us," MacHovec said into the speakerphone.

"Have a good time, guys. I'm going to sleep. I'll get back to you later."

"Have a good one," McElroy said. "And don't leave that phone till we talk."

The living room looked as though it had been designed for smaller people than the Fromm men. But it was comfortable and cheerful, with floral patterns on the sofa and curtains. Family pictures were scattered around, some of them from Mike Fromm's boyhood, when he was a tall, gangly kid. His wedding picture was there, his bride a foot shorter than he, smiling and very pretty.

"Mom died two years ago," Luke said.

"I'm sorry. I lost my mother, too." She realized she had been standing in front of the picture and staring. "I think I need sleep."

"This way. The guest room's upstairs."

The guest room had obviously belonged to Luke's sister. A handmade quilt covered a double bed that half a dozen stuffed animals sat on. Luke dropped off her suitcase and closed the door behind him, saying he would see her later. She gathered up the animals in one big armful and dropped them on a chair. Then she pulled the quilt down, stripped, and got into bed.

She slept soundly for three hours, then got up. The

clock radio on the night table said it was almost noon, and she felt so refreshed that she found the bathroom, where a stack of clean towels lay on the toilet cover, presumably for her. When she got out of the shower, she was a new person.

In her life she had rarely spent a night in a house. Having grown up a New Yorker, she was used to apartment living. She had a friend or two in grade school and high school who lived in a single-family or two-family house in the Bronx, but it still struck her as a different way of living, four walls that looked out onto the outside world. Here there would be no complaints about heavy-footed people running amok, about loud stereos and TVs. Angry wives would not shriek back at angrier husbands only a few feet from the limits of your room. Living in a house gave a new meaning to privacy.

Her hair dried, she stepped out of the bathroom and stopped to listen to the sounds from downstairs.

"Jane? You up?" It was Mike's voice.

"Yes. Hello."

"I just got home. Come down when you're ready. I'll have some breakfast for you."

She was downstairs in ten minutes, the smell of fresh coffee leading her to the kitchen. "Good morning. You're a very hospitable family."

"I'm finally off duty. It's been a long shift. I stopped at the hospital and got to say a few words to John."

"He's OK?"

"He's fine. He asked about you."

"What about what happened last night?"

"He's feeling a little dopey from the anesthetic, so it wasn't a very long conversation, but the gist of it is, there was a third man there. John arrived at the gas station sometime after the guy who was looking for Jerry Hutchins. By the time John realized what was going on, the guy had shot him and gotten his gun. Hutchins got away in his car while the shooter was looking for John."

"How did the shooter get there in the first place?" Jane asked as he filled her coffee mug.

"Didn't ask. We can go back later, but I want you to keep a low profile. Somebody knew you were here. Let's keep you hidden as long as we can. How about some scrambled eggs? I put a little Texas hot sauce in them."

She smiled. "Sounds good."

"I'll join you. This is either my breakfast or my supper, I'm not sure which. But I'm hungry. Let's see if we have some bacon."

He cooked like a master, the smells filling the kitchen and dinette. She could see the kitchen had been updated not too long ago, and she could imagine the pleasure of the woman who had used it.

"We fixed the kitchen up for my wife," he said as he sat down finally to eat. "My son and I did most of it not long before she took sick. She didn't get much time to enjoy it."

"I'm sorry."

"She was too young to die, but you don't have much say in things like that."

"She was very pretty," Jane said. "I looked at some of your pictures in the living room."

"That she was. And about half as big as I am." He swallowed a lot of coffee. "You talk to your people in New York?"

"First thing this morning. They'll be looking for the connection. I hope it isn't anyone on the job."

"First place you gotta look."

"One of the original detectives on the case is on sick leave now. Emphysema. The other one's still on the job. I don't like to think it could be either one of them." She sketched out the case, starting with the Quill homicide.

"I'd be looking at that super of yours," he said. "Sounds like he's on someone's payroll."

"There's another possibility. Last night is just coming back to me. The empty apartment on the top floor . . . Hutchins lived on the top floor. He said someone was living in the apartment. Unofficially."

"Someone who could have killed Quill by mistake and the second man when he got around to it."

"Right."

"Still goes back to the super, don't you think? Didn't he have to know someone was living in an empty apartment? Didn't he show the apartment to people?"

"During the day or early evening. This guy could've come in at night from the roof. Maybe the super knew; maybe he didn't."

"Sounds like a frustrating case."

"A good one."

"Well, it got you out to Omaha."

"You ever hear of a town called Jewell, Kansas?" she asked.

"Yeah, I think so. Very small place a few hours' drive from here. You know someone out there?"

"I may."

"You planning to go?"

"I don't think so. I want to finish up here and get back to New York. I keep hoping you'll get a call that they've found John Grant's car."

"With Hutchins in the trunk?" He looked at her soberly.

She sat with her hands around the warm mug, thinking. "I don't know about Hutchins. I still think he could be on the other side."

"Even with what John said?"

"We'll find out. I think we're going to crack this case this time around." We better, she thought as she drank the coffee.

17

THE CRIME SCENE detectives turned up nothing of interest in the little blue Toyota. There was no blood, no signs of a struggle, no written message stuck between the seats. It appeared that Jerry Hutchins had abandoned the car, tossed the keys, including his house key and some others, into the grass, and taken off on foot. No weapon was found anywhere in the car, and the glove compartment was closed when the car was found. So he probably hadn't been searching for anything in the last seconds he was in the car.

But was he followed and overtaken, or did he just decide he had more flexibility on foot? Nothing at the scene was definitive. Whatever happened, it had been sudden and quick. Tossing the keys meant that anyone following him could not get into Cory's apartment. But whether he made a successful getaway or had been picked up by his pursuer was a toss-up.

Jane gathered all the information she could, then called New York. This time Captain Graves joined McElroy on his speakerphone, and Defino and MacHovec shared theirs. She gave them everything she had and then let Defino and MacHovec report.

Sean had spent the morning trying to trace the company Henry Soderberg had allegedly worked for, QX Electronics. The company didn't exist anymore, but it had occupied quarters in a building in downtown Manhattan four years ago. Defino had chased over there this morning and talked to the owner, who barely remembered the company. His files showed they had rented a very small office on the third floor for about eighteen months, but signed a lease and paid for a full two years. He couldn't remember how many men worked in the office, but he was sure there were only men. At least, he had never seen a woman there.

The telephone company's records showed phone service for QX for eighteen months, all their bills paid on time. But when QX terminated service, which was a few months after the death of Soderberg, they did not leave a forwarding number. A check of Dun & Bradstreet and TRW showed no record of QX's existence. This alone was not telling. They might have been a start-up company, a couple of guys with a brilliant idea, a Microsoft wanna-be that just never made the grade, and with Soderberg gone, half their resources may have been gone too. So they came out of nowhere and went back to the same place, MacHovec volunteered rather poetically.

Where Soderberg came from was still unknown. Stabile, the owner of the apartment building on West Fifty-sixth Street, had no record of any references or former addresses for him. He had a job and he had plunked down a month's rent and a month's security, and that had been enough for Stabile. So at the moment, Soderberg's origins were as cloudy as those of the company he worked for.

"Who claimed the body?" Jane asked almost in the same breath as did a male voice in New York.

"That is the question," Sean said. "Nobody, it seems, for some time. Couldn't find any record in his apartment of his having a family, so they left the body in the morgue after the autopsy. Eventually, maybe a couple of days later, somebody at QX Electronics came in in lieu of next of kin and had him sent to a New York funeral home, but don't ask me what they did with him after that. I haven't tracked it down yet."

"Sounds like he's the key to this whole thing," Captain Graves said. "We'll have to get on it. Jane?"

"Yes, sir."

"I think we can leave the search for Hutchins to the Omaha police."

"I agree."

"It sounds like he doesn't have the answers we need. You up to coming back?"

"I'll call the airline as soon as I get off the phone. I just want to get to the hospital and talk to John Grant before I go."

"Get what you can from him. He can probably identify the shooter, even if it was dark. When they get a drawing, they can fax it to us, see if anyone here can ID him. Meanwhile, we'll be looking into QX Electronics and Henry Soderberg."

That ended her part in the conversation.

"Sounds like you're heading home," Mike said when she hung up.

"There's nothing else I can do here, at least not now. If you find Hutchins, I'd sure like a crack at him."

"We'll hold the room upstairs for you." He smiled.

"I'd like that," she said.

"And maybe we'll get you to that small town in Kansas to see your friend."

John Grant was awake and alert when they got to the hospital. He held out his good hand and shook Jane's. "I have to thank you for what you did. I could've bled to death."

"Thank your wife. If she hadn't called . . . Where is she?"

"Home taking a shower and a nap. She's beat. You must be too."

"I slept this morning. Can you talk about last night now, John?"

"Sure. Let me go back a bit. I left you maybe eleven-thirty, right?"

"About that."

"I drove from the hotel to the gas station. I'd guess I got there about midnight, but I can't swear to it. I left the car off to the side so I wouldn't be in the way if someone came in for gas. The blue Toyota was there, on the other side of the station, the right side. I could see it in the light from these tall lights they have out there. There was a car getting gas when I pulled in, man and woman in it, man doing the pumping. She got out and used the ladies' room, and he went inside and paid Hutchins. I waited till they were finished. When they pulled out of the station, I got out of the car and went to the building and stuck my head inside."

"Did you see any other cars parked there?" Jane asked.

He thought about it. "I don't remember seeing any, but I could be wrong."

"Go on."

"Hutchins was there, sitting on a high stool near the cash register. He was reading a magazine. When I came in, he looked over at me and said, 'Hi,' kind of friendly. I said I just wanted to check in and make sure everything was all right, and he said he was fine, he'd taken Cory home and she was OK, he'd called her. I said if there was any trouble to call nine-one-one, and he said not to worry. That was about all there was. I said good night and went outside to my car. I started the motor and I was just about to pull out when something caught my eye. I could see movement inside the building, where Hutchins was. Someone was inside with him, and I was sure I hadn't seen anyone go in and the place had been empty when I was in there. I got out of the car and started over there when Hutchins flew out the door like a bat out of hell. I called to him but he never stopped. He shouted something like, 'He's after me,' and then a second man came out. I went for my gun and yelled, 'Police, don't move,' and the second man turned toward me and fired. I didn't see the gun until it came up."

He reached his left hand over to his right shoulder to indicate where he had been hit. "I hadn't gotten my gun out and the shot pushed me backward against my car. I slid down on the ground and tried to get out of the light. I heard a car start and the shooter went for the blue car and I dragged myself around the side of the building. I didn't have much use of my right arm, and I was starting to feel kind of woozy. I just kept trying to put distance between myself and the building. Next thing I knew, there was another gunshot and I got hit in the thigh. I must have passed out for a while, because when I woke up my gun was gone. He must have thought he'd killed me."

"Would you recognize him?"

"That's tough. He was wearing a kind of half ski mask, came down just to cover his nose. I'd say he was a little more than medium height, not as tall as Mike over there or me." He smiled. They were two tall men.

"And you're certain he wasn't inside when you were talking to Hutchins."

"I would've seen him. But he could've been in the men's room, or maybe next door in the mechanic's shop. I'm sure there's a door from the shop to the snack store, where Hutchins was sitting."

"And no car."

"Didn't see one."

"So he could've been dropped off after dark, or parked down the road and walked the rest of the way."

"Or he could've come through the woods in the back. I'd take a look-see, find out what's on the other side. Did he get away in my car?"

"Looks that way," Mike said. "Your car was gone and so was the Toyota when we got there. No other cars there. Sounds like this guy planned pretty carefully. Probably expected to get away in Hutchins's car."

"Or leave Hutchins dead at the station and melt into the woods," Jane said.

"He looked like he could melt pretty good. He was lithe, moved like a cat burglar." John took a breath and leaned back. "I don't know what else I can tell you."

Jane leaned over and patted his bare arm. "I'm flying back to New York tonight. I'm sorry I got you in this mess."

He smiled broadly. "Helen's been telling me to take some time off for a long time. She'll be good to me till she gets antsy. By that time, I'll probably be crawling the walls. I hope you come back."

"If Hutchins turns up, I will."

"What about my car?"

"No sign of it," Mike said. "We're keeping our eyes open."

"He'll have dumped it somewhere. Maybe where he had his car waiting."

Wherever that was. "John, do me a favor?" Jane said.

"Sure."

"In a couple of days, replay the whole thing in your mind. If you think of anything else, let me know."

"Will do."

"And get better. We'll keep in touch."

[18]

THE BEST THING she could book on short notice was a flight to O'Hare, where she had to change planes. She would carry on only her handbag, so if she had to run, she could do it without getting winded. They were in no hurry when they left the hospital.

"You should go home and get some sleep," Jane said when they got down to the car. "You've been up since last night."

"No problem," Mike said gallantly. "I've got the next two days off. I'll sleep plenty tonight. It's been nice having a woman in the house. You're the first one since my wife died."

"You and Luke have been very nice to me. Come to New York and I'll show you around."

"We might just do that."

As he was pulling into a slot in the airport parking lot, his radio made sounds. Jane recognized the voice of the woman who had called earlier about the Toyota.

"Hi there, Sarge," she said breezily. "Got some news for you."

"I'm listening."

"Found Detective Grant's car a coupla minutes ago. How's that?"

"That's pretty nice. You gonna tell me where it is or do I have to beg?"

She described a location that meant nothing to Jane, and they ended the conversation.

"Is it far from the Toyota?" Jane asked.

"Coupla miles. When I leave you, I'll go over there and see if there's an easy route between the car and the gas station. Our shooter could have followed Hutchins when he left the station house, kept on his tail after he dropped his girlfriend, then driven around to park his own car on a street the other side of the woods behind the station. If you've got a good map of Omaha, it's not the hardest thing in the world to figure out. How 'bout we get a cup of coffee?"

"Sounds good."

After she checked her bag, they found a table and sat down. He was starting to look tired. "You've been up about twenty hours by now," she said.

"Just about. Don't worry about it. It's not the first time."

"Or the last. I'm relieved that John looks pretty good."

"Me too. We'll be knocking on a lot of doors where John's car was found. I can't tell you I'm very hopeful. You park a car at night and pick it up when it's still dark, there aren't many people who notice it. But then, we may only need one."

"I hope Hutchins is alive. It looks more and more like he's a poor guy who accidentally got caught in something very big and very dangerous."

"I promise you we'll take this very seriously."

She dropped the topic and they talked about other things. Mike had a daughter and Luke had a serious girlfriend. He was glad of that but sorry his wife wasn't around to take pleasure in it.

"Sounds like you had a long, happy marriage," Jane said.

"Not long enough. You ever been married?"

"I don't think I'm cut out for it."

"You have folks?"

"My dad. My mother died several years ago. It was tough. I was adopted," she said suddenly, talking about something she rarely mentioned.

"They were lucky, your parents."

"Maybe. I know I was. My dad always talks about my Irish mother, like it's our secret. He's German all the way back, but I think my mother had some Irish blood in her. She had freckles and a touch of strawberry blond in her hair. So did I when I was a kid, so I guess whoever gave birth to me had some of that, too. But I don't qualify for the Emerald Society."

"Irish cops."

"Yeah. I can still drink their beer on St. Patrick's Day if I feel like it."

"You ever look for your birth mother?"

"Never. And I never will."

"It's all the rage now," he said, "everybody going back to their roots."

"They're welcome to it. I dug mine in the Bronx a long time ago."

"Been a detective long?"

"Almost ten years. I've been at the Sixth Precinct Detective Unit since I got my gold shield. It's down on West Tenth Street. It's been a good life. I've got a partner that's like a brother to me, plenty of dead bodies to keep me working hard."

"You sound like you're kissing it good-bye."

"That's what I'm planning to do."

"Why do I get the feeling you're not all that happy with your decision?"

"Things were changing. They brought in a new captain last year and he's been on my tail from day one. I put in too much overtime; he finds fault with a lot of things. A few weeks ago he pulled me out of the precinct to work on a high-profile case. Then, a week later, he took me off that and put me on the new squad, investigating cold cases. I'm on what we call a telephone call. The assignment comes in by phone and it lasts thirty days, renewable. I'll tell you, it's the best case I've had in a long time, and I'm glad to be out from under my old boss. But when this is over, they'll dump me right back in the Six. I've had no promotion, no second grade, no raise since I got my gold shield. That gets old real quick. I want to keep moving."

"There could be another cold case."

She smiled. "I guess they grow optimists out here."

"Is that your flight?" He cocked his head as a voice made an announcement.

She listened. "Chicago? Let me check."

"That's your flight. I'll walk you over. Maybe I'll flash my badge and give you an escort to the plane."

"Then you promise you'll go home and get some sleep?"

"I promise. After I check out where they found John's car."

A cop is a cop, she thought as they walked to the security checkpoint. She passed through and Mike showed his ID and followed her through the metal detector. At the gate they were just beginning the boarding process.

"I meant that about showing you around New York," she said.

"I meant that about maybe I'd take you up on it."

"I hope you find Hutchins alive."

"We'll give it our best shot." He leaned over and kissed her cheek.

A kiss before flying, she thought. It was a very sweet gesture and she felt touched.

When they called her row for boarding, she blew a kiss to him and joined the line.

On the flight to Chicago she drew a diagram in her notebook with Soderberg's name on the right just below center. Then she drew a line and an arrow to Margaret Rawls on the left, one flight up, then one to Hutchins on the top left, then a line with arrows in both directions between Worthman and Hutchins. Those were the connections, none to Quill, none to Mrs. Best.

Whoever Soderberg was, he knew how to keep his identity a secret, but why? She wondered if there was a family somewhere that had never known he died, or that had received a call one day that his body was being shipped to them with no specifics on how he had died and what he was doing in New York. How would they have reacted to such news? Probably they would have taken it in stride if they were informed. Otherwise, there would be a record somewhere of their calling the police, the medical examiner, perhaps even a newspaper or television program.

But if he was the professional he seemed to be, either there was no family or they knew not to ask. MacHovec would have to dig up the telephone records of QX Electronics and check out calls made after the date of Soderberg's death. Unless they had killed him. Who, she wondered, had cleaned out his apartment?

A lot of work needed to be done, more than she had ever dreamed when they took on the original cold case only a week ago. And then there was Hutchins. Poor Jerry Hutchins had gotten away from New York cleanly, only to get himself in deep trouble because of the reopened investigation. They were just landing in misty Chicago when she stuck her pen back in her bag and closed her eyes.

She did have to run for the plane to LaGuardia after all, and she was glad she had checked the suitcase. She wasn't in as good shape as she would have liked—she'd have to start walking to work, she thought—and she was breathless when she got to the gate.

"Just in time," the smiling ticket agent said, processing her ticket. "Have a good flight."

She sat between two men on the way to New York, one of them engrossed in his laptop, the other making call after call on the phone in front of Jane to people she was sure would have preferred to be left alone. It was night, for God's sake, and an hour later in New York, but he just kept at it, his voice a little too loud, his laugh a little too phony, telling everyone he knew where he was calling from. Jane got a cup of coffee and considered spilling a little on him, but decided against it. Coffee or not, she fell asleep after she handed the cup back to the flight attendant.

The apartment didn't feel quite like home yet, but it was blissfully warm when she walked in. The first thing she did after taking off her coat was to make the mandated call to the office of the chief of department at One PP to notify them of her safe return. The second was to call the office of the chief of detectives with the same message. After that she went to bed and slept well. When she got to Centre Street the next morning, they were all waiting for her even though she was early.

A mass of paperwork had to be completed—no one got an out-of-town trip without submitting every form and document, in at least triplicate, and then closing out each item after returning—but the debriefing would take precedence. They met in Graves's office, which had been set up with chairs in a semicircle opposite his desk. On his credenza was a carafe of coffee and a tray of sweet rolls. MacHovec, to no one's surprise, had already helped himself to both by the time the others arrived. Defino whispered a few obscenities, not quite under his breath and Jane hushed him.

"We all here?" Captain Graves asked, counting heads. Annie had just walked in and sat off to the side with a steno pad on her lap. "Looks like it," he said, answering his own question. "Help yourselves to coffee and then let's get started. Jane? I gather there's no word on Jerry Hutchins."

"Nothing when I left Omaha, and they have my home phone number as well as the numbers here. But Det. John Grant is doing well in the hospital."

"Glad to hear that. Poor guy answers a phone to give

us information and ends up with two bullets in him. OK. You ready to talk?"

She was and she did, going over their stakeout rapidly and then through the interrogation of Hutchins, John Grant's departure from the hotel, the call from his wife, the subsequent discovery of him at the gas station.

"So it looks like somebody knew you were going to Omaha and kept an eye on you when you got there."

"It looks that way."

"And we know what that means." He ran his hand through his perfect hair. "There must be a dozen people on the job who knew you were making that trip."

"Fifty," MacHovec said.

"You're right. It could be fifty, starting with everyone in this room and going on from there. There was a ton of paperwork before you left, Jane, and a lot of people signed off. I don't like to think about this possibility, but we're going to have to, and we'll have to increase security. For all we know, you're being watched, and I mean all three of you."

She had thought about that possibility on the plane. MacHovec and Defino had families, children who went to school, wives who moved around the city in cars and buses and subways.

"Maybe now they've got Hutchins, we have less to worry about," Defino said.

"Maybe. Jane, I cut you off at the gas station."

She went on about finding the Toyota and the keys that Hutchins had obviously tossed. "I think I got some sleep about then," she said. "That was yesterday morning."

"You stayed in the hotel?" McElroy asked.

"No, I didn't. The Omaha police got a little nervous about my safety. I went out the back way and stayed at a sergeant's house. When I woke up, we went to see John Grant and got a pretty good statement from him. I was on my way to the airport so I didn't call in." She described John's visit to the gas station after he had left her at the hotel. And finally she told them John's car had been found while she was on her way to the airport. "So I should hear something today. They're going to canvass the neighborhood pretty good, but it had to be left off at night, so don't get your hopes up."

"But no body," McElroy said.

"Not in the radio message."

"OK," Graves said. He looked more worried than Jane had ever seen him. The easy Hollywood look had dissolved, and today you could believe he was a cop worried about other cops. "We talk about it in this office and your office. Nowhere else. Understood?"

They replied with an appropriate murmur.

"Let's look ahead. We've got two detectives who worked on the Quill case, Bracken and Wright. We are going to have to take a long look at both of them. I know it stinks but we still have to look, if only to clear them. We've got a victim named Henry Soderberg who looked like a poor slob that fell down some stairs while changing a lightbulb. Now he could be the guy Quill's killer was after. You guys turn anything up on him yesterday?" He looked at Defino and MacHovec.

"I think he was born the day he moved into the building on Fifty-sixth Street," MacHovec said.

"Which means he was some kind of a pro," Graves said. "And this company he worked for? QX Electronics?"

"Same thing. Came into being when they moved into that office downtown. Also pros. They paid their bills on time, paid their rent in advance, and paid off the rest of the rent due on their lease even though they moved out about five months before it ran out. No negotiating with the landlord, just paid up."

"And no forwarding address."

"No nothin'. They paid off their Con Ed bill, the phone bill, the rent, gave the janitor a nice Christmas present, and disappeared into the fog. Well, folks, we have a victim and an invisible company. We have to start digging and find out about both."

"Did they get a mover for the furniture?" Jane asked.

"Landlord said there wasn't much, a couple of old desks, an old filing cabinet, some wooden chairs, nothing executive quality. He says they left everything behind, clean as a whistle, not a paper clip anywhere. Landlord rented out the office furnished next time around for a higher price."

"So they carried off their files," Jane said.

"Must have. There've been two tenants since they left. Gordon went down and had a look at it yesterday."

Defino picked up the story. The office was small and the landlord had pointed out the furniture that QX had left. "Could've come from the Salvation Army. There was nothing to show when or where it was bought, where it came from, who made it. The desks are a grainy oak, stained dark, dirty. The chairs look like what my teacher sat on at St. Christopher's."

"Smart guys," Graves said. He shook his head, clearly disturbed. "OK, you know the drill. See if we can find a bank they used, check out all their phone calls for however long they were in that office, get a list for every phone number they paid for, and call the telephone security guys for help if you can't backtrack the numbers yourselves. Then talk to everyone in the building, see if anyone remembers them. I'm sure no one does. They probably never talked to a soul except the janitor they gave the Christmas present to. I don't like this at all. Jane, what are you carrying these days and where is it?"

She took two breaths, knowing what was coming. "In my purse, five-shot S and W Chief when I've got a desk job."

"Starting right now, you carry your Glock, in a holster, where you can reach for it in a second. You will also carry the five-shot as a backup piece. That goes for the rest of the team as well. Got it? We don't know who the enemy is, and he may be our friend on the job. Annie, you talk about this to no one."

"Yes, sir." She looked a little scared, as though this

might be the first time she was involved in something bigger than answering phones and ordering airline tickets.

"That's the QX side of this. Another side is the crime scene building. Hutchins said someone was living in the empty apartment on the top floor."

"It's the last thing he told us. I knew he was holding back, and finally he gave it up. He never saw the person but he heard noises. He said there were rats, but it wasn't rats; it was someone in the apartment."

"Who could walk outside his door and give Soderberg a push when he was up on a stool. Probably took out the lightbulb himself."

"Probably."

"You gotta wear down that super. He had to know. It was his building."

"You know," Jane said, "if someone really was in and out of that apartment, he couldn't have been there when Quill was alive. Quill lived in the apartment underneath the empty apartment. He would've heard footsteps and told Derek. You wake up in the middle of the night and hear someone overhead in an empty apartment— Wait a minute."

"Right," Defino said. "The interview in the Quill file, he said something to a coworker, didn't he? About rats or mice?"

"Same as Hutchins said," MacHovec chimed in. "Lookin' more like we got one guy killed 'em both."

"And holed up on the fourth floor," Jane said.

Nobody said anything.

"And then there's Soderberg," Graves said in the silence. "That funeral home has to have records on who picked him up, where he was buried, or where they shipped him." He made a note on the paper in front of him. "When he took the fall on Fifty-sixth Street, he was an aided case. They must have searched him and taken an inventory of his pockets and wallet. Go to the precinct and look it up. If he was carrying a Social Security card, they would have the number on record. Let's find out when it was issued and where, what kind of earnings it shows. We need a lot of answers. And we need to look over our shoulders. Any questions?"

Nobody asked any. The ones they had couldn't be answered by Graves.

[19]

THEY WENT BACK to their office and Jane sat down at her desk, pushing aside a few telephone messages that had accumulated since she left on Monday. Nothing was from her father, so the rest of them would have to wait for an answer.

Defino stood at the window looking out. You could almost feel his fingers itching to put a cigarette in his mouth, sense his lungs aching to draw in some deadly smoke. MacHovec dropped into his seat with a thud, his face elated.

"Got more work to do today than when we started," he said. "Anybody want to talk about how we break it up?"

"We have to find out who Soderberg was," Jane said before Defino could say anything. "I have a couple of hours at One PP with my trip papers. Sean, you should get started on Soderberg's Social Security. See if he existed."

"Shit, what if he didn't?"

"We'll worry about that later. What do we do about Bracken and Otis Wright?"

That was the worst, investigating two of their own, one with a terminal illness, a guy who had gone out of his way to help, the other a seasoned detective whom they had no reason to suspect. The next step was obvious, but no one wanted to say the words: Internal Affairs Division. At some point IAD would have to be notified and their detectives assigned to work the information-leak angle, cops investigating cops, but not just yet.

"Can't be Otie," MacHovec said.

"Well, it can't be Bracken either," Defino snapped, turning away from the window.

"Let's look at my travel papers," Jane said. "Graves signed off on the trip and Annie typed it all up. Then I took it to the Chief of Detectives' office."

"And sat around while the Chief of *D* gave it a lot of thought," MacHovec said sarcastically.

"It took a while, right, but he signed off on it. Then I went to the Chief of Department. He took less time, and then I went up to the Police Commissioner."

"You remember who looked it over?"

"Some office type, a lieutenant. He made some phone calls, had it brought to an inspector, the commissioner's aide. He took it inside an office and it was signed when it came out." She left a few things unsaid, but that was her business.

"And there's PAAs and God knows who-all, and a lotta people know you're taking a trip. You know what goes on over in the Puzzle Palace. The place is a sieve."

"Your math is great," Defino said.

"He's right, Gordon. But that's the place to look for a leak. Besides Bracken and Wright. And when I finish my paper pushing, you and I should go down to the mortuary that took Soderberg's body. They should have records of who claimed it and where it went."

"I can give 'em a call," MacHovec volunteered.

There were a few seconds of silence. Then Jane said, "I don't want to give them a chance to think about what they're going to tell us or call someone in the family who'll say they should keep quiet."

"She's right," Defino said.

"OK. Your call."

They settled down to work, MacHovec on the phone, Jane with her trip papers, Defino sitting at his desk writing on a pad of paper. When Jane was finished, she left to make the rounds at One PP, agreeing to call Defino as soon as she was finished.

It had gotten cold and the wind was strong. This was where Manhattan began narrowing down, eventually ending at the southern tip, South Ferry and Battery Park, where the Hudson and East rivers merged into one, ready to empty into the Atlantic. The winds from the two rivers blew across the island with great ferocity at the southern end, and even though it wasn't yet winter, it was starting to feel that way.

Jane got her papers logged back in, stamped, re-signed, and closed out. At each location she took down the name of the person she was dealing with, the names of the people at the nearby desks. There was no way of knowing which of them, if any, had leaked information about her trip. Nor was there any way of knowing, at this point, why or to whom it had been leaked. Was it the old battle-ax with the short gray hair and the voice that could almost knock you off your feet? Or the sweet little girl who might have a boyfriend somewhere who needed to know what she knew?

"Try to get it right next time," the battle-ax said.

"I hope you had a good trip," the sweet little girl said.

Finished at last, she borrowed a phone and called Defino. He had been waiting to hear from her and had eaten at his desk. He would meet her in the time it took her to get there.

She hadn't managed to eat yet, but she picked up a sandwich, took a couple of bites, and shoved the rest in her bag. The mortuary was up on the East Side. She caught the Lex and took it uptown. When she got out at Eighty-sixth Street, she saw a familiar lean figure bounding up the stairs to the street. Defino had been on the same train.

"Sean get anything?" she asked when she had caught up with him.

"The aided case card had a Social Security number. He put in a call about it, but I don't think he heard anything before I left. You get lunch?"

"It's in here." She patted her bag.

"We can sit down somewhere—"

"It's OK. I'll eat later. I want to see where this leads."

The funeral home was east of Lexington Avenue, and Defino straightened his tie before they entered. A middle-aged woman sat in the outer office and greeted them with appropriate solemnity. Her eyebrows rose as they showed their shields and IDs. She excused herself and went to an adjoining room.

"Mr. Farrington will see you now." She gestured to the open door.

Edward Farrington was about Jane's age and could have been any businessman sitting in his office. The last time she had been in a similar office, it had been for her mother in the Bronx, where the funeral home had been in the same family for three generations and the youngest generation was getting on in years. Farrington was a relief, a nice-looking executive type dressed as though his business were life instead of death.

"I'm Ed Farrington," he said, offering his hand. "You are police officers?"

"Detectives," Defino said. "We need some information going back about four years."

"I'll do what I can. Please sit. Make yourselves comfortable."

"The deceased was Henry Soderberg," Jane said. She passed a sheet of notepaper across the desk. "The date is approximate."

"Let me check my files."

He left the room, and Jane considered taking another bite or two from her sandwich, but changed her mind. Not in here. As welcoming as this room was with its light walls, pale rug, modern furniture, and light streaming through the window, it was not a place to eat.

Farrington came back with a file folder. "I remember this one," he said. "We received the body from the New York City Morgue."

"That's the one," Defino said.

"He died in a fall. No next of kin, at least not in New York."

"Who claimed the body then?" Jane asked.

"A man named Carl Johnson. No relation. He said he worked with Mr. Soderberg."

The name rang a bell. It was one of the names Defino had mentioned as having worked for QX Electronics. "What ID did he give you?"

"I have his driver's license number written down here. He showed me proof that Mr. Soderberg had been his employee. He had his Social Security number, his home address, and some payroll documents." Farrington looked troubled, as though he suspected he had done something without the proper authorization.

"We'd like a copy of everything you have on file," Jane said.

"I'll be glad to give it to you."

"Where did you send the body?" Defino asked.

"To a funeral home in Arlington, Virginia. It's all in here." He tapped the page in front of him. "Let me have this Xeroxed for you." He went into the secretary's office and returned immediately. "May I ask what the problem is?"

"We're investigating Mr. Soderberg's death," Jane said. "There are some unanswered questions. Did you handle this case yourself?"

"Yes, I did. I remember it mostly because we don't get many bodies from the morgue."

"Do you remember talking to anyone besides this Carl Johnson?"

He leaned back in his swivel chair and looked toward the ceiling. "There were some phone calls before we received the body. I don't know whether they came from him or from someone else. And of course I contacted the funeral home in Arlington."

"Did Mr. Johnson select a casket?"

"No. He said that would be taken care of at home. I remember that he used those words, 'at home.' "

"How was the body shipped?"

"It was flown on a cargo plane."

"Do you know who met it?"

"Yes. That'll be in the file. A representative of the funeral home in Arlington. He had all the paperwork from us."

"Did anyone here look at the body?" Defino asked.

"It wasn't here long. Mr. Johnson was actually waiting in the room next door for it to arrive. Then he signed all the papers and left. We had it on a plane later that afternoon."

"Did Carl Johnson identify the body?" Jane asked.

"He did, yes."

She looked at Defino. He stood and thanked Farrington, gave him his card. "Anyone ever make inquiries about Mr. Soderberg?" he asked.

"Not to me. If anyone called, they would have been told where the body had been sent."

Jane got up and shook Farrington's hand, too. "What was your impression of Carl Johnson?"

"Well dressed. Not as tall as me. Grim. But most of the people I talk to here are grim. I had no particular impression of him."

They walked to the secretary's office and picked up the copied files. She had placed them in an envelope too large to fit in Jane's bag. She held on to it as they walked outside.

"Air's better out here," Defino said.

"Not for long. We should get back, see if Sean's come up with anything and start calling Arlington. So let's go back to the subway."

Defino had already lit a cigarette. "You must be hungry."

"I'll eat at my desk."

"Famous last words."

* * *

"Looks like our boy was born about six years ago," MacHovec greeted them.

"Interesting," Defino said. "That when the Social Security number was issued?"

"Yup. Not much in earnings, unless you're less than six years old; then it's a lot. Only one employer, QX Electronics."

"So he was born to work for them," Jane said.

"Hey, maybe it was the best job in the world."

"Not if it got him killed." She sat at her desk and extricated the sandwich from her bag. She had stopped for a cup of coffee on the way in, and she worked the cover off and took a sip before unwrapping the sandwich. There were some messages, one of them from Mike Fromm. "Let me answer these; then we'll talk."

She was starving now and ate the sandwich quickly, washed it down with the local coffee, which wasn't bad, then dialed Mike.

"How're you doin'?" he asked when he picked up.

"Getting used to breathing fumes again. How's John?"

"He's doing real fine. I dropped in on him this morning. They'll have a hard time keeping him there. I think he's out of the woods, Jane."

"I'm glad to hear about it. I guess there's nothing on Hutchins."

"Absolute blank. But where we found John's car is a straight line through the woods to the gas station."

"So the shooter made off in John's car, maybe caught up to Hutchins, maybe not, and drove around to where he'd left his own car."

"Sounds like the right sequence of events. We've done a pretty thorough canvass of that area, and no one saw anything. And we've done a walk-through search of the woods again—lots of the guys volunteered—but we came up empty. They're examining John's car very carefully, see if we come up with Hutchins's hair anywhere.

He could've been in the trunk and transferred to the trunk of the shooter's car."

"They could be anywhere now," Jane said.

"And maybe Hutchins got away. Maybe he just ran. He hasn't called the girlfriend, and since he doesn't have a bank account, we don't know if he needed money."

"She might send him some if she has any idea of where he is."

"She knows we're watching."

"I hope he's alive," Jane said.

"So how're you doing now that you're back home?"

She had known it was a personal call. None of the preliminary conversation had changed that. "I'm fine. I'm in my office now. I finished my paperwork and we're back at work. The air was better in Omaha."

"Invitation's still open."

"Thank you. Mine too." She was aware of the other two people in the room, of their silence.

"I'll talk to you soon."

She hung up and busied herself moving papers around. He was too nice to care about her. She could not imagine having a relationship with a man fifteen hundred miles from New York, even accepting what an attractive man he was. She was one of those provincial people who thought New York was the center of the universe and it didn't bother her. It was always a surprise to meet someone from far away and see that he had the requisite number of limbs, a brain that functioned more than adequately, clothes that looked like this year's styles.

"Anything up?" Defino asked.

"No. Well, a little." She told him about where John Grant's car had been found.

"But no Hutchins."

"No Hutchins." She cleared up her desk. "I guess we need to contact the funeral parlor in Arlington."

"That where the body was shipped?" MacHovec said.

"By a fellow QX Electronics guy," Defino said.

"Nearest thing to next of kin?"

"So it seems."

MacHovec held out his hand. "Got a number?"

Jane passed it to him. "Here's the file from the New York mortuary. It's got names and addresses."

"That's all I need." MacHovec picked up the phone and dialed. It wasn't a long conversation. When he hung up, he said, "They'll check it out and get back to me. Tomorrow. So don't hang around."

"I've got a list of every name I saw when I was filing my papers today." She passed that over to MacHovec as well. "I don't know what you'll do with it but it's a place to start. And there's a driver's license number for the guy who picked up Soderberg's body. Carl Johnson."

"Nice, clean American name," MacHovec said.

"What does that mean?" Defino said.

"Just offering up an opinion from the gallery."

"Stuff it," Defino said under his breath.

No one had contacted either Otis Wright or Charlie Bracken. Jane hadn't had the time. Defino could have this morning, and MacHovec could have made some phone calls. She didn't blame them for not wanting to do so. It would fall to her and Defino tomorrow.

She decided to take Soderberg's autopsy report home with her. It needed a closer look. She recalled he had broken one of his arms some time ago. That might give her a clue as to whether he was in any shape to screw a light-bulb. And there might be something else that she had overlooked in her first dip.

As usual, MacHovec was the first out the door. She didn't want to spend any more time than she had to in the office, so when Defino stood up, she grabbed her coat and left with him.

On her way home, she stopped at a neighborhood market and bought some necessary items. Her kitchen was empty and she wanted to eat in tonight, go through the autopsy report, get to bed early. On the way out, she saw plastic bags of firewood, not exactly a cord, but maybe a beginning. She picked one up, made a second trip through the checkout line, and went home.

The apartment was pleasantly warm, and she cooked and ate without much fuss. When the dishes were done, she glanced through the small pile of mail, tossing most of what was there. At the bottom was the small letter on crinkly paper.

OK, she thought. I can't put it off any longer. The hell with the autopsy report, the hell with everything else. I didn't throw it away when it came, so I know I have to read it.

Taking a knife out of the kitchen drawer, she slit the top of the envelope carefully and pulled out the two sheets of paper inside.

20

WHEN SHE UNFOLDED the letter, she saw the snapshot. The girl was twenty, with fair hair, a nice figure, and a nice smile. It was the kind of picture that appeared in high school yearbooks, a picture that a boyfriend or father might put in his wallet and pull out to show with pride. Jane took a deep breath and set the photo on the end table next to her chair and began reading.

Dear Ms. Bauer,

I have reason to believe that you are my natural mother. I was adopted a few days after I was born from an adoption agency in New York City. My parents flew out and brought me back.

I have wonderful parents. They have done everything for me that they could. I do well in school and graduated from high school with honors. I am now a student at the University of Kansas, and I am doing pretty well here, too, although the competition is a lot tougher than it was in high school.

I have known all my life that I was adopted. When I was in high school I met a girl who was older and she had looked for her birth mother and found her. I always wondered what my natural parents were like, so I decided to find you. My parents know I am writing to you.

I would like to meet you. I know you're a police officer in New York. I have been putting money away for the last few summers so I can fly to wherever you are. I would like to hear from you. You can write or call me.

> Yours,
> Lisa Angelino

Jane sat perfectly still and let the tears flow when she finished the letter. Nothing in it surprised her, but a lot pleased her. Lisa Angelino came across as a nice person, a bright young woman. Like Jane, she was a natural-born detective, and Jane smiled thinking of that. There was a wholesome and almost shy quality to the writing. Had she been nervous, putting pen to paper? Had she written a hundred drafts and settled on this one? Was her heart breaking because she had not yet heard from Jane?

It had been so many years since it had happened, and Jane had lived half her life since then, the adult half, the responsible half. She had not given much thought to whether she would ever hear from this daughter she had borne, although she had suspected the moment she saw the envelope who it was from.

She had met Paul Thurston in one of those late-teen

summers when everyone's hormones were running wild, when she was thinner, maybe even a little cute, her hair sun-bleached, her freckles prominent. He had been gorgeous; there was no other way to describe him. He was Ivy; his parents lived in Manhattan; he had gone to private school. He had a body that just had to be touched, caressed, enjoyed. She had somehow managed to get through high school a virgin, largely because of her parents and the church. But that incredible summer she gave him everything, her heart, her soul, her body. And she believed he gave her his.

When the inevitable happened, he said he would marry her. That was before he told his parents, before they knew who she was. They had plans for their son, and Jane didn't fit into them. That it was the oldest story in the book meant nothing to her. This was the man she loved, she was carrying his baby, and she wanted to spend the rest of her life with him and their child.

She was terrified to tell her parents, although she didn't need to be. There were a lot of tears, but they stood by her. The idea of an abortion crushed her mother and distressed her father. Jane could no more imagine raising a child as a single woman than she could believe that Paul would come back to her. The irony of following in her own mother's footsteps weighed upon her. She wanted to rid herself of the child growing within her and get on with her life, but she began to dream that her own mother had aborted her. Finally she decided to give birth but then give away the baby. Her parents accepted it.

The last time she saw Paul, he gave her a thousand dollars for an abortion. She knew, spending those last few hours with him, that this was the most difficult thing he had ever done. He was almost in tears at one point, and she felt she loved him at that moment more than she had ever loved him before. He wasn't trying to get away from her; he was prolonging their last time together, as though these were the sweetest minutes and hours they had spent together.

When he walked away, finally, after many last kisses, she knew she had left her youth behind; she had abandoned irresponsibility; she had become a new person. He called only once, a few months later, and she said she was fine, never mentioning she was still pregnant, never offering to give back the thousand dollars. Now the child whose existence was unknown to him had surfaced, along with all the memories and emotions she engendered. The piece of herself that she kept tucked away, never to be exposed, was returning to life. It wasn't a good feeling.

Although she had neither seen nor heard from him again, she knew vaguely what had become of Paul. His name was mentioned in the paper occasionally, so she knew where he worked. When his mother died not so many years ago, there was a small obituary. Among the survivors were Paul and Marla Thurston and their children. They lived in an expensive suburb of New York.

She left the letter on the end table. In spite of all that needed to be done in the apartment, the many cartons that had to be opened and emptied, she had lost her ambition. She picked up some paper that dishes had been wrapped in, scrunched it up, and laid it in the fireplace. She broke down one of the empty cartons and laid the pieces on top of the paper. Lacking a source of twigs, this would have to do. On top she placed a couple of the logs she had bought. Just as she was about to strike a match, she remembered to open the flue. It worked just the way the super had shown her.

The paper caught immediately and burned hotly. The cardboard caught next. The wood was another story. She remembered then that the super had given her a small brick-shaped object that he said would help the fire get started. She found it and tossed it in. It caught, and after a few moments one of the logs began to burn. Success!

She sat down opposite the fireplace and just watched it for a while. If she were still seeing Hack, she would talk to him about this. He was one of the few people in the world she had told about the baby she had given up. She was amazed at her own ambivalence. How could she not know whether she wanted to see this child she had given birth to? She missed Hack's thoughtful appraisals of politics, in government and on the job, of her problems and concerns, of events in the city. The only thing he could not appraise well was his own situation. And here she was, facing the same problem.

She would have to think about it. She would not call or write till she knew what she was doing, however long that took. The child had turned out well. That was something to be grateful for, something, perhaps, to feel ecstatic about. Paul was happy, probably happier than if she had married him. She wondered whether their marriage could have survived. With his parents, probably not.

The fire was beautiful. It was all the things she had hoped it would be, bright and warm and comforting. There was something to be said for being forty and having a wood-burning fireplace in your apartment, for having a job lined up that would pay a good salary, for having loved a great man for a long time and having severed the relationship with no hard feelings.

She got up and put another log on the fire. Then she went to the kitchen and picked up the autopsy report on Henry Soderberg. It would calm her down after the dizzying thoughts about Lisa Angelino and Hack.

In her adult life, which began for her when she gave up the baby, it had always been her work that saved her. When a love affair soured, she worked longer hours, volunteered for special teams and training, forced herself to work hard and think of nothing else. She hoped the insurance business would appeal to her in the same way that police business did. If her head was occupied, she told herself, she could take almost anything, even the entry into her life of the child she had given up.

She remembered that there was a tattoo on the arm of

Henry Soderberg's body. She thought now that she should look at that more carefully. It was the style today for little girls to tattoo themselves, but Henry Soderberg had been an adult of nearly fifty years. A tattoo on his body would reflect something other than what was currently fashionable, perhaps a place he had been or some group affiliation. She turned to the photograph of the tattoo, but it meant nothing to her, except that it had a date in the 1970s. At least it wasn't a love note to his mother. She would ask around tomorrow. If only she could ask him, Hack would know, she was sure. He knew all those little things about men's experiences that never crossed the gender line.

She went to the kitchen and found her magnifying glass. She always kept it with the silverware, which she had already unpacked and arranged in drawers. The tattoo was some kind of snaky creature and didn't make any more sense when enlarged, but in running the glass over the picture of his whole nude body, she saw a color change on his skin, darker on his torso and arms, lighter where he would have worn trunks. He had died in the fall after the effects of the summer's sun would normally have worn off. That would indicate that his skin was permanently tanned from years outdoors. She knew he had left for work in a business suit and he had worked for QX Electronics for some time, so it wasn't a new tan. Maybe he had been a lifeguard for a few years or a beachcomber who needed little money to live on. Whatever the answer, he had spent a lot of years out-of-doors.

Except for the one broken bone, which had apparently healed well, and the new injuries Soderberg had sustained in the fall that killed him, his body was unmarred. There were no healed bullet wounds, no cuts or slashes, no breaks or abnormalities. He had his appendix and his tonsils, and his muscles had good tone. All in all he seemed a tough guy to contend with.

Jane left the file in the kitchen near her bag and got ready for bed. Finally she propped the picture of Lisa

Angelino against her mirror in the bedroom. She might want to look at it a few dozen times before she made up her mind what to do.

[**21**]

EVERYONE WAS IN early on Friday morning. Jane started with her partners, showing a blowup of the tattoo and getting nowhere.

"Maybe it's the day he was married," MacHovec said.

"Doesn't look very marital to me," Jane said. "It looks snaky. And there's no name of his beloved."

"I've seen it before," Defino said. "Long time ago. Sorry. It's gone."

Coffee in hand, Jane went to the second whip and put the picture on his desk. "Military," he said. "Maybe the marines."

She moved on. Graves was on the phone. She went into the first team's office. "This mean anything to any of you?" She handed it to the man at the first desk.

"Sorry."

The second man said, "Yeah, I know this. It's a golden shellback or golden dragon. For when you first cross the equator and the international date line at the same time. Before you cross, you're called a guppy. That's a tattoo, right?"

"Yes."

"A bunch of guys on my ship did it when I was in the merchant marine. After you cross, you're a shellback."

"Nice," Jane said. "So this guy could've been in the merchant marine."

"Or the navy or a troop ship. How old is he?"

"Now? Early fifties."

"Too young for a troop ship. I'd bet on the navy."

"Thanks."

"I like it," Defino said. "He could've been a twenty-year man, built up a suntan, then retired with a nice pension and got a job in electronics. Maybe he worked in that area on board ship. It'd give him a career."

"Then there's got to be a military record."

They both looked at MacHovec, who grinned. "I hear you. Archives are in St. Louis. I don't think they're awake yet out there. I'll get on it."

"What about Bracken?" Defino said. "We haven't found the leak yet."

"I been putting it off," MacHovec admitted. "I'll call him this morning."

Jane felt a wave of sympathy for MacHovec. "Maybe Otis Wright's wife talked to someone."

"I'll give her a call. And we're gonna need a full set of prints on Soderberg for the military archives. If he was born six years ago, he must've served under another name."

"They're in the autopsy file," Jane said. "I saw them. You doing anything about looking for leaks where I filed my travel papers?"

"Yeah, that's a problem. I'm not cleared to see personnel files. McElroy's gonna get them, let me see what he thinks is relevant."

"OK. Anything from that funeral home in Arlington?"

"Nada. I'll give them till this afternoon."

Jane checked in with her father. When she got off the phone, MacHovec was talking to Mrs. Wright in a friendly, schmoozy way. He didn't want to call Bracken, would do anything to avoid it.

Jane picked up her phone and dialed his number. He answered right away. "Charlie, it's Jane Bauer."

"Hiya, Jane. How's it goin'?"

"It's getting complicated. Can I come up and talk to you for a bit?"

"Sure. I'm here."

"Half an hour," Jane said.

Defino was already on his feet. "We're going to see Bracken," he said to MacHovec. MacHovec waved, displaying a look of absolute relief. He was off the hook.

"So," Bracken said, "you still on the Quill case?"

"Sort of," Defino said. "It's taking a few turns we didn't plan on."

"Probably why we couldn't clear it. What's up?"

"We need to know everyone you've talked to about the case since we were here last week," Jane said.

"People I talked to about the Quill case?" Bracken was almost laughing.

"Right."

"The two of you. That's it."

"Think about it, Charlie. I took a trip on Monday and somebody was waiting for me."

"A trip where?" His eyes had narrowed and his brow furrowed.

"Omaha," Jane said.

"Who was waiting for you?" His face was dark. He knew what was going on.

"Never got to meet him. But if he wasn't a killer, he came damn close."

"You find Hutchins?"

"Charlie," Defino said, "we have to know if you talked about this case to anyone. Anyone at all."

Bracken didn't say it, but he knew what they were driving at. You weren't in the business as long as he'd been without making connections quickly. "I didn't give it a thought after you guys left. I don't even remember what day you were here."

"The PAA," Jane suggested. "Your partner. Anyone."

She wondered if he would get angry and throw them out, but he played it very cool. He was old and wise and had a clean enough record that he didn't have to worry. "Nobody," he said. "And I didn't leave any notes lying around because I didn't take any."

"Thanks, Charlie," Jane said.

Out on the street Defino lit a cigarette. "Shit, I hate doing that."

"I know." She looked at her watch.

"Let's get on Derek," Defino said. "See if he knows anything about the guy living in the empty apartment."

"He knows."

"I don't know if he knows what day it is."

"I don't know either. Let's go."

Derek was in the West Fifty-sixth Street building, scrubbing the second floor. He smiled when he saw them, and leaned the mop against a closed door. "So how you doin'?"

"We're doin' fine, Derek," Defino said. "You got a minute for us?"

"I got all the time you need. Where you wanna talk?"

"Right here is fine. It won't take a minute. You remember back when Mr. Quill was killed?"

"I never forget it."

"And you remember everybody that lived here at that time?"

"You know I do."

"And what apartment they all lived in."

"Right you are."

"Now, if someone was living in that empty apartment on the fourth floor, you'd know that too, wouldn't you?"

"Wasn't no one livin' there."

"But if someone was living there, you'd know that, right?"

"Yeah." He said it tentatively, almost like a question.

"Well, we know that someone was living there. We want to know who it was."

Derek shifted his glance to Jane, but she said nothing. "That place was empty, Officer. Wasn't no one livin' there at all. You ask Mr. Stabile. He tell you."

"I know no one was paying rent on the apartment, Derek. But someone was living there. I'd like you to tell me who it was."

"I didn't see no one." He looked from Jane to Defino and back again. "Never. Wasn't nobody there."

"We'll have to talk to Mr. Stabile about this."

"You talk to him. Go on. He tell you, wasn't nobody there. I gotta lotta work to do here, Officers." He went over to the mop and dipped it in the bucket of dirty water at his feet.

"It's important to us, Derek," Defino said. "We have to find that person."

"Who tol' you?" Derek asked with hostility. "Who said we got someone livin' in that empty apartment?"

"The people who lived here told us. They heard him. He made a lot of noise at night."

"What this guy look like?" Derek looked angry.

"Sorry," Defino said. "First we need a name. You know the name. We're gonna get it, you know. It'll be better for you if you're the one who tells us."

"I got work to do." He pulled the mop out of the bucket, squeezing it through the wringers, and started to mop aggressively.

Jane started down the stairs, Defino following her. She looked back and saw Derek focused on his work, his eyes down on the damp floor. "If you tell us," she called back, "we won't tell Mr. Stabile that you knew."

Derek just rubbed the mop hard against the floor and said nothing.

"We'll have to sweat him," Defino said when they were on the street.

"I wish to hell Bracken and Wright had looked inside that apartment. They would've known right away."

"Four years too late for that. Want some lunch?"

"Might as well."

They got back to Centre Street with most of the afternoon left. MacHovec was on the phone, but he waved them in with a certain glee.

"We're gettin' there," he said as he hung up. "Heard back from the Arlington funeral home. Soderberg's body was released to the Navy League in Arlington."

"He was in the navy," Jane said.

"He was an officer in the navy. You don't get to the Navy League if you're a lowly seaman."

"You get a name for him yet?" Defino asked.

"Not yet. I faxed the prints to the archives in St. Louis and talked to a guy there. It'll take a bit, but he'll get back to me."

"Did you talk to the Navy League?" Jane asked.

"They're not very forthcoming, but I talked to them. They talked about privacy and crap like that. Didn't seem to give a shit that it was a police matter."

"How'd you leave it?"

"They'll get back to me. Do I sound like a broken record? My shield number could be retired if I had a buck from everyone who was gonna get back to me with information. Ask me, I'll be the one getting back to them. So what's with Bracken?"

"What you'd expect," Jane said. "He didn't say anything to anyone, didn't make a note, doesn't know why we're asking."

"You believe him?"

"Yeah," Jane and Defino said in unison.

"Then maybe he's your guy," MacHovec said.

"Shit," Defino said. He sat down at his desk and said he'd write up the Fives on Derek and Bracken.

Jane pulled out her checklist. "McElroy give you the personnel files yet?"

"Yeah, I got 'em. You know, it coulda been someone in one of those offices that you never talked to. They pass papers around a lot."

"I know."

"Anyway, here's the way it looks: In the commissioner's office I couldn't get much. In the Chief of Department's office there's a Lieutenant MacGregor who reports to Captain Schwartz who reports to Inspector Rodriguez. The other place, the Chief of *D*, there's a Lieutenant Ferguson who reports to Captain Mulholland who reports to Inspector Hackett." He stopped when he said "Hackett" and looked up at Jane.

$$\boxed{22}$$

SHE FELT THE color drain from her face at the sound of Hack's name.

"You got a problem?" MacHovec said.

"No. Just listening to the names." She hoped her shock had not been read by Sean. Hack's empire extended to an office she had been to twice in the last week. He had to be aware that she had flown to Omaha.

"The way I see it," MacHovec said, as though nothing had happened, "the most likely guys for the leak are the ones right in the offices where you filed the papers."

"Sounds right."

"Any one of them could have a girlfriend connected to our killer except"—he flipped pages in his notes—"except Lieutenant Ferguson, who's a woman. She could have a boyfriend connected." His smirk was obvious.

"You know," Defino said, looking up from the type-writer, "if word of this case got out when we started, even someone higher up could have his ear to the ground. Any of those guys ever serve in the navy?"

Hack had, but years ago, before he came on the job. Still, this additional connection was worrisome. It was worse than that.

"I'll have to ask McElroy to look at their personnel files." MacHovec didn't look happy about it. If this inquiry got too deep too high up, no one was going to be happy. "You know any of these guys?" He addressed the question to the room.

"Heard of Captain Mulholland, I think," Defino said. "But I never worked for him."

"What'd you hear?" MacHovec asked.

Defino turned his hands palms up. "Stand-up guy. Treats his people good."

"Jane?"

"Nothing rings a bell."

"Well, we got a lotta people to talk to. Hear anything from Omaha?"

"I haven't called today. If they'd found Hutchins, we'd've heard."

"So what's with the super?" MacHovec said.

Jane told him. "We're going to have to lean on him. Even if he didn't know someone was in that apartment when Quill was killed, he would've seen stuff lying around when he went to show the apartment. Squatters don't clean up after themselves."

"Professionals do," Defino said.

"True." And if the killer was a pro, there wasn't a chance in hell they'd find him after four years. She picked up the phone and called Mike Fromm. John was doing fine; no one had seen Hutchins; nothing was new. They talked about nothing for a few minutes and then she got off the phone.

"How 'bout we call Stabile?" Defino said. "Let him know we think Derek's holding back."

"What if Derek runs again?"

Defino considered it. "No one ever looked in that apartment. Derek knows that. He's gotta be feeling pretty smug at this point. Here are these two cops who want to know something and they can't do a damn thing to him. It's almost five years later."

"OK," Jane said. "Call Stabile." She got up from her desk and went to the coffee room. One of the men from the first office was sitting at a table stirring a cup of coffee. She sat down with him.

"You find out where your body got that tattoo?" he asked.

"He was in the navy."

"That'll do it. Is it relevant?"

"We don't know yet. Probably not. How're you guys doing?"

"We're creeping. They say it's a cold case. This one is frozen."

"I know what you mean." She stood and sipped her coffee standing up. "I need to run around the block. Too much sitting."

He stood and tossed his empty cup in the basket. "There's no justice," he said.

Jane smiled and returned to the cramped office. Both men were on the phone. She dialed her former partner, Marty Hoagland, relieved when he answered on the first ring. "Marty, it's Jane."

"Jane!" He sounded exuberant. "How's it going?"

"It's different, I'll say that. You got an hour after your shift?"

"Sure. What's up?"

"Just feel like a beer and a friend."

"Great." He told her where he'd meet her and she hung up.

"Stabile thinks we're crazy," Defino said. "He's sure he walked in and out of that empty apartment while they were working on it."

"That doesn't mean anything," Jane said, feeling exasperation set in. "He didn't walk in at two A.M."

"Soderberg was killed in the afternoon."

"None of this means anything, Gordon. Hutchins said someone was living there. I believe him. If Derek knew about it, all he has to do is warn the guy that Stabile is coming. The guy goes up on the roof or down to the first floor. He walks out and he's invisible. Stabile never sees him. Hutchins didn't do this, and he's probably dead because I went to Omaha to find him. I think we have to take Derek to a station house and scare him."

"OK with me." He looked at his watch.

"Not today. Stabile going to talk to him?"

"Maybe."

MacHovec put the phone down. "That was the Navy League in Arlington. Their records are confidential, thank you very much. Very smug lieutenant talked to me. Or didn't talk to me. He knows what went down." MacHovec was sore. He didn't like it when his questions weren't answered.

"Can we get a warrant?" Defino said.

"Shit, this is the military and another state."

"Let's put it on hold," Jane said.

"You got an idea?" MacHovec asked.

"Yes, but I don't want to talk about it. What've we got on this guy Carl Johnson who claimed Soderberg's body in New York?"

MacHovec struggled through paper. His desk was one of those places that started each day looking as though no one worked at it and finished each day looking like a recycling bin. But he had a perfect system of retrieval; ask for something and he laid his hands on it in seconds. "Carl Johnson. Got his address off his driver's license. They had a Xerox of it in the mortuary file. The Manhattan phone book had a bunch of Carl and C. Johnsons, and one of them was at that address." He handed a card to Jane. "I called a bunch of times but no one answered."

"I'll try tonight."

"You ever take a breather?"

"When no one's looking. You check to see if he still has a license in New York State?"

"I did and he does."

"You're good, MacHovec. Got the name, address, and phone number of the Navy League?"

"I will in two seconds."

"Good. I need to see a man about an idea."

She went to McElroy's office but it was empty. She hesitated to talk to Graves, but as she approached his door, he called her in.

"Give me an update," he said.

She did, going over everything she could remember. "We haven't heard back from the archives in St. Louis yet, but MacHovec sent Soderberg's prints to them. It's just a matter of time. I wanted to ask you about something else."

"I'm listening."

"The lieutenant at the Navy League wouldn't give MacHovec the time of day. It's pretty clear he checked up on Soderberg's body and decided whatever he knew was none of our business."

"That's bad news. Getting into military files can be a bitch."

"I'd like to go down to D.C. and talk to them myself."

"Well—"

"Not officially. I don't want any paper trail on my trip. I want to go down there by train on Monday morning. I'll pay for the ticket, and I'll see to it I'm not followed out of my building."

"Jane, if you want to take an official trip, I can OK it, but we still need to have paper to cover your leaving the city. But if you just want to go to Washington on a vacation day, see the sights, say hi to the president, that's your business. But I have to warn you, if you flash your badge around, someone may make a phone call and there could be trouble."

"I understand. OK with you if I take that vacation? I've never been to the capital. I'd like to go before it gets too cold to enjoy walking around."

"I'll tell Annie on Monday morning that you won't be in."

"Thanks, Captain."

"And you might want to make a call or two to let us know you're safe and sound."

"I'll do that."

"Come see me before you leave."

When she got back to her office, MacHovec had heard from St. Louis. Defino was sitting at Jane's desk, which was next to MacHovec's, and looking over the notes MacHovec had taken during the phone call. He jumped up when she walked in.

"OK, we got a name and a bunch of stuff. This guy's faxing it over but he gave me most of the high points. Our boy's name when he entered the navy was Wallace Caffrey. He was born in 1947, entered the navy at age eighteen, got his commission through college and in-house courses, put in twenty years, and worked as an electronic warfare officer. There's your tie-in to QX Electronics. They call guys like him mustangs—up from enlisted ranks to officer grades. The fax'll give us all his assignments and the medals he earned. It should be coming through right now."

"Was he married?" Jane asked. "Is there family anywhere?"

"Yes, and it'll be on the fax."

"Any idea who Henry Soderberg was?"

"Yeah, he looked that up, too. Guy died in the Vietnam War. He'll fax his record over, too. Should be a lot of paper coming across."

"Let's get it Xeroxed," Jane said. "I'm looking for a good book to read this weekend."

There was plenty to read, pages and pages on each man, the real Soderberg and the fake. She noticed that MacHovec put his copy in a jacket and left it in a desk drawer. MacHovec didn't do overtime. But Defino put his where he would pick it up on his way out.

Eventually McElroy dropped in for his preweekend

gab fest. Jane said nothing about her plans for Monday and neither did he. Graves would keep it to himself till Monday morning. Only two people would know where she was going until she got there.

After McElroy left, the three of them went over their checklists and tried to figure out what they knew and what they didn't. Quill's name never came up in the discussion, showing how far they had progressed in less than two weeks. On Monday she and Defino planned to bring Derek to Midtown North on West Fifty-fourth Street, Bracken's station house, and talk to him. She felt guilty not saying anything to them about her trip, but decided it was best not to.

MacHovec left; then Defino looked at his watch. "See you next week," Jane said, looking up from her desk.

"Good weekend."

"Right. Get plenty of reading in."

He gave her a grin, picked up his files, and left. When enough time had passed for him to be on the elevator, Jane looked out, made sure he was gone, and went to Graves's office.

"Sit down," the first whip said. "I've got a little present for you." He handed her a box.

Inside was a cell phone. She looked at it, then looked at him.

"I worry about my people. It's not a gift; it's a loan. When this case is in the bag, you can give it back to me."

"Thanks, Captain."

"It works from as far away as Arlington, Virginia," he said.

She smiled, put it back in its box, and left.

Marty was already at their favorite table in the bar down in the Six when she got there. They had spent more hours after work in this place than any other she could think of, sometimes just the two of them, sometimes with friends on the job. One of them, she thought sadly, was now dead. At least one other had pulled the pin.

Marty had a glass of beer in front of him, about two inches already gone. He signaled the waiter as he saw her and the waiter headed for the bar.

"So how's things? How's your dad?"

"He's fine. I should've called and told you after that trip to the hospital, but it's been hectic. They had his medication wrong. Once they corrected it, he felt fine."

"He still got that loving gal who takes care of him?"

"Saint Madeleine? You bet. I don't know how he'd survive without her."

"Why doesn't he marry her?"

"My opinion? He thinks it would be a slap in the face to my mother's memory. It wouldn't, but that's how he feels."

"OK, I've asked all the polite questions. How're you?"

"Marty, this case is unbelievable."

"I got time. Tell me."

"I can't. I wish I could. Things are happening that are very scary. Basically, the homicide we're investigating was probably a mistake, maybe a contract killing that went bad. We think maybe a look-alike got hit and they waited till the investigation was over and the cops were done in the building to get the right guy."

"Nice. So you're moving along."

"A couple of leaps, a couple of inches. Any movement on the City Hall Park killing?"

"The word is they're nowhere. But I heard something cute that they're not making public. The woman was in a wheelchair."

"Right."

"The ME couldn't find anything in the body to show that she couldn't walk."

"Interesting. She just liked getting around on wheels?"

"They're still doing tox screens, looking for something. Could be hysteria. That won't show up anywhere."

"That's nice."

"Wish you were still on it?"

"Not if they're up against a wall. At least on this case we've learned a few things."

"So how's the new apartment?" They were both out of beer, and Marty signaled for another round.

"It's everything I've ever wanted except for all the cartons I haven't unpacked. The fireplace works."

"Nothing like a good fire. So you're really not gonna tell me about the case?"

"I can't. But the whip just gave me a cell phone so I can make my rings without finding a pay phone. I want you to have the number."

"You know you're worrying me?"

"I'm OK, Marty. I just want someone in the world to know my number, and I can't give it to Dad or he'll call me all day to check up on me." She wrote down the number and handed him the slip of paper.

"OK, Janey. You know you can count on me."

"That's why I'm giving you the number." She sighed unintentionally and he picked up on it.

"So what else?"

"Flora called last week."

"Chief Hamburg?"

"One and the same. She heard I was retiring and she's not happy."

"More to the point, are you?"

"I guess that's the question. Being down here with you . . . the job is half my life, Marty. The Six is half of that. I keep thinking of all the guys I partnered with, the busts, the collars."

"The good times and the bad."

"Yeah." She looked at her watch. "Not like me, is it?"

"It's OK. I know there's a heart of stone under the soft exterior."

She smiled and gave him a light punch.

They finished their beers and Marty paid for all, not accepting Jane's money. "You get it next time," he said affably.

"Just one thing," Jane said. "Let me go first. Give me a few minutes to get to the subway."

"You being tailed?"

"It's possible. And if I am, I'd rather he not know who I met here."

"Hey, I'll go out the back way. But I'll wait awhile first."

"Thanks, Marty. And don't worry."

He grinned and patted her hand.

[**23**]

WHEN SHE GOT home, she went downstairs to the basement. She had a bin assigned to her for which she had to buy a padlock. Every apartment in the building had a bin, and one after the other they were padlocked. Basements were not her favorite places in city buildings. Without dwelling on the inhabitants, she knew they were four-footed, and she had had enough confrontations in twenty years on the job not to want another. And then there were the roaches.

What she was looking for was a way out of the building besides the front door. If she was being watched, she didn't want to be seen Monday morning leaving for Penn Station. But the basement was entirely below ground, and she was not going to attempt to leave through a window.

She went up to the ground floor and knocked on the super's door. His wife opened it and invited her inside. Then she got her husband.

"Hey, Miss Bauer. How's it goin'?" He was middle-aged, white, and had been helpful in the month before she moved in.

"I wondered if anyone had asked about me since I moved in, Frank."

"I don't think so. You want me to ask my wife?"

"Sure, if you don't mind."

He left the living room and his wife came back with him. "You expecting someone?" she asked.

"Sort of. Anyone ask about me?"

She shook her head. "Nobody while I was home."

"Have either of you let anyone into my apartment, like the phone man or the electric guy?"

They both said, "Nobody."

"OK. Just asking. If anyone does ask to be let in, tell them they can't get in till you check with me, OK?"

That was OK with them.

When she left, she walked along the ground floor till she came to what looked like a delivery door. It was marked NO EXIT in big red letters and happily did not have a crash-bar alarm that sounded when you opened it. Jane pushed it open, then stepped back inside. The door closed swiftly and securely. Once outside, there was no easy access; one would have to go around to the front of the building.

She opened it again and held it open with her foot. Outside was a small concrete area between this building and the back of the one facing the far street. Off to the left, a concrete walkway led to the other apartment house and seemed to continue in a narrow alley between it and the one to the left. That meant she could walk out the back door, keep going, and end up a block away from the front of her building. It occurred to her that she could call the Sixth Precinct and speak to one of the cops driving the sector car. They knew every in and out, every alley, every connection in their sector. This was survival information, and every good sector cop and foot patrol officer knew his own area.

But visually, it looked good. She didn't want to try it out right now, because the only way back in was through the front, and if she was being watched, she didn't want her tail to know she had left the apartment house by another door. Next week would be time enough for that.

The wind was starting to chill her. She turned back inside and stood by while the door hissed to a perfect close. She had her exit for Monday morning.

At seven she called the number for Carl Johnson, the man to whom Soderberg's body had been released. A woman answered and said he wasn't there. She wasn't sure when he was coming home, and wouldn't Jane like to leave a message?

Jane wouldn't. In the background Jane had heard a sports broadcast. She wondered if the woman who answered the phone was listening to it or if a man was there, a man who didn't answer phone calls.

She put her coat on and went downstairs. Her 9mm Glock automatic was holstered on her hip, a blazer covering it. She walked briskly over to Sixth Avenue and West Fourth Street and went down into the subway. If someone was following her, he'd get a little exercise. An uptown B train was pulling into the station just as she reached the platform, and she hopped on it. Carl Johnson lived on Central Park West in the Sixties. She rode up to Seventy-second and got off. Coming up to the street level, she saw the Dakota, the huge nineteenth-century apartment house where John Lennon had lived and outside of which he had died. It reminded her of being young and in love with Paul Thurston. She remembered the music that was playing that summer, and she could see the faces of the four young men who had overwhelmed the music scene when she was a kid.

She walked south on Central Park West, staying on the west side of the street. The east side bordered Central Park. Carl Johnson's apartment house was old, but not nearly as old as the Dakota. A uniformed doorman was helping a woman out of a cab as she approached. She waited till he had ushered the woman inside before walking up to the front door.

"Yes, ma'am," he said.

"I'm here to see Mr. Johnson." She had her hand on her shield deep in her coat pocket, but she left it there.

"Mr. Johnson?"

"Yes. Carl Johnson." She took the shield and ID out and watched his face change. "Is he home?"

"Yes, ma'am."

"What apartment does he live in?"

"Ten C."

"Don't announce me," she said. "Just show me where the elevator is."

The elevator was new and streamlined. She was on the tenth floor in seconds and down the hall to apartment C in a few more. She rang the bell and heard someone running.

"Who is it?" a woman called.

"Det. Jane Bauer."

"Who?" The woman opened the door, looked at the shield, and said, "What is this?"

"I'd like to talk to Mr. Johnson."

The woman gave it some thought before saying, "Come in." She then locked the door noisily behind Jane. "I'll get him. Wait here."

"Here" was the foyer. To her left, just after the door, was a kitchen with a dinette at the far end. The appliances were fairly new and the floor was a shiny tile with a floral pattern. Beyond the kitchen, also on the left, was a dining room with a large table in its center and a chandelier hanging above it.

The woman had gone to one of the bedrooms in the back of the apartment. Now she returned, a man behind her. He was wearing casual pants and a sweater over a shirt, although it was warm in the apartment. A slim man of a little more than medium height, he had thinning pale hair and the slight stubble of a man who had shaved early in the morning. His wife stepped back as they reached the foyer.

"I'm Carl Johnson. What can I do for you?"

Jane showed her shield. "I'm Detective Bauer, working with a special squad on the death of Henry Soderberg."

"Henry. My goodness"—he smiled slightly—"that was a long time ago. Have you reopened the case?"

"We have, Mr. Johnson. May we talk about it?"

"Of course. Lena, dear, would you make us some coffee? You'll have some coffee, Detective Bauer?"

"Thank you, yes."

They went down two steps into the sunken living room to the right at the end of the foyer. There were windows on two sides, but none overlooked the park. The room was furnished comfortably, with attractive pieces of crystal and ceramic pottery on all surfaces.

"You were the person who took charge of Mr. Soderberg's body."

"That's right." Not another word, not any explanation.

"Are you related to him?"

"Not at all. We worked together."

"Did his family ask you to pick up the body?"

"I'm not aware that he had any family."

"How did you come to be the person who made the arrangements?"

"As I said, we worked together. When he didn't show up for work, naturally we called him at home. When there was no answer, we called the police. They had a record of his having suffered a tragic accident."

"You said 'we' a moment ago. Who else were you referring to?"

"Three of us worked together. The other man was Ray Kellner. He's long gone."

"He died?"

"No, excuse me. I mean he left New York. We haven't been in touch."

Mrs. Johnson brought in the coffee, carrying it in a glass carafe. She poured it into two brightly colored ceramic cups and offered Jane cream and sugar. Jane took a drop of cream and thanked her. Mrs. Johnson retreated from the living room, leaving the carafe on a warming candle.

"What were the three of you doing?"

"Trying to be Bill Gates, I suppose." He smiled. "Didn't work out. After Henry died, we broke up. Ray went his way and I went mine."

"What were you working at? Software? Hardware? Something else?"

"You could call it software. Without Henry, we couldn't make a go."

"Who were you working for, Mr. Johnson?"

"Just ourselves. We were three not so young men who thought we had a good idea. We used our own cash to back us up. That's about it."

"What part did Mr. Soderberg play in your work?"

"Henry was the marketing man. He was very good. He was lining up buyers for our product."

"How well did you know him?"

"Well enough to trust him, not well enough to know much about him personally."

Jane sipped her coffee and made a show of flipping pages in her notebook. "You had his body sent to the Navy League."

"That was his wish."

"He told you that?"

"At some point, I suppose he must have. It's several years ago and I can't remember exactly what he said or when he said it."

"It seems a very personal thing, telling someone you'd like your body sent to the Navy League if you die."

"When you don't have a family, you have to think of those things."

"What do you suppose the Navy League did with Mr. Soderberg's body?"

"I couldn't tell you. I felt it was my duty to deliver him into their hands. That's what I did."

"Do you have any files from QX Electronics?" she asked.

"Files? We weren't the best-organized people, Detective. We didn't keep any files."

"You had a filing cabinet in your office."

He looked at her, not smiling. "Well, of course we had records of who Henry talked to when he was out selling. When we disbanded, I think we just shredded those papers. We had no product, nothing to sell. There was no reason to keep anything."

"You shredded them?"

"They had names and addresses on them. You can't be too careful these days."

"I don't understand why you and Ray Kellner didn't just continue to work on your product after Mr. Soderberg died."

"It just wasn't the same anymore," he said. "We'd been a threesome. After Henry died, we just didn't have the enthusiasm to go on."

Johnson was winging it, and not doing well at it. She had let him know they were aware of the office, that someone had told them it contained a filing cabinet. He would be on his guard now if he had anything to hide, which she was pretty sure he had. "You made a lot of phone calls for an office that had nothing to sell."

"Henry made appointments with prospective clients," he said quickly. "Ray and I needed equipment; we had experts to talk to. Of course we made phone calls."

"Are you aware that Mr. Soderberg was murdered?" Jane asked.

"Murdered? Surely you're mistaken. The police told me he fell down a flight of stairs."

"He was pushed down a flight of stairs. We have a lot of evidence that points to homicide, Mr. Johnson."

"This is very hard to believe."

"Believe it, Mr. Johnson."

"Henry said . . . some months before he died, Henry said a man living in the same building had been murdered. Do the police think there was a connection?"

"We believe the earlier murder was an error. We think the killer was out to get Henry Soderberg and killed the wrong man on the first try."

Carl Johnson's lips were a straight line and his eyes had become colder and darker than they had been. "Are you sure of this?"

"We are, Mr. Johnson. It's why I'm here tonight. If there's anything else you know about Henry Soderberg, anything in his past that might help us, you should tell me about it."

"I know nothing."

"Who do you work for now, Mr. Johnson?"

"I'm self-employed."

"Still trying to be Bill Gates?"

"Trying to make a living, Detective Bauer."

"Good luck," she said. It was the end of the interview.

The doorman was inside when she got down to the lobby. He was sitting on an armless bentwood chair. When he saw Jane, he jumped up to open the door.

"How long have the Johnsons lived here?" she asked.

"Long time. Ten years anyway."

She said good night as he opened the door and she went out to Central Park West. It was cold now, and she stopped and pulled her collar up. OK, she thought. Get a good look at me, tail. I'm on my way home.

She walked to the subway, went downstairs without looking back, showed her tin at the booth, and went through the exit in reverse. It was one of the perks of the job.

She didn't look around much as she rode downtown. If he was there, he already knew what he wanted to know, that the team had located Carl Johnson and she had talked to him. Her thoughts turned to Lisa, the child whom she had given birth to. In the twenty years since that event, she had not prepared herself for the moment of confrontation. Something in her wanted achingly to see the girl. Something else wanted her to get rid of the letter and pretend she had never received it.

She had lived such an independent life, alone in an apartment, engaging in relationships and breaking them up, earning her own way and paying her own bills, that she had been caught off balance by something that she had no control over. The letter had had the impact of a flash flood. She was surprised and somewhat shaken, too, by the emotions that accompanied her reading of the letter. Maybe if it had happened at a different time, when she was not changing squads, anticipating changing jobs, breaking up with Hack, moving to another apartment, she could handle it better. She smiled to herself as she thought of all the things going on in her life simultaneously. Never a dull moment. Perhaps when she was sitting behind her desk at the insurance company, she would find out what a dull moment felt like. She might even take pleasure in it.

At West Fourth Street she climbed the many stairs up to the street, again without looking back. On the way to her apartment, she stopped and picked up a cup of coffee and a doughnut to eat when she got home.

Finally, sitting in her living room, sipping and munching, she considered the possibility that Hack could be involved in what was looking increasingly like a very big homicide.

24

ON SATURDAY SHE read the military file on the fake Henry Soderberg. She couldn't quite think of him as Wallace Caffrey yet, although if she found any living relatives, she would have to switch names. At the moment, it was uncomfortable.

Under his real name he had spent over twenty years in the navy, visiting more places than she had heard of or could pronounce. He entered the navy as an enlisted man in the mid-sixties and went for SEAL training. As a SEAL he was trained for special operations underwater, beach insertions, parachute drops, special weapons and intelligence gathering, and for a long time in the second half of his career, he specialized in electronics. His combat service started during the Vietnam War.

Also to his credit, he learned several foreign languages, most prominently Korean and Chinese at a place called the Presidio in California.

In his early twenties he married Angie Kim, a Korean girl whom he brought back to the States to live in a house near San Diego. Ten months after his marriage, his first daughter was born, and ten months after his next leave began his second daughter was born. Their names were Tina and Beth Caffrey. There were no addresses for them.

Seven years after taking their vows, Wallace and Angie Caffrey divorced. He spent most of the second half of his time in the navy as a single man. He earned a number of medals and retired from the navy in his early forties.

There was, of course, significantly more information in the file, uncountable details that blurred one's vision. His weapons skills were documented, his education, every ship he served on, every ribbon he earned, every medal he was awarded. There were medical records, shots he had received, life insurance documents; it went on and on. But the outline that Jane sketched on paper as she was reading gave her the important facts: he had been married, he had two children who were likely to be alive, he was smart, he was tough, and he was most likely pretty damn gutsy. So what had he done with those admirable attributes when he left the navy? The military file provided no clue.

The file of the real Henry Soderberg was a sad comparison to his namesake. He, too, had entered the navy as a young man, within a few months of the fake Soderberg. He was a year older, having worked at several jobs for short periods of time. Checking one file against the other, Jane found that both young men served on the same ship for about nine months. It was while they were on that ship that the real Soderberg suffered an accidental death. A month later, the fake was transferred to another command.

It occurred to her that foul play could have been involved. But there was nothing in either file to suggest that. Certainly there was no hint that Wallace Caffrey had played any part in Soderberg's death.

What the death provided Wallace Caffrey with was a name that he could use, a person his own age, whom he apparently knew, with much the same background. The real Soderberg had not lived long enough to acquire a wife. At the time of his death, he had one sister and a living mother. There was no mention of his father. Caffrey, too, had a living mother when he entered the navy. No other relatives were mentioned.

There was a faint hint of trouble in the military life of the real Soderberg. On occasion he was late to assignments.

He failed some tests but passed them the second time around. He had volunteered for the SEALs but quickly washed out of the training course. At one time he asked for compassionate leave and was granted a month to visit his ailing mother. By contrast, Wallace Caffrey had such a splendid record, it practically glittered on the page. He worked himself up from a seaman, going to officer's school and coming out an ensign. Eventually he became an electronic warfare officer, serving in the command center of a battleship.

By that time he had shed his wife, and if he had any relationship with his daughters, it could not have been very deep. He spent little time in the town where he had set up housekeeping, choosing to travel to other parts of the States and to vacation in Europe and Asia. By the time Jane finished the file, she wondered whether she might have had a more enjoyable life had she joined the navy twenty years ago instead of the police department.

The reading of the files took most of Saturday, considering that she slept late, replenishing her energy. In the afternoon, Mike Fromm called. There was nothing new in the case. Hutchins was still missing; no significant calls had been made to Cory's phone; John Grant's recovery was progressing nicely. All of that was just the excuse he used to make the call.

She sensed he was taken with her, and she felt flattered. She knew, too, that she found him attractive. Still, she could not imagine taking on a relationship at such a distance. They were the city mouse and the country mouse, and which of them would be able to change and remain happy? Besides, her emotional life was in turmoil right now. Hack was still a warm memory, and her thoughts of Paul Thurston had managed to aggravate old wounds she had almost forgotten existed. And then there was Lisa Angelino.

It was too much to think about now. She decided to eat out. Maybe if she left the files and letter behind her, she could concentrate on food that she hadn't taken the trouble to prepare. Having had only one meal during the day, she was ready for dinner fairly early. She walked with the weekend crowd through the narrow streets of her new community, checking menus in windows, finally deciding on a restaurant that was fairly empty now but would be reservations-only in a couple of hours. And it was a small enough place that her tail, if there was one, wouldn't be able to come in off the street and sit down without her noticing him.

It was a good meal, a lot better than she would have cooked for herself. She wandered the streets, looking at jewelry and far-out clothes for a while. The weather had turned cold again tonight, and she thought it couldn't be much fun being outside, or even sitting in a car, if the tail had found a place to park.

In her bedroom, she looked at the snapshot stuck in her mirror. The eyes were clear, the smile genuine, the nose closer to Paul's perfect one than Jane's more ordinary one. Did she want this girl in her life? She didn't know. And she didn't know how long it would take her to make a decision. If that was possible.

She made a big brunch for herself on Sunday morning, eggs and sausages and a couple of slices of sturgeon she had picked up down the block. Enough coffee to drown in. She was on her third and last cup when the phone rang.

"Jane, it's Mike." It wasn't the warm, friendly Mike; it was the cop speaking.

"Hi. Good morning. What's up?"

"Bad news."

"Hutchins?" Her stomach tightened.

"He was dumped early this morning or during the night. A jogger found him."

"He's dead," she said, feeling the weight crush her down.

"He's alive, but he won't last. He's been beaten so badly, there can't be a bone they didn't break."

"Shit."

"You couldn't have known," Mike said, understanding her guilt.

She swallowed the impediment in her throat. Her lashes were wet. "I feel terrible."

"I know. I'm not going to give you the speech about how you just did your job. I feel terrible, too."

"Have you told John Grant?"

"I'm about to."

"Did he say anything at all?"

"The jogger says he mumbled a couple of words. I don't know if we'll be able to make any sense of them."

"Thanks, Mike."

"You take it easy, Jane."

"Yes."

"If we learn anything, you'll be the first to hear."

Of all the possibilities one could think of besides the loss of a partner or another cop, this was the worst, the death of an innocent bystander, especially if it was your case. And in this instance, he had been tortured first. What had Soderberg—what had Wallace Caffrey been involved in? She thought again about Carl Johnson. Maybe he was the one Defino should sweat tomorrow, not poor Derek. Johnson had to know what Caffrey was doing, because he must have been part of the same thing.

She called McElroy at home. He was out. She sat looking at Graves's beeper number. Something in her didn't want to call a captain at home. Finally she dialed the number, hung up, and waited.

The phone rang so quickly she thought he must have been waiting for someone to ring him. She gave it to him in a few brief sentences.

"You have Sergeant Fromm's phone number handy?"

"Right here." She gave him both, the station house and his home.

"Hutchins was alive when he was found?"

"Just barely."

"It's interesting. You found Hutchins; the killer didn't. The killer must have traced him to that loft and lost him there. Or never even got that far. You still taking that vacation day tomorrow?"

"Yes, sir."

"I can't caution you enough—"

"I know that. I've found a back way out of my—"

"I don't want to hear about it."

"OK."

"We'll talk tomorrow. I'm sorry this has broken up your Sunday."

She was up early on Monday morning, having slept fitfully. She took the elevator down to the ground floor and walked through the lobby to the back door. On her shoulder was a bag with a change of clothes in case she didn't make it back tonight, although she hoped she would. She inspected the area behind her building from the door, saw no one, and hurried to the narrow walkway that led to the far street. Then, walking briskly, she headed for the subway. Halfway there, an empty cab glided to a stop at a light and she dashed for it.

"Penn Station," she said, shutting the door.

The light turned green and he took off, racing through traffic as though she had said she was late for her train. They rode in silence—the driver an anomaly, a native New York cabbie with nothing to say—till he came to a stop at the station. The fare in her hand, Jane paid and dashed off, getting inside the building in seconds. She bought a round-trip ticket, thinking that that was a sign of optimism, and found the track for the train to D.C. Inside, she picked out a window seat on the far side of the train, shed her coat, sat down, and took a deep breath. She was on her way to her first vacation in months.

25

SHE CAUGHT UP on her sleep and her reading on the trip. At Union Station in D.C. she got a cab to Arlington, Virginia. The trip to the Navy League set her back about twenty dollars, but it gave her an impromptu sightseeing tour.

At the Navy League there were men and women in and out of uniform everywhere. She found her way to the office that MacHovec had spoken to and talked to the secretary, a man in uniform. He said Lieutenant MacPhail had a busy schedule but could spare perhaps fifteen minutes. Jane said fifteen minutes would do it.

MacPhail was young and handsome and wearing a uniform that appeared to have just come out of its box. He welcomed her, offered her a chair, and asked how he could help her. She had not shown her shield to the man outside, and she had given a lot of thought to whether she should do it in here. She had decided, finally, that it was better to show it than not to, even on a vacation day.

"I'm Det. Jane Bauer, NYPD. I'm not here officially. I'm taking some vacation time in Washington and thought I would drop in and see if you could answer a question or two for me about a Navy League veteran who died about four years ago."

"What are your questions?"

"I'd like to find any living survivors of this man." She had written some facts on a sheet of paper, which she handed across his desk. It had Wallace Caffrey's name, naval ID, birth date, and a few other salient facts printed in bold black ink. "He had two daughters, Tina and Beth, and an ex-wife whose maiden name was Angie Kim."

He looked at her handwritten sheet. The names she had just spoken were on it and he made marks next to them. "May I ask why you're interested in this man and these survivors?"

"Mr. Caffrey died about four years ago in what appeared to be an accidental fall. The case was reopened two weeks ago, and we are convinced that his death was a homicide. We're looking for a murderer."

"I don't see how we could help you find that killer."

"Interviewing his daughters and his ex-wife will help us."

"Give me a moment, please." He left the room and she sat back in the chair. She hoped he wasn't going to another telephone to call New York, which would be the end of her visit. She wanted to get up and check the view from his window, but she didn't want to be caught anywhere except in this chair. He was gone a long time, more than ten minutes by her watch. When he came back, he was holding some papers in his hand.

"Mr. Caffrey had a long and distinguished career with the navy," he said, as though he were beginning an obituary. "He died a number of years after he was discharged from the service. It was apparently his wish to have a military interment, and we were able to provide that for him. His daughter Tina Caffrey was notified, and she participated in the arrangements."

"Do you have her address?"

He passed a sheet of paper across the desk to her. "I've given you her address and that of her sister, in case Tina Caffrey married and changed names. The last address for the ex-wife is old, but that's noted also."

"Where was he buried?" Jane asked.

"He wasn't. He was cremated and his ashes were buried

at sea from a ship docked at Newport News, Virginia. It's a service we provide for navy veterans."

"I see." That meant no exhumation. "Do you have any information on what Mr. Caffrey did for a living after he retired from the navy?"

"None at all. He kept us informed of his address, which changed from time to time. The last known address was in New York City. I assume that's where he was living when he died."

"That's right. I see his daughter Tina lived in Virginia."

"Yes. That's probably why she was called when we arranged for her father's cremation."

The other address was in California. She hoped the Virginia daughter had remained in the area and still had a name that could be traced. She folded the sheet and put it in her bag. "Thank you very much, Lieutenant."

He stood and shook her proffered hand. "I wish you luck with your investigation, Detective Bauer. If I can be of further help, don't hesitate to call."

"Thank you."

"Enjoy your vacation. There are many wonderful places to visit here."

The place she visited first was a telephone booth. She called Captain Graves and left a message with Annie that she had arrived. Then she found a Virginia telephone book and looked up Tina Caffrey. The book was a couple of years old, but the name and number were listed. The address was the one the lieutenant had given her. She called the number and heard a mechanical voice tell her the number had been changed. She pulled out a pen and wrote down the new one, thankful the time limit for forwarding calls hadn't expired. The new one was also in Virginia.

The voice that answered was young and girlish. "Is this Tina Caffrey?" Jane asked conversationally.

"Yes, it is."

"Ms. Caffrey, this is Det. Jane Bauer of the New York

Police Department. We are looking into the death of your father, Wallace."

"My father died of an accident."

"May I meet you and talk to you, Ms. Caffrey? I have some questions I'd like to ask."

What could have been a sigh sounded across the wire. "I guess I could. Are you coming down from New York?"

"I'm in Arlington at the moment. I'm at the Navy League."

"The Navy League. I could meet you there."

"That would be great."

"An hour?"

"I'll be just inside the front door."

"And your name was?"

"Jane Bauer. I have my ID with me."

"I'll see you in an hour."

It was enough time to get a bite to eat and settle herself in a chair facing the door. When Tina Caffrey walked in, there was no mistaking her. She had a face that combined the traits of the two sides of her family, but she favored her Korean mother. She was slim, Jane noted enviously, had long, black, silky hair, and beautiful dark eyes. She was wearing a black coat and heels that looked expensive. Jane stood as she entered, and the young woman acknowledged her and walked over.

Jane had her shield and ID out. "I'm Det. Jane Bauer."

"I'm Tina Wilson. I was married last spring."

"Let's sit down."

Tina Wilson wanted to know the whys of Jane's visit, and Jane explained them. Tina listened closely, her face solemn, as though she were hearing bad news. When she was satisfied, she said, "What do you need to know?"

"How well did you know your father?"

"Not very well at all." She stood and took her coat off, as though she had finally warmed up. She was wearing a very dark gray suit and a white blouse. She had no jewelry on except a diamond ring next to her wedding ring. "Not as well as I would have liked. He and my mother divorced when I was a child, and I almost never saw him after that. Not that I saw much of him while they were married. He loved the navy more than he loved his family." She said it with obvious pain. "It was very hard on my sister and me, and I couldn't exaggerate what it did to my mother. She needed a husband and all she got was subsistence."

"Did he keep in touch with the family, even if he didn't see you that much?"

"He usually let us know where he was, the city and state anyway. He sent checks—the navy insisted on that, you know—but things were never easy for us."

"What happened after he left the navy?"

She pressed her lips together, as though trying to decide what to say. "I don't know how to say this. It's something I've thought about a lot. When he left the navy, he sort of went crazy."

"Tell me about it," Jane said.

"He . . ." She took a breath. "Maybe he needed the discipline that the navy brought into his life; I don't know. He had always worked extremely hard. He went to school and learned a lot of things. But when he left the navy, his life seemed to fall apart."

"Did he work?"

"He did, but he wouldn't talk about it. He moved from one place to another. The checks he sent my mother came from a different place every few months. It was as if he was trying to find himself when the truth was that he had left his real self in the navy."

"Do you remember the places he lived in?"

"He was in California for a while; I don't remember what city. Then, suddenly, he was in Chicago, then here in Washington. He stayed here for some time and then he moved to New York. There may have been some other places in between."

"Where did he live in New York?"

"In an awful place in the Fifties. I visited there once."

"You went to his apartment?"

"I was in New York on business. I called him from the company I was visiting and told him I wanted to see him."

"You had his phone number?"

"Yes. He always gave us his number. He said he didn't usually have a listing, so he'd be hard to find if we needed him. He said he would meet me somewhere, but I wanted to see where he lived. He met me outside the front door of the building, one of those tenements that look like row houses."

"I'm familiar with them."

"And he took me upstairs." She was increasingly agitated. "The apartment was all right, I guess. I saw the kitchen and the living room. It was clean and very neat, but my father was always that way. But . . ."

"Something's bothering you."

"I think he was—I can't really believe this—he was living with another man."

"How do you know that?"

"I saw a letter addressed to another name, and on the way out I saw that my father's name wasn't on the mailbox. My father wasn't like that. If anything he was the reverse. He liked women more than he should have."

"Did you ask him about it?"

"I asked him who the letter was addressed to, and he said it was the man he was subleasing the apartment from. But I don't think he was telling me the truth. The letter was opened. The man must have been living there."

"Do you remember what the name was?"

"Soderman, I think. I didn't know anyone by that name."

"What did you talk about when you and your father were together?"

"Oh, he asked about my sister and my mother. I don't think he cared much about my mother but he asked anyway. He wanted to know how I was doing, if I had a boyfriend, what my job was like, the things you ask an old friend you haven't seen for a long time."

"Did you ask him about what he was doing?" Jane asked.

"I did. He said he was in electronic sales. I got the impression it involved computers."

"Was he in good health?"

"From his appearance I'd say he was. He was a muscular man and he always kept himself in good shape. He offered me a cup of coffee, but I was too nervous to drink it."

"How long ago was this visit, Mrs. Wilson?"

"Four or five years ago. I guess it couldn't have been four. He died about four years ago."

"How did you find out he had died?"

"I got a call from the Navy League. They said my father's body had been delivered to a local mortuary for eventual cremation. I was the closest next of kin, at least geographically. He had requested to have his ashes buried at sea. They arranged that for me."

"What did they tell you about how your father had died?"

"Just that he had taken a fall and I guess he had broken his neck."

"Did that surprise you?"

"Yes." Tina Wilson looked directly at Jane. "It surprised me very much. He always took such good care of himself, I couldn't believe he would fall down a flight of stairs. And then I thought, Well, if he's been living with another man in that kind of relationship, maybe something happened to him. Maybe he became ill and lost his balance."

"He wasn't living with another man, Mrs. Wilson," Jane said. Tina's discomfort was so great, so obvious, she wanted to put her at ease.

"How do you know that?"

"I think your father occasionally used other names in his work. The name you saw on that envelope and on the mailbox may have been one of those names."

Tina's face lightened. "That would explain some things I've wondered about."

"Like what?"

"His return address was a post office box. There was no name, just QX and a box number."

"How did you know where his apartment in New York was?"

"He gave me the address over the phone when I called. When I went to the funeral home, and asked for Wallace Caffrey, they couldn't find him. There was some mix-up in names and it took some time till they got it straight."

"I see. Let me ask you this: if you know that your father wasn't having the kind of relationship you thought he was, do you still think he was acting crazy after he left the navy?"

She smiled for the first time since Jane's arrival. She was extremely pretty, Jane noted, with a smile that softened and lighted up her face. Wallace Caffrey had been a fool not to enjoy this beautiful daughter of his. "Yes, I still do. Why didn't he let us know where he was living? Why did he use assumed names? Why couldn't he find a job and settle down in one place? There was something strange going on. I haven't talked to my mother about this, but my sister agrees. I think something snapped in him when he left the navy. I've always wished there were someone I could ask."

"Did you ever know any of your father's friends?"

"Not really. When he was still living at home, sometimes he'd bring someone over. There wasn't anyone I remember, but they were always in the navy."

"Mrs. Wilson, I know this has been a long and painful interview. I don't want to keep you. I want you to know that we are trying to find the person responsible for your father's death. If you think of anything that might be helpful, you can call this number." Jane handed her her card. "You can call collect and you can leave a message with anyone who answers. I will get back to you."

Tina Wilson looked at the card, then held it in her hand. "You know what I think?" she said. "I think my father was working for the CIA. I think he was doing that kind of work. That would explain a lot of things, like the other names, the moving around."

"I will certainly look into that," Jane said. "Tell me, when he sent your mother checks, did he sign them with his name?"

She shook her head. "Not after he left the navy. He sent bank checks, money orders, things like that. It was as if he was trying to hide."

But someone had found him, Jane thought, as she stood and shook Tina Wilson's hand. He hadn't hidden well enough.

[**26**]

JANE WATCHED THE young woman go. She was a happier person than she had been when she entered the building. Her greatest fear about her father had been extinguished. For more than four years she had carried the worry that her father had engaged in behavior that she found troubling. The way her muscles had relaxed, the way she had smiled, the way she had thanked Jane with a handshake showed her relief. Her life had just changed for the better. Tonight she would tell her husband that all her fears had been for nothing. If her father had acted a little crazy, well, maybe he had had a midlife crisis. Didn't everyone nowadays?

Jane checked the train schedule. She had learned more than what she had come for, and there was no reason to hang around. She could catch a train back to New York as soon as she reached the station.

First she called Captain Graves.

"How's it going?" he said.

"Soderberg or Caffrey was cremated and his ashes were buried in the Atlantic, courtesy of the U.S. Navy."

"So we don't have a body."

"Right. I've just talked to his daughter, who lives in Virginia. She came in and we talked face-to-face. Whatever he was doing, he kept it to himself. She thinks he may have been working for the CIA."

"Better hope not or we'll never get to the bottom of this. What are your plans now?"

"I'm getting a taxi to the station and I'm coming home."

"Not much of a vacation. You should stay overnight and see the Washington Monument or something."

"I'll have the taxi do a drive-by."

"Sounds good," Graves said lightly. "How's the cell phone working?"

"I forgot I had it. I'm using the pay phone here."

"Use it if you need it. We'll see you tomorrow?"

"Bright and early."

"Check in with me when you get home."

She did what she promised, had the taxi driver take her past the monument and as close to the White House as he could get, now that it was encased in antiterrorist protection. Surprisingly, she felt a surge of patriotism as she saw through the cab window structures she had previously seen only in books and on film. She was impressed by their size and by the quiet dignity of the monument.

"Can we go by the Vietnam monument?" she asked, leaning forward.

"You bet." When they got there, a grassy area with no

sign of the monument, he directed her to the stairs and said he would wait.

She got out and walked across the grass to the head of the stairs. Below was the dark, stark beauty of the monument. There were names there she would know, the father of a girl she had gone to school with. Jane remembered the funeral, one of the first she had attended.

People were milling about, searching the wall for the name of someone lost. Soderberg/Caffrey had served in that war. So had Hack, but only at the tail end. None of those people on the black wall had made it back, pieces of families gone forever.

She thought of the girl in the little town in Kansas whom she had given birth to, a piece of her family, of her life, that had not been lost, only missing in action. She had to make a decision, sooner rather than later. She walked back o the cab.

"Let's go," she said, and the driver took off with a squeal.

She ate an unsatisfying plastic-wrapped sandwich on the train. Going home she didn't sleep, and she couldn't concentrate on her book. This case, this crazy cold case that had started with the death of Arlen Quill, was becoming a very hot case, the life of Jane Bauer. If only because of timing, Lisa Angelino was mixed up in it. And she had begun thinking about Hack again. She had to find out if Hack was involved in this . . . and what would she do if he was?

As soon as she asked herself the question, she realized she had moved her position from believing he could not be involved to considering the possibility that he was. It was a change she didn't like.

Walking home from the subway, she stopped at a deli for a real sandwich to eat in her kitchen. She kept the tote bag slung over her shoulder like a large handbag to disguise the fact that she had considered staying somewhere overnight, in case anyone was watching and gave a damn. Upstairs, she ate at the kitchen table, reading her mail and drinking a beer straight from the bottle. There was a message on the machine from Defino, left before he knew that she would not be in. Nothing else.

As she finished eating, she remembered her order to call the whip and she dialed his beeper. He called back about five minutes later and she assured him she was safe and had not been followed to D.C.

"They get anything out of the super?" she asked when he had finished his questions.

"The super? Oh, the Fifty-sixth Street building. He flew the coop."

She stifled an obscenity. "We should've taken him in on Friday."

"Don't beat yourself up. Even if he could've told us someone was in that apartment, he wouldn't know the real name. He probably had a deal with the guy, some money off the books to keep quiet."

"Somebody must've wanted Soderberg dead real bad."

"Looks like it. Take it easy, Jane. You've had a big day. We'll talk tomorrow."

She called Defino and apologized for disappearing without notice. He didn't seem bothered, but he told her again about Derek.

"We really missed the boat on that," he said.

"We'll talk about it tomorrow. I'm briefing the whip first thing."

"See you in the morning."

Fatigue hit her the moment she put the phone down. The day had started too early, and as far as she was concerned it was ending now. She tossed the wrappers from the sandwich into the garbage, rinsed out the beer bottle, and got ready for bed.

The first thing Captain Graves did was explain to MacHovec and Defino that it had been his idea not to say where Jane was going, that it had been a vacation day and that anything she had learned was incidental if not accidental. That said, he turned the floor over to Jane, who recounted the previous day's interviews with Lieutenant MacPhail and Tina Caffrey.

They then talked about the missing Derek, an apparent dead end. Then Graves said, "What've you been up to, Sean?"

MacHovec had a file with him. "Looking into employees in the offices at One PP where Jane had her travel plans OK'd. So far nothing stands out, but I'll keep looking."

"Where else do we go?"

"I think we have to bring in Carl Johnson," Jane said. "He's the only person we know who was involved in whatever work Caffrey was doing. I talked to him Friday night and got almost nothing. I think we have to be tougher on him."

"Let's go," Defino said.

Graves asked Jane for the details of the Friday-night interview, then sent them on their way.

Jane and Defino prepared for their visit to Carl Johnson by calling Midtown North and asking for an RMP car, radio motor patrol. The desk officer had the sector car team call her directly. They assured her there were no back doors to the apartments and no freight or service elevators. If Johnson was home when they got there, he would not be able to escape through a back exit. A sector car would meet them at the apartment house to transport Johnson to the station house. They did not call Johnson's number first.

They estimated their time of arrival, and the sector cop said he would be there.

"Looks like you scored in Washington where Mac-Hovec failed," Defino said when they were out on the street, taking an opportunity to jab at MacHovec.

"I think I talked to a different guy. It was just good

luck. The daughter really knew nothing. She wanted a father, but what she got was someone who wrote checks because if he didn't, the navy would take it out of his pay."

"You think this guy Johnson was in the navy, too?"

"No idea. Whatever they were doing, they started after Caffrey left the navy. Maybe long after. QX wasn't in business that long when Caffrey took his fall. But nothing Johnson said really held together. Why would you disband a company that was trying to sell some kind of technological device if the marketing man dies? If the brains of the company dies, that's another thing."

They were down in the subway, waiting for the first train that would take them uptown and then over to the West Side. They had thought about a taxi but decided the subway would be faster. They rode the Lex up to Broadway-Lafayette and changed for a B, which took them over to Central Park West. At Seventy-second Street, they got off and walked back to the Sixties, as Jane had on Friday night. The sector car was already there, parked off CPW so it wouldn't be visible from the lobby.

They identified themselves to the sector car uniforms and went inside. The doorman was a new face and seemed concerned.

They pulled their shields and ID and Jane said, "We're going up to Carl Johnson's apartment. Don't let them know we're on our way."

"I'll keep an eye out," one of the uniforms said, entering behind them.

"He's not up there," the doorman said.

"Is his wife?" Jane asked.

"I think so."

"Good enough."

Upstairs, Mrs. Johnson's feet pounded toward the door. She looked through the peephole and opened up. "What do you want?" she said belligerently, looking at Jane.

"We want to talk to your husband, Mrs. Johnson."

"He's not here."

"Where is he?"

"He's gone. He's left New York."

"Give us an address."

"I don't know where he is," the woman said angrily, raising her voice. "Now get out."

"I'm afraid we can't leave until we find out where your husband is."

"Well, you won't find out from me." She tried to close the door in their faces, but she was no match for Defino.

"You're not cooperating," he said, pushing back on the door to keep it open.

She relented and backed away. "What do you want from him?" she asked. "Why can't you leave him alone?"

"He has evidence in a homicide," Jane said calmly.

"He doesn't know anything about that." The woman sounded as though she was under a good deal of stress. A little pushing and she might snap.

Jane didn't want her snapping. She wanted access to Carl Johnson. "May we sit and talk?"

"I have nothing to say." Mrs. Johnson pulled the door all the way open and let them in. Then she shut the door behind them, turning the bolt.

They stood in the foyer, waiting for her to invite them in.

"Go ahead," she said to Jane. "You know the way. You were here a couple of days ago asking your questions. You ruined my life, you—" She stopped talking and led the way to the sunken living room. "Sit wherever you want."

Jane noticed that many of the beautiful crystal and ceramic objects were gone. The Johnsons were packing. They were leaving New York. "Where are you moving to?" she asked.

Mrs. Johnson dropped into a chair. She was wearing a loose housedress, a floral print on cotton. She looked haggard and miserable. "I'm not going anywhere."

"Where is your husband, Mrs. Johnson?"

"I don't know." The voice was too loud. "I told you that the first time you asked. He isn't here. That's all I can tell you."

"We need to talk to him, Mrs. Johnson."

"Then find him."

Defino stood and went to a window. He looked out for a moment, then turned back to Jane. "She isn't cooperating and we don't have much time. Let's take her down to the station house."

"What?" Mrs. Johnson said. "I haven't done anything."

"You're withholding vital information, ma'am. Get your coat and let's go. We have a car downstairs."

"No!" the woman said.

"Now," Defino retorted. "Let's go now."

"You can't do this to me."

"Yes, we can."

"I have to be here."

"In case he calls?" Jane said.

The woman nodded.

"When will he call?"

"I don't know."

"Tell us where he is."

She shook her head.

"Give us his cell phone number." It had occurred to Jane that she had one in her bag, and figured most of the population of the country did, too.

"I don't know it."

Then he did have one. "Just tell us how you can reach him and you're off the hook," Jane said.

At that moment the phone rang. Mrs. Johnson ran to the kitchen, Defino right behind her. Jane followed and stood in the doorway as the woman picked up the phone, and Defino held it so they could both hear.

It was a short conversation, and when Mrs. Johnson put the phone down, she was in tears. "You have no right to invade my life this way," she wailed.

"It was a friend," Defino said, walking out of the kitchen. He looked at his watch. "We're running out of time. Let's take her in." He was doing a great job of acting.

"Fine with me," Jane said.

"You can't do this," Mrs. Johnson said. "My husband is an honorable man. He doesn't do anything wrong and he never has."

"What's his address and phone number at work?" Defino asked.

"I don't know."

"What's he been doing since QX went out of business?" She shrugged. "He works downtown. That's all I know."

"How do you call him?" Jane asked.

The woman didn't answer. It had to be the cell phone. He had it with him all the time, and his location didn't matter as long as he answered the ring.

"What kind of work does your husband do?" Defino asked.

"He has a job; that's all I know. We live an ordinary life. We have friends and we go to the theater and the ballet. I don't know what you said to him when you were here, but he left the next day and my life has been in turmoil ever since."

"Did your husband suspect that Henry Soderberg's death might be murder?"

"I don't know. I know he was very upset about it. He didn't tell me much about what he was doing, but there was nothing wrong with it."

"Give us your husband's cell phone number," Jane said.

Mrs. Johnson looked at both of them. She took a tissue from the pocket of her dress and wiped her cheeks. Then she picked up a pen and wrote something on a small pad of paper. She ripped the top sheet off and handed it to Jane.

"Does he answer when you call?"

"Always."

"Give me a minute," Defino said, and Jane took Mrs. Johnson out of the kitchen. He would be calling the telephone company now for the ownership of the cell phone.

If it didn't belong to Johnson himself, it might give some indication of whom he worked for.

They sat in the living room, neither of them saying a word. After a few minutes, Defino came back, holding a piece of paper from the kitchen pad.

"Our Mr. Johnson works for the U.S. Department of Commerce and has a pool phone. It's paid for by the communications section of the department. They don't have a record of his name as a subscriber, so I guess he just takes what they give him."

Mrs. Johnson's eyes widened as she listened. "How did you find that out?"

"We call him?" Defino said, ignoring her and addressing Jane.

She nodded. "We'd like you to call your husband," she said. "Is he in Washington today?"

"I think so."

"Dial his number."

They went back to the kitchen and Mrs. Johnson dialed. Defino walked over to listen. Johnson must have picked up on the second or third ring, because his wife began talking. "The police are here," she said. "They want to know where you are. They want to take me down to the precinct."

There was an exchange of conversation, and Defino took the phone from her. "Mr. Johnson, this is Detective Defino of the Special Homicide Squad. Detective Bauer and I want to talk to you concerning the murder of Wallace Caffrey, aka Henry Soderberg."

Defino walked the phone over to Jane and let her listen. Johnson responded to Defino's statement with silence, realizing that the police knew something they should not have known. "Leave my wife alone," he said finally. "She doesn't know anything about my work and she can't help you. I'll come back voluntarily if I have your assurance that you'll let her be."

They worked out a deal over the phone. Johnson would return to New York on the next plane he could get on. He would call Jane's phone every half hour until he was on the plane. He wanted his wife at the airport when they met him. They promised to have her there.

Finally he spoke to his wife again and outlined the agreement. She accepted it and Defino reiterated his own acceptance.

They decided to stay with Mrs. Johnson until they heard that Johnson was on his way and knew which of the three airports he would be landing at. Then they would take the woman to the airport.

"Shouldn't be too long," Defino said, "if he heads out to the airport right away. Hope he comes to LaGuardia. It's a bitch of a ride out to JFK." The tension was gone from his voice. The act was over. They had succeeded.

"Maybe we'll find something out," Jane said. "It's about time."

[27]

CARL JOHNSON MUST have been nervous, because he stuck to the every-half-hour schedule of calls they had imposed on him, and he was on a plane in less than an hour. It was due in at LaGuardia at one-thirty, and they started out for the airport as soon as they got the word.

They were driven in two radio cars, one from Midtown North and one from the Two-oh. Taking two cars from one precinct would leave them short, so they stole a car from the Two-oh for the ride out to the airport. One would later return Mrs. Johnson to her home; the other would take Jane, Defino, and Johnson to the Centre Street office. The plane was only ten minutes late, and Johnson was the second person off. When he saw his wife, he hurried toward her and embraced her. She was sobbing, and he comforted her until she had calmed herself. He had no luggage, so they walked out to the roadway and got into their separate cars.

They drove one behind the other till they exited the Triboro Bridge in Manhattan. Then Mrs. Johnson's car followed One Hundred Twenty-fifth Street across town to the West Side and Jane's car traveled on the FDR south.

The three people in the backseat said little, while the uniformed men in the front kidded around and gossiped. At Centre Street, they sent the sector car back uptown and went upstairs to the only small empty room on the floor, where MacHovec joined them. Johnson called his wife first and made sure she was safely home. Satisfied, he sat at the table and waited.

"What kind of work were you and Henry Soderberg doing at QX Electronics?" Jane asked.

"I spoke to my supervisor before I left D.C.," Johnson said, "and he's given me the OK to tell you what this is all about. May I give you some background?"

"Give us all the background you want. We need to understand what the three of you were doing that would get Soderberg murdered."

"American companies do business with many countries of the world that by law are restricted in what materials can be shipped to them. I am talking about munitions, technology, weapons systems, anything that could be used against the United States."

"Makes sense," Defino said.

"It does, but there are overzealous American companies that don't want to adhere to the rules because there's big money in shipping prohibited technology to overseas buyers. Our job was twofold. One part was to see how honest these companies are and to prevent them from exporting illegal materials. The other side of it was a sting operation. We let it be known that we could obtain and ship the weapons systems used to launch missiles and rockets.

"At one time, those systems would fill a boxcar. Today, because of miniaturization, those chips, circuits, and software fit in a suitcase, making it easy to hand over a whole weapons system to someone walking down the street."

"That's pretty scary," Defino said. "So Soderberg wasn't selling electronic equipment."

"Actually, much of the time he was out trying to buy it."

"What made Soderberg the man for this kind of job?" MacHovec asked from his end of the table.

"In the military, his specialty was electronic warfare systems. He started in communications, encrypted systems, and later countermeasures. He was an investigator and information gatherer. His onboard experience with the working pieces made him the ideal player for this business. And he played the part remarkably well. He was very believable." Johnson closed his eyes for a moment. He looked exhausted, as though he'd been up since Friday night trying to fix the trouble that Jane had uncovered. "Do you suppose I could have a cup of coffee?"

"Sure." Jane stood and took orders. She came back with Annie, each carrying two cups and the requisite extras.

Johnson removed the lid from his container and sipped without adding anything. He took a deep breath and sipped again. "I haven't slept much," he said. "I didn't know until you visited on Friday that Henry had been murdered, although it was a possibility we discussed when he died. Nothing happened after his death, but if you're stirring up the waters, there's no telling what could happen now. Anyway . . ." He drank some more coffee.

"What Henry was trying to do was play the part of a middleman who was buying weapons systems for an Asian country. He wanted to see whether the seller was obeying the law by refusing to sell. Since the potential sellers were private companies, that happens to be the responsibility of the Department of Commerce, and that's who we all worked for."

"Commerce sounds so harmless," Defino said.

"It is harmless."

"But you set up a shell corporation to get the job done."

"That was the easiest way. We had an address, an office, a phone, an e-mail address. You could fax us, talk to us, make appointments with us. We were real people doing a real job, just the job wasn't what it seemed to be. Henry went out and tried to buy systems for a country we could not export it to. When he found a company that was willing to break the law, he worked the case to a point where we had solid evidence, names, commitments, and then turned it over to the department, and they took it from there."

"Were you aware that Henry Soderberg was an assumed identity?" Jane asked.

"I had some suspicions but we didn't discuss it. When Henry didn't come in to work and didn't call in, I called him at his apartment several times, but there was no answer. Finally I called the police and reported him missing. They got back to me after a day or so and said he had died in a fall down some stairs in his building. I called our supervisor in Washington and told him what had happened. It was at that point that I learned Henry's real name as well as his wishes for the disposition of his body. I had the body sent to a funeral home in New York and from there to one in Arlington. It was Henry's wish that the Navy League take care of his interment. I let them know that Wallace Caffrey's body would be arriving under the name of Henry Soderberg."

"Why would he need this identity to do his job?"

"What I was told when I reported Henry's death was strictly on a need-to-know basis, and I've never learned anything further, although I'm sure the department knows all there is to know about Henry. He mentioned he had done some undercover work for another branch of the government prior to our work at Commerce. I don't know the nature of that work, but I believe it was more dangerous and more secret than what we were doing. He could have worked for the CIA, but that's just conjecture. Whatever he did, it's my belief that he kept the name he assumed for that job. What probably happened is that someone at Commerce knew someone at Henry's old job who recommended him for what we were doing. There's a kind of old-boys' network that goes into play when you're looking for an operative."

"What became of Ray Kellner, the third man in your office?" Jane asked.

"When I reported Henry's death, I was told to begin closing down the operation. Ray was transferred to Washington, and he's been working there since we closed down QX." He reached for a pad on the table and wrote on it, then pushed it across to Jane.

"What country or company were you dealing with at the time of Soderberg's death?" Defino asked.

"Several. There were always a number of deals going on at any one time. It wasn't a sequential thing. I had some records in my apartment until Detective Bauer showed up on Friday. When I left on Saturday morning I took them with me, and they are now at Commerce. But I looked them over after your visit." He glanced at Jane. "I think we were working on deals leading to North Korea and China."

"Stings," MacHovec said.

"Stings, yes. But Henry himself was attempting to buy from at least one American company that is no longer in existence."

"Was he personally involved in the Korean and Chinese stings?" Jane asked.

"He was. He had met with a representative of each of those countries at least once."

"Where did he meet them?"

"It depended. Sometimes in a park, sometimes at a coffee shop. He didn't go to fancy restaurants. I saw his vouchers."

"Did he carry a weapon?" Jane asked.

"I don't believe so. But he had been a SEAL in the navy, and that time never wore off. He kept himself in top physical shape at a local martial-arts dojo. I picked him up once and had a chance to watch his workout. It was intense and pretty scary. Which makes it so odd that someone got the best of him."

"Did Henry Soderberg tell you that someone who lived in his building was murdered?"

"Yes. He came in one day and said he had found the body at the bottom of the stairs, just inside the front door."

"Did he say anything else? Did he think that murder had anything to do with him?"

"Not at all. He said it looked as though the man had been followed inside at night and had probably been killed for his money."

"Except no money was taken," Defino said.

"He must not have known that."

"And the man who was murdered had a strong physical resemblance to Henry Soderberg," Jane said.

"I see." Johnson's forehead furrowed. He didn't come across as a good actor, more of an honest and concerned man. "What you're saying is that the victim of that attack was meant to be Henry."

"That's what we think."

"They waited a long time to get Henry."

"The police were in and out of that building for months, investigating the other murder. Whoever killed Soderberg waited till they were finished with their investigation so that no one would make the connection."

"And they made it look like an accident."

"Right. With no police investigation."

"So no connection." He drank some more coffee, then stuffed his napkin into the empty container. "Then what you really want to know is not who we were dealing with when Henry died, but who we were dealing with when the first man died."

"You got it," Defino said.

"And that was months earlier."

"About six months. You have any recollections?"

"There was a deal with two Chinese nationals; I remember that. Both of them met with Henry; I never did. He called them operatives, I know that. Henry went to an agreed destination with a suitcase of what was supposed to be the chips and circuits of a weapons system. He had worked on the deal for some time, and Washington had decided to close it down. The men came with money. They were arrested by the FBI on the spot. End of story as far as we were concerned."

"Why was it the end?" MacHovec asked from his distant position. "Wasn't there a trial? Didn't you turn over evidence?"

"We turned over everything we had. We never heard anything more about it. Maybe they had diplomatic immunity. Maybe the government made a deal and got them back to China. I couldn't tell you."

"Maybe they were madder 'n hell and got someone to kill Soderberg," Jane said.

"You may be right." He looked troubled, as though trying to decide whether to add something. "Let me tell you a little more about it," he said finally. "Henry said that when he met with the two operatives, he noticed someone on a park bench nearby."

"Man or woman?" MacHovec asked.

"That's just it; he wasn't sure. It was a person, a shadow in the dark on a bench. When the FBI took the two men into custody, Henry glanced over at the bench and saw that the person was gone, so he took off to find whoever it was. He was unsuccessful, but that didn't end it. Henry was a tiger. Give him the scent of blood and you couldn't stop him. He contacted people he knew in Washington, put out bait, did everything he could to track down whoever had observed the scene in the park that night. He was sure that person was either a backup for the operatives or an observer to keep them honest with the money, but definitely part of the Chinese team. I would estimate it wasn't long after that that the man in Henry's building was killed."

"Did he keep after this guy after Quill was killed?" Defino asked.

"Till the day he fell down the stairs. And he told me at the end that he was close. He said he could smell blood."

MacHovec sighed loudly. It was one of his habits that made Defino ready to kill. Defino shot him a quick look, as though telling him to keep his mouth shut, but MacHovec had learned to ignore Defino.

"Mr. Johnson," Jane said, "did Henry Soderberg ever tell you there might be someone living in what was thought to be an empty apartment on the top floor of his building?"

At that moment there was a knock on the door and Annie stuck her head in. "Sorry to bother, but he says it's important. It's Detective Bracken."

Jane looked at her watch. "Let's take a break. I'll pick it up." She returned to the office and pressed the button next to the flashing light. "Jane Bauer."

"Jane, Charlie Bracken. We've located Derek, the super."

"Is he alive?"

There was a pause. "Yeah. What did you expect?"

"I didn't know what to expect. Charlie, we're interviewing an important witness. Can I get back to you?"

"Sure. I'll keep him here. He said he's hungry so I'll fill his face."

"Thanks." That was good news. She hung up and went back to the interview room. On the table her notebook was open to the diagram that she had drawn on the plane, showing the connections between Soderberg and the others in the building where he lived. She looked at it as she sat down: Soderberg and Margaret Rawls, Soderberg and Hutchins, Hutchins and Worthman. She looked up. "Bracken's got Derek," she said.

"Hey, hey," MacHovec said. "Dead or alive?"

"Alive and hungry. Bracken'll hold on to him till we're finished here. Where were we?"

"You asked about someone living on the top floor," Carl Johnson said. "I don't understand the relevance and I don't recall Henry talking about it, but he kept a lot to himself. He always said it was safer that way. Also, that wasn't our job."

"There's a possibility that someone was squatting in the empty apartment on the fourth floor, and when Henry came upstairs to change the lightbulb, the squatter came out and killed him," Jane said.

Johnson seemed to be having difficulty coming to terms with what he was learning. "You think this squatter was staying in that apartment waiting for the chance to kill Henry?"

"That's what we think, Mr. Johnson."

"This is unbelievable. Ray and I were just plain lucky then."

"It looks that way."

"I hope my wife is safe."

Jane hoped so, too. They had left LaGuardia in two cars, and if she was tailed, she assumed the tail would continue to follow her car, but there was a chance it hadn't. There was also a chance another tail had been brought in. "Why don't you call her? You'll feel better."

They waited while he made the call, a brief exchange between husband and wife.

"She's all right. One of the police officers is staying with her till I get there."

"I'm glad to hear it." Jane smiled, feeling better herself. She looked at Defino and MacHovec to see if there was anything else they wanted to ask.

"If you find anything in your files from those Chinese operatives," Defino said, "we'd sure like a look at it."

"I understand. I intend to return to Washington as soon as we've packed and the movers have picked up our things. I'm not leaving my wife alone in this city after what I now know."

"You've been very cooperative, Mr. Johnson. We want to stay in touch."

Johnson took the pad and wrote on it. "These are my numbers. I'll see what's on file when I get back to D.C., but it may take a few days. I'll also have to brief my section chief and get her clearance on some of the files, but if it will help in Henry's case, I don't think she'll object. Now that I see what you're investigating, I'll be glad to do anything I can."

They thanked him and got a car from the Chinatown Precinct to take him home and drop Jane and Defino at Midtown North. It was time to sweat Derek.

28

"It's LIKE THIS," Bracken said. "He decided to run after you talked to him—when was that? Friday?—and he took off. He's a little vague about where he spent the weekend."

"Derek's vague about what he had for lunch," Defino said.

"Anyway, either he got thrown out or it rained on him or whatever story he's telling when you ask him next time, he crept back and went to sleep in his own bed."

"Who found him?" Jane asked.

"Stabile, of all people," Bracken said. "Stabile came down to see what was going on, figuring he'd have to clean the super's apartment out and get another guy, and there was Derek, fast asleep."

They followed Bracken to the interview room, where Derek had put his head down on the table and gone to sleep again. Must have been some pretty sleepless days away, Jane thought. Derek lifted his head with a start, stared at them without comprehension, then gradually seemed to figure out where he was and who these people were.

"Detective," he said.

"Hi, Derek," Jane said in her most cordial voice. "Nice to see you again. We've been looking for you."

"I got scared. I went away for a while."

"Well, I'm glad you're back." She sat across from him and Defino sat next to her.

"Lemme know if you need anything," Bracken said, backing out of the room.

"We have some questions for you," Jane said when the door had closed. "It would really be great if you would answer them truthfully."

"Yeah, OK."

"It's about the apartment on the fourth floor, the one across from Mr. Hutchins's apartment. Someone was living there when Mr. Soderberg fell down the stairs, isn't that right?"

"Yeah, that's right."

"Who was it, Derek?"

He made some faces before he answered, wrinkling his nose, pushing out his lips, squeezing his face into a fake smile, rubbing his ear. "It was a lady," he said finally.

"A woman was living in that apartment?" Defino said.

"A real fine lady, yeah, she lived there for a while."

"Tell us about it."

"She come to me one day, ask me do I have a place in that house. I say yeah, somebody move out and we gonna remodel, you know?"

"Did Mr. Stabile know?"

"No, sir. This just between that lady and me. She just want to be there a little while till she get herself together. She got some problems she gotta work on, you know? So I say, they only work on that apartment durin' the day. You can stay there at night, but gotta be real quiet. Can't let nobody know you're there. That was OK with her. She just wanna stay a coupla weeks."

"When did she move in, Derek?"

"I ain't too good with dates, mister. I couldn't tell you."

"Was it before or after Mr. Quill got killed?"

"It was before. Oh, yeah, it was before, 'cause I told her after they found poor Mr. Quill dead, she gotta get outta there. There was cops all over the place."

"And did she get out?" Jane asked.

"I don't know," Derek said in what seemed to be an honest answer. "I didn't see her for a long time. If she was still stayin' there at night, I couldn't tell ya."

"Before Mr. Quill died, did you see her a lot?"

"No. I never see a lot of her. She ain't there much during the day 'cause the men are working."

"Did she have a key to the apartment?"

"Yeah."

"How did she come and go, Derek?" Jane attempted a smile to make him feel at ease.

"She . . . uh . . . I think she come through the roof."

Jane restrained herself from clapping Defino across the back. They had been asking the goddamn right questions, only they hadn't been getting the right answers. "Can you get down to the street from that roof?"

"Not from that roof exactly, but maybe from the next one."

"You can go from one roof to the other?"

"It ain't hard."

All she had to do was wait for Hutchins to leave for work in the morning and then the coast was clear. She could go up to the roof, connect with another roof, get down to the street, and go about her business. Getting back without being seen by Hutchins would be a little trickier, but apparently she had managed.

"Do you know where she went during the day?"

"No, ma'am."

"Did you ever see her during the day?" Defino asked.

"Sometimes."

"OK, let's go back. She moved in before Mr. Quill got murdered. Is that right?"

"Yeah, I think so."

"And you told her to stay away after the murder because the cops were all over the place."

"Yeah."

"But you don't know if she really moved out."

"I couldn't tell you."

"Did you see her there after the cops were gone?"

"Yeah, I see her sometimes. Like in the street maybe."

"You ever ask her for the key back?" Defino asked.

That question seemed to disturb Derek. He scratched his head and looked around. "I don't remember askin' for it back."

"They change the lock on that door after someone moved in?"

He shrugged. "I wouldn't know, Detective."

"What did this woman look like?"

Derek shrugged again. "I'm no good on faces. She was a nice lady. She was good to me."

"You mean she paid you."

"She gave me a little somethin'."

"Was she black or white?"

"White."

"Was she tall or short?"

"Kind of, you know, in between."

Jane nudged Defino and he sat silent. "Was she my age, Derek?"

"Yeah, maybe. She wasn't no kid."

Thanks, Jane thought. "Was she a thin woman? A heavy woman?"

"Thin," he said right away.

"How did she dress?"

He looked confused.

"Did she wear pants or skirts? Did she wear jeans?"

"Pants, like those running pants, you know?"

"Did she have a name, Derek?"

"She told me I could call her Chickie."

"Chickie."

"Yes, ma'am."

Jane sat back. Defino said, "When is the last time you saw her or talked to her, Derek?"

"Long time ago. I couldn't tell you when. It's a long time."

"It's been a long day," Jane said. It was her turn to let out a long sigh.

"You gotta believe it. You want to wrap this up?"

"I think so. Where are you going now, Derek?"

"Back to my place."

"On Fifty-sixth Street?"

"That's the only place I got."

"You going to stay there?"

"Yeah."

"Thanks for talking to us." Whatever it was worth. "If you ever see this woman again, I want you to let us know."

He promised fervently and they let him go. Bracken came in and they sat around for a while, talking about the surprise. Who could have believed it was a woman?

"You think she hung around those six months waiting to get Soderberg?" Bracken asked.

"She could've been watching the building to see if you and Otis Wright were there. Maybe she had another place across the street or down the block that she spent the rest of her time. I gotta believe this was a contract job that she flubbed the first time around," Defino said.

"You know who hired her?"

"Not yet, but we're moving in."

"Let's move out," Jane said. "It's been a long day."

Defino was very agreeable.

She sent Defino home and logged him out when she got to Centre Street. MacHovec, who had already gone home, left notes that he had reached Ray Kellner and he had nothing new to offer, but he confirmed a lot of what Carl Johnson had said. Another note said that a Chinese female worked in one of the offices Jane had visited for her travel approval, the office in Hack's domain. She tucked that one in her bag.

McElroy was on his way out when Jane came by, so she knocked on Captain Graves's open door. "Hey, Cap, we talked to Carl Johnson and Derek," she said.

"Come on in."

She sat down and started with the Johnson interview.

"So we have someone possibly observing Soderberg's meet."

"Man or woman, Soderberg wasn't sure. Now Derek tells us the person squatting in the empty apartment was a woman." She dropped her notebook with the link chart faceup on his desk. On the bottom of the page she had written, *Park bench?*

"A *woman.*"

"About my age, if you can believe Derek, thin, white." She brought him up-to-date.

Graves looked down at the chart and nodded. "So no one may have seen her if she never went up and down the stairs. If you passed a woman in the street, you wouldn't think twice. Maybe she rigged a rope upstairs to swing down and give Soderberg a hard push. You think this Derek could work with a sketch artist?"

"Captain, I don't think he's reliable at all. Maybe what he told us about this woman was true, but you put him with an artist, you're as likely to get Marilyn Monroe as a contract killer."

"So we have a woman who was there four, four and a half years ago. She could be anywhere, any country, as far as that goes. Can't say it looks promising."

"I'll tell MacHovec to check around for known female contract killers. Maybe he'll come up with something. Can't be a very long list. We can also look for help from the Feds on this one. Caffrey was one of their guys. Maybe they'll open up the special files for us."

"Let's hope so." He looked troubled. To become a deputy inspector and trade his bars for a gold leaf, he needed results, and searching for faceless killers wasn't the way to go. "Let's keep at it. Something will turn up." He gave her the upbeat smile and she assured him they had no thoughts of slacking off.

"You missed a call," Annie said as they crossed paths outside the whip's office.

"Who from?"

"Don't know. A man."

Back at her office, Jane cleaned up her desk and went home.

She walked home from Centre Street, feeling the need to stretch her legs. It didn't occur to her until she was halfway there that if she was being tailed, he was getting some unexpected exercise himself, or was it herself? She didn't care; she just wanted to think. Plenty of people knew which cases had been selected for the squad, but she couldn't get away from the fact that someone knew she was making the trip to Omaha. And a group under Hack's supervision knew firsthand. She had known the minute she heard MacHovec mention his name that her love for him had not receded, not diminished, not been replaced by anyone else, better or worse. He had always been her model of the honest cop who had made it close to the top without cheating, without pulling strings, without begging for favors or accepting them when they were offered. He was guilty, if that was the right word, of engaging in a long-term extramarital affair. He would have left his wife and married her if Jane had let him. But she had too many issues in her own life—and he was one of the few people who knew just about everything—that prevented her from agreeing to his wish to divorce. A part of her sympathized with Hack's wife. Another part wanted his children to grow up with two parents.

As she reached her front door, her thoughts had segued to the child she had borne and given up. Maybe it was true that everything in a person's life was interconnected, but the flowchart that was her life was too complicated to follow anymore. Lisa Angelino. She liked everything she knew about her: her name, her looks, her letter, and even the crinkly paper on which it had been written. The notion that she had a child had grown on her these past two weeks, even when she wasn't thinking about it. She had known all her adult life, and especially since she became involved with Hack, that she would never have children of her own. Her parents had expressed sadness that she had not married. But Lisa's letter had changed everything. Some of the essence of Jane Bauer had been passed on to a lovely young woman, and Jane was enchanted with the idea.

Still, that didn't mean she wanted to establish a relationship with this girl, certainly not a close one that would involve flying back and forth, Christmas celebrations, vacations together. The truth was, she didn't know what she wanted, and part of the problem was Paul Thurston.

Lisa had written that she wanted to know who her parents were. Not her mother—her natural parents. Jane thought she knew where to find Paul. The question was whether she wanted to. She had given birth to a child whom he believed she had aborted. He had gone on to marry and have a family of his own. Was it fair to saddle him with this knowledge? She felt that it wasn't. But what if the twenty years had changed his outlook? He understood better than Jane the value of parenthood.

Should he not be given the opportunity—the choice—to decide whether to declare himself Lisa's father?

Upstairs in her warm apartment, Jane checked the messages on her machine. "Jane, it's Mike Fromm. You've been out of the office most of the day, so I thought I'd get you at home. John's doing well. I can't say the same for Hutchins, but he's still alive and drifts in and out of consciousness. He's tried to talk but we can't make much of what he's said. Give me a call at home when you have a chance."

Maybe in an hour, she thought. She felt cheered that Hutchins was still alive. Maybe there was a chance he would survive, that he would even recover most of his faculties and have a life.

There were no other messages. She sat in her favorite chair in the living room and brooded. Mike Fromm was an attractive man, and she had felt the familiar draw of sex from the moment they started talking. It surprised her a little now that the same draw still existed when she thought of Hack. Having lived a monogamous life, having been satisfied with whoever was her current partner, being pulled in two directions was a novel experience.

It was Hack she wanted, and she knew that. If Hack was somehow involved in this business, in these homicides, it would destroy her. It surprised her how much she wanted to talk to him, to hear his voice, perhaps to meet with him and justify it as business.

She got up from the chair, went into the bedroom, and put a pair of jeans on. Then she made dinner, took care of the dishes, and dialed Mike's number at home.

"Hey, good to hear from you. You're not spending much time in your office these days," he said.

"There's a lot of fieldwork on this one. Tell me about Hutchins."

"There isn't much to tell. He's out of it most of the time, but he wakes up every so often. Cory's with him as much as she can. She's the one who heard him say it. Something about Chinese."

"Chinese? As in someone from China?"

"You got it. It was her impression he was telling her about the guy who kidnapped him."

"Mike, this really fits with what we've learned."

"The Chinese are involved in this?" He sounded incredulous.

"Some Chinese people may be. We don't have any names at this point. Did he say anything else? A plate number would be nice."

Mike laughed. "We thought we were lucky to get two syllables out of him, even if they didn't mean much. I don't know what he remembers, and I don't know if he'll remember any more as time goes on. He's still critical. He may go to sleep one day and not wake up."

They talked about other things after that, courtship talk, Jane thought, banter that would lead nowhere if they remained a thousand miles apart. He was considering coming east for a vacation. He had been to New York only once before, and that was with his wife before they had any children. It was when the Empire State Building was the tallest building in the world and Central Park was safe to walk through.

"I would want to see you," he said, "if I made the trip."

"I'll be here. I'll show you around. We can go up to the observation deck on the Empire State Building and walk across Central Park. It's fine during the day, and I carry a gun."

"Hey, that sounds like fun—Central Park, I mean."

"You OK with heights?"

"Don't know. I've never been higher than about twenty stories. No, wait a minute. We went to the top of the Empire State Building that time we came. That place still standing?"

Jane laughed again. "Yes, Mike, it's still standing. I'll take you there, too."

"No, I don't think so. That was then; this is now. I like to leave old memories the way they were."

She thought about that after she hung up. She could see Paul Thurston in a bathing suit and shirt, his legs long and hard, the hair gold against his tanned skin. Whatever he looked like now, it would be different, as she was different. Did she want to superimpose a new memory over the old one?

Shit. She went over to the fireplace and laid a fire, hoping she was doing it as well as the last time. What she wanted was Hack. Between moving and changing squads, flying to Omaha and taking the train to Washington, she had convinced herself that she was over him. She knew now that she wasn't. She was over Paul; she was sure of that. Twenty years was a hell of a long time. She had had better and she had had worse since then, but she was over him. She didn't want to talk to him, though, either in person or over the phone.

She lit the newspaper at the bottom of the fireplace and watched it catch, watched the small flame grow, move upward, ignite the kindling. Her face was warm. Sex was what fires were all about, and sex was what she was thinking about. She hadn't slept with a man since the last time she saw Hack, and that was more than a month ago. She sat on the floor in front of the fireplace, her knees up and her arms around them. Hack would like the fireplace; it had been her first thought when she saw it.

She sat that way for a while. Then, becoming too warm, she scrambled to her feet and went to the kitchen, where she had left the mail. An envelope from her future company was waiting to be opened. She tore it open and scanned the sheet inside. They were looking forward to her arrival; was there any chance she could start earlier than they had agreed upon? There were several workshops she would need to attend in the weeks after she started. Please give us a call, let us know, looking forward . . .

Why did that job suddenly seem so far away? She read the letter again and dropped it on the table, all the bad

old habits she had sworn off returning in this lovely,
clean apartment. She got a beer from the refrigerator and
went back to the living room and the blazing fire. She
curled up on the sofa and drank and watched for a long
time. She wanted to call Hack, get it all out in the open,
whether something funny was going on in his office. She
knew his beeper number as well as she knew her father's
number. Eventually she took the phone over to the sofa
and called her dad. He was glad to hear from her, feeling
pretty good, eating Madeleine's leftovers.

She felt better when she hung up.

[29]

"No shit," MacHovec said. "They sure he said
'Chinese'?"

"That's what the girlfriend thinks she heard."

"So we gotta pull a Chinaman out of a hat and then
work backward."

"Or something," Jane said. "I've got an idea. You guys
keep working. I have to make a call."

In the middle of the night it had come to her. It
was very simple, too simple really, but it was worth a
phone call. Mr. Stabile's secretary answered and put her
through right away.

"Detective Bauer." He sounded happy to hear her
voice. "Have you spoken to Derek?"

"Yes, I did."

"Derek's a good person, Detective. He just doesn't know how to cope when life throws him a curve ball."

"I'm sure you're right. He gave us some useful information. I'd like to follow up on it with you."

"By all means."

"The apartment on the fourth floor, Four B, I think that is, the one on the right . . . who lives there now?"

"That would be . . . just a minute; let me get this exactly right . . . that's Ms. Olivia Dean. Very good tenant, very quiet, pays her rent on time." He was starting to sound like Derek: his world was filled with only the most wonderful people.

"When did she move in?"

"Everyone in the building moved in after the renovation."

"Was she the first tenant in that apartment?"

"Yes. She's been with us for several years."

"How old a woman is she?"

"Well, now . . ." His voice told her the question bordered on impertinence. "I suppose in her forties. Give or take."

"What does she look like?"

"Uh, brown hair, slim."

"Where does she work?"

"At the time she moved in . . . just a moment . . . she worked downtown for some place called Hazelwood Industries." He dictated an address on Walker Street, a street that had its short run from Canal and Centre to Broadway at Church. She could walk there in a few minutes. "But I couldn't swear she still works there. I don't insist that tenants keep me posted on where they work, as long as they pay their rent on time. She always does."

He gave her the phone number he had on file for her office and Jane called it. A woman answered and said she had never heard of Hazelwood Industries or Olivia Dean. They had had their phone number for a few years and they were not on Walker Street.

"Gordon," Jane said as she hung up, "feel like a little stroll over to Walker Street?"

"Sure." He was up from behind his desk before she had a chance to explain.

On the way down in the elevator, she presented her very weak theory that the woman who had squatted in 4B might have decided to stay on after Soderberg was dead. She wasn't a suspect; it would never occur to Derek that she had pushed Soderberg to his death, and maybe she just liked the building, the more so after the renovation.

"Anything's possible," Defino said flatly. "I wonder if Derek's holding back on us."

They went north to Walker and turned left. Crossing Lafayette, Jane noted the opening of yet another Irish pub at the corner of Cortlandt Alley, a tiny street from old New York. The building they wanted was just off Broadway, a textile company on the ground floor. Soon young people with a lot of money would claim the businesses and apartments upstairs for residential lofts. In the meantime, there was no Hazelwood listed in the dingy foyer. But there was a bicycle chained to a metal rack near the mailboxes. They walked into the ground-floor shop, treading on a floor that must have been laid a hundred years ago.

"Help ya?" the rotund man in glasses behind the counter called.

"We're looking for Hazelwood Industries," Jane said. "They're supposed to be at this address."

"Never heard of 'em."

"How long have you been here?"

"Thirty-seven going on thirty-eight years. I'm Eddie."

"And no Hazelwood anywhere in the building?"

"No, ma'am." He had just taken a look at their shields and he was being polite. "But there was a place here a coupla years ago, one of those P.O. box places. The address is Suite one-two-three, but that's really a box number, know what I mean?"

"So Hazelwood could have gotten its mail here and had its offices somewhere else."

"If they had any offices to speak of."

"You remember when the box number place was here?" Defino asked.

"They left about three, four years ago. They were here for a few years."

"Thanks for your help." He wrote down Eddie's name and phone number and they left. Out on the street he said, "I'm liking it better."

"Me too. I think we should pay a call on Ms. Olivia Dean."

Up on Fifty-sixth Street, Olivia Dean was not at home. Jane said she would go back up tonight, but before they left they knocked on the door to the apartment Jerry Hutchins had once lived in.

An older man, looking sleepy, opened the door.

"I'm Detective Bauer; this is Detective Defino," Jane said as they held their IDs up. The man leaned forward to look at them closely. "We wanted to ask you about your neighbor across the hall."

"Never see her."

"How long have you lived here?"

"Three years, four."

"Do you know what she looks like?"

"She's a woman, 'bout this big"—he held his hand about four feet from the floor—"that's all I know. She do something?"

"We just need to ask her some questions," Defino said.

"I never see her," the man said, "maybe once a month, maybe less. I don't remember the last time I saw her. Not for a while."

They thanked him and headed back to the office.

"Fits with what Derek said," Jane said as they walked to the subway. "Maybe she still swings up and down from the roof."

"Like a monkey," Defino said. "So where does she go?

Think she spends her days in a P.O. box on Walker Street?"

"As long as she spends her nights in apartment Four B, we'll find her."

After lunch Stabile called. "Detective Bauer," he said, sounding somewhat tentative, "you remember I told you that Olivia Dean always paid her rent right on time?"

"I remember."

"Well, this is very strange. I was looking through the receipts a little while ago and her check hasn't come in yet. The first of the month was last week."

"Is her lease up?"

"Not at all. It has months to run. I can't imagine what's happened. I tried to call her a little while ago but she's not home. I always have her check by the second or third at the latest."

"I appreciate your calling. If the check comes in, would you give me a call?"

"Absolutely. I wonder what's happened."

"Maybe she had to go out of town on business and she forgot about the rent."

"But it's unusual. Well, I won't keep you."

Jane passed the word along to Defino.

"Interesting. This is looking nice, very nice. Someone tipped her off that we're looking into the Soderberg death, and she's off and running."

"I wonder if we could get a warrant," Jane said, almost to herself.

"MacHovec, you check out this Olivia Dean?"

"Did it while you were out this morning. Big fat zero. Of course, a couple of prints from her apartment might change all that."

"It's pretty thin to get a warrant," Jane said. "We've got nothing but vague guesses. I'll run up there tonight and knock on her door. This'll keep till morning."

She sat thinking about it. It had been such a far-out possibility, that the woman who squatted in the apartment had eventually moved in legally, that she was hesitant to go out on a limb. Still, they told McElroy about it and he took it very seriously. When they got back to their office, Mike Fromm called.

"Got something you're gonna love," he said.

"Hutchins?"

"No. That's still touch and go. I went out to the airport and did some low-tech investigating. I may have found Hutchins's Chinaman."

"Mike, that's fantastic."

"I got the rental car gals to dig deep in their memories and then in their records. Just something we old guys still know how to do. A man with an Asian face and a Chinese name rented a car the day you arrived in Omaha."

"How did he pay for it?"

"With a credit card, if you can believe it." He read off the details. "Gave a New York address and a New York driver's license, for what it's worth. And there's more. He returned the car the day we found Hutchins."

"Fantastic."

"Anyway, it looks like his name is Chong Wang." He spelled it out. "And his address is on Walker Street. I thought New York was all numbers. Where did Walker come from?"

"Walker Street in New York?" She suddenly had the attention of the men in her office.

"That's right." He gave the number and said it could be something slightly different. The girl at the car rental had put the pink carbon copy of the rental contract through the copier and it wasn't as clear as he had hoped. But one of the numbers he speculated on was the address of Hazelwood Industries.

"Mike, I know the place. We were just there this morning. It's a street in downtown New York, down below where the numbers run. I think we may really have something."

"Well, I'm glad to hear it. I'll see if I can get a better copy of this and fax or mail it to you. And in the meantime, we'll go over the car, although I don't expect much. It's been washed and rented out since he brought it back."

"It would be great to have a fingerprint."

"We'll do our best."

She hung up and closed her eyes and took a deep breath. "Oh, sweet Jesus, we may be onto something."

McElroy said he would try for a warrant on the basis of the connection between Olivia Dean and Chong Wang. MacHovec called the Fifth Precinct station house and arranged to have a couple of sector cars meet Jane and Defino at the Walker Street address. Then they took off.

Eddie was in the same place in the ground-floor store. "You're the cops wanted to know about the P.O. box place."

"Right," Jane said. "Now we want to know if a Chinese man lives or works somewhere in this building."

"Chinese?"

"Yes."

"I thought he was a Jap."

"His name is Wang," Jane said.

"I didn't ever know his name, but I see him all the time, going up and down the stairs. Imagine that. He's Chinese. Goes to show."

"You ever talk to him?"

"Nah. He's always in a hurry. Rushes in, rushes out. That's his bike out there."

Defino looked out the door. "The one chained to the rail?"

"Yeah. He takes that sometimes. Sometimes he doesn't. I haven't seen him for a while."

"You know which apartment is his?"

Eddie screwed up his face. "Funny you should ask. I think he lives where that P.O. box place was. How do you like that for coincidences?"

"I like it," Jane said. "Which one is it?"

"Second floor on the right at the top of the stairs. But I don't think he's there."

"Thanks," they said together.

The sector cops were in place, covering the back door, the front, and the fire escape.

"We gotta get this bike looked at," Defino said. "It should have his prints all over it."

"Unless he wears leather gloves for driving. You ready to go up?"

"Let's do it."

They knocked on the unmarked door, standing back on either side. There was no answer and no sound inside. They knocked and called, but there was nothing.

"Stay here," Jane said. "Let me go up the fire escape and see if I can get a look inside." She was down the stairs in a second.

One of the uniforms went up with her, staying low when they reached the window. He slithered to the other side, and Jane leaned over and looked inside. The window was very dirty. A shade was pulled about halfway down and there were no curtains. No lights were on inside. She could make out some furniture, a phone, a table, a couple of chairs. It seemed to be an all-purpose room without a bed, but one could be out of sight around a corner.

"Looks empty," the uniform said.

" 'Fraid so. He might be sleeping. Let's see if he hears anything." She rapped on the glass with her high school ring. There was no response. "Let's go," she said.

Defino met her downstairs. "Crime Scene's coming for the bike. A couple of uniforms'll stick around till they get here."

"Pray for prints," Jane said.

He looked at his watch. "Let's see if McElroy can get us another warrant."

[30]

No one likes to ask a judge for a warrant when he's at home sleeping or having dinner with friends or enjoying a ball game. McElroy had had time to get a request for a warrant to search Olivia Dean's apartment to a friendly judge, but it was too late, he thought, to try for a second one late in the afternoon. They would get the paperwork together and try first thing in the morning. In the meantime, they arranged for the building on Walker Street to be watched overnight.

A crime scene detective called the team just before five to say there were beautiful prints on the rubber grips and on the handlebars, and they would be sent over by morning.

Captain Graves dropped in, having been briefed by McElroy. He was looking a lot more cheerful than the last time Jane met with him. He ordered Jane to stay away from Fifty-sixth Street tonight; they would take care of everything in the morning.

Jane and Defino agreed to pick up the warrant for Olivia Dean's apartment first thing in the morning and then go uptown to execute it. Charlie Bracken said he'd be glad to join them.

Jane walked home feeling pretty chipper. An impossible set of people and circumstances were falling into place in a way that made her shake her head in wonder. She stopped at the store and bought food for dinner. She felt like cooking tonight, making something from scratch that wouldn't taste of a can or freezer burn.

While she cooked and ate, she thought about Hack, about who had leaked word of her trip to Omaha. Someone had. Even if they picked up Chong Wang, there wasn't much chance he would give up names. After putting her dishes in the sink, she decided to call Hack. She picked up the phone and dialed his beeper number. Then she waited. Her phone number would be new to him but he would know that a call to his beeper must come from someone he knew. It might take a minute; it might take ten. If he was at home, in the field, called to a crime scene, it might take longer. She went into her office, took out her checkbook, and started going through her bills.

The phone rang less than five minutes later. When she answered, there was a pause, then a tentative, "Jane?"

"Hack, it's me."

"It's a new number."

"I moved. I need to see you."

"Tell me where to go."

She opened the door after buzzing him in downstairs. The coffee was on and a couple of dishes and spoons lay on the kitchen table along with the ice-cream scoop. Hack loved ice cream, and she had picked up a quart the other day.

The elevator stopped and the door slid open. She felt a kind of adolescent frenzy, a fear in her gut that she was doing the wrong thing, that this would be a disaster, that— He stepped out into the hall and saw her, the smallest smile curling his lips. She went back into the apartment and waited for him. He came in and closed the door without turning away from her.

"You look great."

"You too."

He was holding a small brown paper bag, which he handed to her. Taking it, she felt the cold through the paper. It was ice cream. She smiled. Her eyes began to tear, and she turned toward the kitchen.

"Looks like you were expecting company," Hack said behind her.

She opened the freezer, allowing him to see the quart she had put away as she put his beside it.

"Coffee smells good," he said.

"Hack, I asked you here on business, but I've never missed anyone so much in my life."

"I know." He didn't say anything else for a minute, just stood in the kitchen a couple of feet from her. He didn't have Captain Graves's Hollywood handsomeness. He was more rugged, less perfect. His hair was graying with no silver accents, just plain gray among the black. She thought he was a little thinner than last time. "I won't do anything you don't want me to," he said finally, "but I want to put my arms around you so bad I can't stand it."

She said, "Me too," as she walked toward him, allowed herself the pleasure of holding and being held. Little sounds escaped from both of them. He held her away from him, then kissed her cheeks and rubbed his day-old stubble across her smooth skin.

"I still love the freckles," he said.

She smiled. "There aren't any freckles, Hack. They were there when I met you, but they're gone."

"I see every one of them. Show me around. Then we'll talk."

He admired the fireplace and the floors, the roomy office with all the still-unpacked cartons, the bedroom where he lingered, his arm around her. Then they picked up their coffee and ice cream and sat in the living room.

"How do you like the new squad?" he asked.

"You know about it."

"You know me. I know everything. I put you on it."

"You! I thought—"

"Don't think. I thought you'd like it better. I thought you'd like it so much you'd give up this fantasy of leaving the job for some damn dull insurance company."

"I do like it," she said. "But I need the insurance company money to afford the apartment. And the City Hall case—"

"You'll get a raise on the job that'll pay the rent. And the City Hall case was a dead end. After everyone in the city dried their eyes, nothing was there. That case'll be open for the next ten years."

"It's this cold case I want to talk to you about. It started in Hell's Kitchen."

"I'm listening."

"I went to Omaha last week."

"I saw the paperwork."

"Someone was waiting for me. A killer."

His eyes stayed on her face. He pressed his lips together, then relaxed them. "Who knew you were going?"

"My team, Captain Graves, Lieutenant McElroy, the PAA, and anyone who handled my travel papers."

"You think there was a leak."

"I'm sure of it."

"And it could have been in my office."

"Or mine or the commissioner's."

"You're telling me someone in one of these three offices is on the payroll of a killer."

"Or could be his girlfriend."

"Or his boyfriend, I suppose. What do you know about him?"

"He's Chinese, he's very good at what he does, and the people he works for are illegally buying or stealing weapons-systems circuitry that could be used to launch missiles against us."

"You got yourself a hell of a case."

"Looks like it."

"Somebody checking out my people?"

"Yes."

"I'll do my own checking."

"Thanks, Hack."

He smiled and she knew they were through with business. "Maybe we'll go away for a weekend somewhere."

"I don't know."

"I said your name in my sleep."

"I told you you talked in your sleep. You never believed me."

"I believe you now." His cup was empty and his ice cream long gone. "We done with business?"

"I'm done."

He looked at his watch. "It's up to you," he said.

She went over and sat on his lap, held his head against her, moved her lips through his hair, his ear, shivered with pleasure at his sounds, at the feeling of his arms around her. "It's OK," she said.

"Just OK?"

"I love you, Hack."

"That's a lot better than OK."

She hung on to him after he said he had to go, knowing she had broken a promise to herself. "I wish I didn't love you," she said.

"Wishing won't change it. I don't know where I'd be if I hadn't met you." He kissed her, got out of bed, and started to dress.

She watched him as she had watched him so many other times, a silhouette near the window, a shadow near the bed. This was how she always saw him, in the dark, a beloved shadow. It had been ten years since they met, half the time she'd been on the job. It had been partly that round number that had prompted her to put an end to the relationship, or at least to try.

"How's your daughter?" she asked.

"She hasn't said anything, Jane. I've been very good for the last month and a half."

Month and a half. Had it been that long? "Your wife must know. How could she not know? There could be so much trouble for you."

"There won't be any trouble," he said. He bent over and kissed her. "I stopped smoking after the last time I saw you."

It made her eyes tear. She had wanted him to stop for years. "I'm glad."

"But now that I'm so goddamn healthy, I don't have you to share all those extra years with."

"You're hopeless," she said.

"Think of me when you eat the ice cream," he said, folding his tie and stuffing it in a jacket pocket.

As if she needed something to jog her memory. "Count on it."

He took his cell phone out and made the inevitable call to say when he'd be home and not to bother picking him up at the station. He'd take a taxi.

"I have one of those now, too," Jane said, getting out of bed and reaching for the robe he had gotten her a couple of years ago.

"Give me the number." He put it in his book. "If I learn anything, you'll be the first to hear. I'm sorry I interfered, but I really didn't want you stuck on a case that was going nowhere."

"It's OK. This is the best case of my life."

"Think about it, Jane. Leaving the job?"

"I will."

They walked to the foyer arm in arm.

"You know I'm always there," he said.

"I know."

"I hope you feel as good as I do."

"I do."

"Last kiss then."

That was always the one tainted with tears. Tonight was no exception.

After she closed the door behind him she knew how this case was different. It was the sum total of everything she had worked on in her career. It was all those drug busts in Harlem and Chinatown and Narco, everything that went down in the Burglary Squad, ten years' worth of dead bodies in the Six rolled into one. It was the case that would decide the rest of her life.

She was living in the Six now, after all those years of working there. And the Centre Street office was in the Fifth, Chinatown's precinct, where she had spent some of the best years of her life. In an eerie way it was all coming together, her work, her love, how she wanted to spend the next twenty years.

Hack was clean; she knew that absolutely. They would find the leak. They would find Soderberg's killer. She felt energized and excited, the way she had felt as a rookie, the way she had felt when she got her gold shield. I'm a cop, she thought. Can I ever be anything else?

When she got into bed, she knew how she would handle Lisa Angelino.

31

THE WARRANT TO search Olivia Dean's apartment was ready to execute first thing in the morning. Jane met Defino at Centre Street and they caught the subway uptown together after picking up the warrant at the district attorney's office on Hogan Place. Bracken was already there, waiting in a car down the block. Derek was sitting beside him, looking lost.

"Morning, folks. Derek here has the key to Ms. Dean's apartment and he'll open the door as soon as you show him your warrant."

Derek never said a word and never looked at Jane. When they got upstairs, Derek unlocked the door and then disappeared.

"Fucking Derek," Defino said inside. "He was playing with us. Thought we wouldn't catch on."

They started with the living room, the first room they entered from the door. It was spare but livable: a couch covered with a foam-rubber mattress that could double as a bed, two chairs of a similar design, a television set, a couple of tables. On the floor was a carpet that extended into all the other rooms except the kitchen. If Olivia Dean moved around, no one downstairs heard her. A copy of *People* magazine with an October date lay open on the table in front of the couch; otherwise, there was nothing in the room to make it appear occupied.

They moved on to the bedroom. Here there was a double bed made with military perfection and no spread. The sheets and pillowcases were striped, blue and silver on white. A dresser opposite the bed had two sets of three drawers and, on top, only a glass dish with straight pins, safety pins, and bobby pins.

"Shit, I haven't seen one of these in years," Bracken said, pointing to the bobby pins. "Who uses these anymore?"

Jane opened the closet. Most of the clothes were pants and jackets or other tops of a dark color. She pried open a large box on the floor and said, "Maybe someone who wears a wig."

"You found a wig in there?" Bracken said.

"Nothing flashy, brown, short hair. Maybe she wanted to change her appearance. Maybe every day was a bad-hair day." She backed out of the closet and let them in.

"Looks like clothes for climbing on the roof," Defino said. "You think she wore them out to lunch, too?"

"What are the shoes like?" Jane asked.

"Boots," Bracken said. "Sneakers, coupla pair, one pair black heels. I guess that's for having lunch out. Lotta black stuff hanging here."

"We'll have to inventory the works," Jane said. "Why don't you guys do that and I'll see what's in the dresser."

The first thing she noticed was the jewelry. Everything was inexpensive and there wasn't much: a few pairs of earrings, some bangle bracelets, a silver pin for the lapel of a suit. Maybe contract killing didn't pay what she heard it did. The underwear was not provocative, just standard bras and panties with an emphasis on black. The bras were a small size, and most of the panties had been designed for comfort, not allure.

In another drawer were the kind of socks you wear to keep your feet warm, socks meant for boots and sneakers, not high heels. A few pairs of panty hose were stuffed in a corner.

There were stacks of black tights, plenty of knit shirts and sweaters, many of them also black. Absent were bright colors. This was a woman who kept a low profile, who melted into darkness.

Jane pulled each drawer out of the dresser, checked the space in the dresser and the back of the drawer, then set it on the bed and lifted the front edge to see the bottom. There were no messages or keys or photos taped to the bottom. What was in the dresser was in the drawers.

"Look at this," Bracken said from the closet. He pulled out a box with high-grade rope arranged in circular sections and small metal D rings and nylon loops. "Probably good enough to climb Mount Everest with."

"Or tie some guy up and beat him to death," Defino said.

Jane touched it, rubbing it between her thumb and fingers. It felt smooth and springy, and was a dark red color with a green diamond pattern. "So where is she?"

"How 'bout Omaha?" Defino said. "A nice little lady comes into the hospital to visit cousin Hutchins. Who'd stop her?"

Jane felt a chill. She pulled out her cell phone and dialed Mike Fromm's number. "Mike, do you have Hutchins under guard?" she asked without any preliminaries.

"I've got a man outside his door."

"It's possible that a very dangerous woman is out there looking for him. She's fairly small, maybe forty, could be wearing a wig that makes her look younger or older."

"So small is really all you're sure of."

"That's right. But she may be our kidnapper or a hired killer. She could come down from the roof on a rope."

"The windows are locked. It's cold here. But I'll have a talk with my men. We've got a log of visitors. Cory's there a lot, and an aunt has dropped by a couple of times. I'll check her out."

"Good idea."

"You have prints on this woman?"

"Not yet, but we will soon. We're going through her apartment right now."

"Thanks for the warning."

"Where'd you get the phone?" Defino said when she hung up.

"The whip gave it to me for my trip to D.C. I give it back when the case is over."

"Don't let MacHovec see it. He'll need two."

They did a thorough search, checking out underneath the bed, between the mattress and the box spring, turning over furniture. From the bathroom they took two pill bottles that might have Dean's prints, and from the kitchen a glass on the counter and a few dishes.

Defino slipped on latex gloves and checked the shower, toilet tank, and sink. Then he took out a small penknife, opened it to the screwdriver, and began removing the plates from light switches and electric outlets.

The front closet had a black raincoat in it, a navy-blue single-breasted winter coat with matching buttons, a black leather jacket that looked worn beyond hope, a black nylon shell with a zipper, and a black hooded sweatshirt jacket. On the floor were rubber boots caked with mud and a black umbrella.

There was no desk in the apartment and no mail. The phone in the bedroom was stationary, but the one in the kitchen was cordless, and they tagged and bagged that for prints. They also took the answering machine tape for a sample of her voice.

"She must have left before the first," Jane said. "Stabile

said she hadn't paid the rent, and she always paid on time. I bet the bill's in the mailbox."

"And she's got the key," Defino said. "Maybe Derek has a copy."

They gathered their evidence and found Derek, who unlocked the mailbox without a word. Inside was an envelope from Stabile. There was also a Con Ed bill and a phone bill. All the postmarks were different, but the letters had been mailed in the last week.

"I came back from Omaha a week ago yesterday," Jane said. "That was the first of November. She could have flown out there that day before she got her mail, or maybe the day before when Wang called her to say he needed help."

"So she'd be gone a week," Bracken said. "From the apartment you can't tell."

"But what's she doing out there? Hutchins didn't mention her. No one's tried to harm him since he's been in the hospital. It really doesn't make sense."

"Maybe she's your tail," Defino said.

"I didn't think of that. She could alternate with Wang."

"And you live downtown now, so she stays at the Walker Street place instead of going uptown to sleep."

It sounded reasonable. Bracken seemed surprised that Jane had a tail, and she told him it was still iffy. "We'll go through the place on Walker Street this afternoon. The warrant should be waiting for us by the time we get back downtown."

They split up on that, Bracken driving back to the station house only a couple of blocks south. Jane checked the time. It was still too early for lunch.

"I need an hour, Gordon. I'll meet you back at Centre Street."

"I'll pick up the warrant." He took the things they had bagged in the apartment and hailed a cab to get downtown. When he was in it, Jane hailed the next one and gave the driver an address on Sixth Avenue.

* * *

The building was steel and glass, a perfect rendition of corporate America, with several banks of elevators. She found the ones that went to the twentieth floor and entered the first car that emptied. Three other people stepped on before the doors shut. She hated what she was about to do, but she realized now that she wanted the past to remain the past. In a few minutes that would happen.

The first one out of the elevator, she faced a receptionist who looked up and gave her a friendly look. "I'm looking for Paul Thurston," she said.

"Do you have an appointment?"

Jane showed her shield and ID and said, "I don't need one."

The woman's eyes opened wide. "Down the hall to the end, then left. His secretary will be there."

The hall was vinyl tiled until she reached the circular area at the end. Then it was carpeted, a cool green. Sitting at a desk with a computer was the secretary, just putting down the phone. Around her were closed doors, each of which would lead to a windowed office.

The secretary eyed Jane with a somber face. "May I help you?" she asked.

"I'd like to see Paul Thurston." Jane held the shield in her coat pocket, but she didn't want to show it if she didn't have to. She knew the trouble she could get into, flashing a police ID in a personal matter.

The young woman swallowed. "May I have your name?"

"Just tell Mr. Thurston it's important."

The secretary hesitated, then got up, went to the door directly in front of her desk, knocked twice, and went inside. When she came out, she said, "He'll see you now."

Jane walked inside, feeling the springiness of the carpet, seeing the light from the windows behind his desk, seeing Paul Thurston for the first time in twenty years.

There was no mistaking him. The hair was a little thinner and a little darker but the build had not changed and the eyes were the same bright blue. In a way he looked even better, the cocky puffiness of youth having given way to a slim, sober handsomeness.

"Jane?" he said incredulously.

"Hello, Paul."

"They said—"

"I'm a police detective. I wanted to see you without discussing it with a third party."

"Is this a police matter?"

"It's personal."

He had been standing behind his desk. He came around now and took her coat, hung it in a small closet, and offered her a chair. He sat in one a couple of feet away. "The freckles are gone," he said.

"Nothing lasts forever."

"How have you been?"

It was a question she hated, when people asked for a recap of the years they had been out of touch. She disliked giving recaps as much as she disliked hearing them. "I've been fine," she said, "and it looks like you've been fine, too." On the credenza behind his desk and under the windows there were family pictures. "Something has just come up, some unfinished business. You and I had a daughter twenty years ago."

She heard him suck in his breath. "You got an abortion," he said.

"I didn't."

"It's what we agreed on, Jane. It's what I paid for. You may have had a child, but I didn't."

The remark stung.

"What's happened?" he asked.

"I got a letter from her last month," she said, her voice lower. "I gave her up for adoption. She wants to know who her parents are."

"I'm not her parent. I am anonymous, and don't think for a minute—"

"It's OK; I won't tell her."

"It's not that I don't care. It's just that this is out of the blue. I have a family. It would be very hard. I'm not sure I could handle it." His voice softened.

"I'll handle it," she said. "Thanks for seeing me." She got up and walked to the coat closet. Her hand brushed against the navy-blue coat hanging next to hers and she knew it was cashmere. She took out her own coat and slipped it on before he had a chance to be polite.

"I'm sorry, Jane. There's nothing I can do."

"I understand. Good-bye, Paul." She opened the door and walked on the carpet, then onto the vinyl tiles and down the hall. The elevator came and carried her swiftly to the ground floor. Out on Sixth Avenue she turned toward Forty-seventh Street and the subway. At Thirty-fourth she changed for the Broadway line and took it down to City Hall.

It was all about freckles, she thought. Paul no longer saw them, but Hack did even though they were gone. She would love Hack forever, not that she'd ever had any doubts about that.

[**32**]

THERE WAS A message at Centre Street that Mike Fromm had called. He had not been able to reach the aunt by telephone and he had sent a uniform out to her house. So far nothing else.

Jane and Defino walked around to Walker Street.

"You OK?" Defino asked between puffs.

"I'm fine. Do I look as if I'm not?"

"You look a little spacey."

She grinned. "I'll try to focus. You're right. I'm in ten different places."

They reached the building where Chong Wang lived and went inside. A uniform was in the ground-floor shop, chatting with the rotund Eddie. No one had come or gone from the apartment upstairs since yesterday. The uniform gave them a key that the landlord had contributed.

The key worked perfectly and they went inside. It was a grubby place to live, paint peeling, stains on the plaster from the indiscretions of someone above, dust balls where no one walked. The bed was unmade and the sheets dirty. Defino slipped on a pair of latex gloves. In the closet was a cache of guns.

He whistled. "He's got everything here, big, small, you name it. And enough ammo to annihilate New York south of Canal Street. This guy's a serious shooter, and judging by the type and caliber here, very experienced.

The guys in Ballistics are gonna have a field day testing these."

"We'll need to call to have this stuff picked up. But it has to be done very discreetly. No media. If he doesn't know we're onto him, let's keep it that way."

"Look at this." Defino had the closet door open. "Men's clothes and women's. These could belong to the Dean woman."

Jane went to look. "You're right. They're the same size."

"But they're different. There are party dresses here, skirts. She must have come down here to change. And look at this." He pushed a couple of boxes out of the closet.

Jane opened them. "Wigs. My God, she had a whole wardrobe of them. Here's a blond one; here's gray. And here's an empty box. This is the one she was wearing when she took off."

"What did she do down here?" Defino said.

"Meet people like Soderberg. Maybe kill them if they didn't deliver. You meet a small woman, you're off guard."

"Wang's stuff is mostly black, too. Including ski masks."

"The man who shot the cop in Omaha and made off with Hutchins wore a ski mask."

"OK, let's see what we can put together for Forensics."

Jane went through the drawers and came up with nothing. Defino took a few items for prints. The weapons would be unloaded, inventoried, and then picked up. The uniform said he would stay till everything was taken. Now it was time for another talk with Eddie.

"You're back," Eddie said. "You taking up residence?"

"Not yet," Defino said. "Besides Mr. Wang, anyone else go up to that apartment that you would recognize?"

"Hard to say. People go up and down; I don't really know where they're going. There's a woman though. I sometimes see her with the Chinese guy."

"What's she look like?"

"Not too big. Usually has a knapsack on her back like a hiker."

"What does she wear?"

"I don't look too close. Pants usually. Kinda casual."

"Would you know her if you saw her?"

"Eh. I don't know. I never looked too close."

Defino gave him his card with the usual spiel.

"I don't know what I could think of I haven't told you already."

"Maybe you'll have a dream."

Jane and Defino returned to Centre Street.

There was a message from Omaha that Hutchins's aunt still wasn't home but they would keep looking. Hutchins was starting to come around now, remaining awake for longer periods, and the doctors were optimistic that he might make it.

"But where's the aunt?" Defino said, putting the message down.

"Dean could have a gray wig," Jane said. "She could have the kind of clothes everybody's elderly aunt wears. I hope they know what they're doing there."

"You guys have a minute?" MacHovec said, putting down the phone.

"Sure thing. What've you got?"

"I've been checking out everyone in the offices at One PP. I can't tell you I've cleared people, but the ones I like for this are in Inspector Hackett's office."

"Where the Chinese girl works?"

"Yeah, she's the one. But there's a cop in that office, not Chinese, that's giving me goose bumps. Lotta time off, that kind of thing. And Inspector Hackett. You know he took a trip to China a year and a half, two years ago? Went on some kind of exchange program to help the police set up a detective unit."

Jane remembered. He had been gone two weeks and he had taken his wife, the first time she had ever left the country. Afterward, he gave Jane a beautiful piece of jade that she wore on a gold chain. "Sounds pretty routine," she said.

"Yeah, but how many people do you know who've been to China and had the opportunity to talk to big, important people? Someone could've sat down with him while they were drinking that stuff that goes to your head, and maybe he made some kind of deal."

"I like it," Defino said.

Jane didn't, but she couldn't say anything. "The cop in his office, the one that's giving you goose bumps, did he go to China with Hackett?"

"Good question. Lemme see if I can find out. The whip wants to see us. Time for an update."

"There goes the rest of the day," Defino said. "Not that there's much left."

They went to Graves's office. MacHovec kept quiet about Hack, but they talked about everything else. Graves asked especially about the missing aunt in Omaha. Would Cory Blanding recognize Hutchins's aunt? Jane didn't know. And if the aunt came to visit during the day when Cory was working, if she had the right ID to show the cop outside the hospital room, who would know whether she was the real thing or an impostor?

"You better alert them, Jane. Hutchins may not be of any more use to us, but let's keep the poor guy alive."

"Right."

MacHovec dashed for the door when the meeting was over, and Defino wasn't far behind. Jane called Mike and sketched out their concerns. The aunt hadn't shown up today and still wasn't at home. If and when she came to the hospital, they would detain her.

She called her father then, telling him nothing about her work and doing a lot of listening. When she got off the phone and looked out the window, it was dark out, streetlights on, headlights blazing. She lingered at the window a moment, noticing raindrops on the pane, then got her coat. As she started out the door into the conference area, a phone rang behind her. She went to see if it was hers. It wasn't. It was Defino's. She hesitated, then picked it up, something she didn't usually do.

"Detective Bauer."

"Oh, it's you. This is Eddie on Walker Street. How're you doin'?"

She kept her irritation to herself. "Do you have something for me, Eddie?"

"Yeah, I think so. I think that Chinese guy came back."

"Did you see him?"

"Not exactly. But the bike's gone. Remember there was a bike chained to the rack in the vestibule?"

She shook her head, her emotions flip-flopping. "We took that bike, Eddie."

"What? The cops?"

"Forensics is looking at it."

"Oh. Gee, I'm sorry I bothered you. You got the other thing, too?"

"What other thing?"

"That folded-up thing that's usually chained to the rack, too. I don't know what it was. Something with wheels, I think."

"I don't know what thing you're talking about, Eddie. There was only a bike there when we came."

"Oh. Well, now I think of it, maybe that's been gone for a while. I don't usually go out that way anyway. I use the door to the street." The way his shop was arranged, he had access to the vestibule along the side and to the street in the front. "I'm sorry I bothered you. I never saw the cops take the bike away. I must've been over in the other part of the store when they came."

"That's OK. I'm glad you called. If you think of anything else, or if you see anyone, please give us a call."

"Sure thing."

She made a note to tell Defino about the call. At least Eddie was thinking. She started to leave again. The place was empty even though it wasn't very late. The elevator came and she went downstairs. Outside there was a sudden downpour, people with umbrellas dodging other umbrellas, people without them hurrying for cover, holding soggy newspapers over their heads. She leaned against the wall near the door, hoping it would let up long enough for her to get to the subway. There was a crack of thunder followed by lightning, and a woman nearby yelped. In weather like this finding an empty cab was a dream. She would either have to wait it out or make a run for the subway, which would surely leave her soaked to the skin.

She moved away from the tense crowd near the doors. In her pocket was the little cell phone she had barely used. She could call Hack and ask him if anyone in his office had gone to China with him. He would still be there; he rarely left early.

She took out the phone, turned it on, tapped the ten digits of his cell phone, and then abruptly hung up. It was an excuse to call him. If the suspect cop had gone to China, MacHovec would know it tomorrow, and tomorrow was as good as tonight. She dropped the phone back in her pocket. That was what happened when she saw him again: all the good intentions, the month of not seeing him, of learning to live without him, were canceled out, as though they had never happened.

"Look, it's stopping," a woman's voice said. A handful of people applauded.

Jane walked to the back of the crowd as they started to leave and moved with them out into the damp air. A thin drizzle was coming down, little more than a mist. At least it wasn't below freezing; they'd be in the midst of an ice storm.

She started for the subway, then changed her mind. What Eddie had said was nagging at her. What was "the other thing" chained to the bicycle rack? It wasn't that much of a walk, and maybe she could coax something useful out of him.

She turned onto Walker, thinking more about what she would eat for dinner than what she would say to

Eddie. It would have to be takeout again; there was nothing edible in the apartment. When would she get herself together so that there was food waiting when she got home?

After this case. After this case her life would change. There would be more money, better clothes, no overtime. She would cook, maybe have some friends over, if she could remember who her friends were. She smiled at her joke, stopping for a red light at the corner of Lafayette, where she felt someone jostle her. She started to turn and a man's soft voice said, "Detective Bauer, don't move; don't turn; don't say anything. I can kill you in one second, and I have no reason to keep you alive anymore."

She knew who it was without seeing him. He took hold of her left arm in a strong grip but stayed slightly behind her so that looking to her left she would not see his face. She felt a slight push.

"Cross the street now." They moved together north toward Canal Street. "Where is your gun?"

"On my right hip."

"Keep your right hand where I can see it. Where's your other gun?"

"What other gun?"

"Don't be fresh with me, Bauer. Tell me where your second gun is."

She paused, then decided to tell the truth. "It's on my right ankle." Thanks to Captain Graves.

"If you bend down to get it, I will kill you with it."

"Go ahead."

He tightened his grip and twisted her arm painfully. "Don't be smart. Smart will get you killed."

"Where are we going?" They continued along Lafayette, Wang half pushing her.

"Don't ask any more questions."

She knew he had to be armed, but if he was holding her arm with his right hand, he could be holding a gun only in his left, and that would have to be in a pocket. He wouldn't get very far holding a weapon in an exposed left hand, but he might have something else, something small and lethal that could be secreted in his fist. He hadn't made a move to take her guns, but that could be because of the logistics. He had grabbed her left arm, maybe because there had been no room on her right side and he had been afraid of losing her or knocking over a civilian in his attempt to grab her.

"At the corner we turn right."

Chinatown was little more than two blocks to the right. Damn. He might have a safe apartment there, a room that no one else would enter. He could imprison her and keep her guarded with young armed thugs. The streets were full of Chinese gangs, Ghost Shadows, White Tigers, Flying Dragons, eager to establish reputations that would further their criminal careers. The department was so concerned, they had formed a special unit nicknamed the Jade Squad. Although she would be only a few blocks from Centre Street geographically, she might as well be on the other side of the world.

"We cross the street." It was Centre Street.

They dodged cars, his grip practically stopping the circulation in her arm. He maneuvered her to Baxter Street, where they took a right, then, a few seconds later, to Bayard, where they turned left and crossed the street over an invisible boundary. In moments they had left downtown New York and entered another country. The faces changed; the language changed. A woman berated her young son in the tongue of a country halfway around the world. A handsome young man walking with a beautiful girl switched from perfect English to the language of his parents. They passed a dim sum place that she had eaten in many times, but this time her mouth was dry. Two teenage boys were casually practicing tai chi on the sidewalk. She had done duty on all these streets, looking into gambling, drugs, even allegations of new immigrant women being forced into prostitution, but it didn't help her now.

Now no one looked at them, no one paid the least attention. She moved her right hand, trying to judge whether she could grab her gun before he killed her. The coat was buttoned down to her thighs and the gun was holstered on her hip. She would have to get her hand inside her coat and open the snap tab on the holster before she could reach her gun. And to make matters worse, she was wearing gloves.

Placing the back of her right hand against her right thigh, she tried to slide her hand from her glove as she walked. The glove moved a little and she continued wriggling. If she dropped the glove, she would have a better chance at grabbing the gun—not a good chance, only a better one.

"What are you doing?"

"Nothing."

"I'll kill you if you lie to me."

She let her right hand hang, glove slightly off. They had passed Mulberry Street and came to Mott. He urged her across and they kept going toward Elizabeth. The Chinatown Precinct was on Elizabeth, but she knew he would avoid it. Halfway down the block he said, "Next door, we go in."

There was no number on the door, which was between a restaurant and a laundry. The smell of Chinese food filled the damp air, making her hungry. Keeping his head averted, Wang leaned forward, pushed open the door, and shoved her into a small vestibule with a staircase on the left wall. Inside it was dark and shabby and smelly, and there was nowhere to go but up the stairs to a filthy apartment where she would spend the last hours of her life.

[33]

HE PULLED A ski mask down over his head and pushed
her toward the stairs.

"Go up," he ordered.

He directed her to the third floor, where he used a key
to open a door. "Inside," he said.

He flicked a light switch and she saw a large water bug
cross the floor. Small roaches climbed up and down the
walls. Jane struggled to stay calm. There were different
kinds of fear in life, and although she knew that the
threat of this man was much greater than all the bugs
combined, they were what gave her a chill.

"Stand where you are."

She was nearly in the center of the room and she
stopped dead.

"Turn toward me and show me where your guns are."

She obeyed him, pulling open her coat and raising her
pant leg. As she did so, she looked at him for the first
time. The ski mask covered his face, and he was holding
a gun pointed at her. He was slim, perhaps the same
height as she or slightly taller. Everything he wore was
black and close-fitting. If she had to pick him out of a
lineup, she would have been unable to.

"Take the guns out slowly and set them on the floor.
Use two fingers, left hand only. If you try anything,
you're dead."

She was still wearing her gloves. She pulled them off and stuffed them in her coat pockets. Then she removed the Glock and the S&W and laid them gently on the floor in front of her.

"Kick them over here."

She kicked them with her toe and he picked them up.

"Now sit on the chair behind you."

It was an old bentwood chair with a cane seat that was falling apart. She kept her coat on, sensing no heat in the room. Wang sat on an armchair about five or six feet from her.

"Now pull up your pants so I can see your legs." He wanted to see if she was wearing another ankle holster. She pulled up the pants and stretched out her legs. She had nothing to hide.

"Open your coat all the way."

She unbuttoned the last few buttons and opened it. He got up and walked toward her. She tensed, hoping he would not touch her. He didn't. He picked up her handbag and rummaged through it, pulling out the handcuffs.

"Where is the key?"

"On my key ring."

He found it, took it off the ring, and put it in his pocket. He looked at her ID, went through her wallet, fished around the bottom of the bag, then dropped it on the floor.

"Why are you looking into the Soderberg case?" Wang asked, sitting back down.

"I was assigned to it."

"Don't be smart, Bauer, or I'll kill you. Why is the police department interested in Soderberg?"

"They weren't. We were looking into another case, and his death seemed to be related. We started investigating it."

"What did you learn?"

"Soderberg fell down the stairs and died. His body was sent to Virginia. He was cremated and I believe his ashes were taken out to sea for burial."

"Who did Soderberg work for?"

"An electronics company. They're out of business."

"What kind of business did they do?"

"I don't know."

"You *do* know! Don't lie to me. Tell me what they did."

He must want to know how much she had found out, how successful their investigation had been. She had not herself visited the building where QX had been located; Defino went there while she was in Omaha. But Wang was in Omaha at the same time, and he didn't come back until last Sunday, after he dumped poor Jerry Hutchins. If Wang was working alone, or if Olivia Dean was still in Omaha, he might not know Defino had gone to the QX building or that Jane had visited Carl Johnson. He might not even know of the existence of Carl Johnson till she and Defino went to visit his home a second time. Maybe he didn't know as much as she knew.

She shook her head. She would see how much she could get away with. See what she could find out from him. If she survived this, it would be nice to know where Olivia Dean was.

"Where did you go on Monday?"

Monday had been the trip to D.C. when she left her building the back way. It was probably the morning after Wang returned from Omaha. "To work," she said.

"You lie to me I kill you."

"You kill me I can't tell you anything."

"How did you find Hutchins?"

That would be a sore point. She had done what he had not been able to do. "I found an old friend of his. He told me where to look."

"What did Hutchins tell you?"

"He told me there were rats in the apartment across the hall."

His eyes bit into her. It was the only thing she could see above his chin. "Rats across the hall."

"Yes."

"He lied to you."

"There isn't much I can do about it. He was terrified you would kill him."

"I did kill him."

She tried to keep the surprise out of her face. If he thought Hutchins was dead, why was Olivia Dean in Omaha posing as Hutchins's aunt? It didn't make sense.

What did make sense was that he was an acknowledged killer and she was the next person on his list. No one knew where she was right now; no one would find her in time to save her. She had to try to placate him, string him along by answering questions without telling him anything, figure out how to get out of here or it was all over. Her stomach began aching.

"He didn't know anything," Jane said. "You didn't have to kill him."

"What did he mean about the rats?"

"At the time Soderberg died, someone was living in the apartment across the hall from him, an apartment that was supposed to be empty. Maybe it was you."

"Yeah, sure," he said, his lips curling. "It was me."

He probably knew they had been to the building on Fifty-sixth Street this morning, but he wouldn't know why. The paperwork for the warrant had not passed through any of the offices where the leak could have occurred. And once she and Defino and Bracken were inside, he wouldn't have been able to see where they went. As far as he was concerned, they had no reason to think that Soderberg's killer still lived in that apartment. She wanted to be very careful to tell him only things he already knew. He didn't know she had taken the train to Washington. He might not know she had visited Carl Johnson or what his involvement was with QX. Wang was an assassin who knew more about killing than spying.

"Didn't you kill Soderberg?" she asked.

The lips curled again. He liked knowing more than she did. "Do you think I did?"

"I think it's possible."

"How did you find me?"

"What do you mean?"

"I mean the apartment on Walker Street. How did you find the apartment?"

"We got a tip."

"Someone called and told you you could find me in that apartment?"

"I don't know what they said. The tip came in and I was told." Let him think Olivia Dean had made the call, if she was still in New York. Where the hell was she anyway?

"You're a stupid woman, Detective Bauer, and I don't like stupid women. Tell me how you found me."

"You don't know how the police department works. We have someone who just does research. He's on the computer and the phones all day. He finds something out, he lets us know. He told us to go down to Walker Street and we went."

"What did you do with my bicycle?"

"Forensics is looking at it."

"For my fingerprints and DNA?" He said it with a sneer.

"If they can find any."

"Who is the man who goes everywhere with you?"

She didn't want to tell him. She didn't know how much the mole knew about their team. If it was Hack, he knew everything. If it was someone else, he might know a lot less. Wang seemed to be working with no one else except Olivia Dean. They might not have the manpower to follow both Jane and Defino. She decided to try a lie. "Harry Bittler," she said, using the last name of someone she had known years ago.

"You're lying." He stood up and came toward her, the gun pointing at her torso. As he neared her, he slammed the gun at the side of her face with the force of anger.

She allowed herself to fall off the chair to her left,

diminishing the full impact of the blow. As she went down, she remembered what Mike Fromm had said about Hutchins when they found him. That was what would happen to her. She would be beaten to death and Wang would disappear, leave the country and perhaps never come back. Her death would end up a cold case.

She lay on the floor for a few moments, recovering from the blow. Her head pounded and tears leaked from both eyes. In another apartment, or in another building, a woman shrieked a tirade in another language. Then a child cried bitterly.

"Get up," Wang ordered. "Sit down on the chair. Don't play with me and don't lie to me. Get up," he said, raising his voice. "Do what you're told."

She pulled herself up and brushed her coat off. She didn't want roaches crawling in her clothes and hair. She touched the side of her face gingerly. The skin was broken and there was moisture and it hurt like hell. She sat and drew her coat closer. Something in her mouth tasted like a copper penny.

"Where does this Harry Bitter live?" Wang asked back in his chair.

"Bittler," she said. "There's an *L* in it."

"Bittler." He spat it out, the *L* sounding almost like an *R*. It was the first time he had made that mistake in his English.

"I don't know where he lives. Queens. That's all I know. We don't go home together."

"Who else is there?"

"Captain Graves is in charge of the whole squad. Lieutenant McElroy is second."

"You said someone did research."

"I've never met him. I talk to him on the phone."

"Give me a name."

"Mark Frey." She knew she would have to be careful. Make up too many names and she would get them wrong. Next one, she thought, she would say Paul Thurston.

"And he's the man who knows everything."

"Not everything. He checks to see if people have police records, where they live, that kind of thing."

"I want you to tell me how you found me. I want the truth or I'll do the same thing to the other side of your face. Pretty soon you won't have a face left."

She bent her head over and closed her eyes. The truth wouldn't hurt anyone. "I remember now," she said, looking up. "The Omaha police found the car rental you used. Your license had the Walker Street address. That's how we found it."

"How could they find the car rental?" he asked angrily.

"I don't know. I wasn't there. An Omaha cop called and said he'd done some old-fashioned investigating. He came up with your name and address."

Wang stared at her. She realized as she spoke that she had nearly divulged the fact that the Omaha police might know that he was Chinese. If they knew that, Hutchins was still alive. If he was alive, there were other things he could talk about. Answering his question was a mistake.

"How did the cop know it was me? A lot of other men rented cars at the airport that day."

"He said it was the only one from New York."

He stood up and approached her. She tensed, waiting for the blow, but he stopped and stood halfway between their chairs.

"Did he know I was Chinese when he was asking questions at the car rentals?"

"I don't know what he knew. He gave me a name and address and we went down to Walker Street."

"Hutchins is alive, isn't he?"

"You said you killed him."

He stepped forward and whacked the left side of her face. She started to fall but he broke it and pushed her back up, putting his masked face close to hers. Her eyes were tearing badly, her head was pounding, and she was beginning to sweat. Both sides of her face were stinging.

"You tell the truth when I ask you a question or you will die sooner instead of later. Is Hutchins alive?"

He's a madman, she thought. It doesn't matter what I tell him; he's going to kill me. The panic that was just below the surface threatened to undo her. He had to know the answers to these questions if Olivia Dean was in Omaha, but his pleasure was taunting her, terrorizing her. And he was succeeding. The pain in her stomach was worse and her face was on fire. This was how she would die, in fear and pain.

"Answer me," he shouted.

"I haven't talked to anyone in Omaha for a couple of days. Maybe he's alive; maybe he's dead." Her voice shook.

"But he was alive when they found him."

"He was alive," she said wearily.

"Was he talking?"

"No. He was in a coma. He was expected to die. Maybe he has died." She reached her right hand into her coat pocket for a Kleenex.

"What are you doing?" he screamed.

"I need a tissue."

"You take anything else out, I kill you."

"There's nothing else in there." As she said that, she felt something hard. My God, she thought, the cell phone. As she pulled out a tissue, her glove came out also and fell to the floor. The phone was in her pocket. Maybe the phone could save her life.

She pressed the tissue against her eyes, then, very softly, on each side of her face. It came away with blood. She looked at it and set it on her lap where he could see it.

He had stood as she did this. Now he kicked the glove away from her. "You talked to Hutchins, didn't you?"

"I haven't seen or talked to Hutchins since we interviewed him at the station house in Omaha. He left and went to the gas station. I never saw him again."

"You're lying."

"I'm not lying. I'm—"

But he was in front of her again, pummeling her with his fists. She felt pain everywhere, her upper arms, her shoulders, her face. He stood back, retrieving the gun, which he had left on his chair for the assault.

Why was he asking these questions? she wondered. What did it matter whether she had spoken to Hutchins in the hospital or not, where his bicycle was, who her partner was? Maybe he was just revving himself up to kill her and this was the way he did it. He admitted to her that he had killed Hutchins—although he was wrong—and that meant he didn't expect to let her out alive. But he was wearing a face mask, so maybe there was a chance he would let her go.

She wanted desperately to live. She loved Hack. She cared about Mike Fromm. She wanted to talk to Lisa Angelino and say all the right things to her, whatever they were. She wanted to sit in front of a hot fire in the apartment she now called home.

Wang had begun pacing, as though he were trying to decide what other stupid question to ask her that would give him an excuse to beat her some more. He stopped now and faced her. "What do you know about the Rawls woman?" Once again he had difficulty with the *R* and *L*.

"She was just a woman who lived in the building. She went back to Tulsa and you killed her there."

"She wasn't 'just a woman,' Bauer. She was Soderberg's girlfriend. If I know that, you know that. And you know where she worked too, in the Federal Building. She was an agent of the government. She was working with Soderberg."

Jane felt a chill. She had never asked where Margaret Rawls worked. She had assumed it was just a job, and it probably had been. Federal jobs were often word processing and secretarial.

"So you killed her for having dinner with Soderberg. And all the others in the house on Fifty-sixth Street?"

He gave her a faint smile. "I couldn't take a chance. They knew him. He talked to them. He went to their apartments. He told them who he was and what he was doing. They all ran from that building like frightened mice after he died. They ran because they knew. All except Hutchins. Hutchins stayed. Then he disappeared. Then you found him and went after him. He told you things. What did he say?"

"He didn't know anything. None of them knew anything," Jane said, feeling the sadness of the loss of innocent lives. "They were just—"

There was a commotion in the hallway. Feet pounded up the stairs and someone banged on the door.

"Don't move," he said. He turned his back on her and opened the door. Two young men were there, and the three of them spoke in agitated Chinese.

Jane put her right hand in her pocket, but one of the young men peered over Wang's shoulder and stared at her. She let her hand hang and stared straight ahead. The conversation was brief. When it ended, Wang slammed the door and walked over to her. On the way, he picked up a rope from a table.

He tied her ankles together and her wrists together behind her back. Her torso was tied to the back of the chair. Then he grabbed a roll of duct tape, tore off a piece, and pressed it over her mouth. Then he left the apartment.

This guy is nuts, she thought. He's crazy. He kills because he loves it. She fought back the urge to be sick.

[34]

She looked around, trying to find something she could use to cut the rope or scratch off the duct tape. She couldn't remember ever feeling this much pain. Her handbag was still lying on the floor where he had half emptied it. The cuffs were gone, but she might have a small mirror in there or some keys he had missed. She moved the chair inch by inch to where the bag lay. Her hands were tied behind her but she could move her fingers. She had no idea how long Wang would be, and if he came back and found her half-untied, he'd finish the beating he had only started before he left. Still, it was her only chance.

She reached the bag and managed to get it between her feet, although they were tied together. She tried lifting it as she bent over, afraid she would topple forward and hit her head on the bare floor. It seemed to take forever, but she found she had some play in her knees. He had done a hasty job of tying her up, or maybe he just ran out of rope. In any event, she kept trying to raise the bag, first between her feet, finally between her legs, then toward her face so she could lean over to get the leather strap over her head. The rope was around her chest, giving her very little distance to move forward. It was try and fail, try and fail, pray Wang didn't return, hope something in that bag would get her loose.

Suddenly she felt the strap touch her nose. She almost cried with joy. Come on, Janey, you can do it, she told herself. Keep trying. One more try, one more try.

It was exhausting and depressing, but little by little she worked the bag up between her legs until she held it tightly between her knees. Wriggling, she moved it up till it was between her thighs, then, finally, almost on her lap. The zipper was open and only half the contents still inside, but she was just able to get her face to touch the zipper, and she started scratching the zipper against her face and the duct tape, over and over.

She could feel progress, and that alone kept her working at it. Suddenly she was able to expel air from the right corner of her mouth. After that, it was almost easy, pulling the tape against the zipper until her whole mouth was exposed. She opened her mouth and breathed through it. Then she grabbed the front of the bag between her teeth and hauled it up on her lap so it touched her stomach.

She was just about to see what was left inside the bag when she heard the thunder of footsteps and shouting on the stairs. Dear God, she thought. Don't let it be Wang.

Someone banged on the door, then banged again and called in Chinese. Jane hung her head as far forward as she could, although she couldn't hide the open bag on her lap. There was a sound of a key in the lock; then someone burst in.

He said something, perhaps asking her a question she could not answer, then, sounding disgusted, went out and slammed the door, turning the key again before he raced downstairs.

It was like a reprieve. He had not seen the duct tape hanging from the side of her mouth, had not noticed the bag on her lap. She tried to see inside the bag, hoping she could snag something with her teeth, but there wasn't much left in it, and the logistics seemed impossible. That meant she could not untie the rope keeping her hands behind her.

OK, use your brain, Jane. Think. She wriggled her hands and realized that her coat was unbuttoned and had opened as she had worked the bag up to her lap. In fact, the coat was no longer covering her lap. With some more wriggling, she might get the right-hand pocket near her hands.

She worked at it, relieved to see that her efforts were producing results. She bounced on the chair a couple of times, pulling the back of the coat more and more to the left so that the right pocket came closer and closer to where her hands were tied behind her. It was slow and tedious and her whole upper body was hurting from Wang's blows. But she had to do it, and soon. Wang had been gone a long time now. If he came back, it was all over.

Suddenly her left hand felt the slit of the right-hand pocket. She worked her hand into the pocket and touched the phone. A minute later she held it in her hand. She could pull it out but she couldn't see it, and she would have to operate it blindly. She got it out, carefully set it in her left hand, still tied closely to her right, and got it open. Her best bet was 911, if she could find the two digits, which she wasn't sure she could do. There were several buttons on the phone, one of which turned it on. She was confident she could find that one, but where to go from there?

And then she remembered the redial button. Who was the last person she had called? She couldn't remember. She knew she had taken the phone out when Defino was there because he had made a crack about not letting MacHovec know, but whom had she called? Shit. She couldn't remember. Which left 911.

And then it came to her. She had dialed Hack's number while waiting for the rain to subside on Centre Street. That was the last number in the phone's memory. If she could find the redial button, it would call his cell phone, which he always had on him.

She closed her eyes and tried to picture the phone. The

on-off switch was in the middle in red, which wasn't much help right now. Where was the redial button? Somewhere along the top. Left or right. Her instinct said left, and she would go with that. If she screwed up, she'd try for 911. She pressed the middle button and heard the dial tone, the most beautiful music of her life. Then she pressed the button to the left and heard the tinkle of ten beeps in a row. You did good, Janey. It rang once, twice, three times. Where the hell was he?

"Inspector Hackett's phone," a woman said, barely audible.

Oh, shit. "This is Detective Bauer. Can you hear me?" She had to raise her voice, taking a chance that someone outside would hear.

"Detective who?"

"Bauer. B-A-U-E-R. Tell Inspector Hackett this is a ten-thirteen. I am—"

"Detective, Inspector Hackett cannot take your call. Please call your squad." And she hung up.

I will kill her, Jane thought. I will wrap my hands around her neck and strangle her. She was panting with anger. She waited half a minute. Wherever he was, he would return for his phone. He was never without it. He would answer and he would save her. He had to.

She pressed the on-off button again and heard the dial tone with somewhat less enthusiasm. Then she pressed the button to its left once more. It rang twice and she thought, The bitch is going to let me die.

On the third ring, it was picked up. "Hackett."

"Hack," she said, almost shouting, "it's Jane Bauer. Ten-thirteen, Hack. I'm tied up in a room in Chinatown, Bayard Street between Mott and Elizabeth. No number on the front door. Between a restaurant and a laundry. Third floor right. The door is locked. They're going to kill me when they get back."

"Hang on. I can hardly hear you. Bayard Street, between a restaurant and a laundry, third floor right." He was talking loudly himself now.

"That's it."

"Leave the phone on as long as you can. We'll try to trace it. Are you all right?"

"I'm alive."

"Stay with me." He called, "Mike," and started shouting instructions. She heard him say "We have a ten-thirteen," and then there were other voices.

She sat back, holding the telephone carefully, hoping Hack would get there before Wang did. Her coat was half off her right side and she was feeling cold, but there was hope now and that would have to keep her going.

"You still with me?"

"Yes," she shouted.

"They're on their way."

She knew it wouldn't be Hack who broke through the door, but it didn't matter. He was clean and he loved her and he would save her.

The footsteps on the stairs were so quiet, she didn't know anyone was there till she heard the key in the lock and saw Chong Wang enter the apartment.

35

HE STARED AT her, his eyes darting around, and it hit her that he was no longer wearing the ski mask. His bare face was her death sentence. He didn't care anymore whether she saw his face because he had come back to kill her. Time had run out.

The open handbag was back on the floor and her chair was near where it had been when he had left. But the duct tape was hanging from her left cheek, the coat was off her shoulder, and behind her back she was holding an open cell phone that emitted occasional noises.

"Who was here?" he said.

"One of your friends. He walked in and walked out."

He ripped the duct tape from her face. "How did you get this off?"

"It got loose." Her voice was that of a frightened child.

He smacked her face with his bare hand, left and right, bringing tears. She wanted to hurt him. She had never wanted to hurt anyone so much in her life. She strained at the ropes to kick him or knee him, but she couldn't.

From a distance came the sound of a siren, but in New York there were always sirens. She didn't know what to do about the phone. It was impossible to get it back in her pocket, but she could turn it off if she wanted to. He had not walked around behind her, but if he saw it, that would be the end.

Suddenly he dashed away into a room she could not see. Maybe he thought someone else was in the apartment. He was jittery with fury, banging things around, slamming a door, then kicking it open. Then he was back. He took the gun out of his pocket and rubbed it as though it were a fine piece of furniture.

"I'm tired of you and it's time for you to die," he said.

"Tell me one thing," she said, playing for a few seconds more. "About Olivia Dean. You killed her, didn't you?"

"What do you know about Olivia Dean?"

"Just that she's missing. I think you killed her."

"She started asking for too much. It had nothing to do with Soderberg. That was years ago. We were finished with her and she was a bother. It was better to get rid of her."

"I see." There was an explosion of sound from the cell phone and she thought, Oh, Jesus, this is it.

"What's that?"

"I don't know."

He looked around, then walked to the back of her chair. He grabbed the phone out of her hand and started shouting in Chinese. Then he held the phone to his ear and said, "Who is this?"

Come on, Jane thought. For the love of God, get here while I'm still alive. Get here, get here. The distant siren had stopped. Wang continued to talk on the phone, threatening to kill her. Finally, he threw the phone against the wall.

The gun was still in his hand. He leveled it at her. He was wired and ready to kill. His eyes burned with the thrill of it. In the moment she had left, she thought of her father.

They came through the door like a battering ram, three of New York's finest shouting at Wang, *"Police, don't move,"* and then firing. The multiple gunshots threw Wang backward. The space was short, less than ten feet between him and the cops. The gun in his hand dropped to the floor as he fell, and bounced away.

When the noise stopped, she said, "Thanks, guys," her voice so weak it hardly made a sound.

"Detective Bauer?" one of them asked.

"I think so."

"Hang on there. We'll get you free." A knife went through the ropes, and a sturdy hand helped her stand. "You need an ambulance."

"I just want to get home."

"We'll take you to Bellevue." It sounded more like an order than a suggestion.

She stood for a moment, swaying, tears on her cheeks, then leaned on the young cop who had cut the rope. She felt cramped and achy from the waist down. Above the waist was more serious pain. When she took a deep breath, her chest hurt.

Without looking around, she picked up her bag,

stuffed the contents back in, and put the strap over her shoulder. "He has my cuffs and keys," she said. "And my guns."

"We'll retrieve them for you when the crime scene unit comes."

She was aware that a uniform was bending over Wang and picking up his gun.

Going downstairs wasn't easy. A uniformed sergeant helped her, giving her welcome support. Outside only the sky was dark. The street was being closed off with yellow tape that said CRIME SCENE DO NOT CROSS, and lights were being set up in the entrance. There were more police vehicles than she had seen outside a station house parking lot in a long time. She looked around as the sergeant led her to the waiting ambulance. A door opened on a car halfway down the block and a man got out and stood in the middle of Bayard Street. Jane gave him a small wave and got into the ambulance. Then they took her to Bellevue.

Captain Graves showed up and Defino and then McElroy. MacHovec called. The doctors cleaned up her face and told her she had abrasions but no broken bones or teeth. The worst damage was where the zipper had scraped away her skin and left a nasty wound that they medicated and covered. An X ray indicated a possible rib fracture, but that would take care of itself. "Just don't laugh too hard," the doctor said without a smile. There was pain medication if she needed it.

Mike Fromm called, having gotten the word from Defino. That was nice of Gordon, she thought.

"And by the way, if you still care, we found the aunt."

"Hutchins's aunt is OK?"

"She was sleeping over at her daughter's house. No question of who she is."

Hack called about midnight. "How bad does it hurt?" he said.

"It's OK. I'm fine. I think they'll let me go home to-morrow." Her voice was still weak.

"I apologize for my PAA."

"I wanted to kill her. How long has she worked for you?"

"A couple of years, maybe three."

"Did she go to China with you, Hack?"

There was a pause. "Yeah. She did."

"She could be the leak."

"I'll take care of it tomorrow."

"I'm too tired to talk."

"I'll see you first thing in the morning."

He arrived with flowers, beautiful flowers, yellow roses and orange mums and lots of other things. "For your new apartment. I like it, by the way. I like it a lot."

"Is Wang dead?"

"Yeah. They weren't taking any chances. All three guys tapped him. I guess our training is paying off. Frank Graves tells me this is about weapons systems getting to the Chinese. The PC will be meeting with the Feds later today. They'll want a piece of the case, or at least the information that closed it."

"That's what Soderberg was working on, finding Americans who were selling it to the Chinese and grabbing the middlemen who were getting it to China. He set up a sting and put a couple of them out of business."

"This guy Wang do him?"

"A woman did. She's missing, and he admitted to me last night that he killed her. I think I know where to find her."

"I hope you'll let me know."

"You'll hear, I promise."

He leaned over the bed and kissed her lips. "Gotta go. I have a date with my PAA."

When he was gone, she called Eddie on Walker Street.

"Hey, hey," he said. "Detective Bauer. You the one I heard about on the TV last night?"

"I wouldn't know, Eddie. I haven't turned my set on for a month. But it could have been. I was on my way over to see you when this happened."

"See me about what?"

"You said there was something else chained to that rack where the bicycle was."

"Yeah, right."

"What was it?"

"It was all collapsed. It was flat against the wall. It wasn't a baby carriage. It wasn't a kid's stroller, too big for that. It could have been like a small wheelchair."

"Thanks, Eddie."

She lay back on the pillows and looked at Hack's flowers. She knew exactly where Olivia Dean was.

She was home before noon, driven by a sector car. There was a message to call Captain Graves, and when she reached him he said he wanted to drop over this afternoon, if she was up to it, bring some food, and debrief her. If it was all right, Defino and MacHovec would join him. It was fine with her, especially if they brought the food.

"You still in a lot of pain?" the whip asked as they trooped into her apartment. "The son of a bitch really beat you."

"It looks worse than it is. I'm fine."

The men took care of the food, which was very nice. There were salads and cold cuts and bread and a couple of half gallons of Coke. She had made coffee before they arrived. While they ate, she told them what had happened. Graves's tape recorder was on the whole time.

"That phone saved my life, Boss. I think it's gone now. He smashed it against the wall. The Communications Division is gonna be bent out of shape."

"We'll get you another one in fourteen-carat gold. Not to worry."

"So what've we got?" Defino said. "Wang was the guy in Omaha, right?"

"Right."

"Do we have the leak yet?"

"We should hear about that soon. There are a couple of suspects."

"So where's the Dean woman?" MacHovec asked. "Gone to China on a slow boat?"

"I don't think so. I talked to Eddie this morning before I left the hospital. Remember he said there was something else chained to the rack where the bicycle was? Well, I got him to guess it might be a small wheelchair."

"But Dean was an athlete," Sean said. "What did she need a wheelchair for?"

"What did she need the wigs for? What did she need the party clothes for? It was how she worked. She had a lot of props, and the wheelchair was one of them. She had a falling-out with Wang—he said she wanted more money—and he killed her in City Hall Park."

There was utter silence. Then the whip said, "Holy shit, multiple clearances, all with results."

"Her body's still in the morgue. We've got plenty of fingerprints and plenty of DNA from the apartment on Fifty-sixth Street. They shouldn't have much trouble matching it."

Graves was beaming. "I'll make the call right away," he said. Then he shook his head. "No. This is your case. MacHovec, you know how to make a phone call."

MacHovec grinned and went to find the phone.

[36]

THE MATCH ON the prints came by late afternoon. The DNA would take longer, but who needed it? Before the end of the day it was announced that Inspector Hackett's PAA had been arrested. The charges began with endangering the life of a police officer and went on from there. The Feds would have seconds with her later.

The story that developed, much of which was reported in the local media, was that the PAA, Emily Wilson, a middle-aged New Yorker with superb secretarial skills, had been approached in China two years earlier and asked to be alert to information on the Soderberg case and a couple of others that were not reported. There was a modest retainer for her vigilance and a promised large bonus for actual information, which she was supposed to telephone to Mr. Chong Wang.

Jane healed and was relieved to hear that Hutchins was truly on the mend. Her father said he always knew she would solve the City Hall Park Murder, and as always, he was very proud of her.

The police department decided to award her a Meritorious Commendation, and she had a chance at the Medal of Honor. On Medal Day at One PP, the Chief of Detectives was unavoidably busy at something, and Inspector Hackett stood in for him. The picture of the smiling Hackett and the smiling Jane Bauer was on the front of

e *Daily News* and the *Post*. The *Times* used it in the
Metro section.

Hack called her afterward—they had not spoken since
he left the hospital—and said he had always wanted a
picture of the two of them that he could hang on the wall
in his office, and he thought he had worked this one out
pretty well.

"Nearly got me killed," she said.

"Then there wouldn't have been a picture. Can I ask
you what your job prospects are?"

"Captain Graves wants the three of us to continue in
the cold-case task force."

"Sounds like a good idea to me."

"Defino hates MacHovec and I spend half my time
keeping them from killing each other."

"It's good training. You didn't answer my question."

"I told the insurance company I'd be staying on the
job."

"You won't regret it, Jane."

"It'll mean bread and water if I keep the apartment."

"You'll figure something out," he said cavalierly.
"You'll get a raise. The promotion list is making the
rounds, and I recognized a few names from your office, a
couple to first-grade detective and a handful to second.
And maybe someday you'll have a roommate."

She didn't answer that. "It's a great picture. We look
so happy."

"We were happy."

"Dad's framing his. He can't keep his eyes off it."

"A man with good taste."

She smiled at the picture after they hung up. There was
a letter in the mail from Mike Fromm. He and his son
were planning a trip to New York next month. How was
the first week of December? She thought it was just fine.
The tree at Rockefeller Center would be up and lighted,
New York at its brightest.

The ordeal in Chinatown still gave her nightmares.
She knew that working in insurance would never give
her bad dreams, and for a couple of days after she left the

hospital, she had thought it was really what she wanted
And then something changed. She couldn't let go of th
job. Or maybe it couldn't let go of her. It was part of he
in a way that nothing else in her life was. Who would sh
be without it?

She called Flora Hamburg and they got together fo
dinner, Flora with her white hair and shopping bag an
her weapon on her ample hip. Flora never said a word
never asked her what she wanted to do. But when sh
picked up the check, she reached into her shopping ba
and pulled out a framed copy of the famous picture.

"You look great," Flora said. "Even that son of a bitc
Hackett looks good."

There had been article after article in the papers. Th
mayor was deliriously happy with the success of th
squad. First-Grade Detective Jane Bauer was emblemati
of the best of the police force. Her partners were grea
men, and the squad had more than proved itself.

And then there was Jane Bauer herself. She was grate
ful the past was past, more grateful than she could ar
ticulate that she was alive and well enough to work. Th
investigation of the murder of Arlen Quill had turned
into the case of her lifetime, almost the last one, sh
thought, with a familiar echo of fear. She sensed a prid
that she kept to herself in what she had accomplished: th
observations that had become leads, the frail strands o
possibility that she had picked up and run with till the
panned out. Who could have imagined a simple homicid
would lead to a complicated international conspiracy?

It was over now, the questions answered, the last o
the pieces neatly fitting into the puzzle, time to move on
time to tie up the last loose end in her life.

She got a fire going, made herself a mug of coffee, and
got the phone. Sitting down in her favorite chair, she dialed the number of Lisa Angelino.

If you enjoyed this mystery, look for these
novels featuring intrepid investigator
Christine Bennett

THE APRIL FOOLS' DAY MURDER

by Lee Harris

For his favorite charity, the high school drama
club, Willard Platt fakes his own murder as an
April fool stunt. But the repeat performance later
that day is the real thing. And some say he
deserved it. Investigator (and ex-nun) Christine
Bennett is troubled by Willard's widow, who roams
the road at night, and his son, who has a troubled
marriage and bizarre secret life. Behind this
family's respectable facade, violent passions are
seething. For this is not the first tragedy to strike
them. Nor will it be the last.

It's party time for a killer. . . .

THE HAPPY BIRTHDAY MURDER

by Lee Harris

Sleuth Christine Bennett is moved by two poignant mementos treasured by her late Aunt May. The first is a sad little note mourning the death of a young man lost in a Connecticut wood; the other, an obituary honoring a wealthy local manufacturer who committed suicide just after his splendid fiftieth birthday celebration. Why did her aunt never mention these virtually simultaneous tragedies? With her investigative instincts irresistibly whetted Chris slices through the layers of the past, and uncovers the horrible truth that murder was just the icing on the cake.

Mayhem knows best. . . .

THE MOTHER'S DAY MURDER

by Lee Harris

Investigator (and former nun) Christine Bennett is appalled when a young woman claims to be the natural daughter of Sister Joseph, beloved Superior at St. Stephen's and Chris's dearest friend. But after the girl is murdered, all the evidence leads the police to believe she was telling the truth—and that Sister Joseph is the prime suspect. As Chris frantically searches for the truth, it seems only a miracle can save Sister Joseph from a life behind bars.

Published by Fawcett Books.
Available wherever books are sold.